ST. MARTIN'S

MINOTAUR

MYSTERIES

Other titles from St. Martin's **Minotaur** Mysteries

St. Martin's Paperbacks is also proud to present
these mystery classics by Ngaio Marsh

PRAISE FOR JULIA WALLIS MARTIN'S
THE BIRD YARD

"Will definitely appeal to fans of Elizabeth George and P. D. James."
—*Booklist*

"With her nuances and her vivid, memorable scenes, has been likened to Minette Walters."
—*New Orleans, LA Times-Picayune*

"Intense, this novel gives readers an instant jolt with its stark depiction of evil lurking in the decaying back alleys and crumbling infrastructure of Manchester, England . . . Martin has worked a keen note of malevolence into her novel and created a gripping story that has firm psychological underpinnings."
—*Publishers Weekly*

"Well-constructed, beautifully written. It will definitely rank among the best crime books of the year."
—*Yorkshire Post*

"A nail-biting thriller . . . a remarkably mature novel."
—*Manchester Evening News*

"Immaculately crafted, chilling and . . . compulsively readable." —*Cambridge Evening News*

"This author's career [is] going much the same way as [Minette] Walters'."
—*The Bookseller*

PRAISE FOR THE EDGAR-NOMINATED
A LIKENESS IN STONE

St. Martin's Paperbacks Titles
by Julia Wallis Martin

A Likeness in Stone
The Bird Yard

THE
BIRD
YARD

JULIA
WALLIS
MARTIN

St. Martin's Paperbacks

THE BIRD YARD

Copyright © 1998 by Julia Wallis Martin.

Library of Congress Catalog Card Number: 99-16428

ISBN: 0-312-97138-9

Printed in the United States of America

St. Martin's Press hardcover edition / September 1999
St. Martin's Paperbacks edition / June 2001

St. Martin's Paperbacks are published by St. Martin's Press, 175 Fifth Avenue, New York, NY 10010.

10 9 8 7 6 5 4 3 2 1

For my son.

ACKNOWLEDGMENTS

My thanks go to Superintendent Mike Hoskins, Metropolitan Police, Clubs and Vice OCU. Also, to Duncan Campbell, Greg Dinner and Russell Murray.

PROLOGUE

November, 1997

The vast metal ball hung from the jib, held still by its own dead weight. He felt the weight of that ball as if it were an extension of himself, a responsibility that kept him in the cab for hours on end.

Operating cranes of this nature was a vocation of sorts. It kept men like him apart from the rest of humanity, his workmates bringing the occasional offering of tea or cigarettes. He took their gifts as a god might take any sacrifice, mindful that their lives were in his hands and aware that the slightest sign from him could send them running for cover.

Below him, on ground that glittered with frost, two workmen came out of a house. Victorian and four storeys high, it stood at the end of a row, its downpipes lurching from crumbling walls like badly broken limbs. It stood as testimony to the days when properties such as these were inhabited by people whose families could not be considered *old* or *connected*; people made cruel by the fear of family scandal or the sudden loss of their comparatively insignificant wealth. They clustered together, away from the terraced slums that had spread to the north. The slums were gone now; only these houses remained, the downward spiral from flats to squats having led some years before to an order that condemned them.

His workmates gave the all clear, then retreated to wasteground that stood between these and a second row of properties.

He watched them retreat and noted where they stood. There were twenty-odd men on this job and he could have told you where each of them was at any given moment. Their lives depended on his knowing, and he kept his eye on them all, watching the patterns they made as they drifted apart then came back together like flotsam.

Positioning the crane came automatically. Fifteen years on the job and you stopped having to think about it. All he thought of was safety, because some of the casual labourers could get a little careless. It wasn't the threat of masonry falling down around them that he worried about. No one would be stupid enough to stand close to a building that was about to be brought down, but the less experienced among them didn't appreciate that dust could be a killer, that thin shards of brick could blind them, that splinters of wood could pierce like a bullet and scar or maim a man.

They were standing well back, safety helmets on, their mouths covered by masks, their eyes protected by goggles. Some were leaning against a fence of corrugated iron that marked the boundary to what had once been vast garden. But it was no longer a garden — not what he would have called a garden at any rate.

Mesh fixed to the fence swept up to the roof of the house. At first, he took this to be some bizarre attempt at security, but as the crane rumbled past, the birds contained by the mesh began to swarm, and it was then that he recognized the garden for what it was: an aviary of gigantic proportions. He slowed the crane and watched as some of the birds made for trees planted within it. Others made directly for the house, where they darted through open windows, and the oddness of it, the mere fact that the house was clearly an extension of the aviary, pulled his mind from the job for a moment. But only for a moment. Safety was everything, and he dragged his attention back to the task of checking his workmates' positions: they were still where he'd seen them seconds ago, well away from danger, and mindful of his approach.

He turned the crane away from the aviary, the noise of the engine deafening, and as he lumbered across the wasteground towards the property he was about to demolish, he reminded himself that the birds were none of his business. The area had long since attracted the more dysfunctional elements of society, and if somebody had wanted to build a gigantic aviary, that was their affair; just so long as they understood that he had his job to do, that ultimately the crane would move in and the birds would have to go.

At moments like these, he felt all-powerful; as though, if he wanted to, he could bring down the entire world with that large metal ball, and as he pulled a lever that felt surprisingly light in his hand, the ball began to swing, gathering momentum, blotting out a sun the colour of ice.

There was a real skill to demolition. People didn't know that, he thought. People didn't appreciate that you couldn't just go smashing into a building, not even a relatively small building such as this. There was a certain satisfaction in knowing, almost instinctively, where the weak spot was, positioning the ball *just so*, giving the wall what seemed like the gentlest of taps, then sitting back and watching it come down.

But it didn't come down. That was the thing. It didn't come down at all. The side of the house bowed but withstood the contact whereas the wall at the front shuddered and imploded.

He knew what had happened: the side wall had been repointed or perhaps even rebuilt at some stage, whereas the mortar that held the brick at the front had disintegrated on impact. The masonry it was meant to hold had collapsed to reveal the rooms within, and something within those interior rooms was drawing his workmates towards them.

They moved slowly, faces raised to the sky, skin made pale by a film of dust from mortar reduced to a powder, and as he watched them, some removed their goggles, others their masks. He shouted out to keep them back, to tell them the house was unsafe, but none of them acknowledged his cry of warning.

Exasperated, he jumped from the cab and stormed towards them, dust raining down from the still, cold air. Then he saw what they were looking at and stopped, mid-stride, appalled.

The implosion had revealed a pair of alcoves. The one nearest the road had been sealed over at some stage, but as the wall caved in, plasterboard had fallen away to reveal a bundle of rags.

There was something about those rags, thought the driver, something that spoke to some primeval fear within, for he saw, almost immediately, that they weren't rags at all, that in fact, they were clothes that loosely concealed a shape, which made him recoil.

He spoke to the foreman. 'Jacko,' he said, 'where's your mobile?' The foreman reached into the pocket of a duffelcoat, pulled out his phone and said, 'Who do you want me to call?'

For a moment, the driver wasn't sure. Who *did* you contact first – the boss or the authorities?

He pulled the goggles from his face, as if by doing so he could also rip the image from his eyes, but the image remained: a birdlike neck, and lips peeling back from the teeth.

A sound he recognized, a sound that sometimes wove its way through his dreams, forewarned him of danger. 'Police,' he said, and the house,.as if deeply offended, hurled bricks from the rooms above as the men started running for cover.

Fourteen years with Greater Manchester Police had given Detective Superintendent Parker sufficient experience to know that the victim had been walled up alive. No one had arranged the body like that, and no one had closed the eyes, which were so finely skinned that the iris could be seen beneath the lids.

In life, that bundle of rags had clawed at the walls, had cried, had screamed out for mercy, and his cries had gone unheard. Parker considered the possibility that he had suffocated, but thought it more likely that the cause of death would prove to be dehydration. Then again, thought Parker, perhaps not. Perhaps the fact of his incarceration, the certainty that he'd been left to die had done the trick.

He studied the small coiled form, the fingers to the mouth and, because he could imagine only too well what the victim had suffered, found he couldn't stand to dwell on what he might have gone through prior to death, so he forced himself to concentrate on the room where he had been found.

The alcove was divided from its twin by a cast-iron fireplace, paper hanging from the chimney breast like strips of shredded skin. There had once been some pattern to it, some border where in other houses picture rails were fixed.

Behind him the strobe-like effect of a flashing blue light blinked against his surroundings, and as he turned to signal a uniform to switch the bloody thing off, he saw bricks, rubble, debris, all of it covered by frost. Even the workmen looked frozen, cold and shock having turned their faces the colour of powdered stone.

He stared across wasteground to the houses opposite. These, too, were properties that had once been owned by the professional classes, but Parker had only ever known the area as a drug dealers' paradise. Now, not even the junkies remained, rotten floors and biting cold having driven them away. The entire row was unoccupied, with the exception of the house with its makeshift aviary. As he made his way towards it, finches swarmed like schools of tropical fish towards the trees. Some flew into the house; others found holes in the mesh and escaped, only to return, for although the yard was far removed from the habitats that had allowed their various species to evolve, it represented security and they were loath to leave it.

Eventually, the aviary and the house from which it protruded would be razed to the ground. Parker didn't know when, and he didn't much care. He only knew that his prime suspect was in there, watching him, and he caught the movement when Roly stepped back from a window. He melted into the shadows and remained there, but not before Parker had seen him, and not before Roly saw Parker make his way to Roly's Yard.

CHAPTER ONE

October, 1997

Along with the office that went with his rank, Parker had inherited a photograph. In it, bobbies wore the type of uniform most members of the public would still recognize today, although their faces were adorned by sideburns of extraordinary proportions. They had stood in three rigid lines awaiting the flash from a camera, and if, for many of them, it had been the only time in their lives that they had been photographed, there was no indication in their oddly solemn expressions that they felt any sense of occasion.

They were standing to attention in front of a building that no longer existed, a building that had been demolished in the sixties to make way for the station that Parker was based at now. The surrounding buildings were in keeping with this brighter, newer building, but its window looked out on a city that his forebears would have had little difficulty recognizing.

As he looked out on to landmarks by which he had first learned to navigate as a boy, it struck him that he knew every square inch of Manchester. He felt he belonged there, and saw nothing remotely unadventurous in bringing his own kids up a mere stone's throw from where he himself had been born. Their friends were the sons and daughters of people Parker had known all his life, and there was nothing wrong with that, he thought, nothing wrong with continuity, and the feeling of security that could be derived from it.

Detective Inspector Warrender broke into his thoughts by knocking on the door, then walking in. 'Sir?' he said, and Parker turned from the window.

Warrender, ten years younger than Parker, was sharp, good at his job, and even better at knowing instinctively when to take something straight to a senior officer. 'We've got a missing kid.'

Parker wondered whether Warrender had any idea of the extent to which those words could turn him cold. Some time ago he had come to the conclusion that it was something to do with having had kids of his own. Warrender, still unmarried, still 'playing the field', as he put it, couldn't possibly know that the news of a child having gone missing or come to harm always had a greater impact on parents. 'How old?' he said.

'Twelve.'

Twelve, thought Parker. His youngest boy was twelve, his eldest fifteen – and driving him up the wall with bands like Oasis, Blur, and the Verve.

'When was he last seen?'

'Yesterday afternoon.'

'Runaway?'

'Maybe. His home life could be better, and he's been known to play truant from school.'

Already, Parker was assessing the situation. Twelve was a bit young to be buggering off on a whim, though you never knew – hormones could kick in with a vengeance even at that age, though some kids took off over minor problems that seemed insurmountable to the emotionally immature.

'Something else,' said Warrender. 'He vanished about a hundred yards from where Joseph Coyne disappeared.'

That was enough for Parker. 'Let's go,' he said.

8

CHAPTER TWO

Half an hour later, Parker knocked at the door to a semi on a council estate that had the distinction of being one of the largest in Europe. 'Mrs Maudsley?' he said, showing his ID. The elderly woman who had answered the door led him through to a room where other officers were already present. They stood when Parker walked in, and stayed standing even though he acknowledged their deference.

She was nervous, this elderly woman, aware that Parker was something very senior to the uniforms who had taken details relating to her grandson's disappearance, and also superior to Detective Inspector Warrender who had followed in their wake. Parker picked up on her nervousness and reassured her swiftly. 'This is routine, Mrs Maudsley. Gary's only twelve, so we want to find him quickly, don't we?' He smiled, and it didn't wash.

'You don't think something's happened to him?'

Under normal circumstances, Parker would have replied that youngsters disappeared every day of the week. Most trailed home in a day or so, the argument, fear or sheer curiosity that had led them to try their wings having paled to insignificance by comparison with the discomfort of spending a couple of nights on the streets. Some, however, didn't come home of their own accord, and when that happened, the police started a search, logged their name on the missing persons index and hoped for the best. 'The odds are against it,' he said, and that was true enough in that, statistically, most kids who did a disappearing act were found safe.

'All he did was nip to the shop, and that was it. I haven't seen him since.'

She might just as easily have been describing the way in which Joseph Coyne disappeared, thought Parker, and Mrs Maudsley added, 'Just like that lad from Adelphe Road.'

'We don't want to go jumping to conclusions,' said Parker, comfortingly, but she wasn't listening.

'Nobody's ever found him. I see his mother from time to time. She's not the same person.'

Parker, who still kept in regular contact with Joseph Coyne's mother, was only too aware that she wasn't the same person, just as he knew that, of late, she'd been putting rather more faith into what clairvoyants and mediums had to say than in anything the police might come up with. Part of him didn't blame her in that the police had very little to go on, and even less to say by way of explanation or comfort. Consequently, her 'Where do you think he is?' was invariably met with some platitude, and it must have come as a relief to find someone prepared to commit themselves one way or another. He only hoped she wouldn't come up against someone who would take advantage of her vulnerability and encourage her to part with what little money she had in order to receive 'advice' from the other side.

The last time he'd seen her, he'd promised that the investigation into Joseph's disappearance would never be wound down, and she'd interrupted as if telling him something he didn't already know: 'It's been five years, Mr Parker. Chances are, he's *dead*.'

Mrs Maudsley added, 'One of your lads found our Gary's watch,' and Parker, turning to Warrender for confirmation, was told that it had been discovered at the top of the road. He was also told that Warrender had seen a boy of roughly Gary's age hanging around. Warrender had approached him with, 'Are you a friend of Gary's?' but the boy had replied that he wasn't, that he'd just seen some coppers pickin' up the watch and he'd wondered what was goin' on, that's all.

Warrender had said, 'What's your name, son?' but the lad had edged away, and Warrender had asked a female officer to see if she could get anything out of him. She'd returned a short time later and had told him the boy's name was Nathan, that he lived locally, that he went to school with Gary, but that he wasn't particularly friendly with him, and Warrender, who was more interested in the watch than in Nathan, had left it at that.

'Strap was broke,' said Mrs Maudsley, and then she fell silent, as if afraid to suggest that it had been wrenched from Gary's wrist.

'Straps break all the time,' said Warrender, 'especially flimsy, plastic straps,' but she wasn't daft. She gave him a look with pale grey eyes that were cloudy with age, but astute.

'Do you have a picture of Gary?' said Parker, and Mrs Maudsley nodded towards a school photo standing on the mantelpiece.

Parker studied it as if lifting the image of Gary Maudsley clean off the photographic paper and imprinting it on to the fabric of his own memory. Gary was a fresh-faced kid, the hair light brown, his grin more of a smirk, the tie of his school uniform imaginatively knotted. Cheeky little bugger, thought Parker, but something lay behind that grin, something that spoke of his life as having been hard. 'What was he wearing yesterday?'

'Bomber jacket and jeans,' said Mrs Maudsley.

Mentally, Parker stripped the photograph of its school uniform and, in his mind's eye, redressed the boy. It made a difference: Gary seemed older, a little more streetwise perhaps.

'Where's his mother?' said Parker.

'Morocco,' said Mrs Maudsley. 'She writes from time to time.'

Say no more, thought Parker. 'What about his dad?'

'Sheffield. He married again after Frances upped and left.'

In those two brief comments, Parker had Gary's life in a nutshell. His mother had buggered off, and his dad had left Gran to bring up a kid who didn't fit into the new life he'd made for himself. It happened all the time. 'Well,' he said, 'a lot of kids take off for a day or so, and then they turn up safe.'

That alone was a greater reassurance to Mrs Maudsley than anything else he could have said. Maybe Gary was out there, somewhere, perfectly all right, in which case she'd kill him when she got her hands on him. She smiled a fraction.

'Can I see his room?' asked Parker, and she took him upstairs to where, already, a couple of officers were searching through Gary's belongings. They acknowledged Parker but carried on, and Parker stood by the door, watching them work.

The room overlooked the back of the house where the strip of lawn that passed for a garden was divided from identical strips of lawn by hedges that were high and untidy.

'This is it,' she said, and Parker nodded. As rooms went, it was typical for a lad of twelve, the posters on the walls mainly relating to bands Parker's kids listened to — Blur, Oasis. No surprises there.

There was a bird-cage by the bed, minus the usual mirror, and cuttlefish shell that Parker associated with the hobby of keeping cage-birds, and, indicating it, he said, 'Gary kept a bird.'

'It died,' said Mrs Maudsley. 'He'd only had it a week or so. Found it dead one mornin'.'

Unusual, thought Parker. He wasn't an expert on cage-birds, but he was under the impression that, sensibly cared for, they lived for a good few years.

His eye passed over a plastic cassette case and settled on muddy clothes hanging out of a bin. A badge on the side of the shorts informed him that this was Gary's PE kit and, lightly, he said, 'He left you a bit of washing, then?' She smiled a little shakily, and Parker continued, 'Better get it clean — you never know when he'll need it. I was a great one for giving a filthy kit to my mam the morning of a game.'

'You think he's all right, then?'

Parker didn't reply. Maybe that strap had caught on something, or maybe it had been wrenched from Gary's wrist — he didn't know, but the very fact of it worried him, just as it had worried Warrender.

'Where the hell is he?' she said suddenly, emotion she'd held in check spilling over into words that sounded as if they'd been spoken in anger.

He couldn't look into those pale grey eyes, afraid that his own might betray a fear every bit as great as that which had her in its grip. 'We'll find him,' he said, but he didn't add that he'd promised much the same to Joseph's mother or that, to date, he had failed to keep that promise.

CHAPTER THREE

Within twenty-four hours of Gary's disappearance, the where-abouts of every paedophile known to be living in the Greater Manchester area had been spewed from a computer, but the name that leapt out at Parker was that of Douglas Byrne.

Parker, who knew him of old, had questioned him when Joseph Coyne went missing, and now, as he stood in front of the shop where Byrne ran his business, Parker was reminded of nothing so much as the corner-shops of his childhood. In places such as this, he'd bought fags in ones and twos, had dipped his hand into plastic trays to pull out sweets that were dusty, had gazed up at shelves where meat was tinned and stacked beside bottles of Tizer. The thought of the sticky red liquid brought the taste to mind, and with it the slightly damp smell of countless slovenly women, the sheer weight of their body-mass crushing the backs of their slippers to squalid flatness.

Shops like these, shops that were as integral a part of his childhood as the sight of a woman sweeping the pavement in front of her own front door, were gone now, and the businesses that replaced them were of the here-today-gone-tomorrow variety. In that regard, the shop had lasted longer than most in that video shops as small, ill-situated and badly stocked as this were failing by the dozen. But Parker wasn't there to look at the books or to question how Byrne paid his bills.

The shop was a front for under-the-counter stuff. That much Parker knew.

He and Warrender walked into the chaos of videos crammed into makeshift shelving without thought to genre or condition. Their covers spoke of the film industry having stopped dead somewhere around the mid-seventies, odd images half obscured by yellowing, dog-chewed plastic.

There was a counter of sorts, and Byrne, with his immaculately kept finger-nails and hair that was receding before its time, was standing behind it.

The minute he saw Parker, he appeared to shrink a fraction in a way that suggested resignation as much as nervousness. 'Dougie,' said Parker.

Byrne replied, 'I'm not talking to you without a solicitor present.'

'This isn't about Joey,' said Parker.

Byrne slipped out from behind the counter, locked the door to the shop, then turned to Parker, saying, 'So what's it about?'

Nodding in the direction of the upper rooms, Parker said, 'Upstairs.'

Byrne led them through to the back, then up a flight of stairs that led to a bedsit. It wasn't the first time Parker had seen the room, and if it was small and dark, at least it was clean and functional – more than Byrne deserved, in Parker's view.

Byrne indicated the only available chair, as if inviting him to use it, but Parker preferred to stand, as did Warrender, who positioned himself by the door. Although the proximity of the man and his belongings made Parker feel like scrubbing himself down, he attempted to sound non-judgemental as he said, 'Local lad's gone missing.' He produced a photograph of Gary Maudsley and passed it to Byrne, adding, 'Know him?'

Byrne slumped on to the bed, holding the photo in hands that were white and soft. He looked at it for a good few seconds, then handed it back to Parker. 'No.'

'Not even by sight?'

'Should I?'

'He lives locally – I thought he might have come into the shop at some point.'

'Well, he didn't.'

Parker replied: 'I'd hate to find out down the road that he ever *was* in this shop. It wouldn't look good for you.' Byrne made no comment, and he added, 'Think carefully, Dougie. You've never even bumped into him on the street, maybe?'

'Not that I can remember.'

'You said you'd never laid eyes on Joseph Coyne, but it transpired that you'd been seen talking to him the morning he disappeared.'

Byrne stood up, agitated, and went to the window where he gazed out on the street below. He said, 'I told you, he walked up to me, asked me the time,' and Parker, who had always felt vaguely insulted by the lack of imagination that had prompted Byrne's feeble explanation of his conversation with the missing boy, let it go, for once. Turning from the dismal outlook to face Parker, Byrne added, 'There's countless blokes done worse than me. How come you're goin' at me?'

'Joseph lived less than a mile from this shop. You were seen talking to him the morning he disappeared, and now another lad's gone missing, one who also just happens to live about a hundred yards away from here.' Byrne looked shaken as Parker added, 'You see my point, Dougie. I'd be bloody daft not to question you, wouldn't I?'

'When is it going to stop? That's all. When do I get the chance to shake off the legacy of one stupid mistake?'

His voice had become a whine, and Parker, who hated him all the more for it, said, 'Some legacies are bequeathed for life, Dougie. You can't molest a kid and expect society to forget.'

Byrne looked up sharply, beads of sweat breaking out on a forehead that reminded Parker of nothing so much as a slab of lard. 'I know how the police think – you can't have been done for molesting a kid and *not* know how they think – so I know what you're thinkin', Mr Parker—'

'Smarter than me, then,' said Parker. 'Half the time, I haven't a clue what I'm thinkin', Dougie – too bloody busy with paperwork.'

'—I'm a soft target. Pin it on me, and suddenly your life gets a lot easier. It stands to reason I'm gonna be accused.'

'Calm down, Dougie. Nobody's accusing you of anything.'

'And anyway, how do you know that anyone's responsible for anything? For all you know, he might just have fucked off with a mate!'

He was right, Parker had to give him that, but he was far from finished. 'Where were you, yesterday?'

'Here.'

Parker didn't react to it. He just watched the soft white fingers as they fondled the flabby white palms. 'Can anyone confirm that?'

'It was quiet. Hardly anybody in – there never is in the afternoons. I'll have to have a think . . .'

Parker smiled down at the man, wanting nothing more than to pick him up, pin him against the wall, and push him through the brick. He allowed his tone of voice to do the job for him as he said, 'You do that, Dougie, you have a think, and when you've thought, give your solicitor a bell. Tell him to cancel any holiday arrangements he might have in mind – chances are, you're going to need him shortly.'

They left him and walked out on to the street where the air seemed sweeter somehow, then made their way round the side of the property to a pair of large wooden gates.

Parker opened them to reveal the area that stood at the back of the shop. There had once been a lawn of sorts, but now there was only soil, the earth impacted and rutted by the wheels of Byrne's mini-van.

Up against one wall stood a concrete bunker, and looking at

it now, Parker could recollect a time when coalmen had lugged hessian sacks into his own backyard, emptying them into one that was similar. Those days were gone, along with the smog that had hung over houses like these, but in properties where owners were too idle to rid themselves of these unsightly reminder of the past, the bunkers remained.

He walked over to it, lifted the lid, and found it empty, the interior wet with damp, the sides stained black with coal. Five years ago, it had stood several feet to the left of where it was now positioned, because during his initial investigation into Byrne, Parker had ordered his men to shift it and dig out the ground it covered. His men had dug to a depth of several feet, but they hadn't found Joseph's body. What they *had* found, was a metal flyte case that had been buried quite close to the surface. They had lifted it out from the soil.

Once back at the station, Parker had invited Byrne to open it, but the man had denied that the case was his. He had then been obliged to watch as one of Parker's men had jammed a chisel under the lock and wrenched it apart. He had seemed infuriatingly satisfied when Parker had seemed bewildered by its contents, but that lack of comprehension had been momentary: the flyte case hadn't contained pornographic videos, photographs, address books, or any of the items Parker had hoped to find, but clothing catalogues.

It hadn't made sense to Parker, not until he'd flicked through them and had found substantial sections devoted to children's wear. Most of the garments had been modelled by six to nine year olds, their faces bright with happiness, their smiles devoid of guile. The knowledge that Byrne had used these images for his own gratification had made Parker want to vomit. Worse than that, it had made him want to succumb to the temptation to beat the shit out of the man. He had turned to one of his officers, his voice shaking, '*Get him out of here,*' and Byrne had been led back to the safety of his cell.

In thinking back to those catalogues with their images of

children in fireproof pyjamas, Parker realized that you couldn't make any child fireproof, not with men like Byrne on the street, predators who were waiting their chance to grab them.

Is that what had happened to Gary? thought Parker. He hoped to God he was wrong.

'What now?' said Warrender.

Parker closed the lid of the bunker. 'We get a warrant to search the place, and we watch him. Put him under surveillance.'

He looked up and found that Byrne was staring down at them, his face pale, his mouth sullen, as if he were being picked on, for reasons he couldn't quite fathom.

CHAPTER FOUR

Twelve-year-old Brogan Healey gazed up at the glass-domed roof. Rain had washed away the worst of the dirt and a dim, uncertain light fell like a blanket over the units below. Most were temporary; mere stalls set up in what had once been a fish market. Others, like Moranti's Emporium, were more permanent fixtures. Its bowed window was filled with ornate, bamboo cages; some were large, some were small, but each contained a brightly coloured finch.

The last time he'd peered through the window he had seen a cheetah's head, a stuffed fox, a snowy owl in a glass case, and a bell-jar of foliage that was running riot. Now, these things were gone, but new and equally interesting items replaced them: an array of antique and collectable perfume bottles, pre-war Ovaltine tins, and lengths of silk concealed the plain plaster wall at the back of the shop.

He walked in to find Moranti, elderly and dishevelled, sitting on the type of wicker basket into which pheasants were loaded after a shoot. His clothes had a certain cut to them, particularly the gabardine coat with the wide lapels: its size seemed to draw attention to his lack of height, his roundness.

'Got any jobs?' said Brogan.

Moranti was accustomed to receiving a steady stream of potential employees, most of them lads who thought a job at his curiosity shop would be preferable to a paper round. Without exception, they were often big for their age, and they handled the birds as if they were rats, crushing the delicate frames in overlarge hands. Consequently, he glanced at the boy's hands rather than at his face. They were small.

'What kind of job?'

'A Saturday job.'

Moranti eased himself away from the wicker basket and walked over to him. 'What use would you be to me?'

'How do you mean?'

'I mean, what would you know about finches?'

A Blue Monarch fixed him with eyes both black and still. 'A bit,' lied Brogan.

Moranti reached down and pulled a cloth from one of the bamboo cages to reveal a sudden splash of colour. 'What do you make of that?' he said, but Brogan didn't reply. The bird was dead, that was as much as he knew.

'It's a Gouldian finch,' said Moranti, and it seemed incredible to Brogan that this purple-throated bird, its underbelly gold, had ever lived and flown.

'Some of these birds are expensive,' said Moranti. 'Rare, do you see?'

Brogan saw.

'And one of the things you never do is hold them like *this*.' He clenched his fist with the thumb uppermost to illustrate the way the majority of people attempted to hold a finch.

'Is that what killed it?' said Brogan, and Moranti looked up at the glass-domed roof, a slice of grey paler than the rest where a pane had fractured to let in the cold morning air.

'I left it in a draught,' he admitted. 'That's something else you never do.' Unexpectedly, he smiled, making them conspirators. 'But that's for me and you to know, eh?'

'I won't tell no one,' said Brogan.

Moranti reached into the cage, scooped the body from the litter, and handed it to Brogan. 'Now,' he said, 'when you pick up a bird, you make your hands a cage, like this, see. And you leave a little space for its head — let it see out if it wants.'

The bird lay limp and cold in Brogan's hands, but he tried to imagine what it might feel like if the feathers were warm.

'Good, good,' said Moranti. 'Now, give it to me.'

As he took the bird and covered it in a handkerchief, it seemed to Brogan that there was something of the magician's trick about his movements, as if, at any moment, he might whip away the cloth to reveal that the bird had gone, but Moranti rolled up the handkerchief and put the bird in his pocket. 'Now,' he said, 'try this one.' He scooped a Banaquit out of a cage, appearing to catch it mid-flight, and placed it in Brogan's hands with a flourish.

Softly, and with more confidence than he felt, Brogan cupped the bird so that its head was free to move although the body was contained. It struggled and flapped but he didn't tighten his grip, reasoning that it would be better to let it escape than to kill it.

'Good, yes, you've got it,' said Moranti, and, as if realizing that Brogan had indeed got it, the bird settled. 'You like it?'

'Yeah,' said Brogan. 'It's great.'

Moranti said nothing for a moment. His last boy had been small and delicate, much like one of the birds. To date, he hadn't replaced him, although since he'd disappeared, boys had walked into the shop week in, week out, asking for jobs. None had seemed suitable for his purposes, somehow, not until now, and he said, 'Supposing I say yes. When could you start?'

Brogan wasn't sure he'd heard him right. 'Start?'

'I thought you wanted a Saturday job,' said Moranti.

Brogan held out his hands and Moranti cupped them, the boy transferring the bird in as expert a manner as anyone could have hoped for, considering it was the first time he'd attempted it with something alive and flapping.

'Now, if y' like.'

'I don't pay much,' Moranti warned. 'Three pounds a day.'

'I'd do it for that,' said Brogan, and this was true. He'd have done it for less, for nothing perhaps, if only because a job of any description would give him something concrete to do with the time he spent out of the house, wandering the streets, looking for one good reason why he should ever go back home.

'In that case, we give it a try. Your first job – you come with me.'

He followed Moranti out of the unit, the floor gritty under his shoes. Sand on concrete, a safety precaution, a leftover from a time when the floor was awash with blood and offal and ice.

Brogan knew the market well enough, but had never before had cause to leave it via the back entrance. It gave out on to a square of hardcore where stall-holders' vehicles were parked up tight. Moranti made for a van. 'Seat-belt,' he said, reversing out even as Brogan got in.

He backed into a road that Brogan had walked down with his mother, when he was still small enough for her to insist that he held her hand. The recollection brought not so much a lump to his throat as a gaping hole to his stomach. A part of him was empty, and the fact of it was brought home to him in the simple things – a scrap of fabric from a dress she had made which he found at the back of a cupboard, the shoulder bag that hung on a peg in the hall. Among its contents were treasured fragments of his first few years of life – a wooden button, the charm from a rattle, a plastic toy that had tumbled out of a cracker.

Two years on, the implications of her death registered in ways that made him ashamed. In walking into the kitchen to find unwashed clothes spilling from a laundry basket, he would think of her, just as he would think of her when the sight of his unmade bed took him by surprise.

Of late, it had begun to register in the silence that was enveloping the house – a silence so powerful it could drown the blare from the television, the phone ringing, and he ate his meals in that silence, a plate on his knee, chewing each mouthful as if what he found on the fork were some foreign language.

It registered now, as Moranti drove past the shop where his mother had bought some wool, because knitting him a jumper was one of the last things she'd done. Sometimes he held up the front section, stood in front of a mirror and imagined her pinning the shoulders, checking it for size. Soon, his arms would be far too long for the sleeves. It didn't matter. The bobbled and cabled jumper with its centrepiece that depicted the tree of life would never be stitched.

'Where are we going?' said Brogan, and Mr Moranti patted the corpse in the pocket of his coat.

'I want my money back,' he said. 'We're going to Roly's Yard.'

The inner city fell away to be replaced by the shell of a factory surrounded by walls that bore notices warning people off. Brogan read the words UNSAFE and PROSECUTION, then turned his attention to houses awaiting demolition. They were unlike any they had passed so far, standing tall and square, a flight of steps leading to boarded-up doors; tiles missing from the roofs, the gutters and metalwork stripped for scrap.

A strip of wasteground divided them from a row of similar properties, their massive gardens overgrown, the boundaries that defined them having long since fallen away.

Someone had made some attempt at redefining one of the boundaries with a fence of corrugated iron, a pair of makeshift gates the only access, and mesh swept up from the fence to the roof of the house itself to form a cage. He'd seen something like it dangling from a Christmas tree in a store, his mother stopping to wait as he examined it with hands that were minute by comparison with her own. 'What is it, Mummy?'

'A toy,' she'd replied, and Brogan had imagined an entire town of similar houses, some of them with carefully painted people peering out of the carefully painted windows.

Moranti struggled with the gates, tearing at the chain that

held them closed. It fell to the ground at Brogan's feet, and Moranti left it there, pushing at the gates until they opened, their jagged edges scraping on the ground.

Brogan followed him through and walked straight into a nylon net that draped from the mesh above. It touched his face in a way that reminded him of the entrance to a ghost train, and he staggered back as finches of every description took fright and panicked. Some made for trees that had been planted around the aviary. Others flew skyward, their progress halted by the mesh. They clung to the wire with slender claws, their bodies upside down, keeping the strangers in view by twisting their heads into impossible angles.

Many appeared to fall as they freed themselves from the wire, only to turn mid-flight and head towards the house, entering via open windows. A bird the size of a plum flew past, its tail as long as Brogan's arm, wafting in flight like a long, thin reed, turquoise turning to green. And then it was gone, and Brogan looked the length of the yard to find that it was much as he imagined the surface of the moon to be.

What had once been a grassed area was now nothing more than bare earth. At some point, an attempt had been made to concrete it, but the concrete had sunk before hardening, and small craters had been left where rain had settled into pools. Most were no more than inches deep, husks of seed floating on the water, ebbing towards the edges, sitting there like scum.

A bright red bird, its back dusted with a smattering of stars, swooped down and landed gently in a pool. It dipped a nervous beak into the water, then rose up, as if it had made some inspection of the boy and had returned to the trees to report back. 'It's only a boy, a very small boy, like the others who've been here before him.'

Roly stood in the yard, a boy-child of a man. Small and dark, his movements timid, as if, like a deer, he might at any moment take fright and run. He dipped his hand in a polythene bag, pulled out a fistful of seed, and scattered it on the ground as Moranti called from the gate, 'That Gouldian you sold me.'

The hand to the bag, the seed to the ground, a Zebra darting to Roly's feet, the back of its wing speckled like the coat of a fawn. It seemed an effort for Roly to form the words as he shouted back to Moranti, 'Wh-what about it?'

'Dead,' said Moranti.

'You sh-should care for them better.'

'You telling me I don't know how to keep my birds?'

Roly pinched the corners of the bag between his index fingers and thumbs, flipped it a couple of times and tied the ends. It was reminiscent of the way in which Brogan's mother had tied his sandwiches for school, and the emptiness returned to punch him hard in the gut. 'There's a high mor-mortality rate to keeping finches.'

'It's even higher when people sell you diseased birds.'

'I sold you a healthy bird.'

'So healthy it's dead,' said Moranti.

Roly's speech impediment worsened as he took offence at the comment. 'What – do you – w-want?'

'A refund.'

A cardboard box stood by a nesting shed, the damp lid having collapsed inwards to reveal the remains of finches. They were Scarlets, mostly, their feathers red as though each had been pierced through the throat.

'How – do I know it's d-dead?'

Moranti dipped his hand into a pocket of the gabardine coat, brought out the bird and handed it to Roly, who studied it as if by doing so he could determine the cause of death. He turned it in his hands, the fingers deft, the tiny stiffening form so feather light he could flip it over with a finger and thumb.

'I s-sold you a bl-black-headed Gouldian. This is r-red.'

'You sold me a red,' said Moranti.

'Black,' said Roly, but he reached into a back pocket and drew out some money. He peeled a fifty-pound note from a bundle, handed it to Moranti, then tossed the corpse into the box with the Scarlets. Then he approached Brogan and smiled a little nervously, as if expecting the boy to turn his back. Brogan noticed a slight imperfection to his lip, something that wasn't noticeable unless you got up close.

'You li-like finches?'

'Don't know,' said Brogan, shyly. 'I don't know much about them.'

'Well,' said Roly, a little more confidently, 'what-whatever you do, don't listen to Mr Moranti. Every time I s-sell him a bird, it comes back wrap-wrapped in a — r-rag.'

It wasn't a comment Moranti cared to hear. 'Come on, let's go.' But as he made for the gate, Roly raised a hand and snapped his fingers.

Instantly, the birds became unsettled. They didn't simply dart away but began to swarm round the yard. Round and round they went, like a plague of terrible insects, and Brogan covered his eyes as one of them smacked against his face.

Moranti stood at the gate. 'Brogan,' he shouted, but Brogan couldn't move, afraid to take his hands from his eyes.

Roly continued to snap his fingers, whipping the birds to a frenzy, and then he lashed out, lowered his hand and opened his palm a fraction. The birds appeared to settle, and Brogan took his hands from his face to find a bird on Roly's outstretched palm. It cowered there, too stunned to move, unaware that it was free, that it could hop from Roly's palm and flutter to the ground or fly to the trees. 'Y-yours,' said Roly. 'If you w-want.'

Brogan took it from him, cupped it in his hand and felt its heart hammering under the plumage.

'A — T-Tiger finch,' said Roly, and although it was plain and brown, the feathers dull by comparison with many other finches, it seemed to Brogan a beautiful thing, a soft and terrified thing. He wanted the bird to know that he couldn't have liked it more — not even if it had been the plum-coloured bird with the fabulous turquoise tail.

28

Moranti had left the yard, and, finding himself alone, Brogan panicked and ran towards the net, but as he ducked beneath it, Roly called after him, 'Y-you can come back, if you like.'

'What for?' said Brogan.

'To see the birds.'

Brogan looked unsure about that and, hurriedly, Roly added, 'I'll give you another b-bird.'

Brogan could hear Moranti revving the van. 'All right,' said Brogan.

And then he was gone.

CHAPTER FIVE

Searching Byrne's property had proved a waste of time. Deep down, Parker had known that would be the case, but he'd had to go through the motions as a matter of procedure, and you never knew your luck: Byrne might have made a mistake, might have left something somewhere to indicate that Gary had been to the shop, to his bedsit, to some small part of the property to leave a clue as to what had become of him. But there was nothing.

Parker, who hadn't allowed himself to hope for too much, had reminded himself throughout that if Byrne was in any way responsible for Gary's disappearance he wouldn't have been stupid enough to keep anything incriminating on the premises. Even if he were innocent (and Parker doubted that), he would have disposed of anything relating to children the minute he learned that a local lad had disappeared, and the media interest was such that Byrne would have known within hours that Gary had gone missing.

Notwithstanding this, Parker had obtained a warrant and he and his men had gone through the house like a double dose of salts. 'Don't forget the roof,' Parker had said, and after searching obvious hiding places such as the water tank and the space between the floorboards and the ceiling of Byrne's bedsit, his men had obliged by yanking the insulation from the eaves and lifting slates.

Then Parker had ordered the bunker to be moved as before, and yet again the ground that it had been standing on had been dug to a depth of several feet. He had anticipated that nothing would be found, and nothing *had* been found, but he had ensured that his men then examined the rest of the area to the back of the shop to try to ascertain whether the soil had been disturbed. It hadn't. 'Rock solid,' Warrender had said. 'So where do we go from here?'

Parker, who had fewer options than he would have liked, had now spoken to both Gary's parents and had decided to arrange for the Maudsley family to make an appeal through the media. He didn't for one minute suspect that any of them was concealing information, but he had to cover all the angles, and he intended to take advantage of a form of psychological profiling that had rarely been used five years earlier when Joseph Coyne had vanished: the appeal would be watched repeatedly, not only by every man on the team but by psychologists who would try to determine whether any member of the family knew more about Gary's disappearance than they were admitting.

The Maudsleys hadn't been comfortable with the prospect of facing television cameras, and Parker had done his best to reassure them: 'It's nothing to worry about. Nobody's out to make you look stupid, or responsible for what's happened. It's simply a way of letting the entire country know that Gary's disappeared. You never know, somebody might come forward with information as a result, so it has to be worth it, doesn't it?'

The Maudsleys had agreed with that, but the idea of those cameras still worried them, and Gary's dad had said, 'What do we have to do?'

'You'll be sitting behind a long table in a large room,' said Parker. 'There'll be microphones on the table, and there'll be cameras, and there'll be reporters, but I'll be right there, looking after you, so if anyone asks a question that you don't know how to answer, give me the nod and I'll do the talking for you.'

Reassured, they'd agreed, and the appeal had been made. It had been broadcast during the six o'clock news the evening before, and now Parker had gathered together his team to watch a recording of it.

The room where they were watching it was within the station and, if not for the fact that it was unusually small, Parker and his team might have been forgiven for thinking they'd been plucked out of the incident room and dropped into a cinema. They sat in semi-circular rows with the lighting dimmed, and there was an air of anticipation, as if they were about to be granted a preview of some major cinematic production, but the image on screen before them was no work of fiction.

Gary Maudsley's dad looked nervous, but Parker tried not to read too much into it, reminding himself that nerves were only to be expected in the circumstances: not only was his son missing but sitting directly in front of him were press photographers, reporters and camera crews, all recording his every word. As if that wasn't enough for him to contend with, his ex-wife was beside him, and despite the effort they made to appear united in front of the press, it was easy to pick up that their relationship was anything but amicable.

From time to time throughout the broadcast Frances Maudsley glanced at her ex-husband, with a sly, venomous look that laid the blame for their son's disappearance firmly at his door. Not that she thought he'd done anything to Gary – Parker knew that much from the brief, bitter why-ask-me-I-was-in-bloody-Morocco interview that had taken place in his office within hours of her arrival at Heathrow – it was more that she feared being branded by the press as a lousy mother, which was why she was trying to deflect attention from herself by saying that Gary's dad could have done a lot more for their son than he ever had.

Parker had refrained from pointing out that at least Gary's dad had stayed in the same country, he hadn't buggered off to live with someone he'd met on holiday. He'd also refrained from asking her how she'd managed to come by the thick gold Rolex — and Parker knew the genuine item when he saw it — clipped around her wrist. 'Do you work in Morocco?' he'd said.

She'd replied that she couldn't get a permit and that, in any case, her boyfriend was well off so she didn't need to. Parker's deliberate silence had prompted her to gaze out of his office window to a view of the city beyond.

For some days now, a steady rain had deepened the grey of the buildings, and it was obvious to Parker that whatever architectural strength and beauty there was to some of Manchester's better-known landmarks, it was all lost on her. She'd said, 'Don't you ever want to just ... get on a plane and go?'

'Go where?' said Parker.

Her voice had almost softened. 'Somewhere warm,' she'd said. 'Somewhere where it doesn't bloody rain.'

Parker had followed her line of vision to clouds that seemed so low it was almost as though a blanket of smoke had settled on the city. But for him this was home, and no amount of sun would coax him to leave it for anything other than a fortnight's holiday somewhere pronounceable.

'I'd have taken him with me, if I could,' she said, 'but I couldn't. You know what it's like with blokes and other people's kids — they don't want to know.'

'Some do,' said Parker, but he didn't doubt that her boyfriend wasn't among them. He wouldn't have wanted a woman with baggage any more than Gary's stepmother had wanted his dad with a twelve-year-old lad in tow. 'I love our Gary,' Frances had added. 'If anyone says I don't, they're a bloody liar.'

No one had disputed her word, but Parker thought back to a card that had been shown to him by Gary Maudsley's gran. *Happy Birthday, Gazz. Missing you always. Mum!*

On seeing that card, Parker had tried to imagine how he might have felt if his own mother had been absent on his twelfth birthday, and from that had come the realization that some kids learned from necessity the art of dissociation.

As he looked at the image on screen, it seemed to Parker that it was Gary's mum who was dissociating herself from the reality of her situation. Her son was missing and yet she sat there, her face blank, fiddling with her cuticles, pushing them back from highly polished nails, the Rolex catching the light from a flash-bulb and looking like a fake.

During the appeal, Gary's father had spoken for the family, his voice picked up by a microphone and amplified for the benefit of reporters.

There had been some difficulty in editing the film, and his lips appeared to move before his words were heard. The effect was unnerving, particularly when his voice broke as he said: 'If anyone's seen our Gary, or knows where he might be, please . . . tell the police.'

He had looked at his elderly mother, as if hoping she might come out with something more original, something that would prompt some member of the general public to go forward with information they might otherwise have withheld, but Gary's gran said nothing. She stared at the people in front of her, people who, with pencils poised, awaited a comment that she would never make, then lowered her eyes. 'He's only twelve,' said Gary's dad, and then, as if it had only just occurred to him that his son might be watching, he had added, 'Gary, if you're listening, you're not in any trouble . . . Just come home.'

Just come home, thought Parker. If only it were that simple.

He signalled the officer operating the equipment and, as the lights came up, Parker scanned the faces of people he knew well, people he worked with, socialized with, held together as a team. He knew their backgrounds, their dreams, their aspirations, and knew also that most of them, male and female, had kids of their own. Like him, they were one hundred per cent committed to finding Gary alive. Like him, they had a suspicion that Gary was already dead.

CHAPTER SIX

Roger Hardman had spent his life on the land, and although this particular job was new to him, the land, as such, was not. It was a different county, that's all, one that was unfamiliar, the shape of the trees as new to him as the shape of the people he found himself thrust among.

His new employer, the National Trust, had told him to open up rights of way on an estate situated to the south of Manchester, recently bequeathed by someone called Fenwick. By all accounts (and Hardman was only going by what people had told him), Fenwick had amassed a fortune in business and had retired to Colbourne House, where he had devoted the remainder of his life to keeping himself to himself.

Hardman didn't blame him for that, but he did blame him for blocking off all known rights of way throughout the estate, and now, as he fought his way down a bridlepath that had been all but obliterated, it struck him as obscene that, in this day and age, one individual could amass sufficient fortune to buy a thousand acres and prevent anyone else from enjoying its considerable beauty. It seemed odd, too, that someone should go to such lengths in life to keep people off their land then bequeath it to the type of trust that would open it up to the public. Perhaps, thought Hardman, Fenwick had suffered a stab of guilt towards the end and had tried to alleviate it by altering his will, or perhaps he had simply wanted to keep his land out of the grasp of distant and not-much-liked relatives.

Whatever the case, when alive, Fenwick had let most of his land to neighbouring farmers, but pockets such as this woodland had been left to their own devices. It was surprising what became of neglected woodland: Hardman knew better than anyone how impenetrable it could become. Trees could be choked by undergrowth, and paths such as this one became barely negotiable in no time. It had once linked villages to either side of the estate, but that was generations ago. Nowadays, the villages no longer existed, and the path led nowhere as such.

The wood itself was of no particular interest, thought Hardman. No pond to fish, no magnificent view, just forestry that had grown so dense, it might have been nightfall in there. Winter was almost upon them, but many of the trees still held their ragged leaves, and it seemed to Hardman that they conspired to block what light there was from a mournful sky. He carried a scythe and hacked with it, his progress slow, his sixty years telling on him now, but he swung it in slow, easy strokes, an old hand, and far too canny to catch himself unawares. He knew what the long, curved blade could do to the calf of a man's leg; knew he wouldn't be the first to catch an artery and die in less than two minutes. No one would find him, or at least not for a while, and certainly not in time. They might find the spot where he'd cut through the wire to get to the path in the first place. They'd also find where he'd sliced his way through the undergrowth and, by charting his progress, they'd come across his body. He didn't much fancy that.

He put the scythe down for a moment, wiped his brow with the back of his hand and looked up. The position of the sun told him it was lunch-time, just as it told him that the path wound east, which meant he'd reached half-way. If he could find a spot to sit a moment, have a bite to eat . . . but there was nowhere suitable, just trees, darkness and a treehouse of sorts, well off the path to his left.

He felt the ground, found that it was damp, and reasoned that in an hour or so, with luck, he'd have the job finished. Lunch could wait, he decided, so he lifted the scythe and continued, stopping only when curiosity caused him to wonder who might have built the treehouse.

Kids, he decided, but Fenwick had died without issue, so it must have been built by the children of a family that had once owned the estate. Colbourne House was prestigious enough for minor gentry, and it had no doubt accommodated more than its share in its two-hundred-year history. Still, to build a treehouse so far from the gardens struck him as strange, and he tried to picture the children who had built it, seeing them in breeches and those odd buttoned boots, a snatch of lace or velvet at their pale, slender throats. He wouldn't have wanted to be a child a hundred years ago, privileged or not, and if he had been, he wouldn't have built a treehouse in a wood where the trees were gnarled into shapes that could seem almost demonic to a child's eyes.

In leaving the path to take a closer look, he realized he'd been wrong. Whatever it was, this thing, it wasn't a treehouse. Its shape and proportions were difficult to discern, ivy having distorted it and made it part of the background so effectively that he might not have seen it at all if he hadn't just happened to glance at it from a particular angle.

It was supported on poles that had been stripped of bark, planed smooth, and driven into the ground to form a rectangular construction. It looked like some kind of scaffold or the frame to a four-poster bed, but the base, instead of being at a level that would make it possible for a person to climb in, was at shoulder height. Ivy had smothered the base with a mattress of green; the leaves moving softly, a bird dipping down and swooping its length, then fluttering into the trees, and on the soft, still wind, he caught the sound of a dog's single bark from many miles away.

He stretched out the hand that still held the scythe and used the arc of steel to touch the ivy. The tip of it lifted a tentacle of green, and in a nervous, jerking movement, he whipped it away to reveal what it concealed.

He knew, of course, that what he'd found were bones, and he wasn't a stranger to death, so it wasn't of death itself that he was afraid. What he feared was the fact that he had reached out, and had revealed with his scythe, a thing that was touched by evil, and he threw the scythe to the ground. He would never retrieve it again, feeling it to be tainted, unlucky, and all the more likely to carve through his flesh and bring about his own untimely demise.

Poor young bugger, he thought, for even as he stepped back and away from the scaffold he knew the remains were small. Boy or girl, he didn't know, but this had been a child.

He turned now, and ran, stumbling down the path, feeling the trees closing in, feeling that he was in danger. Death had been to this place, had visited a child there, had left its remains to the birds, and he ran as if that thing on the scaffold might lift itself from the bed and beckon him back, the teeth grinning, the voice child-like: *You'll never forget me you know. Every day for the rest of your life, you'll remember the way you found me, and it will haunt you, Roger Hardman, that I promise . . .*

CHAPTER SEVEN

Parker stood at the entrance to Colbourne Wood. It had been taped off at the point where Hardman had cut through the wire, and uniformed men were standing around, miserable in the rain.

It was growing dark, and Parker anticipated that they had less than an hour before the team would have to rig up lights. Ideally, they ought to see the remains and get the lie of the land before cluttering the scene with equipment, and he wished the pathologist would arrive so that they could get on.

The news of what had been found had reached his ears within an hour, Hardman having fled from the wood in search of the nearest phone. He'd called the police, and first on the scene had been a patrol from one of Greater Manchester's sub-divisions. Uniforms had asked Hardman to show them the exact location of the remains, but nothing they could say or do had persuaded him to set foot back in that wood. 'Follow the path,' he'd said. 'You can't miss it ...' and they'd done precisely that until they'd reached the structure that Hardman had described as ... a *scaffold*. One of them had lifted the ivy a fraction, had seen the remains and had returned to the patrol to radio Headquarters.

The information had gone straight to the incident room, and the man who had received it had placed his hand over the receiver before calling to Warrender. 'Neil, the remains of a kid have been found.'

'Where?'

'Colbourne Wood.'

'I'll get the guv'nor.'

Parker had been found and had gone to the incident room where he'd almost grabbed the receiver from the man holding the call. His brief, pertinent questions had elicited the information that the remains were skeletal, and he had ordered the uniforms to secure the scene before he ended with the words, 'I'm on my way.' He had then arranged for scene-of-crime officers to meet him at the wood along with Sherringham, the pathologist.

As he and Warrender left the station together, Warrender had said, 'It can't be Gary, guv. Assuming he's dead, there's no way his body could have decomposed so fast.'

Parker had been aware of that, just as he had been aware that Warrender hadn't added what each of them was thinking: the remains could well be those of Joseph Coyne.

They had walked out of the building and into the kind of rain that had reminded Parker of Frances Maudsley's words: 'Don't you ever feel like going somewhere warm, somewhere where it doesn't bloody rain?' and now, as Parker looked at his immediate surroundings, he was able to relate to her desire. Wherever that warm place might be, it wasn't Colbourne Wood, where the branches of the tightly packed trees entwined as if to keep intruders out of their space.

A couple of vans were parked up alongside the fence, the scene-of-crime officers sitting in them, waiting for Parker to give the order for them to enter the wood. All wore waterproofs over their dark blue overalls, and all seemed grimly subdued. There was no doubt about what had been found in that wood. Those uniforms from the sub-division had confirmed it. Therefore, in a very short space of time, they would be confronted by a skeleton, and though none of them was exactly spooked by the prospect, the fact that it had been described as that of a child put a different complexion on things.

Hardman was leaning on a rotting post, staring into the wood. The sky was heavy with the type of cloud that dispensed rain in sheets, but he took no notice and kept his eyes fixed on the trees as Parker walked up to him. 'Mr Hardman?'

He gave a nod

'Must have been a shock for you. How are you feeling?'

Hardman looked him full in the face. 'Cold,' he replied. 'Otherwise, all right, all things considered.'

'Can you tell me how you came to find the remains?' said Parker, and Hardman gave him the details.

Parker asked, 'Would you be prepared to show us where they are?'

Hardman seemed to shrink away, as if the mere suggestion of going back into that wood was out of the question, and Parker left it, not wanting to do anything that might result in the man keeling over on him. You never knew with elderly people and, in Parker's view, one body a day was plenty. 'You want to get yourself indoors,' he said. 'Do you live near?'

'Rented house in the village,' said Hardman.

'How about one of my men giving you a lift?' said Parker, but Hardman returned to his former pastime of staring into the trees.

'I'm all right,' he said.

A car drew up, one that Parker recognized as belonging to the pathologist. He walked over to it, and as Sherringham wound down the window Parker peered in to see him dressed for the weather in an oilskin jacket, his black trousers stuffed into wellington boots. 'Where's the body?' asked Sherringham, getting straight to the point.

Parker replied, 'I'm told it's off a bridlepath, about three-quarters of the way into the wood.'

'You haven't seen it, then?'

'Not yet,' said Parker. 'We've only just arrived.' He indicated the men in the vans. 'We're all set if you are.'

'Right, then,' said Sherringham, pulling a black leather bag from the passenger seat and climbing out of the car.

As Parker led the way towards the cordon, the scene-of-crime officers piled out of the vehicles and pulled their hoods against what was now a torrential downpour. They were joined by Warrender who climbed from Parker's saloon, and the group followed Parker towards the point where Hardman had cut through wire.

Once there, Parker paused and looked along the length of the path as far as he could see. Bramble and thorn were strewn on the ferns that lay to either side of it, and up ahead it disappeared into darkness. It was almost as though the trees were closing ranks, thought Parker, shutting them out, and he scanned the trunks for some sign of light between them. There was none. Just darkness leading to darkness, and the certainty that if they left the path, they'd soon be lost to that darkness.

'Not a pleasant place,' said Warrender, and Parker wondered whether that was precisely what the National Trust had felt on inspecting the land so recently bequeathed to it along with the house. Someone senior had probably taken a look at the wood and come to the conclusion that it was high time something was done to make it accessible, to lighten it up, to rid it of its malevolent, watchful air. To be responsible for a wood like this was a bit like being responsible for the type of pond that children couldn't resist – the type of pond that sat there, half hidden by reeds, just waiting for a tiny foot to tread too close to the bank.

He stopped himself. He wasn't a man to let his imagination get the better of him, and thoughts like that belonged to children, not to full-grown men. But as they walked through the cordon, Parker looked back to Hardman, still leaning on that post, watching them go, and read in his expression the expectation that none of them would ever be seen again.

44

They took the path in single file, treading with care for fear of trampling some clue as to how the remains had come to be where they were. It sounded as though they had been there for some time, in which case, there was little hope of finding clues, fresh or otherwise, but the precaution had to be taken.

Earlier, Warrender had asked Hardman how big the wood was, and Hardman had replied that it covered a good forty acres, but that meant nothing to Parker. He was a city boy, born and bred, and he couldn't have marked out an acre if his life depended on it. All he knew was, the wood was old, and, for the most part, it consisted of good old-fashioned English trees, the type he'd climbed as a kid. None of this pine nonsense that Parker tended to think of as vaguely foreign. These trees meant business, and over hundreds of years, their trunks had not only thickened but had contorted into shapes that gave them twisted limbs, screaming mouths, watchful, vengeful eyes.

The afternoon light was fading fast and visibility decreasing by the minute, yet Parker didn't want his men to use torches until it became absolutely necessary: something within him felt that it was important to see his surroundings as the child might have seen them before its death. You never knew, thought Parker; that might prove important, and he wanted his first impression to be accurate.

There was, of course, always the possibility that the child had been taken to the wood at night, just as there was the possibility that Hardman was mistaken. This may not be the body of a child at all: in a wood as old as this, there was no telling how long the remains had been there, and it was conceivable that what had been found were the remains of an adult murdered at a time when people were smaller than they were today. Not likely, he admitted to himself, but it was just possible, and in strange, remote little villages such as had existed as recently as a hundred years ago, a form of rough justice was sometimes meted out in the cruellest and strangest of ways.

He reminded himself that, at this stage, nobody knew

whether they were dealing with murder, though he had to concede that the likelihood was remote of a person taking themselves into a wood, building a scaffold, lying on it and waiting to die of exposure or starvation. Therefore, for the moment, Parker was of the opinion that they were about to find the remains of a person – child or adult – who had been murdered. The question of when that person had been murdered was one that only a pathologist would be able to answer. Sherringham might conclude that the remains had been there for a century or more, in which case, Parker's men would be relieved to learn that house-to-house enquiries would not comprise a major part of the investigation. On the other hand, Sherringham just might say that the flesh had only recently fallen away from the bones, in which case . . .

Odd, thought Parker, the way in which the remains of murder victims invariably came to light. He'd seen it many times: walls crumbled, riverbeds ran dry and trees fell to the ground, their roots unearthing bones that were instantly recognizable as not being those of an animal.

At the same time, he realized that the fact of the matter was, it was incredibly difficult to dispose of a body. England was small. It was also overpopulated, and people from towns and cities seemed to be driven, in ever-increasing numbers, into the country. They went in search of peace. And what they found was death: secrets kept for many years by soil, and rocks, and trees.

These particular trees were doing their best to keep whatever secrets they could by ensuring that he and his men were unable to see where they were going, but the path that Hardman had cut was almost as good as a thread leading them to the scene.

No sooner had Parker thought this than the path stopped, abruptly. He scanned the ground for some sign of the ferns having been flattened, found the trail he was looking for, and peered into the darkness in the hope of seeing what it was that had first caught Hardman's attention. He could see nothing untoward, just woodland so dense that the light had been shut out completely. Then he picked out the shape of two trees standing side by side. Between them, as if forming a bridge, there appeared to be something fitting the description of the scaffold, and as he approached it, he saw the scythe that Hardman had flung to the ground.

He moved towards it, the men behind him, and stopped in front of the scaffold. The ivy that the uniforms had lifted had fallen back into place and Parker could see nothing of what lay beneath it. He lifted a tentacle of green, felt it cool in his hand, then had the strangest sensation — as if the plant were entwining itself round his fingers.

He crushed a stem, an unnecessary act, but one born of a desire to reassure himself that this was merely a plant and that he could pull it out of the ground by its roots if he chose to do so. And yet he also had the feeling that, if he were to do so, it would quickly take root again and grow back stronger than ever. He drew it away from the platform, and saw a skull in which the teeth were perfect. A garment had been fastened around the throat, but whatever it once was, it was now all but rags — like the body, there wasn't much left of it, and the ribs, the pelvic girdle, the skull itself — all were small, the bones having about them a newly minted quality, as if they might be plastic, rather too white to be real. Hardman hadn't been mistaken, thought Parker. These were the bones of a child.

He let the ivy go, and turned to face his men, but it seemed suddenly to Parker that they were melting into the darkness. He could see the whites of their eyes, could hear them breathing softly, but nobody spoke, and nobody moved. He felt completely alone. If this is Joey, he thought. If this is down to Byrne . . .

He looked again at the scaffold, the bones now wet with rain, as if the skull was weeping, as if he could hear a childish voice that said, *You found me, then.*

CHAPTER EIGHT

It had been a good day for Brogan. Not only had he found himself a job, but he'd been given a bird.

He'd left the yard at a run, and as he'd dived into the van, he'd shown the bird to Moranti. 'I'm gonna call him Tiger.'

Moranti reached into the back and produced a small oblong box, four inches long, and two inches in diameter. Brogan passed him Tiger, too nervous to try to put him into the box himself.

Moranti took the bird from him and eased it in, then handed it to Brogan to hold. There were holes punched into the cardboard, and Brogan tried to imagine what it might be like for the bird, crouching down in there. It would be dark, he decided, and Tiger would see pinpricks of light, like stars. He'd be warm, because he was holding the box so close and under his coat, and he'd feel secure because every time Moranti took a corner, he adjusted the position of the box to prevent the bird from being thrown around.

Periodically, he felt the vibration of Tiger's claws as he scrabbled to gain some purchase on the smooth, cardboard interior, but for the most part, he stayed still. He was the first pet that Brogan had ever had, and he spoke to him softly through the holes punched into the cardboard, aware that Moranti was watching him, bemused.

Once they were back at the Emporium, Brogan had wanted to put the bird in a cage, but Moranti said it would be better to leave him to settle.

'He hasn't got no food.'

'He wouldn't eat any even if you gave him some, not until he's settled,' said Moranti. 'You leave him for the moment, yes?' and he passed a tin to Brogan. 'Polish the counter,' he said.

By lunch-time, Brogan had polished not only the counter, but the case that housed the stuffed fox and the cut-glass perfume bottles.

The lengths of silk that covered the back wall had been straightened, and the velvet seat of the carved wooden chair had been brushed clean. Then he made a start on the finches, lifting them out and putting them into a holding cage while he cleaned out the litter, replaced the seed and refilled the water feeders.

Some of the birds were so scared they sat and trembled in his hands. Others pecked in anger, the point of their beaks like tiny pricks from a needle, but none escaped and none was hurt, and all were returned to their cages without so much as a feather out of place.

'You're a good boy, Brogan ... a good boy.'

Lunch had come in the form of baps bought from the delicatessen. They'd sat on the wicker basket to eat them, Moranti watching his customers but leaving them to browse. Most were women, some with children, their fingers sticky on the surfaces that Brogan had already polished. After lunch, he took a rag and started to polish again, but all the while, he looked at the box that held his Tiger finch, and because he was pleased with the boy, Moranti relented and produced a bamboo cage from the back of the shop. He inspected it to see if it was sound, then handed it to Brogan. 'A few loose bars,' he said, 'but we can soon sort that,' and he showed him how to weave the raffia so that it bound the bars, tucking the ends away so they were neat as well as secure.

Brogan scrubbed it down with a solution that Moranti

assured him would keep the bamboo from cracking as well as disinfect it, and after he'd done all he could with it, Moranti said, 'Now for Tiger.'

The box containing the finch stood on the counter, next to the till, and Brogan, who had spent the entire morning wanting to pick it up, to shake it gently, to talk to the bird inside, now hesitated. He bent towards the box, resting his ear on the cardboard, and heard nothing. He didn't know what he would do if Tiger was dead, and it seemed possible to him that he might have died of fright in there, shaken out of his senses, walled up in the dark.

'Come here,' said Moranti, and he plucked the box from the counter, opened the lid and tipped the panicking finch into one of his hands. 'Nothing to it,' he said.

His fingers had closed on the bird to conceal it completely, and now he opened the bamboo cage, put his hand inside and opened the palm.

The bird was gone.

Brogan looked into the cage, but he couldn't see it. He looked at Moranti's hands. They were empty.

Frantically, he grabbed the box and tipped it upside down. He'd *seen* the bird in Moranti's hand. It *couldn't* be lodged in the box. And yet he peered in to make sure, finding that, as he suspected, the bird wasn't there. 'Where is he?' said Brogan. 'What have you done with Tiger?'

Moranti, seeming bewildered, looked up at the glass-domed roof as if expecting to see the Tiger finch flapping against the fractured pane of glass. Then he looked at Brogan's face and saw that the boy was on the verge of tears.

'He's gone,' said Brogan, who couldn't quite believe it, and then he saw Moranti smile and he looked in the cage again. The Tiger finch was there, and yet a moment ago the cage had been empty. He knew it was a trick, but didn't know how Moranti had done it, or why. He knew only that, for one brief moment, he had felt a sense of loss that was every bit as great as the loss he'd felt at his mother's death. Strange how that loss could come to him out of nowhere, sparked by events that couldn't compare with the greater loss of her death yet seeming somehow magnified by the fact of it. 'You shouldn't have done that,' he said, and he walked away from the cage.

'Brogan,' said Moranti, 'what about your bird?'

But the boy had picked up the rag and was rubbing at the counter in small defiant movements, his back to Moranti. 'You could have hurt him,' he said.

'I know what I'm doing.'

'Tiger's mine.'

'Brogan . . . I'm sorry.' For the rest of the day, Moranti caught him glancing over at the cage as if expecting the bird to be gone. This is a child who has lost many things, thought Moranti, and he decided never to play the trick again. It seemed to him a terrible thing that now the boy wouldn't look at the bird. 'Don't you want him?'

'No.'

'Shall I sell him — give you the money?'

'Do what you like.'

'Don't you want to work for me no more?'

There was the briefest of hesitations. 'I didn't say that.'

'I don't want no boys who don't look after a bird that relies on them, Brogan.'

'Tiger doesn't rely on me.'

'Who else is there to feed him?'

'You can feed him.'

'He's your bird. Why should I look after him?'

Brogan turned from the counter. 'You could have *killed* him,' he said.

So that was it, thought Moranti — the ultimate loss. Better not to want something, to love something, than to lose it in the end. 'I have gentle hands,' he said. 'I can handle the birds.' Now Brogan went to the cage and looked in on the finch.

He found that it was cowering on the litter, its wings slightly fanned, its breath coming sharp and quick. 'You've hurt him,' said Brogan, simply.

'Not me,' said Moranti. 'I never hurt the birds.' But Brogan thought back to that splash of colour lying dead in a cage. Moranti had left the Gouldian in a draught. Moranti couldn't be trusted. 'Where will you keep him?' said Moranti.

'In my bedroom.'

'Your parents won't mind?'

'No,' said Brogan, who wondered what his mother might have said. Initially, she'd have told him he couldn't keep it, that she'd be the one who would end up cleaning the cage. Then she'd have told him he'd have to ask his father, and Brogan's protests would have enabled her to anticipate what his father's reaction might be, so she and Brogan would have conspired to keep the bird a secret. 'Keep it in your room,' she'd have said. 'And don't let your father know.'

The covered market was shutting down for the night. Already, the mock-Victorian gas lamps had been dimmed. Stallholders were pulling down the shutters and Brogan, whose work was finished for the day, added, 'I've got to get home.'

'Here,' said Moranti, dipping a hand in the till. He pulled out five pounds and Brogan, who recalled that they'd settled on three, said, 'I haven't got no change.'

Moranti, who still felt guilty, replied, 'Keep it. You've earned it,' and after he'd taken the money, Brogan picked up the cage. The Tiger finch was still lying flat on the litter, its wings extended. 'I think he's hurt.'

'He's fine,' said Moranti, but as Brogan made for the door, the Diamond Firetail flapped lazily at the bars of his own bamboo cage, its various levels filled with devices that Moranti had slipped in for the bird's amusement. For the most part, it ignored them, seemed, in fact, to avoid them, and Brogan wondered whether there was any point in giving finches toys to play with. For all he knew, the devices might even upset the birds in some way, and it confirmed his suspicion that

Moranti didn't really know much about them. To him, they were just an addition to the many curious objects that littered the Emporium, and when they died, as the Gouldian had, he wasn't concerned that he'd lost them. All he cared about was getting his money back.

He wondered whether to take his bird to a vet, just to be sure, but he didn't know any vets, and even if he had the money to pay one, he wasn't sure that a vet would look at a finch. He hovered in the doorway, watching as Moranti emptied the till into a small drawstring bag. It was navy blue and a miniature of a bag that Brogan's mother had bought for his PE kit when he was still at primary school, and he felt that familiar stab as he said, 'Got any books?'

'What kind of books?'

'Books about finches.'

'No,' said Moranti. 'What would you want with a book?'

'I just want to know about finches, that's all.'

'Try down the library,' said Moranti.

'Now?'

'It'll be closed. Try Monday, after school.' He produced a cloth and walked up to Brogan, draped it over the cage that held his finch, and said, 'To keep him warm, to stop him getting scared.'

Brogan adjusted the cloth, and was about to walk out of the Emporium when Moranti added, 'Roly knows all about finches.' He pulled the string on the navy blue bag, shutting the money up tight. 'You got a problem with Tiger, you go ask Roly.'

He left the covered market and walked the two miles home to a suburb where it seemed, at times, as though someone had turned back the clock. Most of the roads were tarmacked now, but these were streets where terraced houses stood in rows, and some were still cobbled, the stones smooth, the pavements narrow and cracked.

54

He stopped in front of a house in the middle of a row, and found that, as was usual for a Saturday, a box had been left on the doorstep. A couple of weeks back, the lid of a similar box had been opened, but nothing had been touched, and Brogan had imagined some passer-by finding it, opening it and discovering that it contained nothing more than groceries. The fact that they'd left it alone had made him realize that the potential thief had felt a stab of pity for whoever the food might be meant for, and ever since then he had hated to find a box on the step.

He left it where it was and walked into the house carrying the cage, which he took straight up to his bedroom. Then he went back down for the groceries, kicking the front door closed as he struggled into the house with the box. He took it through to a kitchen where cheap pine units fought for space along a wall that had once been occupied by a Welsh dresser, left to his mother by grandparents Brogan had never known. There had been something sad about his mother's insistence on keeping it polished, as though she hadn't quite come to terms with the fact that she was housed in the middle of a terrace, that the cottage she might have dreamed of would never become a reality, that this was all she amounted to, all she would ever own.

The dresser had been sold, and Brogan hadn't known why, though he remembered, vaguely, that at the time, his father had been out of work and other items of furniture had also been sold. There had been a walnut cabinet crammed with china, tiny cups and saucers edged with gold, minute, fragile animals, a duck, a dog, a foal.

Now there was a sideboard where the cabinet had been, its top drawer filled with bills, receipts, photographs, the paraphernalia of everyday life. Its lower drawers held oddments, the sort of rubbish cleared from the house of every person who dies leaving others to sort through their belongings and wonder why this or that had been kept.

It was here, in the kitchen, that he remembered his mother best. If he kept his back to the door, he could almost imagine that nothing had changed, that she was in the next room, just out of sight and behind a lightweight ironing board. He had grown so good at this that he could almost catch the smell of the hot, damp clothes, which seemed to permeate the house, though neither he nor his father had ironed anything since her death.

There was another smell, less than welcoming, the smell that creeps into a house when cleaning becomes superficial and corners, crevices, surfaces and soft furnishings are not attended to. There was only so much Brogan could do, and he did his best because she would have wanted it that way.

He put down the box of groceries on a unit, pulled bread, cheese and salad cream out of it, and made a sandwich of sorts. His mother would have insisted that he got a proper meal, and at this time a couple of years back, he'd have walked in to find her peeling vegetables, braising meat or pulling a pie from the oven. Not that she was any great shakes as a cook. A plain cook, his father had called her, but there had been nothing plain about watching the expert way that her hands whisked sugar and butter into a filling for the cake that sometimes appeared for 'people who managed their cabbage' – 'Oy, you little monkey, get your fingers out of that bowl!' – but he always got the fork with the thick, creamy substance clinging to the prongs.

He took the sandwich up to his room, where the matching wallpaper, curtains and duvet cover depicted a design more suitable for a very young child. It didn't strike him as inappropriate: he had never known it to have been decorated in any other way, though a photo of him peering from a cot had made him realize that there had once been a time when the walls were powder blue.

There was a cheap vanity unit in one corner, more suitable for a girl than a boy, the laminated surface pink, the mirror oval, a crude design of flowers painted on the wood and protected by scratched glass. It was flimsy, and old, its drawer crammed with wrappers from sweets, cuttings from comics, legacies from a time when, for lack of more conventional toys, he had cut figures from the *Dandy*, had pasted them on to the cardboard back of a cereal packet and made up stories to amuse himself for hours at a time.

He sat on the bed, the cage at his feet, the sandwich to his mouth, and as he chewed, he rocked, quietly, not knowing he was doing it, not knowing what he was looking at as he stared out through the window to the houses opposite, with their blank, square windows and nets that were all the yellows and greys of a world unwashed.

He reached down and drew the cloth from the cage. Tiger still sat on the litter, too scared to sit on the rod that served as a perch. His small bright eyes looked up in fearful expectation, and Brogan struggled to think of a way of comforting the bird. 'You'll be all right,' he said. 'I'll get a book, and if it doesn't tell me what to do, I'll take you to Roly.'

He spoke through a mouthful of food, the word nothing more than a mumble, the houses opposite fading to become a gigantic aviary, a heavenly chaos of colour. 'Roly,' he repeated.

CHAPTER NINE

At seven a.m. the following morning, Parker called in at the station to be briefed by the men who had worked through the night, most of whom were monitoring as best they could the practical problems associated with a major investigation.

Julie Coyne had already phoned in and Parker knew that, before the day was out, she'd be down at the station. 'If she turns up, try to persuade her to go home. If she won't, put her in one of the interview rooms and tell her I'll see her as soon as I get back.' He added, as an afterthought, 'Though don't ask me when that'll be.'

He turned to the morning papers, which had been brought in, and scanned them, not out of curiosity but necessity: the police, ever wary of the possibility that at any point in any investigation one of their officers might be persuaded to sell information, liked to keep an eye on what the press had managed to find out with a view to discovering how they'd come by the facts.

Much as he had anticipated, the story was being carried on the front page of every national paper, but the press had precious little information other than that the bones of a child had been found and they had embellished what few details they had with rumours that the child may have been the victim of a cult.

It was an interesting speculation, and since the thought had also occurred to Parker, he didn't blame them for latching on to the possibility. It certainly appeared to be the type of case in which the ritual of the kill appeared to have been as important as the fact of it, which wasn't a happy thought, in Parker's view.

His eye was drawn to paragraphs picked out in fluorescent ink by members of the team, but Parker found nothing that caused him undue concern. The press had discovered that the remains were skeletal, and knew also that they lay on a scaffold, but this was information they had probably got from Hardman. It was too much to hope that they wouldn't have harangued whoever had discovered the remains into divulging what little they knew.

Warrender came on duty and Parker told him to stay at the station. He didn't seem put out; nor did he seem to feel that he was missing out on the action. Parker wondered whether, like himself, he wasn't all that keen to return to Colbourne Wood. He'd seen what there was to see, and it was something he wouldn't forget in a hurry.

But Parker couldn't afford the luxury of not returning to Colbourne, and a short while later he left the station, to find that, already, the M62 looked more like the M25. He sat in the traffic, which moved at a steady fifteen miles an hour, and turned off the motorway to find that the roads that led towards the wood were jammed with vehicles. Uniforms were blocking the road, turning people back, and as Parker pulled up within yards of the cordon he realized he had a serious problem: news of what had been found had spread. There were hundreds of people at the scene. Even as he climbed out of the car, some were breaking the fence and running across the land that surrounded the wood. Someone had had the foresight to call in for back-up, and uniformed men were there in far greater numbers than Parker would normally have placed at the scene of a crime. Mounted police had also been brought in, and they positioned themselves at strategic points, covering the wood from every angle, ensuring that nobody got to the trees and gained access to the scene.

Hardman was leaning against the rotting post as if he'd been there all night. Parker walked up to him, told him his scythe had been found and that he'd get it back in due course, but Hardman wasn't having any of it. 'Don't want it,' he said. 'Keep the bloody thing – bury it. Better still, chuck it on a fire.'

A man in his mid to late fifties was standing next to Hardman, his clothes casual, slightly shabby. There was something about him that made Parker want to take a closer look at him, and the man turned as if sensing that someone was watching him. There was something in his expression, Parker thought, a look that went beyond curiosity: he seemed genuinely upset, as if what had been found had some particular meaning for him.

Parker had half a mind to talk to him, find out who he was, how far he'd come, but as if anticipating it the man moved off, and Parker's attention was taken by the press who had homed in on Hardman.

For the most part, Hardman ignored them, or made monosyllabic responses, his eyes still fixed on the wood. Some photographer would get an award-winning shot of that leathery face, Parker thought. Enough of them were trying, but Hardman seemed not to notice. All he saw was the wood, and some private horror that had him in its grip.

Parker, who had gone to supervise the removal of the remains, entered the wood to be greeted by a different team from the men who had arrived with him the afternoon before. They didn't need him to organize them. They knew their job, and Parker was careful not to get in their way.

Sherringham wanted not only the bones but the platform on which they lay, and Parker watched as this, along with a fair proportion of the ivy that covered it, was freed from the poles.

Once the structure was dismantled, the site lost some of its horror and he wondered what the press would say when they got the chance to see it. They would find it hard to equate the spot with the picture they'd drawn of the place. For the most part, it would look like any other area of the wood, the trees dense, the foliage thick, and if not for the men who were combing the ground, there would be little to indicate why it had aroused such emotion in those who had seen the scaffold.

The scene-of-crime officers lowered the platform on to a lightweight support. Four feet wide and six feet long, it took the weight, and had handles that enabled them to get a decent grip. It was covered by a plastic sheet, the whole thing secured by tape, and at a nod from Parker, the men got into position, lifted the support, then carried it like a stretcher down the path.

Parker followed them silently and, as they reached the cordon, saw the men pause when they were faced by the enormity of the crowd.

The sight of the platform prompted those closest to it to surge forward, but before Parker could bark an order, uniforms linked arms to form a solid line and Parker realized that there was some advantage to having in the area one of the best football teams in the country: crowd control was almost second nature to these men.

Horses appeared to back up the uniforms, and kept the crowd contained, but getting the remains to the unmarked van was a slow and difficult process. At every step of the way, people pressed forward repeatedly, and at one point, the men carrying the platform were rocked by a gang of lads who'd broken through the line of uniformed men.

The last thing Parker wanted to see was the remains of a child spilled into the road, and he shouted a comment that stopped them in their tracks: *This is a kid, for God's sake.*

A silence came over the crowd. They stood back as the platform was eased into the van, and even after the doors were closed, the silence remained for some time.

There was nothing further he could do there so he headed towards his car with the intention of returning to the station. Much of what he would do in the future depended on what Sherringham could tell him about the remains, but whatever else the pathologist might say, one thing was for certain: these were not the remains of Gary Maudsley. Therefore, Gary was out there, somewhere . . . and Parker intended to find him.

CHAPTER TEN

Parker didn't need a medium to tell him that when he got back to the station Joseph Coyne's mother would be there, waiting for him, and he wasn't surprised when Warrender greeted him with the words, 'You've got a visitor. Mrs Coyne. I've left her in one of the interview rooms with a WPC.'

'Thanks,' said Parker. 'I'll go and have a word.'

The interview room was pleasant enough in that the walls were lined with hessian and the furnishings, although sparse, were comfortable. Its only shortcoming was the lack of radiator, and it was cold in there. Julie had kept her coat on, something long, beige and lined with a yellowing fleece. It was a far cry from the type of coat she might have worn some years ago, thought Parker, but come to think of it, she didn't flash her body parts around the way she used to. Everything about her seemed subdued, sombre, more thoughtful, as if she were saying, 'Let me have him back, and I'll be good.'

And maybe she would be, thought Parker, though God only knew, she'd learned in the harshest way possible that her child was precious and that she had had a responsibility to set him a standard, to fulfil her duties as a parent. He wouldn't wish that kind of lesson on anyone and, in any event, she'd long since paid her dues: she had aged out of all recognition since her son's disappearance and looked a good deal older than a woman in her early thirties. But it wasn't just her appearance that had changed; her attitude to life had undergone a transformation, and it was difficult to equate this softly spoken person with the loud, sometimes aggressive woman who had reported her son missing five years ago.

The first time Parker had interviewed her, he had sat in the sitting room of her tiny, two-bedroomed flat, and she'd chain-smoked as she answered questions he'd asked for the sole purpose of trying to build up a picture of Joey's home life.

'How long have you and your husband lived here, Mrs Coyne?'

'Two years, and he isn't my husband.'

'What's his name?'

'Chris.'

'Chris what?'

'Hill.'

'Where is he?'

'Out.'

'Where?'

'You tell me.'

She'd shaken a mane of hair that was bleached to breaking point, its volume almost drowning a small neat face. The gesture seemed mildly threatening somehow: there'd been something of the animal about it, the female of some species warning off a predator. 'Why are you asking me all this?'

'I need to know,' said Parker. 'We want to find him, don't we?'

She'd calmed down, but she hadn't softened.

'Is your partner Joey's father?'

'No.'

'So where's his father?'

'Saudi.'

It had taken Parker the best part of three days to discover that by 'Saudi' she had meant prison, and when he'd challenged her for wasting his time, she'd turned wide, innocent eyes on

66

him and had claimed that everyone knew what 'Saudi' meant, and what kind of copper was he, what chance did he have of finding her boy, if he wasn't even well up on local slang?

'Saudi' was a new one on Parker, who was in fact well up not only on local slang but on women like her, women who convinced themselves that the 'gifts' from boyfriends they saw from time to time didn't count as payment for sexual favours: women who wouldn't have classified themselves as occasional prostitutes, women who saw their kids as a bind, women who entered into relationships with men like Christopher Hill, men who would ultimately drag them even further into a life that would prove harder tomorrow than it had been today.

Initially, Hill had been questioned at length by Parker, but once Byrne's existence had come to light, Parker had laid off him. The fact that he'd been eliminated from Parker's enquiries had no doubt come as a relief to Hill, but the damage done to his relationship with Julie had proved irreparable: that he had been questioned at all had left her with doubts she couldn't quite dispel. He'd walked out, but it was no great loss, thought Parker. Christopher Hill, terminally unemployed, a petty thief, more of a nuisance than a cause for concern to the police, wasn't as bad as some of the men she might have picked up. At least he hadn't knocked her around or stolen what money she'd had, but he hadn't been much use to her, either.

Now, as he walked into the interview room, he found her, as he had known he would, staring into a cup of tea that had grown cold. He spoke to the female officer who was sitting with her. 'Maureen, how about a fresh cup?' and pulled up a chair, adding, 'Make that two.'

Julie Coyne looked up at him, her hair shorter now and a light brown, its true colour. She hadn't slept the night before. Parker could see it in the heaviness of her movements as she reached out, touched his hand and said, 'Is it Joey?'

'I don't know,' said Parker. 'I'm waiting for the patholo-gist to—'

'I do,' she said. 'It fits ...'

She'd lost him. 'Fits with what?'

'A few months back, I went to see a woman at the spiritualist church. She's genuine,' she added, hurriedly. 'She's worked with the police.'

Parker could imagine the ad at the back of some local paper. It would refer to this woman, whoever she was, as having worked with the police at some stage and that would inspire confidence in people who, for the most part, couldn't afford to part with the twenty-odd quid it would cost for a sitting.

'She said that he was happy now, *at peace.*'

Parker swallowed the euphemism for death with something approaching fury. He wanted nothing more than to tell her that nobody, *nobody*, had the right to imply her son was dead.

'She said he'd been in pain but that was over.'

She was on the verge of tears, and Parker didn't know if he could stand it. 'Julie,' he said, holding her hand a little tighter, wishing to God that Maureen would come back with that hot, sweet tea.

'She said he was thinking of me when he died, and that he watches over me.'

Parker fought the urge to snatch away his hand and slam his fist on the table. She felt the tension ripple through him and drew her hand from fingers that had frozen with fury. 'What did I say?'

'She told you all this,' said Parker, 'but she didn't happen to mention where we might find his body?'

He had expected the comment to bring her to her senses, but her face lit up at the memory of something the woman had said. 'Oh, yes,' she said. 'She told me he was staring up at trees, that there were birds ...'

'But she didn't give a location?' said Parker, and the ice in his voice had melted to be replaced by something akin to profound sadness.

'She couldn't,' said Julie Coyne. 'Those on the other side aren't allowed to give information like that.'

Pity, thought Parker. Life would be so much easier if they were. Anger made him blunter than he had intended to be, and he said, 'If the remains are Joey's, we'll soon know.'

Notwithstanding that she'd told him only seconds ago that she believed Joey was dead, she started to cry. 'Tell me he isn't dead, Mr Parker. Tell me it isn't *him!*'

Maureen walked in carrying a tray, and Parker felt himself a coward as he stood up, indicated the chair he had just vacated and said, 'Take care of her, Maureen. Then get a patrol to take her home.'

He walked out into a corridor, stood beneath a vent that blasted cool, dry air into his face and breathed deeply. The truth was, he was torn. Part of him wanted the ID to be positive in that five years was a long time and he wanted the lead that might help him prevent another death, but at the same time, nothing would have overjoyed him more than to see Joseph Coyne, now seventeen, saunter into his mother's flat and say, 'Mum, I'm home.'

CHAPTER ELEVEN

In some respects, the room where Sherringham was examining the remains was similar to an operating theatre. The table in the centre was stainless steel, the lamps above of a type that could be manoeuvred into a variety of positions. Right now, they were shining down on the platform, which overlapped the table by several inches.

Sherringham had ordered that as much as possible of the ivy should be left *in situ* and his reasons for this were twofold: in places, the ivy was binding the bones together, and it was also binding the skeleton to the platform. By leaving the ivy intact, he had succeeded in ensuring that the skeleton had not been much disturbed, and that what he was seeing now was pretty well what Hardman had seen when he found it.

Over the years, the ivy had wrapped, vine-like, under and over the bones, had twisted its way into every crevice and crack. Now the ribs were a cavity filled with withering leaves, their surface wax-like underneath the glare of the overhead lamps.

Some of the plant had been pulled out by the roots to which clods of earth were clinging, and tendrils draped from the platform to the floor of the lab. It was as if they were searching for purchase on the sterile, shining floor, thought Sherringham. He touched the ivy and found it cold, like the hand of a corpse, and although there were few things that Sherringham felt uneasy about touching, he didn't like the feel of it, and he drew his hand away.

The skeleton had been photographed at the scene, but now that he had got it to the lab, Sherringham photographed it again from every angle. The shots would be compared at a later date to determine how much, if at all, the remains had shifted when the platform was disturbed, but he knew even now that the ivy had done its job.

He moved to the head of the table and looked at the skull. It was easy to see where the bones had knitted in infancy. Dental records would confirm the child's age, and they would also confirm whether these were the remains of Joseph Coyne.

He walked round the side of the table, and began to remove the ivy, clipping it away with a tool that looked like miniature pruning shears. It fell to the floor at his feet, and lay in great swathes round green rubber boots that trod it underfoot. At one point, an assistant swept it away, leaving him free to work, to pick and pluck at the leaves that had grown inside the ribcage and were smothering the spine.

It was a long, slow process, Sherringham wanting the skeleton free of everything that could conceal any part of it from his acutely observant eyes, yet unwilling to disturb it if he could help it. A lesser man might have whipped away the ivy in a few swift strokes, but Sherringham took his time, using tweezers where necessary, clearing the bones as effectively as the teeth of a predator might.

And then he was done, and the bones lay before him, gleaming white beneath the lights that shone down from above. He measured it, examined it, and recorded his observations via a microphone fixed to the lapel of his green overalls.

He concentrated his attention on the garment that had been fastened at the neck, found that it was held with a strip of Velcro, and undid it before his assistants lifted the skeleton and moved it to an adjoining table, leaving the garment behind.

Sherringham picked it up and studied it. It was a small

cotton cloak of some sort, the strip of Velcro roughly stitched, the hem uneven in places.

He spread it out, and photographed it, then cut a tiny section from the hem. This he sealed in a sterile polythene bag and labelled for the lab. Ultimately, it would be analysed and it would be possible to confirm what the material was and possibly even where it had come from. It may once have been black – that was something the lab would tell him when they'd analysed the dye – but it was now various shades of grey, and something about the way in which the body had decomposed had caused the dye to fade leaving an impression of the spine and ribs, as if the garment were some sort of Turin Shroud.

He recorded these findings too, and made some written notes, then turned his attention to the platform. An impression of death had been left here, too, in that the area on which the body had lain was discoloured, the wood that had supported it having been shaded from the sun by flesh and bones. The resulting effect was bizarre, as if a shadow of the body still remained, and as if the area that surrounded it had been bleached to form a contrast.

Sherringham took slivers of wood from each individual piece that made up the platform, bagged them all and labelled them, again for the lab. He was fairly sure that the platform was made of railway sleepers sliced lengthways into thirds, but it was just as well to have the lab's view of the type of wood, its age, and from where it may have originated.

He turned his attention back to the remains. Without soft tissue, there was little to give any pointer with regard to how the child might have died: lungs would have told him whether the child had been asphyxiated, other organs would have enabled him to take samples in order to determine whether drugs or poisons had been used.

He didn't relish the thought of having to tell Parker there was too little to go on to establish the cause of death. The possibilities were endless, and he would list them in the hope that one or more might fit with something Parker discovered in the course of his enquiries. Of all these, one had sprung to mind the instant he had clipped the ivy from the bones only to find that the limbs fell away from the torso. Perhaps, thought Sherringham, the child had bled to death.

Parker would want to know what had made him venture that theory, and Sherringham now looked again at the skeletal remains. Without the tangle of green, the limbs lay flat on the platform, severed at the major joints.

The body had been dismembered.

CHAPTER TWELVE

Roly left the market, crossed the road to an old arcade and walked into a bookshop where he saw Byrne. This was their usual rendezvous. The first Tuesday of every month they met without the need to confirm the arrangement, and if either didn't show, the other assumed that something had come up.

Byrne was at the usual spot, standing in front of a section where books of a type that interested him were shelved. Biography, autobiography — works of non-fiction from which he derived comfort when he discovered that others had lived lives sadder than his own.

Roly walked up to him, plucked a book from the shelves, and let the pages fall open where they would. Byrne kept his voice very low as he said, 'I've had a visitor. Parker. Wanted to know if I'd ever spoken to Gary.'

'What did you t-tell him.'

'That I'd never set eyes on him.'

Roly flipped a page.

'I need to get out of Manchester for a while, but it costs,' said Byrne. 'I need a deposit for a flat, rent, food ... I can't afford it.'

Roly shut the book, plucked out another and, again, let the pages fall open. 'I was hopin' you might help me out,' said Byrne.

'C-can't,' said Roly. 'I haven't got no money.'

'You *must* have,' argued Byrne.

'If I had, w-would I be living somewhere like M-Mousade Road?'

Roly had him there. For the life of him, Byrne couldn't imagine why Roly would want to live as he did if he had the money to live elsewhere.

'I can't go through it again,' said Byrne, and now he sounded desperate. 'I got questioned when Joey went missing. I know what to expect. Parker will go at me for months.'

'C-can't,' said Roly.

They were joined by a third party, a woman with a boy that Roly judged to be five, perhaps six. The child stood by his mother for a moment, then slipped away to play at a computer in a corner of the shop that was stacked with children's books. He sat beneath a bulb set into the ceiling, some silver-backed thing that shone directly down on a head of gold. It gave him an almost ethereal quality, as if he'd been dropped from the heavens, and he manoeuvred the mouse with a confidence that Roly could only admire.

'You've *got* to help me,' said Byrne.

Roly snapped the book shut, the sound like the breaking of a bone, and as he put it back on the shelf, Byrne raised his voice a fraction: 'People like us should help one another out.'

'C-can't help you,' said Roly. 'No one can help you, Dougie — not if P-Parker's determined.'

Byrne cast his mind back a couple of years. There'd been someone he knew who'd been released from prison having served a sentence for child molestation. Greater Manchester Police hadn't wanted him on their patch: they'd paid his expenses and shipped him off to another part of the country, made him somebody else's problem. Byrne, who knew what it was to be persecuted, had formerly been determined to remain on his home turf. He hadn't intended to oblige anyone by moving away, and he had long ago decided that, if it came to it, he wouldn't be persuaded to leave Manchester against his will. But Parker hadn't tried to persuade him to leave. On the contrary, Parker had made it clear that he wanted Byrne where he could see him. One day, Parker hoped to get the evidence he needed to charge him with the murder of Joseph Coyne, and Byrne suspected that Parker sensed that day was drawing close.

He felt much as he imagined an impala might feel in the dead of night, blind to what was going on around him but certain that a predator was crouching in the grass a mere few feet away. He woke in the night, certain that he could smell Parker in the room, feel Parker's breath on his face. For the first time ever, he envied the man who'd been shipped to another county, wished, in fact, that he'd been shipped off with him, and the panic these feelings induced in Byrne gave him courage of a kind. 'I'll come to the yard,' he threatened. 'Parker'll follow me there.' But the threat seemed to make no impression and, short of grabbing Roly by the throat and making it clear that he meant it even though it would arouse the curiosity of those browsing around him, Byrne felt helpless to do anything about it. He stormed out of the shop.

After he'd gone, Roly turned his attention to the child who sat at the computer, his mother having gravitated to shelves where volumes were dedicated to astrology, cookery and sex. Her son sat alone, clicking a mouse against apples, owls and garden gates to make a story progress in the manner that he wished to see it progress, and as Roly watched him, it occurred to him that anyone could have drawn the child away without his mother's knowledge. Anyone could have lured him to the door, slipped him out into the street and into a waiting car. He knew how easily these things were done, how careless parents unwittingly were, and how easy it was to take advantage of a stupidity that almost amounted to complicity.

An apple fell from the tree and smashed, blood red, to the ground. A pale horse appeared on the far green hills, and the child drew it to the apple as if coaxing it to feed. A worm writhed from the apple. The pale horse shifted shape and became a reptile. The child drew away from the game, and Roly drew away from the child, aware, even as he did so, that cameras installed for security purposes monitored his movements.

CHAPTER THIRTEEN

Parker stood in the incident room, in which photographs of the scaffold dominated noticeboards fixed to every wall, and briefed his team. The men keeping Byrne under surveillance had reported back after following him to a covered market where he had bought duck-liver pâté, black olives, a creamy cheese spiced with peppers – Parker was put in mind of prisoners who'd gone into jail incapable of putting a meal together only to emerge as amateur chefs, food one of their few pleasures in life.

His men had followed Byrne to a bookshop where Parker suspected that he had met a contact. During their conversation, Byrne had seemed to grow agitated, and he'd left the shop abruptly, but after he'd walked out, his contact had remained, had appeared to be watching a child who was playing at a computer.

Parker's men had split, one following Byrne, the other sticking with his contact. Byrne had been followed home, but his contact had entered a nearby covered market where Parker's man had lost him in the crowd. The detective had returned to the bookshop where he requested footage from security cameras that monitored the customers. It was made available, and Parker and his team had studied it intently.

Although the quality was poor, it was possible to determine

that Byrne's contact had been white and in his early to mid thirties. He'd been of medium height and medium build, and his hair was short and dark.

Great, thought Parker. Why these people couldn't oblige by making themselves conspicuous was a constant source of misery to him. There had to be countless men who fitted such a description, but life was never easy in Parker's line of work.

There was one clear shot of the contact's face, but it didn't ring any bells with Parker, who had come to know by sight a number of paedophiles living in and around his patch.

That meant nothing, thought Parker. There were paedophiles all over the globe and most of them would live and die without coming to the notice of the police. One thing was sure, though: he hadn't wanted to be seen talking to Byrne. It was just possible that he was an innocent individual who was nervous of being seen with a convicted child molester in case he was tarred with the same brush. But even as he thought it, Parker didn't believe it. Child molesters set themselves apart. Decent people didn't associate with them. Therefore, any suspicion that fell on Byrne's contact was probably justified, and it troubled him that he didn't know who the man was. He had been under the impression that he had Byrne taped, that he knew where he went and with whom he tended to associate. Clearly, that wasn't the case – but, then, if he had the resources to watch men like Byrne twenty-four hours a day from the moment they were released from prison to the moment they died, it was far less likely that kids like Joey and Gary would have gone missing in the first place.

'I want to know who he is,' he said to the team, 'if Byrne is seen talking to him again, the minute they part company, I want him brought in.'

His briefing was interrupted by a call from Sherringham. 'We've got an ID. The dental records have confirmed the remains to be those of Joseph Coyne.'

It was an odd thing, thought Parker, but from the minute he'd first set eyes on the bones, he had somehow suspected that the match would be positive, but to have it confirmed came nevertheless as a shock.

Sherringham hadn't known what to expect by way of reaction, but it hadn't been the sadness that lay behind Parker's voice as he replied, 'That's terrible news for Julie.'

'There's worse,' said Sherringham. 'He was dismembered, possibly prior to death.'

Aware that he was being watched by his men, Parker also knew that his reaction to the news had given him away. Certain members of the team had seen him deal with cases so bad that even the press had declined to report the full details, and would have grasped that what he was about to tell them now was news of the worst possible kind.

After Parker ended the call, he confirmed their suspicions, then returned to his office having left complete silence in his wake. He needed some time on his own, a space in which to think uninterrupted, and as he looked out on the city, he thought about Byrne. He'd misjudged him. He'd had him down as responsible for the abduction of Joseph Coyne, but he hadn't imagined him to have been capable of committing a crime so horrific. His first reaction was to bring Byrne in and go at him until he confessed what he'd done. There had once been a time when Parker might have got away with it. Trouble was, times had changed. People like Byrne had rights. If Parker were to break him down by methods now considered unacceptable, his case against Byrne would be thrown out of court on the grounds that his confession was unsafe. In the light of there being only circumstantial evidence against him, Parker needed a confession, and if he couldn't get it one way, he'd get it another. Question was, how?

He knew that to stand a chance of trapping Byrne, he needed a greater understanding of how his mind worked, where his weaknesses lay. He recalled once having read an article in the *Police Review*. It had centred on a criminal psychologist who had contributed to the compilation of a database of offender profiles. He'd recently published a paper on the type of murder in which the ritual of the kill appeared to have been as important as the fact of it. Parker felt he had nothing to lose by talking to the man.

He left his office, went down to the police library three floors below, and looked up the article in the relevant issue. A telephone number was given, but even as Parker wrote it down, he wondered whether he was clutching at straws: he'd heard conflicting reports about the usefulness of criminal psychologists. Some seemed to compile fairly accurate profiles of the person the police eventually found was responsible for a particular type of crime, but others had been known to throw an investigation right off track by encouraging them to focus their attention on the wrong type of suspect altogether. It was just possible that a criminal psychologist might take one look at Byrne and tell Parker he was on to the wrong man. But then Parker considered what he knew about Byrne. It was all superficial. A criminal psychologist might just show him what Byrne's true weaknesses were, and once they were revealed to him, Parker would use them against Byrne to break him down.

He left the library and made for the incident room where he spoke to Warrender. 'Phone this number. Ask for Murray Hanson.'

The name meant nothing to Warrender, but the words 'criminal psychologist', scribbled beside it, brought a wry smile to his lips. He didn't know a great deal about the ins and outs of offender profiling other than that the idea had taken root in America; the FBI had given credibility to what he, personally, felt was a hit-and-miss pseudo-science. On those grounds alone, he decided that he wouldn't be holding his breath, but Parker wasn't a man to whom he cared to put this view, and all he said by way of response was, 'Sir.'

Hanson had been about to leave the clinic when his secretary buzzed him to tell him that a Detective Superintendent Parker was on the line.

Although it had only just gone four, the Friday-night traffic that filed through this suburb of London was already nose-to-tail, and Hanson knew he'd be caught in it whether he took the call or not. He leant against one of the radiators in an office he shared with another senior psychologist, feeling the warmth seep through the fabric of his coat. In buildings as old and inconvenient as this, the archaic central-heating system made little impact, and it was only by pressing up against the radiators that anyone could tell if it was actually on. 'Put him through,' said Hanson.

'Mr Hanson?' said Parker.

'Speaking,' said Hanson.

'I'm a Detective Superintendent with Greater Manchester. I got your name from the *Police Review*.'

'I've contributed a couple of articles,' Hanson confirmed.

Parker put a face to the voice and judged Hanson to be a man in his mid to late thirties. That was relatively young for someone who was obviously successful in his field, so Hanson was clearly bright, and dedicated with it. He detected a slight Mancunian accent from the inflexion, and because it served to make him feel that he was talking to someone from his own patch, he sounded slightly less formal than he might have done as he added, 'I hope I haven't caught you at an inconvenient time.'

'I can talk for a moment,' said Hanson, and then, in a move that Parker felt was astute, he added, 'What was the subject of the article?'

'It mentioned that you'd been instrumental in setting up a database of offender profiles.'

Hanson recalled that article, and recalled also that it had generated correspondence: certain senior police officers appeared to hold the view that the type of crime committed in America differed vastly from that committed in the UK. They had therefore let it be known that, in their view, a database of offender profiles was little more than an interesting curiosity, a fad that would have its day and then be forgotten. Parker added, 'It also referred to a paper you recently published – the one about incidences of human sacrifice.'

'I'm just one of many who've made a similar study,' said Hanson.

Parker, who wouldn't have thought that that type of murder was commonplace enough to warrant extensive study by a number of individuals, replied, 'That may be so, but yours is the only name I've got at the moment so I wondered if we could meet?'

Hanson said nothing, so Parker added, 'You've probably heard what was found at Colbourne yesterday.'

'I read this morning's papers,' Hanson confirmed.

'I'm heading up the investigation.'

Hanson, who had guessed as much the minute he discovered who Parker was, said, 'I could send you a copy of the paper I recently published if you think it might be of help.'

'I was rather hoping you'd—'

'But other than that . . .'

Parker began to wonder whether it was his imagination or whether Hanson genuinely sounded defensive. 'I wondered if you'd like to take a look at what we've got – give an opinion.'

'You're in Manchester,' said Hanson.

It wasn't imagination, Parker decided, and his tone hardened as he said, 'It's a three-hour journey by train, surely—'

'I don't have any plans to visit Manchester.'

'Maybe not, but in the circumstances—'

'I'm sorry, but I'm working to an incredibly tight schedule at the moment and I really don't have time—'

'Now wait a minute—' said Parker, but Hanson cut across him with the words, 'If you hold, I'll find the name of someone in your area. There are plenty of people who—'

'You're said to be an *expert*,' said Parker. 'Or have I been misinformed?'

Hanson wasn't about to fall for that. If Parker could get him to admit that he was regarded as an authority in this particular field, it would be difficult for him to fob him off with a colleague who might not be held in such high regard. 'As I said, I'm busy.'

'So am I,' said Parker.

'You have my sympathy,' said Hanson.

Parker took stock of the conversation. For some reason – and he couldn't for the life of him think why – they were arguing. He had half a mind to slam down the receiver, but a mixture of professionalism, curiosity and determination to get his way prevented him from succumbing to the luxury. He forced himself to sound civilized as he said, 'Save your sympathy, Mr Hanson. Save it for the relatives of Gary Maudsley.'

'Who's Gary Maudsley?'

'Twelve-year-old lad who went missing a couple of weeks back. I think there's a fairly good chance we'll find his remains on a similar scaffold, given time.'

'Mr Parker,' said Hanson, 'the fact is, I don't—'

'Hard to say how many other lads will go missing before we—'

'I said, I don't have any intention of coming to Manchester.'

Parker was sure he couldn't have heard him right.

Hanson added, 'You'll have to ask somebody else.'

'I don't want somebody else.'

'I'm willing to give you a list of names.'

'I don't want somebody else,' Parker repeated.

Hanson, tiring of the conversation, decided to end it abruptly. 'In that case,' he said, 'I can't help you.' And then he cut the call.

Parker sat in the incident room staring at the receiver, which he still held in his hand.

'What's up?' said Warrender.

'I've just spoken to Hanson.'

'Solved it for us, did he?' said Warrender. 'When do we pick up the killer? Or is he having a word with him to get him to give himself up and save us the petrol?'

Initially Parker had been stunned. Now he was angry. He slammed down the receiver, stood up and turned to Warrender, saying, 'Phone the clinic back. Ask for the fax number.'

As the order was carried out, and the number placed on his desk, Parker pulled a chair up to one of the computers and wrote to Hanson. He took the letter to one of two fax machines in the incident room, dialled the number, and watched as it went through.

Warrender knew well enough when to ask Parker questions and when to keep his mouth shut; he kept his distance. He didn't know what Parker had written in that fax: he was merely glad it wasn't addressed to him.

Hanson was leaving the building when his secretary called from the doorway to her office, 'I've just got a fax from Greater—'

'Put it on my desk.'

The secretary had worked at the clinic long enough to have seen any number of psychologists come and go, and she wasn't overawed by any of them. 'It's from the police and it's marked urgent,' she pointed out.

Hanson hesitated, but only for a moment. There were plenty of other people who were qualified, and willing, to help with Parker's enquiries. Hanson was qualified but he wasn't willing. He wasn't going to Manchester, and that was the end of the matter. 'Hold on,' he said, and retraced his steps, heading for the office he'd just left.

'Don't you want the fax?'

'No.'

He disappeared into his office and emerged some moments later with a list. He took it into his secretary's office and handed it to her, saying, 'Fax him back with a copy of this. I've marked a cross against a couple of names. That should keep him happy.'

Hanson's secretary took the list and looked at it. 'What about the fax?'

'File it,' said Hanson, and then he was gone.

After he had left the office, his secretary reread Parker's fax. She had been told to file it, and she obeyed, but she would have preferred to have left it on Hanson's desk. Parker had made comments that she felt he ought to see, if only because it sounded to her as though Parker intended to take the matter further if he didn't respond. Also, Parker had clearly misjudged Hanson in that he wasn't arrogant, obstructive or self-opinionated, and she wondered what had been said between them to prompt such remarks.

The car park flanked her office and she caught sight of Hanson as he crossed it, then climbed into a battered C-reg Saab. He was too young for her by a good twenty years, and the only emotions he aroused in her were maternal: a good-looking man like that ought to be raising a family, not chasing round town after girls who were probably totally unsuitable.

And then she stopped herself as she realized that, although she'd worked for him for a good while now, she knew little about him. Women never phoned him at the clinic, and if ever she asked whether he'd done anything interesting over the weekend, he merely replied, 'Nothing much.' In short, if someone like Parker had asked her for a profile of Murray Hanson, she'd have found herself hard pushed to tell him anything, other than that he was quiet, that he kept himself to himself and that, generally, he was well liked by his colleagues and the junior members of staff. It sounded so like the profile of a serial killer that the thought of it made her smile: she'd have to tell him that – he'd probably laugh.

Warrender picked up the fax that had come through from the clinic and took it to Parker, who had left the incident room and gone into his office.

He was standing at the window, a habit of his, and Warrender wondered what he was thinking about. The scaffold, maybe, or Byrne. More likely, he was thinking about his brush with this guy Hanson.

He stood there, deep in thought, and Warrender had half a mind to leave him in peace. Then Parker turned and saw him. 'What is it?'

'This just came in.'

Parker took the fax and read it. It hadn't been written by Hanson but by a secretary acting on his behalf. It was nothing more than a covering note to accompany a list of people who might be better placed to help with Parker's enquiry. There was neither reference nor response to the comments Parker had made, and Parker got the distinct impression that Hanson either hadn't read the fax he'd sent, or didn't deem his comments important enough to warrant a response.

The psychologist's attitude seemed the height of insolence to Parker, and the anger that had subsided in the moments since he'd left the incident room resurfaced with a vengeance.

'Phone the clinic. Get him on the line.'

Warrender left Parker's office, and moments later, the phone on Parker's desk began to ring. Parker whisked the receiver to his ear, prepared to hear Hanson. What he got was the secretary, who apologized and told him Hanson had left the clinic. She sounded middle-aged. She also sounded cautious. She, at least, had read the fax, thought Parker. 'Do you have his home telephone number?'

'Yes,' she confirmed, 'but I can't—'

'Give it to me.'

'I'm afraid I—'

'Now,' said Parker.

He waited while she got the number, then wrote it down as she dictated it, and asked, 'Does he have a fax at home?'

'Yes,' said the secretary, and she gave the number with no further prompting from Parker.

'Thank you,' said Parker. He hung up, left his office and returned to the incident room, where he went to the noticeboard and pulled down photos of Joseph Coyne and Gary Maudsley. He took them to Warrender saying, 'Get a computer printout of these photographs — something I can put through a fax — then put them on my desk.'

If Hanson thought he was in for a quiet Friday night, he was much mistaken, Parker thought.

He would have preferred to hit him with what he had to say the instant Hanson walked through the door to his home, but before he did so, he had a duty to tell Julie Coyne that they'd found what was left of her son. It wasn't a task he was particularly looking forward to, and on those grounds alone, he wanted to get it over with as quickly as possible. But there was another, pressing reason why it had to be done straight away: if he were to leave it until morning and the press somehow got hold of the news before he'd had the chance to break it to her, he'd never forgive himself.

He left the incident room and went in search of the female officer who had sat with her in the interview room the day before. At least, thought Parker, Maureen, with all her years of experience, would know what to expect when the news was finally broken.

Outside, Julie Coyne's flat looked much the same as ever, a maisonette on a sprawling estate that was less than a couple of miles from Gary's home.

Inside it had undergone a total transformation – much like Julie, thought Parker, grimly. It wasn't just the lick of paint, the fresh wallpaper, the flowers on a table set for the meal she would make for herself alone; the drab velvet curtains had been replaced by light, floating cotton ones, the carpet was new and this one, unlike the old one, didn't have cigarette burns on it or the imprint of an iron that had fallen as she pressed a blouse in front of the electric fire. Even that was gone: she'd had central heating put in. At one time, he'd have asked her where she got the money. Not any more. He knew where she worked, knew that she'd been promoted and was out of the typing pool. He was glad for her. And sad for her. So incredibly sad, he didn't know how to say it, but it turned out he didn't have to.

'It's him, isn't it.' she said.

'Julie . . .' said Parker.

He'd never been much good at this. He didn't know anybody who was, if he were honest. Maureen seemed to lead him, rather than her, to the chair, to sit him down, to place her hand on his arm. But Julie Coyne stayed standing.

'I knew anyway,' she said, lightly. 'The woman at the church . . .'

How long, thought Parker. How long will it be before it hits her?

'He's happy now,' said Julie, her face illuminated by the light that filtered through those floating curtains. *'At peace.'*

He couldn't help thinking of Gary Maudsley's gran. She wasn't at peace. Right now, she was standing at the window as Julie Coyne had for the best part of the last five years, waiting for a lad who hadn't come home.

CHAPTER FOURTEEN

Murray Hanson was living with a radiographer, which wasn't entirely unusual for a clinical psychologist. Their hours had been equally unsociable at one point in their respective careers, and they had been thrust together by circumstance as much as by mutual attraction.

Right now, she was standing with her back to a kitchen window that gave out on to a garden. Situated, as they were, within a half-hour drive of central London, they were lucky to have a garden. He earned the kind of money that normally wouldn't have stretched to a house with a garden in one of London's more desirable suburbs, but he'd looked around until he'd found a two-bed cottage of sorts. Small though it was, the mortgage was crippling, partly because he insisted on paying all the bills himself, but the house, like the garden, was his, and he wanted to keep it that way.

Much of the garden was paved, and in what passed for a rockery, a toad had taken up residence. He fed it woodlice when he could find them, flicking them towards it and watching with fascination the speed with which the tongue flicked out to catch them.

If ever he sold the house, it would be on the understanding that the toad had a life interest in the property, and that was what Jan wanted, a life interest in the property – a life interest in his *life*, in fact. She'd been dropping hints of late, and he didn't blame her. Two years into a live-in relationship, most women would do the same. She was thirty and, although she hadn't said so in case it scared him off, she wanted children, security, the knowledge that the roof over their heads belonged to her as much as to him; the knowledge that he intended to stick around.

He'd made the usual excuses, had referred to his first disastrous marriage, but knew it wasn't fair to string her along. The time had come for decisions. He would either have to take the plunge or tell her he couldn't commit to more than he was already giving.

Relationship problems were common enough – he dealt with them every day, along with the agoraphobics, the juvenile delinquents, and the sexual deviants that had first brought his work to the attention of the police, but right now, she wasn't talking about 'where their relationship is going'. She was standing at the window, her pale hair loose and falling on to a sweatshirt that he seemed to recall having bought for himself some months ago. He hadn't worn it yet. He hadn't had the chance. Every time he looked for it, he found it in the wash, or in the bag she took to the gym, or draped round those delicate shoulders. He liked the way it drowned her with its sheer size, liked the very smallness of her, the doll-like, fragile build.

'You're not listening,' she told him. 'Someone called Parker phoned just before you came in. Police, I think. I said you'd be back any minute.' She saw the look on Hanson's face and added, 'What's wrong?'

Even as she spoke, Hanson heard the phone begin to ring. He turned and walked out of the kitchen and into what had once been a large utility room. The units that had lined its walls when Hanson bought the cottage had been stripped out, the walls replastered and ragged, the tiled floor covered by two brightly coloured rugs.

He flicked a switch on the wall but it was the lamp on the desk that lit, its glow softening the harsher lines of a computer that was wired up to the web. That computer was his link with criminal psychologists the world over; there would come a day when the database was global.

Beside it, a phone that was also a fax was flickering into life, the ringing tone having been replaced by the whir as a fax began to come through.

Hanson left it a moment, then lifted the edge of the paper and saw the letterhead of Greater Manchester Police. He whisked it out and read it, aware that Jan was watching him, aware also that his expression was giving him away.

'What is it?' she repeated.

He made no reply, but put the fax, face down, on his desk, and watched as two further pages were printed out. He picked them up and studied them.

The first was the picture of a boy, and although it hadn't come out well enough for Hanson to determine the colour of his hair or school uniform, it did at least depict the smirk of a kid who'd been full of life.

Not any more, thought Hanson. Not if he'd fallen victim to the person responsible for reducing the boy in the second photo to bones on a wooden scaffold.

Jan walked up and looked at both the photos. 'Why are you so angry?'

Hanson was silent. The murder of a child was enough to make anyone angry, but if he were honest, his anger was due, in no small part, to the way in which Parker had invaded his privacy.

Jan turned with the intention of leaving Hanson's study, but as she did so the phone that was linked to his computer began to ring.

For a moment, Hanson was tempted to leave it. He had guessed who it would be, and his position hadn't changed: he'd sent a list of names; Parker could take his pick.

The answerphone kicked in as Jan reached the door, and she recognized the voice as belonging to Parker.

'Hanson,' said Parker, 'if you're there, pick up the phone.'

It was less a request than an order.

'Aren't you going to answer it?' said Jan.

Hanson snatched up the receiver. 'What do you want?'

'I take it you've read my fax.'

'Just,' said Hanson.

'There, now,' said Parker, softly. 'That can't have been too hard.'

Jan walked out of the study, closing the door behind her.

'How did you get my number?'

'Your secretary gave it.'

'She had no right.'

'She had no choice,' said Parker.

Hanson wondered how best to end the conversation and whether he could counter Parker's threats with a few of his own. 'You have no right to invade my privacy like this, no right to use bullying tactics.'

'Mr Hanson,' said Parker, and he suddenly sounded weary, 'I'd have phoned you earlier, but I was with the mother of Joseph Coyne. I've just had to tell her that what we found on the scaffold is all that was left of her son, and it wasn't a pleasant experience to watch her fall apart.'

'Mr Parker, I—'

'So you're coming to Manchester if I have to get you picked up and brought down here for questioning.'

'You can't do that.'

'Watch me,' said Parker, adding, 'I could bring you in, make no mistake—'

'You've got no grounds.'

'I'd find some.'

'You're out of order—'

'Maybe,' said Parker, 'but you might say I'm desperate.'

He didn't sound desperate so much as determined, thought Hanson. 'I have no plans to go to Manchester.'

'So you said.'

'That's why I sent you a list of people who—'

'I'm not interested in them. I want you.'

'Why me?'

'You're the expert.'

'Any one of my colleagues could—'

'I want you,' repeated Parker, 'and either you come, or first thing tomorrow I contact the governing body of whatever association happens to monitor your profession and tell them you've behaved in an unprofessional manner.'

'So you said in your fax.'

'I meant it,' said Parker. 'So what's it going to be?'

Hanson walked into the kitchen to find that Jan was folding his sweatshirt and putting it into the hold-all she used for the gym. 'What did the police want?'

'Parker investigated the disappearance of a boy whose remains have been found in Colbourne Wood. He's got another missing lad and he wants me to go and talk to him.'

'Are you going?'

He watched her fastening the Velcro straps, slinging the bag across shoulders that looked too tiny to bear its weight. 'I don't think I have much choice.'

'Where do you have to go?'

'Manchester.'

She froze — a momentary thing, but it didn't escape him.

'When?'

'First thing.'

She unfroze, but she didn't relax. Hers were the movements of a woman who was making a conscious effort to make herself appear untroubled by a situation she found deeply threatening.

She wouldn't ask whether he had any intention of making contact with his ex-wife while he was there, he knew that. In all the time that they'd lived together, she'd never once lowered herself to ask whether he still loved her, and she never would. Just as well, thought Hanson, because if she knew the answer to that one, he doubted she'd be able to handle it.

'Manchester's a long way away,' she said, lightly, and instantly, he got to the subtext of the comment, substituting time for distance, the past for the present. Lorna was yesterday. Jan was today, but she, who wasn't confident of his commitment to her, was confident of one thing: even now, after all these years, the wife who'd left him for somebody else would just have to snap her fingers . . .

. . . and that would be that.

CHAPTER FIFTEEN

Hanson hadn't wanted to give in to Parker, but he had come to the conclusion that it would be easier to do what he wanted than to explain himself to a powerful governing body. He had also come to another conclusion, one that had been creeping up on him for a while. It was about time he took some of the type of advice that he was always doling out to other people: *deal with the past, get it into perspective, then get on with your life.*

With that in mind, he packed a few clothes, put them, along with his briefcase, into the car, and drove up to Manchester, both to oblige Parker and to deal with a past that had become an emotional constraint that dragged him back each time he tried to plan for the future.

The route he chose took him past the grammar school he had attended, and he recalled that, as a boy of fourteen, he had sat in one of those classrooms, trying to absorb the finer points of some mathematical equation. It hadn't been easy. Outside, playing fields stretched into the distance as far as the eye could see, and on that long, hot afternoon, the click of wood on willow had filtered into the room to be ignored by him despite his love of the game, for he had known even then that he was fortunate, had known that for a lad of his background to have been given the gigantic step up and out of what amounted to poor circumstances was privilege enough for a lifetime. Consequently, while most of his classmates, their faces shining from the heat, had dreamed at desks arranged with almost military precision in horizontal rows, he had kept his head down and worked.

He had been a favourite with one of the masters, Parris, whose unassuming movements had been dramatized by a scholarly gown that seemed rather too large for his frame. He had taken Hanson, along with a couple of other boys, for extra tuition, not minding that their parents couldn't pay, their academic achievements reward enough for the hours he spent coaching them after school. The boys had known little about him, it seemed there was little to know: his wife was a local magistrate, his sons lived abroad. Devoted to his garden, he seemed to them to be a man who had certain standards, a man who lived by those standards and expected his pupils to do likewise. He was unremarkable. So unremarkable that he wasn't even a figure of fun. He was just *Parris*.

But on that day in June, he became something other than just *Parris*. He became a legend. He assumed a larger-than-life status and ensured that long after the names of other masters had been forgotten by every boy in the school his would be remembered.

Outside, a sixth-form batsman stared dismally into the eyes of a boy who would ultimately become a county-level bowler. Inside, Parris stared dismally into the eyes of a classful of boys who were due to take an end-of-term exam. Minutes into the lesson, the headmaster walked into the classroom and guided Parris into the corridor where two men were waiting by the door. They had glanced in at the boys in a manner that suggested that any one of them might, at some stage, come to their attention and ought, therefore, to be made note of now. The boys had glanced back as Parris merely acknowledged them with that quiet, almost deferential way he had, and followed them down the corridor.

Hanson had heard their footsteps recede on a floor so

highly polished, they would have seen the soles of their feet reflected in the shine. Then there had been the solitary sound of the headmaster's footfalls when he had returned, alone, some moments later to take the class for the remainder of the period. He had been pale, strained, and somehow less of a man than Parris whom Hanson had held in awe. To Hanson, Parris would always be 'Sir', notwithstanding that ultimately he had served twelve of a fifteen-year sentence for taking tea to his wife in their terribly English garden, then smashing her head with a hammer as she lifted the cup to her lips.

He never explained why he did it, and from the moment that he had witnessed him being arrested, Hanson had been seized by the desire to learn what motivated people to kill.

CHAPTER SIXTEEN

The headquarters of Greater Manchester Police was much as Hanson remembered it, an award-winning concrete block several storeys high. He left the car in an area designated for visitors, was checked through Security, and waited at the front desk for Parker to come and get him.

When he materialized, he proved much as Hanson had imagined him, an intelligent-looking man in his early forties. There was the suggestion of a sense of humour behind that solemn exterior, but there had been nothing humorous about the threat Parker had made on the phone, and on the whole Hanson wasn't feeling over-friendly.

'Good journey?' said Parker, extending his hand.

As they shook, Hanson tried to prevent the reluctance he felt at being there from showing in any way. He just wanted to get the whole thing over with so that he could leave. 'Not bad,' he replied.

They weighed one another up, each knowing that Parker had won this one, and that Hanson was at a disadvantage, not only on that score but because he was on Parker's territory. Then Parker led him deeper into the station.

Hanson had grown accustomed to the interior of a number of police stations over recent years and was unimpressed. The building had been designed to cater for the needs of a force that covered a massive area. It was vast, functional and plain, its corridors leading off to rooms that varied in size but were similar in design and furnishing.

He followed Parker into a lift that ejected them on the fourth floor, then down a corridor where breeze-block walls were painted a dour off-grey. It might have been leading to cells, but one of the doors off it opened into an incident room, where Parker's team were working, its walls smothered with photos that showed the scaffold from every conceivable angle. It was as if the walls were a carpet of green, thought Hanson, an advert for a luxurious woodland retreat.

As he looked at the photographs, Parker studied him, hoping that his expression would give some clue to what he might be thinking, but there was nothing. In more ways than one, Hanson seemed a bit of a closed book.

In the knowledge that Parker was watching for a reaction, Hanson turned away from the photographs. He had no intention of voicing his thoughts just yet, but there was nothing he could do to prevent those thoughts from ringing an alarm: the killer had built that scaffold in preparation for a crime he had known he would commit, and that did not bode well.

'What do you think?' said Parker.

'Bizarre, but not unique.'

The comment intrigued Parker, and Hanson elaborated, 'Tibetans and certain tribes of Native Americans buried their dead in a similar way.'

'Well, we don't get many Tibetans round here,' said Parker, bluntly, 'and I can't say we've had much bother with any Apaches.'

Hanson followed him into an office that led off the incident room. He took in the details at a glance, the photograph of uniformed men by the cabinet, the neatness, the sparseness of the furnishings. Parker was either extremely well organized or he had an army of people taking care of the paperwork. Having considered the little he knew of the man, Hanson decided it was the former.

'Let me take you through what we've got,' he said, and Hanson sat down and listened to the details, much of which he knew from what had been reported in the press. He broke in at one point to clarify some facts: 'You say that Joseph Coyne disappeared from a local estate?'

'Five years ago, and with all the hallmarks of an abduction,' Parker confirmed. 'Gary Maudsley went missing from the same estate, just less than two weeks ago.'

'Do you have a suspect?'

'Douglas Byrne,' said Parker. 'A paedophile. I questioned him extensively when Joseph disappeared, but came nowhere near close to pinning him down.'

'You think he abducted him, though.'

'Yes,' said Parker. 'I do.'

'It's no simple matter to abduct a person. It requires planning, organizational skills, a certain degree of intelligence to pull it off successfully.' He noticed that Parker was thinking that through, and added, 'Would you have said that Byrne had the necessary skills?'

'It's difficult to say. He left school at sixteen then almost immediately committed a minor sexual offence against a child of eight. That led to a custodial sentence, the first part of which was served in a juvenile detention centre. After he came out, he was limited to certain types of job owing to the nature of his conviction.'

'So what's he doing now?'

'He runs a video shop.'

Parker paused to see what reaction these words would produce, and saw it in the smile of resignation on Hanson's lips.

Parker slapped a file on the table, the words *Property of the Chief Constable* stamped on its dark blue cover. 'By the time you've read this, you'll have as much information about Byrne as I do.'

'What drew your attention to him rather than to some other suspect?' said Hanson, who didn't doubt that Parker would have been spoiled for choice in a city the size of Manchester.

'He was seen talking to Joseph the morning he disappeared. He denied having spoken to him. He also denied having committed the offence for which he was ultimately convicted until the evidence proved so overwhelming there was no point in continuing to deny it. Unfortunately, in this case, we don't have any evidence, and he's not about to admit anything.'

Aware that Byrne's home and workplace would have been searched as a matter of course, Hanson said, 'What did the searches produce?'

'A few fairly innocent photos of children, nothing pornographic.'

To the majority of paedophiles, the most innocent of images would suffice, thought Hanson, as Parker went on, 'We found nothing to link him with Joseph, and I can't afford to repeat what amounted to a futile exercise. *This time, I have to get him.*'

Hanson picked up the file, flicked through it and found it flimsier than he would have expected, in view of Parker's having had his eye on Byrne for years. 'I take it this is the abridged version?'

'You'll find what you need in there. If there's anything further you want, you have only to ask,' said Parker. 'Where are you staying, by the way?'

'Guesthouse, out towards Bury.'

Parker reached into the filing cabinet and drew out a cassette. 'Do you have access to a video and television?'

'I've no idea, but I can probably get my hands on one. Why?'

'Take a look at this,' said Parker, handing him the cassette. 'It's a copy of an appeal made by Gary's relatives.'

Hanson, who knew what he was expected to look for, also

knew that Parker would have run it past other psychologists. He knew, too, there was no point in asking what conclusions any of his colleagues might have drawn: Parker would expect him to form and express his own opinion with regard to the likelihood of any of the relatives having had anything to do with Gary's disappearance. 'I'll take a look,' he said. 'How long before your men will have finished searching that wood?'

'It runs to a good forty acres,' said Parker. 'Then there's the rest of the estate to consider — another thousand, give or take.'

That alone told Hanson all he needed to know. He could imagine the painstaking search, the sheer manpower it would involve, the technology that would be employed, the *time* it would take. Another lad was missing, and if there was one thing the police didn't have it was time.

He put the video cassette in his briefcase along with the file on Byrne. 'There's a favour you could do me, if you would.'

'Oh?'

'There's someone I'd like to look up, if possible. He lived in Greater Manchester when I was at school.'

Parker didn't respond, and Hanson could imagine that, in all probability, he was working out some way of pointing out that he had enough to do without supplying Hanson with the address of some former acquaintance. 'His surname was Parris,' said Hanson. 'His Christian name was Mallory.'

He realized immediately that the name meant something to Parker, and wasn't surprised. Parris's crime had aroused such local interest that it would have been odd if Parker hadn't known of him.

Parker replied, 'The crime was committed a long time ago. It's highly unlikely that we would hold a current address on file.'

Odd, thought Hanson. It didn't seem so very long ago since he had been sitting in that classroom, but Parker was right: the likelihood of the police or prison authorities being able to supply a current address was somewhat remote. 'I take it your interest is professional?' added Parker.

'Not entirely,' Hanson admitted. 'He taught me maths.'

'Then I take it you passed your exams?' said Parker, drily.

'You might say I wouldn't be where I am today if not for him.'

'I'll see what I can do.'

Hanson knew by Parker's body language more than by the silence that followed that this was as much as Parker wanted at this stage, and he rose to go. Parker got up, too, made it clear that he'd guide him down the labyrinth of corridors and back to Reception where Security would sign him out.

They walked through the incident room, larger and lighter than many Hanson had come across, in which additional phones and manpower added to the atmosphere of frenetic activity. Calls were coming in from the general public, and even as he passed a desk, he heard a uniform taking details from somebody who believed they'd seen Gary on a flight to Southern Ireland. The officer hung up, giving Parker a wry smile and saying, 'That's the fourth flight he's been seen to catch since he went missing.'

Par for the course, thought Hanson. He turned to Parker and said, 'What do you want most out of this?'

'How do you mean?'

'Do you want him stopped, convicted, held up as an example to everyone else who thinks they can commit a crime of this nature and get away with it? Or does a promotion hang on it?'

The word *promotion* seemed to appal Parker. 'Nothing hangs on it except the safety of other kids. I've got two lads of my own – I know how I'd feel if one of them disappeared.'

'You want him off the streets,' said Hanson.

'More than that, I want Gary Maudsley back, alive and well.'

Wordlessly, Hanson turned back to the photographs. Instantly, Parker was on to him, and he said, 'You think he's dead.'

Hanson, who had seen the scaffold and knew, perhaps better than Parker, what they were dealing with, merely said, 'I need more information.'

'Where would you like to start?'

'The wood,' said Hanson. 'Show me where you found the body. Let me see the scene.'

In walking back through the wood, Parker recalled having woken the night before to stretch out his hand before him having dreamed that he held a scythe in a fist clenched in fear.

In his dreams, he had followed the path that Hardman had cut, and he had been alone. Now, he had Hanson for company, and all around them uniforms were searching among the trees. There were two hundred men, in total, not all of them here: others had been allotted acres of woodland on other parts of the estate where the undergrowth was equally thick and progress equally slow, the thorn and bramble in places up to their thighs.

On open land, they would have attempted to move forward in a long, unbroken line, but here they stumbled, fell, and made their way as best they could, the occasional expletive reaching Parker's ears as thorns pierced clothing, tore it and embedded themselves in flesh.

Hanson looked up, his eyes scouring the treetops just as those of the men around him were searching the ground. 'Where does the bridlepath lead?'

'Nowhere,' said Parker. 'There were villages at either side

of the estate at one time, but we're talking a hundred years or so ago.'

'What happened to them?'

'The family who owned it had the locals evicted. Their cottages were demolished.'

'Any particular reason?'

'I think they just got tired of the local peasants tramping across their land.'

They wouldn't get away with it today, thought Hanson, yet he couldn't help drawing a parallel between that and the lack of power that prevented protesters from stopping a road being built straight across their gardens. Nothing changed, he reminded himself. The weak, the vulnerable, the powerless were invariably victimized, stripped of human dignity, treated as commodities — he looked around him — were murdered.

'Over there,' said Parker, leading the way to a rectangle of tape that cordoned off the poles that had supported the wooden platform.

The platform and the remains had been removed, but Hanson could imagine that the ribcage had ultimately proved as great an asset to the ivy as the poles that had enabled it to get an initial purchase. An evil thing, ivy, he thought. A keeper of secrets that refused to be confined to the soil, a demonic plant that reached up to the heavens by whatever means it could.

'Can I touch it?' he said.

'Go ahead,' said Parker, and as Hanson reached out to one of the poles Parker had the feeling that they were being watched. He knew that was absurd in that they were surrounded by his men. At any given time, one or more of those men could and did appear among the trees, and all of them had better things to do than to watch Parker and Hanson. And yet the feeling persisted. It was something to do with the place itself, he decided, the darkness induced by the foliage, the dimness of the light. It also had something to do with the fact that Parker felt more at home in town. Places such as this were alien to him; they stirred in him some primeval fear of being hunted down, of being taken by surprise by a lethal foe.

Hanson sensed his unease, and attributed it to the fact that Parker would be subconsciously aware that the danger to any child of his own couldn't be negated until the murderer was caught. It was a stress that every parent among his men would grapple with, and that fascinated him. On one level, assuming that they recognized this fear, they would rationalize it by telling themselves that the killer didn't even know their children existed: on the other, they wouldn't be able to shake the fear that their child might be next. He said, 'You mentioned something about the boy being dressed in a particular garment.'

'A cloak,' said Parker. 'It was fastened round his neck with a strip of Velcro.'

'Anything else of interest found at the scene?'

Parker cast his mind back to some of the points Hanson had made in the article published in the *Review*. 'You mean signs painted on trees, the presence of some kind of icon?'

'Anything you can think of,' said Hanson.

'Nothing.'

'Just the scaffold.'

'You say that as though it isn't remarkable in itself.'

'It's remarkable,' Hanson admitted, 'but, like I said, it isn't unique.'

The feeling of being watched increased and Parker, who had been fighting the urge to spin round and look, now succumbed and found himself gazing at a civilian. That the man had got past his officers didn't please Parker, but this was nothing by comparison with the fact that he recognized him as the person he'd seen standing beside Hardman the day that the scaffold was taken from the scene. He started towards him, and watched him melt away deep into the trees.

'Wait there,' said Parker, and followed. He caught him easily, grabbing him by the arm.

As Parker had noticed the first time he saw him, the man was in his mid to late fifties. He wore the same slightly shabby casual clothes, but he seemed troubled rather than aggressive. Parker eased his grip. 'This is the scene of a crime,' he said.

'I'm only looking,' he said.

'You were here yesterday.'

'I live near here.'

'Where?'

He gave his name as Gifford and an address which, as he had said, was local enough, in that it was a short drive from the town of Colbourne.

Parker escorted him personally from the scene, and watched as Gifford made for a small pick-up truck. Noting the registration was second nature to him and, after deciding to make sure that Gifford's address checked out, he returned to Hanson, who was waiting where he'd left him.

'Problem?' said Hanson.

'Not sure,' said Parker. 'Someone I saw here yesterday. We'll check our records, find out whether he's more than just curious.'

Hanson, who knew better than most people how places of macabre interest could draw members of the public, wondered whether what had been found in those trees would ever fade from public memory. There was every chance that the grandchildren of people who had been at the scene when the remains were removed would warn children of their own not to go there and the usual suburban myths would develop in relation to the place. In many respects, thought Hanson, it might be no bad thing if the wood were to be buried under concrete, or if a motorway were to obliterate all trace of what had been found there.

'So,' said Parker, 'what do you think?'

Hanson turned his attention back to the scene before him. 'There's nothing to suggest idolatry, or Satanic worship,' he said. 'Therefore I'd say there's a chance you could be right. It's the work of an individual. The motivation is most likely to have been sexual, which, in view of the boy's age would indicate that the killer was a paedophile.'

'Byrne,' said Parker.

'Let me read the file. Then let me talk to him. If Byrne is your man, I'll know.'

Even as he spoke, Hanson saw a series of images of the way in which the scaffold might have been constructed and realized that Joseph might have helped his killer to build it. He tried to block a flood of dialogue from his mind.

Hold this for me, Joey — that's right, good lad.

What are we making?

A treehouse — it'll be our own secret hideaway from the world.

I won't tell no one.

And then had come the ivy, that green and malignant thing, its cool and searching tentacles reaching up, growing across the body like a blanket. *There now*, Hanson imagined it saying. *All safe and warm. All tucked up for the night!*

He stooped and picked up a feather, the tip of it the kind of metallic green he had always associated with dragonflies. Amazing, thought Hanson, that birds of the British Isles could be so colourful; you'd never think it. From a distance, the sparrows, although cleaner than their city cousins, still looked brown, and although he knew that chaffinches and tits could swoop out of nowhere in a flash of unexpected colour, he wouldn't have thought any of them could lay claim to this vibrant turquoise blue.

'What have you found?' said Parker.

He let the feather go and it fell to the ground like the seed from a sycamore tree. He watched it spin, its progress as slow as that of the men around them, but infinitely more graceful. It belonged there, he decided. Ultimately, it would become a part of the ground to be covered by leaves, to be picked up, come spring, and used in the construction of a nest that would, perhaps, be built by a bird of the same species.

'Nothing,' he said.

CHAPTER SEVENTEEN

Parker had suggested that, instead of returning to the station, they find a pub and get a bite to eat, but the journey from London, the briefing, and the drive out to the scene had left Hanson feeling that the only thing he wanted right now was to head for the guesthouse in Bury.

Parker had asked him where he intended to stay, and Hanson had told him, but he hadn't added that he and his former wife had once owned the property, or that the people to whom they had sold it had taken advantage of the spacious rooms by offering bed and breakfast to passing trade. Parker was hardly likely to be interested, thought Hanson, though he might find it odd that he should want to return to his former home. He found it odd himself, and didn't intend to mention it to Jan, who would find it threatening.

Bury was a twenty-minute drive from the station, which made it convenient for Hanson in that he anticipated that Parker might call him in every time there was a major development. He was prepared for that, but what he wasn't prepared for was that the minute he pulled up outside the house memories he'd blocked from his mind came flooding back to catch him unawares.

Considering it was almost twelve years since they'd moved in, he was surprised by the detail he could recall, the V-necked sweater his wife had worn, the ivory blouse, the navy skirt, and the gold button earrings inherited from her mother.

He thought he had hauled those memories out, dealt with them and put them away for good, but now they surfaced with a vengeance, and he wished he hadn't come.

The front of the house hadn't changed, he thought, the hedges that surrounded it blocking out the light from the lower rooms. The gates were missing. He and his wife had kept them closed. He couldn't remember why. The new owners had taken them off the hinges, and had put a notice on the stone pillar that had supported them. *Vacancies.*

He drove round to the back, parked where he'd always parked, and walked to the front of the property, catching himself as he reached into his pocket for the key and pressing the bell instead.

He wondered whether he'd be recognized as the former owner, but eight years was a long time, and he and the Judds had met only once. It had been Lorna who had dealt with the details of the sale, agreeing prices on carpets, curtains, and the large gold mirror fixed to the wall in what he assumed would now be used as a dining room. The new owners wouldn't remember him, he decided, and it certainly seemed to be the case when Mrs Judd opened the door, and gave absolutely no indication that she remembered him.

He recognized her. Now that it came to it, he realized he would have known her anywhere, but this had less to do with her penchant for grey, overlarge tracksuits than the distaste he'd felt for the thought of someone like her occupying the home that he had renovated for a woman of Lorna's elegance.

At the time of the sale, he had pictured Mrs Judd cluttering the hardwood sills with tasteless figurines. The impression she had made on him had remained, and, in looking at the house, he found it justified.

When booking the room by phone, he had given the name Franklin and had described himself as a conference organizer.

He had also stipulated that he wanted a room that looked out on to the road, but as she led him up the stairs, she told him, 'The back rooms are quieter.'

'I'd prefer a room at the front,' he insisted, but when she gave in and he walked into what had once been his and Lorna's bedroom, he wondered whether he'd been wise. It was almost as if he could picture Lorna sitting on the bed that had once been their own, the particular look she wore when she was about to initiate sex. How many other couples had slept in that bed since the house was sold? How many people had brought back strangers as Lorna had, in the end? He imagined an endless procession of people picked up in bars, in clubs, or at the type of convention he had told Mrs Judd he organized; people who sought consolation in the type of one-night-stand that Lorna had used to end their marriage.

During the division of their possessions, she had suggested that he should have the bed on the grounds that it was far too big for her flat, and he'd told her to sell it to the Judds for whatever she could get. They'd bought it, and now, here it was – a memorial to his failure as a man.

He looked past it, taking in the details of the room. Odd that it looked much the same, even though its furnishings were unfamiliar. The dressing table was no longer there, but the fitted wardrobes remained, and he recalled that the day Lorna had walked out, he had come home to find her makeup gone. That was all. Such a simple thing, yet he'd known, and it was enough to make him open the door to the wardrobe now and stare at its interior as if willing her clothes to appear.

Cold anger; that had been his initial reaction. The pain had come later, and if he had chosen to dull it by launching himself into his work, well, that was nothing unusual. Most men would have done the same.

'Breakfast is served till nine thirty,' said Mrs Judd. 'After that, we clear the tables.'

'I'll be down by eight,' he assured her.

'How long are you staying?'

'It's difficult to say at this stage. A few days, perhaps longer.'

He doubted she needed the room. There might be passing trade in the form of sales reps, and the surrounding hills drew their fair share of ramblers, but there were no holiday-makers as such, and businessmen tended to stay in hotels closer to the city.

A kettle stood on a tray alongside a cup, a saucer and a sugar bowl stuffed with tea-bags. 'Help yourself to tea,' she said, and he noticed that the outside of the kettle was dulled by limescale, the crockery coarse and off-white.

Noticing the absence of a television, he said, 'I need to watch a video – something to do with my work. I don't suppose you could arrange for me to have a TV and video in my room?'

'There's a TV and video in the sitting room.'

'This is something of a confidential nature,' said Hanson, and he saw a flicker of suspicion cross her face. She thinks it's pornography, thought Hanson, and he wondered what her reaction might be if she knew just how much pornography he was sometimes required to watch to research a particular deviation.

He came to the point. 'It's nothing I wouldn't watch in company,' he said, 'but, for reasons I'd rather not go into I'd prefer to watch it in private.'

Her suspicion deepened. 'People have the use of the sitting room until eleven,' she said. 'After that, we prefer that our guests retire to their rooms.'

She'd latched on to something about him. Maybe his face rang a bell, or something about him didn't ring true. It was possible that, when giving his name and occupation, he had sent out a signal that she'd picked up on subconsciously. Whatever it was, she now clearly felt uncomfortable with him for reasons she couldn't quite pinpoint. He saw it in her body language, and heard it in her voice as she added, 'Will there be anything else?'

'Nothing, thanks,' he said.

After she left him to it, he took a shower in what had long ago been a dressing room but was now an *en suite* bathroom. He'd built it himself, had splashed his face with ice-cold water in it the evening that he'd come home to find Lorna gone.

Now, the water was more a trickle than a gush, limescale blocking the showerhead. Hanson adjusted the temperature but gave up in the end and stood beneath a dribble that ran lukewarm, then cold.

After he'd dried off and changed, he left his room and went downstairs to the hall, taking the briefcase with him, and never taking his eyes off it as he used the public payphone under the stairs. He dialled his own home number and, when Jan answered, thought his voice sounded strange as he said, 'Hi.'

Her voice had an edge. 'Hi,' she replied. 'Good journey?'

'Not bad,' he replied, in an echo of the reply that he'd given to Parker.

'I was worried,' she said. 'I'd hoped you might phone as soon as you arrived,' and Hanson was aware that she was trying not to allow herself to sound critical but that his lack of consideration had hurt her.

'I'm sorry,' he said, 'I should have thought ...'

'It doesn't matter.'

It did and, like the silence that followed, it spoke volumes.

'Where are you staying?'

'A guesthouse in Bury.'

'Give me the number,' said Jan. 'I'll phone you back.'

This had been his house, the home he had shared with Lorna. He didn't want to give her the number to his past, notwithstanding the fact that the number had changed. 'It doesn't accept incoming calls.'

'So where can I reach you?'

Nowhere, at the moment, thought Hanson. 'It's difficult right now, but I'll give you a ring tomorrow.'

'How long are you staying?'

'Hard to say.'

'Did your meeting go well?'

'Fine, but I can't talk.'

He knew he sounded wooden, and hoped she'd attribute it to his fearing that their conversation might be overheard. 'Sorry,' he said.

'What about?'

Everything, thought Hanson. Sorry I can't commit. Sorry I'm screwing up. Sorry I told you I loved you, and meant it, but can't seem to get it together.

In what he took to be an effort on her part to reach out to him, she suddenly said, 'The house feels empty without you,' and he could relate to that. This guesthouse, with its cheap figurines, its tacky furniture and the paintwork that had yellowed since he'd applied it eight years before, felt empty without Lorna. He'd known that it couldn't possibly be or feel the same without her, and yet he had allowed himself to imagine that he would be able to handle it, that by coming here he could lay the ghost of their relationship. 'I'm running out of change,' he said, and Jan said nothing at all.

He wished he could put a note of warmth in his voice and say something to bridge the gulf that had opened up between them, but he couldn't think of anything, and then they were cut off.

He stood there for a moment, the case at his feet, the receiver warm in his hand, and tried to visualize what she might be doing, how she was reacting. It was as if he were staring in at the window of the home they had shared for the past two years and watching a stranger walking from the kitchen to the living room, then crumpling into an armchair to work out what was going on between them. Maybe she'd come up with some answers. If so, she'd be doing better than him. Right now, despite his profession, he found himself incapable of analysing what he was doing here, why he had come. He wondered whether, if not for the case that had brought him back to Manchester, he would have felt the need to come back at all.

'A problem, Mr Franklin?'

He turned to find Mrs Judd observing him from the doorway to the living room. No, he thought, not the living room: the *dining* room, the small square tables having given the room where he and Lorna had spent the greater part of their time together a totally fresh identity.

He replaced the receiver. 'Cut off,' he said. 'I'll try again, later.'

She melted into the room, and he had the feeling she was watching him. He'd lost count of the number of patients who'd come to him exhibiting all the characteristics of paranoia. *People watch me, suspect me of things,* and his comforting reply was predictable enough: *Lots of people feel that, it's not necessarily true ...*

In this case, it was most definitely true. He couldn't see her, but he could sense she was there, standing behind the door and trawling her mind for details that would enable her to place where she'd seen him before.

He picked up the briefcase and walked into the sitting room. Finding it empty, he closed the door behind him and sat in one of the chairs that faced the TV. He pulled the case on to his knee, turned the combination locks and pressed the clasps, which unlocked with an almost silent *snick*.

Almost immediately, Mrs Judd opened the door and walked in. Hanson pressed the clasps back into place. She didn't speak, but left it to him to say, 'You did mention that I could use the sitting room.'

'I wanted to make sure you knew how to operate the video.'

Hanson considered the equipment, which was basic if not archaic. 'I'm sure I'll manage,' he said, but she walked towards the television, turned it on, and held out a hand, saying, 'If you give me the video, I'll put it in for you, make sure you don't have any problems.'

Hanson opened the briefcase, pulled out the cassette, and saw that there was nothing on the casing to give any indication of what it might be. He handed it to her and she drew it from the cover, slotted it into the machine and pressed the button marked Play. The screen became a snowstorm, largely because Hanson activated the remote, flicking the television to a dead channel.

Mrs Judd moved towards the door, her voice deadpan as she said, 'How long did you say you intended to stay?'

'I didn't,' said Hanson. 'Depends how long I'm needed.'

As she opened the door and walked out, it occurred to Hanson that life would be a great deal easier if he were to explain himself, but he was having enough difficulty explaining himself to himself and he didn't feel like baring his soul to this woman.

He got up and went to the door to close it tight behind her, then used the remote to find the channel that tuned into the video.

He watched the tape a number of times, noting the way in which Gary's dad held on to his composure. He felt that, in all honesty, it was virtually impossible for him to assess whether the man was hiding something with regard to his son's disappearance. To make comparisons relating to body language he needed to talk to him in an environment where he felt unthreatened. Then he could get some idea of how the man responded when at ease and when under stress. This would give him some idea as to whether he was as near devastated as he now appeared to be. One thing was clear, though, thought Hanson. Gary Maudsley's dad was no fool. His son had gone missing from within a hundred yards of where Joseph Coyne was believed to have been abducted. At the time when the appeal had been made he'd been gone for almost a week. There was no trace of him, bar the watch ripped from his wrist. It didn't look good.

He listened again to the tone of voice, the choice of words when Gary's dad had pleaded for anyone with information to come forward. He could almost imagine Parker's 'What do you think?'

Hanson knew what he thought: Gary's dad was out of the frame. Parker would be relieved. He had Byrne down as Gary's abductor and didn't want the issue clouded by some psychologist suggesting he should work on the boy's father, just in case.

Hanson turned off the television, rewound the tape, and returned it to the briefcase, which he locked. A cursory glance at his watch informed him that it was gone nine o'clock — his stomach had been telling him that for the past three hours at least. Time to get a bite to eat and call it a day, thought Hanson.

He left the sitting room, and as he walked out of the door, Mrs Judd appeared at the foot of the stairs. 'Going out, Mr Franklin?'

Hanson, aware that her attention was focused on the briefcase as much as on him, tightened his grip on its handle. 'Just a brief stroll, Mrs Judd.'

'We lock the doors at eleven.'

'I'll be back by then,' he assured her, and walked out of the house, stepped on to a path that had once been flanked with shrubs, and headed for a parade of shops where he and Lorna had sometimes grabbed a takeaway on evenings when neither could be bothered to cook.

He tried to refrain from looking back but found himself unable to resist the temptation. He saw what he'd suspected he would see: the figure of Mrs Judd staring after him from a downstairs window. He could understand her reservations: she obviously had a better memory for faces than he had given her credit for. As for his reluctance to go anywhere without his briefcase, he knew he couldn't afford to let it out of his sight. If the file it held were stolen, the police wouldn't trust him a second time with sensitive information, and he, for one, wouldn't blame them.

Hanson sat in the Saab, tucked down a side street and well away from the nearest street-light. Up ahead, a block of upmarket flats blotted out a night that was cloudless, and on the seventh floor, Lorna passed periodically in front of one of the windows. She was too far away for him to be able to distinguish her features clearly, but that didn't matter. The woman, with her dusky skin, her soft, dark hair, was Lorna. No mistake.

He'd often wanted to see where she was living, had been able to visualize it from a set of plans obtained from the local authority. The flat was bigger than he'd imagined, a twenty-foot living room, two double bedrooms and a kitchen fifteen by twelve. It looked too big for one person, and he knew she was living alone, but he also knew that she entertained a lot, that people stayed over, that she liked her space.

He'd mentioned that to Jan, who had remarked that he seemed to know an incredible amount about his ex-wife, considering he hadn't set eyes on her for years, and Hanson had replied that they had mutual friends, that he couldn't help it if, from time to time, they happened to mention how she was, what she was doing, who she was seeing. 'I'm interested, that's all.'

'Interested?' said Jan. 'I'd have said obsessed.'

'You know nothing about obsession,' said Hanson, meaning it as a joke. 'That's my province.'

'Yes,' she'd said softly. 'I'm beginning to realize that,' and now, as he sat watching Lorna, Hanson had to admit that to an outsider, his behaviour might appear obsessive. But it wasn't. He knew the difference, and he could say with total confidence that it wasn't. He should know: he'd lost count of the number of times he'd tried to explain to his patients that it was important to recognize and acknowledge their own obsessive behaviour if they hoped to free themselves of it. He was just curious, that's all.

He wondered about the flat and whether she felt safe. Security was reasonable but not what he would have called good: an intercom from each flat to the entrance door plus a neighbourhood-watch scheme being less than useless against a professional burglar. Even Hanson could have got in if he'd wanted, and he recalled a comment made by one of his patients: 'I only wanted to talk to her, but she wouldn't talk to me. I'd never had the chance to tell her what she'd done to me ... how much I'd suffered.'

Few of us act out our fantasies, thought Hanson. Most of us are too afraid of where they might lead. He had considered this in the light of what his patient had subsequently done. *I didn't mean to hurt her.* And now, as he sat watching Lorna, Hanson could relate to his patient's desire to break in, to shake his ex-wife by the throat, to get it across to her somehow that what she had done was something that had destroyed the very fabric of his self-esteem. *I'd like to kill her,* he thought.

CHAPTER EIGHTEEN

As Byrne walked into the yard, birds swirled round like mosquitoes, and Roly came out of the nesting shed to see who'd walked in. The minute he saw it was Byrne, he disappeared back into the shed, and Byrne walked up to the doorway.

In looking into its depths, he saw that row upon row of cages lined its walls, a different species of finch in every compartment. There had to be half a dozen varieties in there, some of them not fully fledged, others ready to try their wings or to be sold, never knowing what it was to fly. He wondered what it was about them that Roly was so obsessed with. To Byrne, they were just birds, neither beautiful nor ugly. 'Roly,' he said.

'I t-told you never to come here.'

'I had no choice.'

Roly lifted a Banaquit out of a cage and cupped it in one hand. With the other, he plucked a pipette from a mug, glutinous liquid glistening from the end as he dripped it into the bird's beckoning beak.

'We need to talk.'

'I'm b-busy.'

He returned the Banaquit to the cage and reached into another to lift out a couple of fledglings. He placed them in one of several small cardboard boxes kept stacked by the door, then pushed past Byrne who followed him to the house.

Here, in the kitchen every surface, from the mottled green units to the thick wooden pelmets that ran above the window-frames, was encrusted with filth. The smell of it caught at the back of Byrne's throat, and he gagged at the unexpected stench. 'Jesus Christ, Roly!'

He watched, in something approaching fascination, as Roly placed the fledglings in a cupboard over the cooker. 'What are you doing?'

'B-breakfast.'

For a minute, Byrne took this to mean he was going to eat those scraps of life with their barely discernible cries, and, frankly, it wouldn't have surprised him if he had.

'The heat from the cooker k-keeps the cupboard – k-keeps them warm,' said Roly, but Byrne had lingering doubts. There was something about the man, something of the predator: he could almost imagine him catching the birds mid-flight, his mouth a gaping cavern, the birds swallowed live. He pushed the image away. Of late, his imagination had been running riot enough on account of Parker without him letting Roly get to him.

Roly lit one of the rings, the flames leaping up with a popping sound that Byrne hadn't heard for years. He had forgotten that sound, and the smell of gas. It came to him now, briefly, and with it the recollection of himself as a child, watching his father light a similar cooker with an instrument that resembled a pen. Try as he might, he'd never been able to flick it into life, the flint that ignited the device having worn to the metal, but his father had had the knack: he'd been the only person in the house who'd been able to crack it. 'The other day, in the bookshop,' he said.

'What a-bout it?'

'I was saying that Parker—'

'You were saying you w-wanted some m-money,' said Roly.

'Okay, so I want some money. Give me some and I'll go.'

Roly shut the cupboard door and indicated the kitchen, the yard, the general filth and decay. 'C-can't. G-got none.'

'You *must* have,' Byrne argued.

Roly pulled a pan from under a unit, set it on the gas and watched fat that had solidified from an earlier meal melt and liquefy. 'W-want some?' he said, but Byrne, who wasn't altogether sure he could stomach food cooked in that pan, didn't reply. A short while later, he left Roly and wandered into the back room. He had lived in some squats in his time and he wasn't a stranger to squalor but, nevertheless, he paused in the doorway, appalled by the filth and the smell.

Clouds of finches beat at the window with fragile wings. At times, it was hard to discern which were in the aviary and which in the room. The window, in any event, was slightly open, and the birds could choose to enter and leave at will.

He took great gulps of air, settled into an armchair, and had the strangest feeling, as if he were in a large glass aquarium rather than in what amounted to an extension of the aviary. He felt as if he were somehow on display, as if people in the outside world might be pressing their faces against the fence and looking in on the spectacle of two unnatural men displayed in an unnatural habitat, for he knew that this was how the outside world, in all its ignorance and insensitivity, perceived men such as they.

He thought back to some of the things that had been said to him by the police after he was arrested for caressing a child and complimenting him on his beauty – that was all it had been, a compliment, and yet the police had sullied that compliment, had made him feel dirty, and Byrne had found himself incapable of making them understand that he cared for the boy. He'd wanted to make him feel welcome, that was all. Besides, the boy had wanted to be with him, had wanted to be touched, had *enjoyed* it, for God's sake.

Byrne had bought him a compendium of games – something that had turned up in court and was referred to as an exhibit. There'd been another exhibit, which the prosecution had described as unsuitable viewing for a child. *This man is a danger to young children.* Those words had haunted Byrne down the years. How the police could say such a thing was a mystery to him. He'd fed the boy, had clothed him, had been *there* for him, and contrary to what the police had said, Byrne had gone out of his way to keep him safe, had walked him home at night through streets that were dark to a home where no one noticed where he was half the time. And yet the police had referred to him as a monster, a view shared by one of the lifers who got him in the lavatory and rammed a piece of piping up his backside. *How does it feel, Dougie, you wicked bastard?*

To have a lifer call him wicked had struck Byrne as bizarre, and he'd laughed, until a combination of pain, shock, and terror curdled the laughter so that it had turned to screams of agony. A warder had sauntered by, eyes fixed dead ahead, ears shut off to the sound of a child molester *getting his due*, and after he'd been returned from the prison hospital, Byrne had found the pipe lying giftwrapped on the floor of his cell. There'd been a tag attached to the wrapping, one that had been signed by every prisoner in the block, and he'd been kept in solitary after that, housed, for his own protection, in a cell where, periodically, he'd been tempted to smear his own excreta on the wall by way of protest. He'd never done it. To have succumbed to that temptation would have been to give them the evidence they needed that he was an animal, when *they* were the animals, not him: he was a lover of children, and he had no intention of allowing anyone to rob him of his dignity in the face of such a fact.

A bird flew down from a pelmet and landed by his feet. He was surprised at how tame it was, how tame the majority were. Some flew on to the arm of the chair, hopped on to his hand, walked up his arm and pecked at the pale, freckled skin as if the liver spots might be grain. On finding him of little interest, they flew off to view him from the picture rail, or to lift their tails and deposit a dropping on or beside him.

Such filth wasn't merely squalor, it was a statement, Byrne decided. In prison, he had wanted to smear his excreta on the walls but hadn't succumbed to temptation. Perhaps, by allowing the birds to do the job for him, Roly was making some kind of protest against a world he felt had rejected him. Byrne didn't know: he'd never been much cop at working out what made people tick. All he knew was, Roly was as weird a bloke as any he'd ever come across. Chances were, if ever he ended up in the nick he'd be transferred to some equivalent of his house and aviary, the new surroundings more sterile, but the faces peering in on his world more of a reality than the fantasy spectators that Byrne had imagined to be staring in from outside.

Roly appeared with a fry-up and handed a plate to Byrne, who stared at the food. The bacon, sausages, and mushrooms looked reasonable enough, but the egg didn't look like any he'd seen before. It wasn't the egg of a chicken, he knew that much, but it couldn't be a finch's egg because it was too big.

He stabbed at the yolk, a deep, almost blood-red yellow that turned his stomach cold. It ran into the grease like serum, and, unable to face it, he lowered his knife. 'The egg,' said Byrne. 'What is it?'

'S-swan.'

Byrne had a vision of Roly wading into water, a great white ghostlike shape rising up at him as he reached out to raid its nest. *You weird, weird bastard*, thought Byrne, but for fear of offending him he spread some of the yolk on to the bread, and cut it into slivers. He put a piece into his mouth, and found that it tasted rich and not unpleasant. It had a stronger flavour than that of a chicken's egg, a creamier texture, a taste that stayed in the mouth long after the rest of the food was eaten.

He finished the meal, regardless that each mouthful was more difficult to chew than the last, the grease like lead in his stomach, the aftertaste making him retch, and put the plate on the floor, vaguely disgusted that a couple of finches seemed interested in what was left of the egg. It seemed cannibalistic to him, the way they pecked at the slivers of yolk, and in the end he couldn't watch.

Roly stood up and took the plates through to the kitchen, Byrne padding after him, whining at his heels. 'What do you say, Roly?' But Roly, engrossed with his fledglings, appeared not to hear.

As a charm of finches flew through the door, Byrne was suddenly unnerved. It wasn't just the meal, the filth, or the faint suggestion that something wasn't right: it was the way in which those birds came in and out. He beat at them with his soft white hands and said, 'What if somebody were to tell Parker that Gary and Joseph came down the yard regular?'

'Is that a th-threat?'

'You're leaving me no option. If it'd get Parker off my back, I'd tell him those two lads came down here.'

He could sense the way in which Roly was thinking it through, weighing up the likelihood of Byrne spilling his guts to save his skin.

'This m-money,' said Roly. 'How much do you n-need?'

'Thousand, maybe more.'

'A th-thousand?'

'I need a room – there'll be a deposit – and then there's food, electricity . . .'

'Th-thousand quid,' said Roly. 'That's a lot of m-money, Dougie.'

'You can afford it.'

'M-maybe I can, but I can't just p-pull it out of nowhere. Y-you'll have to give me time.'

'How long?'

'A couple of d-days,' said Roly.

'Tonight,' said Byrne. 'I want it by *tonight*.'

He took a last incredulous look around the kitchen, then left, Roly watching from the window as he hurried across the yard and out through the gates.

Warrender found Parker in the police canteen and, much though he hated to interrupt his cooked breakfast, pulled up a chair, sat down and said, 'Byrne's just been followed to a house in Mousade Road.'

Parker knew the area, had spent more than his fair share of time policing it in the days when the houses were occupied by tenants. 'Do we know why he went there?'

'No, but we know the house is occupied by a squatter.'

'I didn't realize anybody had stuck around.'

'Well, somebody has,' said Warrender.

'Do we have a name?' said Parker.

'Barnes,' said Warrender. 'Roland Barnes.'

'How did you come by that?'

'I phoned the council,' said Warrender, 'asked them whether they knew of any squatters living on Mousade Road. They've been trying to get him out for the past few years.'

Good luck to them, thought Parker.

'Chances are he'll have to shift in a week or so, whether he wants to go or not.'

'Why's that?'

'Houses are coming down.'

Parker could visualize the way in which council officials, armed with an eviction order, would knock on the door to the squat, get no answer so break in and remove Roland Barnes, even if they had to carry him out. After that, they would give a demolition team the go-ahead to move in with the type of heavy machinery that could leave a row of houses looking like a war zone. All that would be left of the former squat was a pile of rubble, valuables having been plucked out, sold for scrap or to dealers who fancied they knew a bargain when they saw one. Fair enough, thought Parker. Most of them did, and houses in roads like Roumelia and Mousade could no doubt produce their fair share of marble hearths and brass fittings.

'What do you want to do?' said Warrender.

There were two options, Parker decided: he could bring Dougie in and question him, or he could pay Barnes a visit, find out something about him and question Dougie on the back of what he knew about Barnes. He stabbed at an anaemic yolk and watched it congeal on a plate that was cold to the touch. 'I'll check it out,' he said.

'Want me along?'

'No, let's keep it casual – I'll take a look-see, and then we'll take it from there.'

CHAPTER NINETEEN

It had been some years since Brogan had last used the library, and yet he recognized instantly the corner of the room set aside for children, its lowish table dwarfed by mahogany bookshelves.

In turning away he saw again his mother at the counter, her raincoat stained, her boots in need of a polish, the cardboard library ticket seeming bulky in her hand.

A slow and painful process of elimination, born of ignorance as to how books were categorized, ensured that it took him some time to find volumes devoted to cage-birds, and of these, the majority related to members of the parakeet family. All contained full-colour sections illustrating the various species, and here he found African Greys, South American Greens, Australian Macaws with feathers afire. Yet none of the birds depicted touched a chord, and it was only a simple wash drawing in *Finches of the World* that made him draw breath and hold it deep for a moment.

He took it to the counter, and spoke to a middle-aged woman better suited to a sweet shop than to this quiet and intimidating place, 'Can I take this out?'

'Are you a member?'

He felt the colour flood to his cheeks, and although he wanted to tell her that he thought he probably was, that his mother might have made him a member at some point, he couldn't bring himself to attempt the explanation, certain the words would come out wrong, certain she wouldn't believe him.

He turned away but the librarian called him back and waved a form. 'Take this home and get one of your parents to sign it.' He took it from her as she indicated the book and added, 'Want me to put it aside?'

He mumbled an embarrassed thanks, and recalled that the last time he'd been here, life had been less complex. What he wanted, he had asked for, pointing pudgy fingers up to brightly coloured books and saying, *'Mine!'*

'What's your name, love?'

'Healey,' said Brogan, and as she wrote it down, he fled, not even knowing whether he'd pluck up the nerve to go back for it.

Elaine opened the door to her three-bed semi, her two young children behind her, and Brogan was hit, almost physically, by the sheer strength of the perfume she had splashed down the front of her dress. He'd seen her do it — open the bottle and slosh on the eau-de-Cologne that she bought cheap from the market.

She didn't look like a singer but that was what his dad, who backed her on keyboards, insisted she was. Brogan had once seen her dressed for the job, a long black skirt slit to the hips, the spangled top, its straps digging deep into broad, fleshy shoulders. They talked about the Labour Club as if she were making a début at the Royal Albert Hall, and his dad had once made some reference to knowin' a bloke who could get her on a show called *A Star Is Born.*

Now, as she stood at the doorway, her hair damp, one cheekbone slightly glossy, she didn't look much like a star, born or otherwise. The makeup she wore was thicker than usual, and yet it failed to conceal that she was past her best, that she'd never see forty again or that her skin, like her figure, was thickening. Something else the makeup failed to conceal was a bruise that was fading to yellow. From its colour, Brogan could determine roughly when she'd taken the belting that had produced it.

As a child, he'd felt his mother flinch as he reached up to touch the evidence of his father's temper. Most of the bruises appeared before an item of furniture was sold, and he had come to associate the sight of them with an impending loss.

As he wondered what might have been in the house that Elaine had recently lost, an image flashed into his mind: the hugeness of his father's hand as it crushed a cardboard mobile that his mother had painted with care. That hand could come out of nowhere at times, a hand capable of sending him spinning across the room and into another universe, a world where stars exploded behind his eyes until he felt as if he were trapped in some bizarre and crude animation. Only the Toms and Jerries of this world saw stars like those, but they got up and carried on within moments of being sent spinning. Brogan, like his mother, usually took to his bed until the sickness that invariably followed had subsided.

In the past, his mother had appeared by his bedside, her hand cool on his head, her voice barely a whisper, 'Shush, love, your dad'll hear you,' and Brogan would shut up, the dread of making his father even angrier more terrifying to him than lying in the small dark room had ever proved to be, for the company of the imaginary ghouls that clustered around his bed was infinitely preferable to the threat of his father coming at him again with, 'What's the fuckin' racket?'

'Dad – I wasn't cryin' . . .'

His mother would never come again to tell him to cry quietly, but there was some consolation to be had in the fact that now it was Elaine who had the problem of keeping his father's temper under control. He wondered how she was managing, looked again at the bruise to her cheek, and came to the conclusion that she wasn't.

'Is he in?' said Brogan.

'I'll get him.'

She walked back into the house, leaving the door half open to a hall that was papered from ceiling to floor in sunflowers. He'd once seen something like them on a school trip, a coach-load of kids all gawping up at these flowers in a vase. He'd forgotten it until he saw the wallpaper, but now it came flooding back, the way he'd got home and his mother had said, 'What did you see that you liked?'

He didn't like them any more, not now he'd seen them as wallpaper in the hall of Elaine's house. It cheapened them, somehow, made them look like plastic instead of like the flowers he'd sometimes seen in his dreams.

His father came to the door, his eyes half shut in a way that suggested he and Elaine had been working the night before. He wondered what they'd earned. Twenty, forty quid – cash up front and the DSS none the wiser.

Brogan held out a couple of brown, official-looking envelopes. His father took them with indifference and dipped into a pocket for the roll of notes that seemed always to be there. He peeled off a tenner, handed it to Brogan, and said, 'Did you get the food I left?'

Brogan took the note. 'Yeah. Thanks.'

'Managin' okay?'

'Yeah.'

As he pocketed the money, Brogan's fingers touched the form from the library. He pulled it out. 'Will you sign this for us?'

His father took it from him, fished for a pen and leant the form against the sunflower walls. He signed his name, the slow and deliberate signature of a man for whom the words on the page had no meaning, the letters mere shapes that he'd learned to form from necessity, and handed it back, saying, 'Might drop by in a day or so, see how you're doin', eh?'

Brogan folded the form. Over and over he folded it, crease for crease, making it small, making it safe. *Finches of the World.*

As Brogan walked down Roumelia Road, sounds he couldn't identify mingled with a wind that whistled through the houses, circled their dismal rooms and left through cracks and crevices in glass and brick and stone.

The cage swung softly beside him, the Tiger finch still lying flat on the litter, its wings outspanned. The book had been a mine of information to Brogan, who now knew more about the country of Tiger's origin than any geography teacher could ever have hoped to teach him in a term of intensive tuition. He knew what he should be eating, where he would like to nest, what supplements he needed, but he didn't know how to heal him, and Tiger was clearly hurt.

Moranti had told him that Roly knew all about finches, and Brogan, in sheer desperation, had brought his bird in the hope that Moranti was right.

There were vehicles parked up on the wasteground, a dumper truck and a van that gave the name of a local firm. Two men holding clipboards were standing in front of the houses, making notes, commenting, but neither looked at him as he rattled on the gates to Roly's Yard. He pulled at the chain that held them, heard its rattle magnified as it bounced off the back of the houses. The sound of the chain unnerved him, but because he didn't know how else to make his presence known, he shook it again and, moments later, saw it whip free from the gates.

The gates opened, but only a fraction, and Brogan held up the cage. 'Tiger's hurt.'

Roly opened the gates wider, took the cage from him, and led the way down the yard to the nesting shed. The odour of the birds was strong, but it was an odour to which Brogan was already accustomed, something he'd breathed all Saturday down at the Emporium. At Moranti's it mingled with other scents: the perfume from the scent bottles, the cloying, mousy smell of the stuffed fox, the thick, sweetish varnish on the lid of a lacquered box.

'H-how did he get hurt?'

'Moranti squashed him.'

Roly put the cage on a chair and reached inside. The bird made no protest as he picked it up, lifted it out and inspected it.

'Is he badly hurt?' said Brogan.

'N-not really sure,' said Roly. He turned the bird in his fingers in much the way that he'd turned the corpse of the Gouldian. 'W-when did he last eat?'

'I dunno.'

Still with the finch in his hand, Roly reached up to a shelf and pulled a pipette from a mug. He laid it down on the counter and used his free hand to lift a bottle down from a cabinet resting against one wall. He unscrewed the lid and dipped the pipette into the liquid. 'What's that?' said Brogan.

'Glucose,' said Roly.

He fed the bird with tiny drops of fluid.

'Will he die?'

'M-maybe,' said Roly. 'He'd better stay w-with me for now.'

The thought of leaving his finch behind was what had prevented Brogan from bringing Tiger sooner. Somehow he'd had a feeling that Roly might take the bird away from him, on the grounds that he obviously hadn't taken good enough care of him. 'It wasn't me,' he said. 'It was Mr Moranti.'

'I know,' said Roly. 'N-nobody's blaming you.'

'He tipped him out the box and tried to hide him, that's what did it.'

'He's always d-doing that,' said Roly, and he smiled, which made Brogan lighten up a little.

'What if he dies?'

'I'll give you another.'

'I don't want another,' said Brogan. 'I want Tiger.'

He watched as Roly put the bird in one of the nesting boxes, and after seeing him settled, said, 'I'm sorry.'

'It wasn't your fault.'

In one of the neighbouring cages, two of the Zebras had produced a hatch, their dull brown feathers much the same colour as the litter into which they flattened themselves in fright. They gazed up at Brogan with eyes so small it was almost impossible for him to imagine that they were eyes at all. Not even insects had eyes as tiny as those, thought Brogan. 'You take better care of your birds than Mr Moranti.'

'Th-that's why mine survive and his d-don't,' said Roly, who dipped his hand into one of the cages, and brought out a White-eyed Oriental. He tipped it into Brogan's hands and watched him stroke the bird, his touch immensely gentle. 'What did Moranti do to that G-Gouldian finch?'

Brogan thought back to the glass-domed roof and the slice of ice-cold air that had descended from the dome. 'Left it in a draught,' he said.

'I thought as much.'

'They've fixed the roof,' said Brogan. 'Some of the shop-owners moaned because the rain was getting in.'

Roly took the bird from him and put it back in the cage.

'I'm glad you c-came back,' he said. 'I l-like you, Bro-brogan.'

'I like you too,' said Brogan, and Roly touched his cheek, caressing it so gently, the tip of his finger felt like the tip of a feather against his skin.

CHAPTER TWENTY

Parker pulled up outside the gates to the yard, the wasteground to his right. He could remember a time when there had been houses on that land, and it struck him as odd that some of the roads had been demolished while others had been left standing. He could only assume that the council had encountered problems in evicting owner-occupiers. It was easier, in some cases, to wait for certain occupants to move on or die off – the entire area was littered with strips of wasteground such as this that bore witness to the fact that the council was seizing whatever opportunities arose to fell the houses without having to pay compensation.

Warrender's description of the yard had given him some indication that the garden had been converted into an aviary, so he was prepared for the wire mesh that stretched from the fence to the roof of the house. Even so, as he approached the property it struck him as one of the oddest things he'd seen in that the interior of the house was clearly an extension of the aviary. He could almost imagine what those upstairs rooms must be like. Given the chance, he intended to take a look, if only to have his suspicions of squalor confirmed, but failing that, he would be satisfied with taking a good hard look at Roland Barnes.

He found the gates chained but not locked, and he pulled

the chain through, pushed open the gates, and walked into the net that draped from the mesh above. It caught him unawares, snagging on the buttons of his jacket as he tried to free himself. For a moment, he felt like an insect caught in a web, and he slashed at the net in irritation as much as anything.

Once free of it, he ducked under and into the yard, and took a good look at the scene that now lay before him. It was then that Parker felt a stab of apprehension. He wasn't an easy man to frighten. There wasn't a back street in Manchester that he hadn't plunged down at some point in his career, and the darkness that had enveloped him had often contained the unknown, but the minute he entered the yard, he felt that he was dealing with a different kind of unknown.

The sky above was wide and clear, and the trees that strained towards it were spaced so that he could see what lay beyond them, yet he was gripped almost immediately by a feeling that he might never get out of there. It didn't matter that he could just as easily turn on his heel, duck back under the net, walk through the gates, climb into his car and drive as far away from the place as petrol would allow, the feeling remained. And when he saw a figure emerge from the shed, it increased. This was Byrne's contact. Parker couldn't swear to it, but he looked very like the image on the security video. 'Roland Barnes?' he said.

Roly picked up a yard brush that rested against the shed.

'Detective Superintendent Parker. Greater Manchester Police,' said Parker, showing his ID. 'I'm making enquiries into the disappearance of . . .' A boy appeared in the doorway to the shed, and, taken aback, Parker stopped mid-sentence. '. . . a young lad,' he finished.

Roly started to sweep the yard with slow, methodical strokes.

'I won't take much of your time,' said Parker. 'I just need a word.'

Roly ignored him, the swish of the brush invasive, rhythmical and insolent.

'Mr Barnes, could you just stop sweeping for a moment.'

Roly leant the yard brush against a wall, picked up a dustpan and brush, and continued.

'Mr Barnes, could you just stop that.'

'I w-won't be a minute,' said Roly.

Parker suddenly lost patience. '*Now!*' he shouted.

The birds soared into the air, but as quickly as they had taken flight, they settled, and then there was stillness.

'Now,' said Parker, softly.

Roly put back the dustpan in its place, and Parker took a good look at the boy before indicating the house. 'Inside.'

They entered the kitchen and Parker was almost knocked back by the smell. It was no different from the smell of the yard, but it was stronger, and no air circulated to minimize it. Even so, he took pains not to show his disgust as he said, 'That's quite some aviary out there.'

Roly led the way into the back room, but he didn't reply.

Parker absorbed the geography of the room, its furnishings, its open window, the birds, the pelmets and doors. 'I take it you breed them?'

All he got by way of response was a nod from Roly.

'Sell them?'

Another nod.

'Who to?' said Parker, making for the window, gulping at the air and finding that it wasn't much of an improvement.

'Just p-people,' said Roly, and Parker realized that his reluctance to say more than was necessary was probably due to the speech impediment.

Outside, the boy was creeping out of the shed. Inching out, thought Parker. He wondered who he was.

He turned from the window to find Roly standing in the doorway to the kitchen, watching him. It was hard to know what to make of him: anyone living in as great a degree of filth as this ought, by rights, to be filthy himself. None of it seemed to fit. He produced a photo of Gary, saying, 'Local lad, Gary Maudsley, went missing a couple of weeks back.'

Roly took the photo.

'Know him?'

Roly shook his head and handed back the photo.

A movement from within the yard caught Parker's eye. He turned his head and saw the boy walking into the shed. 'Who's the kid?' he said.

'D-don't know,' said Roly, and it seemed to Parker that he was genuinely struggling to form even the simplest reply. He suddenly felt for him, and softened a fraction. 'Take your time,' he said.

Roly added, 'He ju-just turned up and a-asked to l-look at the b-birds.'

'You must get a lot of that,' said Parker. 'Kids wandering in, wanting to look around.'

A nod from Roly.

'But not Gary.'

And now a shake of the head.

'Mr Barnes,' said Parker, moving away from the window, 'do you know anyone by the name of Douglas Byrne?'

'Y-yes.'

'When was the last time you spoke to him?'

'Today.'

'And where was that?'

'H-here.'

Parker hadn't expected Roly to be quite so open. 'What brought him here?'

'He w-wanted to b-borrow some money.'

'Why?'

'He didn't say.'

'Friend of yours, is he?'

'Not r-really.'

146

'So why would he think you might lend him some money?'

'He was d-desperate – he was trying everyone he knew.'

'And how do you know him?'

Roly indicated the houses opposite. 'He used to l-live in a squat down Roumelia R-road.'

Out in the yard, the boy walked out of the nesting shed carrying a small, polythene bag. The ends were tied, and Parker watched as he loosened them, dipped his hand into the bag and scattered seed on the ground. He didn't have much of a knack for it, and the seed hit the ground in dollops. Some of the birds darted down to feed, but most remained in the trees, watching him, made nervous by his jerky, uncertain movements.

'How long has it been since you last saw Byrne – before today, I mean?'

The answer was instantaneous. 'Just a f-few days back.'

'Where?'

'B-bookshop,' said Roly. 'I b-bumped into him.'

Was that the truth? wondered Parker, or had the meeting been arranged? 'How come he didn't ask you for money then?'

'He did.'

'And you said no.'

'I haven't got any m-money,' said Roly. 'I t-told him I c-couldn't help him.'

It stood to reason, thought Parker. Maybe that was why Byrne had left the shop so abruptly. 'Clearly, he didn't believe you?'

'P-pardon?'

'Why would he come here, today, if he believed you – if he thought you had no money?'

'I d-don't know.'

The boy crouched down to a finch, extending his hand towards it, offering seed on his palm. From here, it was impossible to see anything of the bird other than the dusty, feathered back, but Parker wasn't looking so much at the bird as at the boy. 'Well, if you think of anything that might be of interest to me, or if Byrne should call again ...'

'I'll l-let you know,' said Roly.

As the door to the house was opened, the finch took fright, and Brogan followed its line of flight as Parker walked over to him. 'You seem to have a way with them,' he said.

The finch was now nothing more than a dot in one of the trees. 'Scared of me,' said Brogan. 'Not used to me yet.'

His voice hadn't broken, and there was a quality to it that made Parker want to protect him. 'What's your name, son?'

He answered shyly, much as a younger boy might. 'Brogan.'

'Brogan what?'

'Healey,' said Brogan.

'Where do you live?'

'Arpley Street.'

There was a note of warning in Parker's voice. 'You're a long way from home, Brogan.'

The comment seemed lost on the child, and Parker wondered how best to get him out of there without making it obvious that he wanted a chance to talk to him alone.

'Tell you what,' said Parker, 'Mr Barnes has a few things to do just now, so why don't you let me drop you off at home?'

Roly gave the slightest nod as if to say that maybe Brogan should go along with Parker. 'Okay,' said Brogan, and Parker led him out, lifting the net as Brogan ducked under, then closed the gates behind them.

He led him towards a car that came as something of a disappointment to the boy. It was the first time he'd seen the inside of a police car, unmarked or otherwise, and he found that there was only a police radio to mark it out as being any different from any other saloon. He had somehow expected more.

'Seat-belt?' said Parker, and Brogan did as he was told, clipping it into place as Parker fired the engine and drove down Roumelia Road.

The wasteground flashed past to the left. In the weeks since Brogan had first seen it, a three-piece suite had been abandoned there. Behind it, the corpse of a burned-out car lay on its roof, the upholstery gone, the metal blackened, the steering-wheel ripped out.

'Known Roly long?' said Parker, conversationally.

'No,' said Brogan.

'How did you get to meet him?'

'Through Mr Moranti.'

'Mr Moranti?'

'Someone I work for down the covered market.'

'You look a little young to be working,' said Parker.

'Saturday job,' said Brogan.

'Ah.' That explained it, thought Parker, who had reckoned as much but had wanted it spelt out. 'Hope he's paying you well?'

'Three quid a day,' said Brogan, and Parker was touched by the note of childish pride.

'That's a good whack,' he said, kindly.

'Yeah. One of my mates says he gets twenty, but I don't believe him.'

'Very wise,' said Parker. 'Not even I get twenty quid a day.'

'Honest?'

'Honest,' said Parker, feeling that what with tax, insurance and everything else that disappeared from his salary, it wasn't too far from the truth.

He kept a hand on the wheel and used the other to pull out the photo of Gary Maudsley, passing it to Brogan and saying, 'Ever seen him before?'

Brogan took the photo and looked at it. 'No. Why?'

'He's gone missing from home,' said Parker.

'Has he run off?'

Dear God, I hope so, thought Parker, the alternative being too appalling to contemplate. 'Possibly,' he said.

'Is he a friend of Roly's?'

Parker replied, very cautiously, 'Roly said he didn't know him.'

'So what made you ask Roly if he'd seen him?'

'We're asking a lot of people,' said Parker.

Handing the photo back, Brogan said, 'What do you think's happened to him?'

'We don't know,' replied Parker. 'That's what we're trying to find out.'

The area fell away, to be replaced by evidence of industries that had long since gone to the wall, their premises left as derelict as the houses that surrounded them, and Parker drove the rest of the way in silence, stopping the car in front of the house that Brogan directed him to.

As he killed the engine, he turned to Brogan, suddenly very serious. 'I've got a lad about your age, and I'll tell you something, Brogan, if he was going down that yard, I'd be out my mind.'

'Why?'

Parker struggled to explain, constrained by the fact that he couldn't go round telling people he had a gut feeling about somebody. Also he wasn't yet sure for himself what it was that bothered him about Roly. 'It's not a good thing for a lad of your age to hang around with men they don't know very well. Understand me, Brogan? Understand what I'm trying to say?'

As Brogan got out of the car, Parker leant across and added: 'Are your parents in?'

'There's only my dad.'

'Your dad, then.'

'What do you want wi' me dad?'

'Quick word, that's all,' said Parker, doing his best to reassure him.

'I've haven't done nothin'.'

'Nobody said you had.'

'He's out.'

'Out where?' said Parker, but Brogan didn't reply.

He decided not to push it. He'd call on Brogan again, and he'd keep on calling until he managed to get a good look at his father, weigh him up, tell him his son had been found at Roly's Yard. In the meantime, Parker satisfied himself with, 'Don't go down the yard eh? Not any more,' but Brogan closed the door to the car and turned towards the house, fishing in his pocket for a key on a piece of string.

The years peeled away for Parker, and once again he was standing in Julie Coyne's flat, reaching out for the key on the string that she'd handed across with the words, 'This is the spare. Joey wears the other round his neck.'

Brogan's father, wherever he was, probably had a spare just like it, thought Parker, and he only hoped he wouldn't find himself holding out his hand to take it from him, examine it, and tell him that if any of his officers came across anything like it, they'd try it in his lock and see if it fitted.

The birds were swarming, the recent visit from strangers having unsettled them. Often, they went undisturbed for weeks, the only person they saw being Roly, and he was nothing to worry about unless, as was currently the case, he was lashing out at them, his hand like the tongue from a lizard catching flies. It was incredible how he managed it, the sudden flash of movement that was both expert and horrific, the speed with which he could catch a bird mid-flight, the gentleness with which he managed to hold it for a moment – and then the decision. Sometimes, he would release the terrified creature. At other times, as now, he would snap its neck and toss it into the box.

CHAPTER TWENTY-ONE

The minute the blue saloon appeared in front of the house, Mrs Maudsley came out to greet him. It was as though she'd been standing at the window, waiting, thought Parker, and he only wished he was bringing something more than reassurance.

She looked worn, thought Parker, the last couple of weeks having added another ten years to the seventy-odd she owned to. 'No news,' he said, aware that although she would be frustrated by that, she would also be relieved. At least he wasn't walking in to tell her they'd found Gary dead.

'Joseph Coyne's been found, then?' she said.

'I'm afraid so,' said Parker.

'It's definite, then. It's *him*?'

'Yes,' replied Parker. 'Definite.'

She looked very old, and he put an arm around her. 'It doesn't mean we'll find Gary dead, Mrs Maudsley.'

'Why are you here?'

'I just came to see how you are.'

'Well, now you've seen,' she said.

'I know it's hard.'

'What are you *doing*?'

Everything we can, thought Parker, but all he said was, 'Gary had a bird, didn't he?'

He followed her into the house and watched as she squatted

down to light the gas fire with a twist of paper. It blackened the element guarding the flame, then turned to ash that was airborne for the briefest of moments before the spark that carried it expired.

'What about it?'

'What kind of bird was it?'

She eased herself to feet that seemed minute beneath ankles that had swollen with age. 'Hard to say, now,' she admitted. 'Summat fancy.'

'Can you describe it?'

'Small, I remember that. He used to be able to hide it just by doing this.' She held out her hand, the joints arthritic, and curled her fingers with difficulty.

In doing so, she made Parker realize that the bird must indeed have been small, and he said, 'What colour was it?'

'Green,' she said.

'Just green?'

'Green all over, like a leaf. Even its beak was green.'

Parker felt a stab of disappointment. It didn't sound exotic.

'Like a little green canary,' she added, as an afterthought.

'Where did he get it?'

'Pet shop.'

'Where?'

'Down Tib Street.'

Tib Street, with its multitude of pet shops, no longer existed as such. Parker tried to steer her gently into the present. 'You sure?' he said. 'It can't have been Tib Street, Mrs Maudsley. It must have been somewhere else.'

'I can't think of anywhere else, not unless . . .'

'Go on.'

'He had a job, a while back, down the covered market.'

The temperature suddenly dropped, or so it seemed to Parker. He felt as if he'd been drenched in ice-cold water. 'How long ago was this?'

'Last Christmas. And then he stopped going. Said he'd got sick of spending his Saturdays cleaning out the cages.' She turned towards a coffee table jammed against the corner of the room. It held an African Violet, the petals the rich deep purple that Parker invariably associated with church vestments, and beneath it, magazines were strewn in some parody of neatness. She leant down, pulled them out and, with them, a book, which she held out to Parker, who took it and turned to the title pages. It was a library book, overdue by several weeks.

'I kept on at him to take it back, but he never got round to it.' She sounded guilty, and Parker, who felt she had enough on her plate, reassured her with a smile accompanied by, 'I've got a library book at home — I've had it so long I'd have to mortgage the house if I took it back.'

She smiled, and he was touched by the way she cut the smile short, as if remembering that her grandson was missing, that not even jokes were funny at the moment and that maybe they would never be funny again. She took the book from him and thumbed through it, finding an illustration of the bird that Gary had kept before handing it back, saying, 'There you go.'

Parker looked at an illustration above the text that described the bird's country of origin. It depicted a finch that was green. 'Greenfinch,' said Mrs Maudsley. 'Pretty little thing.'

'Can I take this?' said Parker.

She wasn't listening: her thoughts having drifted back to a time when she'd told him to get rid of the bloody chirping thing. 'Eh?'

'The book. Can I take it?'

'It's due back down the library.'

'Don't worry about that — I'll sort it.'

He left the house and climbed into the car. Mrs Maudsley shut the door and retreated into the house in the expectation that Parker would just drive away. But he didn't. Not immediately. He thumbed through the book until he found the page depicting the finch. Beneath the illustration he read the words:

> *There are thirteen species of these birds, now known as Darwin's finches, their main differences being in the shape of their bills and their feeding habits.*

He turned the page and learnt that *Geospiza magnirostris* had a heavy, seed-crushing beak whereas *Certhidea olivacea* had the bill of an insectivorous bird.

Parker didn't give a shit about *Geospiza magnirostris* or *Certhidea olivacea*; neither was green and neither had been kept by Gary Maudsley. What Gary had kept was a *Camarhynchus pallidus*, and he tried to imagine him getting his tongue round the Latin. He probably wouldn't have bothered, thought Parker. Chances were, he'd have called it a Woodpecker finch and left it at that.

He closed the book, fired the engine and pulled away from the house. As he made for the top of the road, he imagined Gary trying to visualize the bird in its natural habitat. Chances were, he would have failed. Like Parker, Gary was unlikely to have known the first thing about the Galapagos Islands other than that they, like the birds that lived there, were clearly exotic.

Parker threaded his way through the crowds that jammed the covered market in late afternoon, and walked into the Emporium to find Moranti sitting on a large wicker basket. 'Mr Moranti?' he said.

Moranti stood up. Parker wasn't his usual type of visitor, and he knew instinctively that he wasn't a potential customer.

Parker produced his ID. 'Detective Superintendent Parker.'

Moranti watched him warily as he looked round the unit. 'That's quite a collection of birds.' He glanced along the cages. 'Where do you get them?'

Moranti seemed to take a moment to reply, and he only did so after he'd thought it through. 'All over.'

As if baffled by the reply, Parker said, 'All over where?'

'The country,' replied Moranti.

'All over the country?' repeated Parker, as if he'd just been made privy to some kind of trade secret. 'You can breed birds like these in our climate?'

'You can breed them anywhere if you know what you're doing.'

'Must be a lot of work, seeing to them all.'

'It can be.'

'Got any help?'

'A lad comes in, Saturdays.'

Thoughtfully now, Parker turned this piece of information over as if it were new to him. 'A lad.' And then, as if struggling to recall the details, he said, 'Let me see now ... Didn't you have a lad working for you a while back, smallish, light brown hair?'

He couldn't be certain whether Moranti was suddenly frightened or just unsure as to where this was leading. 'Yes,' he admitted.

'What was his name?'

Moranti's voice was barely audible. 'Gary Maudsley.'

'Are you aware that Gary went missing a couple of weeks ago?'

The voice grew even quieter. 'Yes.'

'But you didn't contact the police.'

'No.'

'Why not?'

'I didn't think it was important.'

As Parker digested the comment, two of the birds started to fight, their cries shrill, their wings beating against the bars of a cage. 'Not important?' he said.

'Not relevant,' said Moranti.

'Not relevant to whom?' Parker asked.

157

Moranti replied, 'The police.'

'I see,' said Parker, and he peered into one of the cages at a bird with crimson wings. It edged along the perch, keeping him in view in much the way that Parker was using the mirror that hung in the cage to watch Moranti as he said, 'My lad would probably like a bird like this ...' He drew away from the cage, turned a pair of cool, thoughtful eyes on Moranti, and said, 'How much is it?'

Moranti, who knew that Parker wasn't in the market for a bird but might well be in the market for causing him a serious problem, didn't respond. He waited for what he suspected might be coming next. His suspicions were confirmed when Parker said, 'Have you ever had a lad called Joseph Coyne working for you?'

Moranti stroked the palm of one hand with the fingers of the other, as if he held a finch and was smoothing down its feathers.

'Mr Moranti ...' said Parker.

The fingers continued to smooth.

'Joseph Coyne,' said Parker. 'Did he work for you?'

The invisible finch was now being plucked by those fingers. Parker imagined its feathers as they floated to the ground. 'Do you ever buy birds from Roland Barnes?'

Moranti's reluctance to reply provided the answer, and Parker built on it. 'Did you ever take Gary or Joseph down to Roly's Yard?'

'No,' said Moranti.

'Sure?' said Parker.

'I never take no boys of mine down to Roly's Yard.'

'Why not?'

'I want them here, to watch the shop. I do the buying, not some boy I employ to work Saturdays.'

One of the birds was attacking the side of its cage. Its beak was short and tough, and it wouldn't have surprised Parker if one of the bamboo bars had splintered and split.

'Who's working for you now?'

'Young lad called Brogan,' said Moranti, and once again, it seemed to Parker as though there had been a none-too-subtle change in the temperature, summer turning to winter with the flick of a God-like switch.

'Well,' said Parker, his voice as cold as the air that carried his words, 'let's hope this new lad of yours doesn't just ... *disappear*, eh?'

'What's that supposed to mean?'

Parker didn't reply. He took one last look at the birds, as if seeing a great deal more than was obvious to the naked eye, then sauntered towards the door, opened it and walked out.

Parker pulled up in a side road, he and Warrender leaving the car out of sight and walking to the front of Byrne's shop to find it closed.

The street lamps were lit, one of them casting a yellowish hue on Parker's coat as he banged on the door. There was no sign of life in the room above, not that Parker had expected Byrne to oblige by walking to the window at precisely the moment he could have done with seeing him there. Nevertheless, he had the feeling that Byrne wasn't merely avoiding them: he wasn't there.

They walked round to the back and found the gate unlatched. Parker pushed it wide, saw Byrne's van, and then the bunker directly ahead. He'd always felt drawn to that bunker, he didn't know why. He'd already checked it out and had found it to be empty, yet he checked it again to make sure.

The same glittering blackness. The same stained walls.

'Any ideas?' said Warrender.

'He's local, born and bred. He could be anywhere, with anyone.'

'I'll check out his known relations.'

Parker knew Byrne's background better than Warrender's, and knew that even his closest relations had cut him out of their lives after his conviction. 'Don't bother,' he said.

He closed the lid of the bunker, a splinter coming away from the edge and embedding itself in his palm. As he drew it out, and sucked the spot of blood that emerged from the wound, he thought back to what he'd seen of that other yard earlier in the day, and he came to the conclusion that he'd be better off using the manpower at his disposal to watch Roly rather than Byrne. 'Byrne's lying low,' he said. 'He'll surface, soon enough.'

CHAPTER TWENTY-TWO

Parker's night had been broken by dreams in which he found his younger son at Roly's Yard. There was nothing new in this. Throughout his career, he'd substituted family members for victims, but since he knew of other officers who experienced the same, discomforting phenomenon, he assumed it was normal. Even so, he wished there were some technique he could adopt to prevent it happening and it occurred to him that it might be an idea to mention it to Hanson. Right now, though, he didn't intend to pull his mind from the purpose of their meeting: Hanson had now had a chance to evaluate the contents of the file on Byrne, and Parker was anxious to hear his view.

He checked him through Security and led him up to his office, making a stab at small-talk but finding it difficult in the circumstances. 'Did you find your way to the guesthouse all right?'

'Yes.'

'Comfortable?'

'Yes.'

'Good,' said Parker, abruptly, and Hanson knew intuitively that Parker had asked the question out of courtesy. In reality, he wouldn't have cared if he'd kipped on the platform at Piccadilly, provided he had read the file and was about to make some valid observations. He pulled up a chair when Parker gestured to him to sit, and wasn't surprised when Parker got straight to the point.

'So, how are we doing?'

'That's difficult to say,' said Hanson. 'I've read the file, but I haven't talked to Byrne and, as you are no doubt aware, even if I had, criminal psychology isn't an exact science, so I—'

'In your opinion, is Byrne our man or not?' said Parker, bluntly, and the remarks that Hanson had been about to make evaporated.

He had hoped to have the opportunity to lead up to what he was about to say because he was certain that Parker wasn't going to like it. He had intended to begin by explaining that he had read the statements and reports relating to the original investigation into Joseph's disappearance with a view to trying to build up a picture of Byrne. All he'd seen was a frightened man who had stuck rigidly to his story: he didn't know Joey, though he had admitted to having asked him the time on the morning that he was assumed to have disappeared. Byrne insisted that was coincidence, and a jury was likely to concede that it was conceivable. An elderly, purblind individual had said she *might* have seen a boy who *might* have fitted Joseph's description hauled into a van that *might* fit the description of a vehicle owned by Byrne, but *nobody* had seen Gary pulled into a similar vehicle.

Granted, Byrne hadn't been able to come up with the name of anyone who could corroborate that he'd been in his shop on the afternoon Gary had gone missing, but the boy hadn't been seen outside it, either. Therefore, there was little evidence to support Parker's assumption that Byrne was responsible for the alleged abduction of Joseph Coyne – and that was all it was, *alleged*.

Hanson had then intended to move on to material that related to more recent information. Byrne's every movement had been watched since Gary Maudsley's disappearance, and the police had been able to establish that, some days ago, he had gone into the old covered market in central Manchester. After leaving it, he had gone to a bookshop where he met a contact. There had been a young child in the bookshop and the mother had wandered away, giving Byrne the opportunity to approach him, but Byrne hadn't taken it. In fact, he wasn't known to have reoffended since being released, and when Hanson considered the nature of Byrne's first offence, he couldn't help feeling that, although serious, it didn't put him in the category of dangerous offenders. Byrne had succumbed to a temptation to molest a child, but the offence had stopped short of penetration, and he hadn't taken steps to ensure that the child wouldn't divulge what he had done.

'I'm waiting,' said Parker.

Hanson suddenly decided not to bother attempting to defend his view or persuade Parker of its validity. He just wanted to get the session over with so that he could pack his bags and get the hell out of Manchester for good. 'There are certain things we don't know,' he said, 'like whether Joseph was abducted or if he was sexually abused, but we're making those assumptions.'

'There are times when we have no choice but to do that,' said Parker.

'It isn't a criticism, it's an observation, as is the fact that we currently don't know whether Gary Maudsley is a second victim.'

'But that said . . .' prompted Parker.

'That said,' agreed Hanson, 'if we stand by those assumptions, then you're dealing with a predator, somebody with a history of sadistic sexual offences.'

'Let me tell you the rest,' said Parker. 'Background, environment, role models, the possibility that he himself was an abused child, perhaps even hereditary factors for all we know — all these things have played a part in who this man has become. Right now, he's in his mid to late thirties, he lives alone, he's—'

'Very good,' said Hanson.

'Now tell me something I don't know,' said Parker, and Hanson resigned himself to the inevitable I-don't-need-you-to-tell-me lecture as the other man went on, 'I've been with the force for nigh-on fourteen years. It isn't the first time I've come across a crime committed by someone who is clearly incapable of empathizing with another human being, a person devoid of conscience – the type of person we label a psychopath.'

'Which brings me to Byrne,' said Hanson, and he wondered what Parker's reaction was going to be. 'Byrne isn't a psychopath. He isn't even dangerous.'

'Try telling that to the parents of the lad he molested.'

'He isn't a killer,' said Hanson. 'You're looking for a killer, and you're also looking for somebody who obtained a perverse pleasure from building that scaffold, someone for whom the ritual of the kill was every bit as important as the fact of it.'

'That's your professional opinion?' said Parker. 'Byrne isn't a killer?'

'It's highly unlikely,' said Hanson. 'He's a paedophile, granted, and paedophilia, like rape, is about power, not sex, but Byrne doesn't crave what many perceive to be the ultimate power – the power to take another human life. On the contrary, he seems able to content himself with images of children that you described as innocent. Think about it.'

Parker thought about it. He also thought back to the yard, the birds, the lad he'd found with Roly. Byrne had always disgusted him, but he'd never frightened him. That yard had frightened him, had caused him to dream a dream in which he had found his youngest boy lying on a scaffold. 'I had a dream,' he said.

Hanson, aware of a subtle change in Parker, replied, 'It's no easy thing to deal with a case of this nature.'

Parker looked up with eyes that were bloodshot from staring into the darkness for hours after he woke. 'What about you? What do you dream of at night?'

The simple things, thought Hanson, a house, a wife, a child – but the child is never mine, and the house is falling down. He had gone there expecting Parker to fight his corner, to argue his case, to attempt to persuade him that he hadn't spent the best part of five years investigating someone for nothing, but the man now sitting in front of him suddenly appeared not to want to do that.

'This power,' said Parker, 'this desire for control over other living things . . .' He thought about the birds, so small, so utterly defenceless, then rose slowly to his feet. Hanson did likewise, as if summoned to do so. 'Come with me,' said Parker. 'There's something I want you to see.'

From their vantage-point on the wasteground, Parker and Hanson had a good view of the gates to Roly's Yard. The chain that held them closed was dull, the links beginning to oxidize to a deep and bloody red.

They stood by the corpse of the burned-out car, the only splash of colour the almost violent yellow of the vast industrial skips, and close to where they stood, a starving bird was scavenging for food it couldn't find.

Parker didn't lack imagination, but he did lack the poetic turn of phrase that could describe in prosaic terms what he had felt as he entered the yard, yet he managed to describe it vividly enough to furnish Hanson with more than just an impression of what lay behind those gates. He also described the Emporium and spelled out what he saw as a link between Moranti, Byrne and Roly. 'Gary once worked in the covered market. Brogan is working there now. Byrne was seen entering the covered market prior to meeting Roly at the bookshop, and one of my men followed Roly to that same covered market after his meeting with Byrne was over.'

Parker's description of Moranti and the Emporium intrigued Hanson. It also troubled him, because although Moranti had denied taking Joseph and Gary to the yard he had obviously taken Brogan, so it seemed likely that he'd taken his predecessors. 'Bit of a coincidence, don't you think?'

'I do,' said Parker, 'and in my line of work, we're not all that keen on coincidences.'

Hanson watched the bird, its feathers dull and ragged. Not the type of bird that looked as though it might have come from the Emporium or the yard. Somewhere, thought Hanson, there had been a bird with a fabulous turquoise plumage. A feather from that plumage had ended up in the wood, and he hadn't realized its significance. He told Parker, who said, 'There must be dozens of feathers lying around.'

'Not like this,' said Hanson, and as he began to describe it, Parker saw a vision of it spinning to the ground.

They stood in silence a moment, Parker growing agitated, angry with himself. 'I pulled the surveillance team off Byrne yesterday afternoon.'

'Was that wise?'

'I don't have endless resources, Murray. I thought the men currently at my disposal would be better employed watching the yard.'

'I don't see anybody.'

'Maybe not,' said Parker, but he glanced towards Roumelia Road with its boarded doors and windows and it wasn't necessary for him to elaborate.

'If I were you,' said Hanson, 'I'd get him back under surveillance. He led you to Roly. My guess is that even if he isn't the killer, he's somehow involved in the deaths of these boys and there's no telling who else he might lead you to.'

As if to reassure himself, Parker blurted out, 'Nothing too drastic can have happened in under twenty-four hours. If it had, I'd know about it.'

Hanson, who could think of plenty that could happen in under twenty-four seconds, refrained from mentioning that Byrne might have done anything: he could have done a runner for all Parker knew. Clearly, however, Parker was aware that taking the surveillance team from off Byrne had been a mistake. But, with luck, it wasn't too late to rectify that mistake.

Hanson said, 'Pity your men saw Byrne entering the market, but didn't actually see him enter the Emporium.'

'Maybe he didn't go in. Maybe he and Roly arranged to bump into Moranti in one of the delicatessens.'

'What for?'

'You're the criminal psychologist,' said Parker. 'Why would they want to meet?'

Hanson spared him an account of the network paedophiles build among themselves, one through which they exchange support, information and obscene material. He said, 'Where do you go from here?'

The bird had gathered up the courage to scratch an area of soil only yards from their feet.

By lifting their eyes a fraction, they brought the gates into view and Parker replied, 'I'm going to organise my men with a view to making a thorough search of that yard.'

'How long will that take?'

'Couple of days.'

'Why so long?'

'You'd be surprised,' said Parker. 'I need to talk it through with my own superior officers, then formulate a plan, obtain warrants and inform the local council — it is, after all, their property.'

Hanson wouldn't have expected a problem there. There would be no reason for the local authority to deny the police access to the yard, and Roly, as a squatter, would have no legal right to prevent the police from entering it.

Parker went on, 'An operation of that nature takes time to put together, but we can't hang around too long — those houses are coming down, every last one of them. This time next week, Mousade Road won't exist any more. Neither will the roads that surround it.' Even as he spoke, Hanson formed a picture in his mind of one vast tract of wasteground. 'Superstores,' said Parker. 'That's what's going up, apparently. Superstores and a Toys 'R' Us.'

The starving bird flapped lethargically to the rim of a skip, then almost seemed to fall rather than fly into its interior as Hanson said, 'Search the yard, by all means, but if Roly is your man, and if you're looking for the remains of other kids, you're wasting your time.'

Parker wasn't having it. 'Oh, really!'

'There'd have been a particular purpose to the way he went about murdering that boy, some reason for him leaving the remains on a scaffold. You recognised that there was an element of ritual to the kill. That's what drew you to me.'

'What are you getting at?'

'I'm saying that the likelihood of him burying some of his victims on a scaffold in a wood only to bury others in and around a house is highly remote. It wouldn't fit in with who he is and why he does what he does.'

'So I'm just supposed to hang around every wood in England waiting for him to pop up with a couple of poles and a railway sleeper, am I?'

'I didn't say there weren't methods we could—'

'I'm searching that yard,' said Parker, and Hanson knew he'd be wasting his breath if he tried to persuade him not to.

'Go ahead, but you won't find anything there.'

'We'll soon find out,' said Parker.

Parker had no choice but to take the matter to the Assistant Chief Constable because he intended to request ground-scanning radar, and at five K a day, that would be expensive. However, in Parker's view it would be a justifiable expense: a scanner would be able to determine what lay beneath the ground and behind the walls and floors, so would give a good indication of where the police should focus their attention. He'd only ever seen it used on a couple of occasions, the monitor revealing information that meant nothing to him, the images on screen changing as a probe was passed over earth or stroked against a wall.

Operating it was more than a skilled job, it was an art, but that was no excuse, thought Parker. Ground-scanning radar ought to be there, at his fingertips, whenever he required it. If he could have had his way, he'd have had a scanner stashed in his office, but there were only two firms in the country who could offer such technology, and this was a source of considerable irritation to Parker. He felt that the police ought to own equipment of that nature outright.

Assistant Chief Constable Chalker, who wore his fifty-odd years rather better than Parker suspected he would himself, was in full uniform, the hair almost white, but the face relatively unlined. He looked what he was, a man who was remarkably fit for his years. Astute, worthy of his position, and worthy also of the respect that his men had no hesitation in showing.

He considered what Parker had told him, then asked a few questions of his own. 'Is there anything to indicate that either Gary or Joseph ever went to this yard?'

'Not as such, sir, no, but we have every reason to suspect—'

'And there's nothing on record to indicate that Roland Barnes has ever been convicted of a sexual offence against a minor?'

'No, sir.'

'And the boy who was there?'

'Brogan,' said Parker.

'You haven't yet had the opportunity to talk to his father?'

'I've had a female officer go to the house. Healey wasn't there, so she talked to a few of the neighbours. They reckon he doesn't live there – they think he's left the lad to his own devices.'

'Have we made an active effort to trace where Healey is?'

'Warrender found out that he's claiming income support. Next time he signs on he'll be followed, and we'll soon know where he's living.'

Chalker said nothing for a moment. Thinking it through, thought Parker, who hoped that, as a result, he'd come to the conclusion that he himself had drawn: that yard had to be searched, and searched very thoroughly. Chalker said, 'Hanson believes the yard is unlikely to yield a result.'

'He might be wrong,' said Parker. 'Can we risk it?'

Chalker, mindful of the cost of a search on that scale, said, 'It's a massive and expensive undertaking,' and Parker thought back to what he knew of the type of house in which Roly lived. Without even seeing the interior, he could visualize its layout with its multitude of rooms set on four distinct levels. The basement would have to be ripped apart and walls would have to be examined. Floorboards would have to come up. Alcoves, pantries, stairwells – there was no end to it. He said, 'I don't dispute that but, God knows, it could be a graveyard. We simply can't risk the council moving in and discovering remains. If it came out that we had had our suspicions but hadn't conducted a thorough investigation because of the cost . . .'

'I realize that,' said Chalker, 'but the fact is, *you* brought Hanson in, and Hanson is of the opinion that we won't find anything of interest at the yard.'

'He could be wrong.'

'I can't justify it,' said Chalker. 'Not on what you've put in front of me today.'

It was the response that Parker had anticipated, yet he couldn't help wishing that Chalker had seen the yard for himself before making such a decision.

'Search the yard by all means, but stick to the resources already at your disposal.'

By that, Parker assumed he meant the men on his team, and although he'd have trusted his life to any one of them, none had X-ray vision; none could see through walls, floors or solid earth. A scanner could.

As if tapping into the vision of the task ahead Chalker broke into his thoughts by saying, 'In my day, all I had was a team of men. We often got the result we were looking for.'

Parker, who was aware that statistics appeared to dictate that the number of serial killers had increased over the past thirty years, knew the truth of the matter was that the police had just grown more efficient. This was due, in part, to the technology now available to them, and it was this very technology that Chalker was denying him the opportunity of using. 'In your day,' he said, 'killers often got away with murder.'

'I'll pretend I didn't hear that,' said Chalker, and Parker left his office without waiting to be dismissed.

Parker went out of the station, and headed not for home but for some park he hadn't seen for the best part of thirty years. He wasn't sure why he'd gone there, but he sat on a bench and watched several kids fooling with a roundabout. It was falling apart by degrees, the wooden slats rotted through, the mechanism grating as they tried to make it spin. There was the suggestion that it might once have been painted blue, the paint long gone, the roundabout now toning in with the colourless swings and a slide.

They seemed too young to be out alone at this time of night, and it struck him that they were probably of a similar age to Joseph and Gary. He watched them as he'd never before watched kids of this age play. Half the time, they looked almost teenage. The other half, they looked as though they belonged there, as though they were clinging to some vestige of a childhood which, for the most part, had been hard, as his had been.

Some time later, they grabbed their bikes and rode off into the dark – no lights, no reflective gear, just a bunch of kids bumping on and off the pavement, unmindful of being invisible to the traffic. Then he eased himself up from the bench, which had infused some of its cold dampness into him, and drove home, the circuitous route he had chosen through the back streets leading him past the house where he'd been born.

He was offended to find that its plain front door had been replaced by something a little more ornate and was struck by the power that former homes could exert on an individual. It wasn't dissimilar to the house where Brogan lived, a two-bedroomed affair with a bathroom installed as an afterthought by parents who'd been accused of 'going all posh!'.

He'd been happy there, that was the difference, but then, he'd had parents who'd loved him, and that, too, was the difference. He didn't know where Brogan's father was, but he knew he wasn't around — not often, at any rate. Parker was beginning to get the impression that Healey, wherever he was, paid little more than lip-service to parental duty, and that wasn't love, it wasn't enough.

Nowhere near enough.

CHAPTER TWENTY-THREE

The roof had been repaired in the old covered market, a fresh pane of glass set high into the dome like a jewel among paste replicas of what the glass should be. The sun shone through it, unhindered by dust, to donate a shard of light on the units below, and as Brogan walked in, he found Moranti sitting on the basket. The minute he saw him, Brogan knew something was very wrong. 'Mr Moranti?' he said.

Moranti stood up. 'Brogan,' he said, 'I can't have you work here no more.'

He fished in the pocket of his gabardine coat, brought out a five-pound note, and handed it to Brogan, saying, 'You're a good boy, Brogan. Good boy, but go now, please.'

'But what have I done wrong?'

'Nothing,' said Moranti. 'The police came to see me. They said I was breaking the law – you're too young to work in the shop.'

'That's not true.'

Moranti looked at those childish hands, so gentle with the birds. 'I'm very sorry, Brogan. You have to go.'

Brogan walked past him, and as he stepped out, Moranti added, 'Don't go down to the yard,' but Brogan wasn't listening. Parker had lost him his job. That was all he knew.

He left the covered market and crossed the road to the

station, where he caught a bus that he knew would drop him in the vicinity of the yard. During the ride, he looked out at surroundings that had grown increasingly dismal the nearer he got to the suburb, and he found himself noticing things he'd never noticed before: the trees were losing their leaves and the few species of domestic bird that had remained to brave the winter were fluffing inadequate feathers against the cold. Many looked fat despite lack of food, their feathers giving the lie to skin and bone, and it brought to mind the scrap of a poem cut from a magazine, something his mother had pasted on to a card. She had leant it on a shelf of the dresser that once dwarfed the kitchen and when he had seen it, his father had said, 'What the bloody hell's this?' But he hadn't destroyed it. He hadn't crumpled it up in his hand as he'd crumpled up her life; he'd merely read the first few lines, then put it back as before, except that the card lay flat for a while and his mother had left it like that, only putting it upright again after tea, when his father had gone.

On reading the poem, Brogan had understood why his father had laughed; its sickly sentiment being a far cry from anything that he could be expected to relate to or draw comfort from. Yet Brogan had searched for it in the drawer after his mother's death, knowing she had hidden it there after the dresser was sold. He hadn't been able to find it, and suddenly it had assumed an importance that was out of all proportion to the effort she had gone to in cutting it out and pasting it, in keeping it for months. In thinking of it, he remembered her. There was so much he wanted to tell her, about Roly, about the finches, and so much he wouldn't want her to know, about his dad and Elaine.

He got off the bus and minutes later, as he crossed the wasteground, he, too, fluffed what few clothes he wore as if they could somehow protect him from a coldness that came from within. There was an emptiness inside that wasn't entirely due to lack of proper food. It had something to do with wanting to be held, and he crossed the road to the yard, then rattled on the gates in the knowledge that Roly would hold him. Roly would ruffle his hair with hands that were gentle. There was nothing large or threatening about those hands. They didn't come out of nowhere to deliver blows for minor misdemeanours. His voice was never raised and his words were never hard. All he got from Roly was warmth, comfort and the welcome that kept drawing him back for more.

He knew the minute the gates were opened that here too, something was wrong. It was almost as though Roly was reluctant to let him in, and Brogan wondered whether Parker had had a word with him as well as Moranti. 'What is it?' he said. 'What's wrong?'

Roly drew him into the yard and chained the gates behind him. 'I've got b-bad news,' he said, and he led Brogan past the nesting shed and into the kitchen.

'What?' said Brogan, looking around, half expecting Parker to appear demanding to know why he'd gone back to the yard when he'd specifically told him not to.

Roly pulled a shoe-box from a shelf, put it on the draining board and slowly lifted the lid. 'I d-did my best,' he said.

Brogan stared down at Tiger. He seemed so small, his feathers dull and matted. Roly had arranged him on a bed of cotton wool. Brogan's voice was small. 'Can we bury him?' he said, and he picked up the box as Roly led him out and into the yard.

He let Brogan pick the spot, a corner by the fence where the metal was curling away from the wooden frame that held it, and crouched beside Brogan who dug with his hands, and made a hole that was big enough for the shoe-box. But at the last moment, Brogan said, 'I don't want him buried in that box.'

'W-what, then?' said Roly, and Brogan reached in for the bird, but when he picked it up, the wings came away in his hands and he almost dropped it in shock. 'His wings,' he said.

Roly explained, 'That's to set him fr-free. You under-st-stand me, Brogan. I had to s-set him free.'

Brogan, who didn't understand, studied the spots of blood that had congealed where the wings had been ripped from the body.

'That's not him,' said Roly. 'That's not h-him in your h-hand – that's all that's left behind.'

Brogan cradled the bird for a moment, then placed it in the grave, its wings beside the torso with the scraggy, twisted neck. He'd managed to keep his tears in check until then. Now, they streamed down his face and Roly pulled him close. 'Moranti killed him,' said Brogan.

'He didn't mean t-to,' said Roly.

He let him cry for a while, then led him back to the kitchen where he opened the cupboard above the cooker. The interior had been turned into a mesh-lined bird-cage, and although he couldn't see the birds in that cupboard, Brogan could hear them. As Roly reached in and brought one out, he said, in a voice that was cracked from the recent tears, 'Why do you keep them shut up?'

'They s-settle better if you keep them enclosed for a while.'

He lowered his hands, then opened them, and Brogan looked at the bird as if he had revealed some precious jewel. Against a backdrop of such utter drabness and filth, it seemed like some sort of bird-of-paradise, the shimmering blues and greens of its back seeming hand-painted somehow. It was as though someone had made a sketch of it, leaving a precise and careful child to colour the various sections with felt-tipped pens.

'Only a f-freak of nature has that kind of beauty. S-sometimes I think they're the only proof we've got that there's a God.'

Brogan cupped his hands, and Roly tipped the bird into them as he added, 'The s-secret ... the secret with Gouldians is, you have to handle them s-soon as they feather,' and Brogan stroked its back with the tip of a finger. The bird seemed quite at ease.

'Would you like him?' said Roly.

Brogan, who couldn't imagine anything he wanted more than he wanted that bird, just held it close.

'He's yours,' said Roly.

CHAPTER TWENTY-FOUR

The news that a Mrs Palmer had turned up asking to see Parker in connection with the Gary Maudsley case took Warrender down to the front desk.

He found her sitting on a padded bench that ran round the reception area, and he also found that she was younger than he'd expected, her name having put him in mind of a middle-aged woman. One day, she would become the type of woman he had initially imagined her to be, the jawline sagging, the waist thick and the clothes ill-fitting and cheap. Right now, she was tiny, trim, and slightly overawed by her surroundings.

'Mrs Palmer?' he said.

She stood up as he spoke, and Warrender drew her aside. 'You say you have information?'

She fumbled in her bag and drew out a segment from a watch strap. Warrender took it from her and studied it. Initially, he didn't know what its significance was, and then it dawned on him that it matched what was left of the strap from Gary's watch.

'Where did you get this?'

'It's our Nathan's.'

'Nathan?'

'My son, Nathan. He did a swap with Gary. He gave him a CD, and Gary gave him the watch.'

The name Nathan Palmer rang a bell with Warrender, and now he placed it as being the name of the boy that he'd seen at the top of the road the day Gary was reported missing.

He fingered the plastic, feeling it soft, stressed, the grey having lightened to white as it stretched and then snapped. 'How did it get broken?'

'He and a lad from his school were messing around. This other lad grabbed his wrist.'

'Where were they at the time?'

She sounded more frightened now. 'Top of Gary's road.'

'It's okay,' said Warrender. 'Don't get upset.'

'I know I should have come forward.'

It was only then that Warrender realized she'd known about the watch for some time, and the implications were serious. If the watch hadn't been ripped from Gary's wrist, then maybe he hadn't been abducted. Maybe he'd gone missing from somewhere else. 'How long have you had it, love?'

She didn't reply, and he said, 'It's okay, really. Just tell me.'

'Weeks,' she said.

'Why didn't you come forward?'

'I meant to, but I kept putting it off.'

Warrender knew how it was. People sometimes kept information to themselves for years, afraid of getting involved and justifying the decision not to do anything by telling themselves that what they knew wasn't important. Sometimes, it took a renewed media interest to convince them that they had a duty to go forward, that if they didn't, the perpetrator of a serious crime might not be brought to justice. 'It's okay,' he said, again. 'You've done the right thing.'

She seemed close to tears as he asked, 'How old is Nathan?'

'Twelve.'

The thought of her having a lad of twelve staggered Warrender, and she waited for his reaction as he calculated what her age must have been when Nathan was born. He said, 'Did he and Gary hang round together much?'

Her reply was instant. 'No.'

It was a lie, and Warrender knew it. 'You sure, love? Because this could be important – even more important than the watch.'

She faltered now. 'I don't know, but I don't want him questioned. He's—'

'I know,' said Warrender, 'he's only a lad – but he might be able to tell us whether Gary ever talked about the places he went, the people he knew.'

'I'll ask him,' she said.

'No,' said Warrender, softly. 'We will.'

Warrender took the information straight to Parker who was tempted to interview Nathan himself, but the news that Brogan had been seen heading for the yard prompted him to leave Hanson to deal with Nathan while he headed for Arpley Street to wait for the boy to get home.

Hanson, who welcomed the opportunity to show what could be done if the right techniques were employed, suggested it might be best if he were left to interview Nathan alone, in his own home, and now, as he sat in the front room of the Palmer household, Hanson had a good view of St Michael's church. The steeple soared into the sky, a post-modern metal spike that jutted from a yellow brick tower, its shadow falling across a playground and the Portakabin annexes to a school that hadn't been built to cope with the sheer volume of pupils for which it now catered.

'Nathan,' he said, and the lad glanced at his mother. 'Do you know who I am?'

The lad shook his head and Hanson said, 'I'm not a policeman, and I'm not here to cause you a problem.'

Nathan weighed him up and looked as though he didn't

quite believe it. He was, thought Hanson, fairly typical of many lads of his age, his legs skinny, his knees, like his face, enormous and indicative of the fact that, ultimately, he would develop into one of those tall, gangling types who are all height and no strength in late adolescence. That was years in the future, though. Right now, Nathan Palmer looked every inch a twelve-year-old, and Hanson was handling him with care.

'Truth is, we've got a bit of a problem, Nathan. We're trying to find a friend of yours, Gary.'

At the mention of his name, Nathan looked sharply away, as if the steeple suddenly held some kind of fascination for him.

'And we're not having much success.'

Nathan kept his eyes fixed firmly on the shadow from that steeple, as if, with luck, it might reach across the road and block out everything that was happening to him.

'That your school?' said Hanson.

He nodded.

'You don't have far to walk, then.'

Nathan kept his eyes fixed on the shadow. 'Is he ever coming back?'

That was the thing about kids, thought Hanson. You could never quite predict how they were going to react. Nathan might have spent the next couple of hours talking about school, his friends, his family, his hobbies — anything but Gary. Instead, he had come to the point, and Hanson saw it as a good sign on the whole. 'We don't know,' he said, 'but we'd like to try to find him, and to do that, we need to try to discover what the circumstances were when he went missing. That's why the watch is important.'

'What's the watch got to do with it?'

'We thought it was wrenched from his wrist. Now we know that it wasn't, we can forget that idea and think about where Gary might have gone the day he disappeared.'

'I don't know,' said Nathan, and the comment sounded

defensive, as if he were afraid that Hanson thought he knew where Gary was, and wasn't telling.

'I know,' he said, reassuringly. 'Nobody thinks you know where he is, or anything like that, but we're hoping you may be able to tell us where he *might* be.'

'How would I know?'

Hanson explained in the simplest possible terms: 'It works something like this, Nathan. In order to find out where Gary might be, we need to find out as much as we can about who he knew and where he went. That might mean secret places – places that only certain of his friends might know about.'

The lad was listening, at least, and at the mention of the word 'secret,' he hadn't denied that he and Gary had any. Hanson had known many an individual to fix on the word and deny they had any secrets. We all have secrets, thought Hanson, and he thought about the guest-house, his reason for going there, and that, very soon, his secret might be out. He said, 'I know I probably seem pretty old to you, but it isn't that long ago since I was twelve.'

Nathan now took his eyes from the shadow and looked at Hanson. His expression gave him away in that he seemed to find it almost impossible to imagine this man ever having been twelve.

'And what I remember ... What I remember most is that sometimes I went to places that my parents didn't know about. And you know why they didn't know?'

Nathan shook his head.

'Because I didn't let them find out. You know why?'

Again the lad shook his head.

'Because I knew they wouldn't have approved if they'd known.'

He let the boy absorb the thought before he said, 'Same with people – if I had friends I thought they might not approve of, I didn't bring them home, and you know what?'

In a voice that Hanson had to strain to hear, Nathan replied, 'What?'

'That's okay,' said Hanson. 'It's perfectly normal. Nobody should ever expect you to tell them everything about yourself. We all have our secrets, and we're all entitled to keep them to ourselves.'

Nathan didn't look too sure, but Hanson continued, 'Trouble is, we've got a bit of problem here, Nathan, because Gary's gone missing and we don't know what's happened to him.'

He noticed the way in which Nathan's mother squeezed his hand extra hard at that, as if relating to what Gary's family must be going through right now. She was probably thanking God it was them and not her, thought Hanson, and she was probably also feeling guilty for thinking such a thing. He said, 'When something like that happens — when someone goes missing, I mean — secrets have to be told because it may make the difference between finding that person alive ... or not.'

He didn't want to frighten the kid, but at the same time he had to get it through to him that this was serious stuff. 'So, if you and Gary ever went anywhere that your mum wouldn't have approved of, you have to tell.'

He'd put that badly. 'What I mean is, I think Gary would have wanted you to tell. I think he'd have said, "It's okay, Nathan, you can tell, I'd do the same for you." What do you think?'

'Nat,' said Nathan. 'Gary called me Nat.'

Hanson said, 'When we care about someone, *really care*, we often give them a nickname, or shorten their name. I'm glad that Gary called you Nat. It means he liked you a lot. He saw you as a friend. Were you, Nat? Were you his friend?'

There was no immediate reaction.

'Did you like him enough to want to do whatever it took to get him found?'

That hit the mark. Hanson saw it in physical signs, the

sudden slump to the shoulders, the way that he glanced out of the window to St Michael's, and followed the shadow of that steeple as it fell across the Portakabin classrooms.

To Nathan, it didn't seem five minutes since he and Gary had hidden behind them, smoking, and Nathan, who hadn't seen much of him lately, had said, 'What you bin up to then?'

'Workin',' said Gary.

'Nice one. Where?'

'Down the covered market.'

'Who for?'

'Moranti.'

Nathan had exhaled as Gary said, 'He took me to see this yard.' He had stopped then, as if unsure that he should say anything more, and Nathan, who couldn't have given a toss one way or another whether he told him or not, had left him to it. 'Full o' birds,' said Gary. 'You've never seen anything like it,' and the following weekend, he'd taken him to see.

Right from the start, Nathan had sensed there was something wrong with that place. He'd hated the way the net had caught at his face, and had hated, also, the way the birds rose up as if to attack. He'd said, 'Where is he then, this *Roly?*' but Gary hadn't replied.

The brightness had gone from the day, the sun no longer warm on their backs, the yard more shadow than substance. Gary had continued to shout for Roly, and Nathan had been aware that the yard echoed in a way that a place of this type could not, in reality, echo. His voice had faded away on a breeze that had seemed to chill them through, but Roly hadn't appeared, and as the seconds ticked by, Nathan had grown increasingly afraid.

'Look at them,' said Gary. 'Amazing, or what?' but despite his having described the birds as amazing, Nathan had realized from the start that not all the finches were beautiful: some were demoniac in type, their plumage dark, their eyes watchful. He had spotted a cardboard box standing by the nesting shed, and had gone over to it. The lid, damp from rain, had collapsed inwards to reveal the remains of finches, Scarlets, Gary had said, their feathers red as though each had been pierced through the throat, and he had drawn away from it, his hand to his mouth, the stench incredible.

'It's only birds,' said Gary.

'Yeah, but how did they die?'

'The weather,' said Gary. 'They can't take the cold,' but Nathan had felt there was something terribly broken about those tiny, scarlet things, something inexplicable about their being there at all. He had looked up, had seen a figure staring down from a window, and had panicked then, running for the net, Gary shouting after him, 'Nat, where you off?'

He didn't know, and he didn't much care. All he had known was that the yard and everything in it had spoken of danger.

'What is it?' said Hanson, but it wasn't to him that Nathan turned, it was to his mother, his voice breaking as he said, 'You know you said never to smoke?'

She squeezed his hand.

'Gary smoked,' he said, 'and he gave me a fag.'

She squeezed again.

At last, thought Hanson, because he recognized the admission for what it was: the drip of information that might become a flood, the confirmation of what Parker had suspected – Gary Maudsley had gone down the yard. He smiled at the lad in front of him and said, 'Me, I smoked like a chimney when I was twelve,' and the lad launched into a confession that had been on his mind since he saw a photo of the missing Gary Maudsley in the press. *Have you seen this boy?* it said, and Nathan, who hadn't seen him lately, had thought, *No, but I know where he's gone . . .*

CHAPTER TWENTY-FIVE

Parker could almost have timed it to the moment when Brogan turned the corner at the top of the street, and he saw at a glance that he nursed a cardboard box in his hands, one that was just about the right size for a finch.

He saw him fish for the key that hung from the string round his neck, and as he lifted it to the lock, Parker couldn't help allowing his imagination to furnish him with an image of Roly wrapping that string round his hand and strangling him with almost casual ease.

He pushed away the image, climbed out of the car, and called out, 'Brogan.'

The lad swung round on him but didn't speak, and Parker broke the impasse by saying, 'Where did you get the bird?'

The lie was quick and convincing: 'Moranti gave it me.'

'Kind of him,' said Parker, and if his tone was dry, he didn't doubt it was lost on Brogan, who twisted the key in the lock and opened the door.

There was something especially child-like about the way he then stepped across the threshold and tried to close the door on Parker, as if by doing so he could make him disappear. It put Parker in mind of the way his eldest had played hide-and-seek as a toddler. Parker would count to ten, and instead of running off to hide, his son would simply stay in the room but turn his back on him, convinced that because his dad was now invisible to him he would be invisible to his dad. Parker had played along, pretending to search the house in a vain attempt at finding him, but, right now, he wasn't in the mood for pretending to be invisible and he jammed his foot in the door. 'Mind if I come in?'

'What for?'

'I'd like to talk to your dad.'

'He isn't in.'

'I'll wait.'

'He won't be back till tonight.'

'How about a cuppa, then?' said Parker, and he pushed his way gently into the hall, knowing that short of ordering him out, there was nothing Brogan could do but let him in.

He closed the door and followed Brogan into a back room, watching as he put the box on a table strewn with crockery.

'Where've you been today?'

'Working.'

'I thought you only worked Saturdays?'

'Mr Moranti was sick. I had to look after the shop.'

'You should be at school.'

'I couldn't let him down, could I?'

'How did you know he was sick?'

'He phoned.'

Parker had tried to contact Brogan's father by phone and had learned that the Healeys phone had been cut off, but he let it go. 'Well, it was good of you to help him, just this once.' He smiled, but Brogan didn't return the smile.

'Sit down a minute, Brogan. I don't bite.'

Brogan edged round the couch and sat in the only chair as Parker indicated a photograph on the mantelpiece. 'That your mother?'

The question had been unexpected, and Brogan merely nodded.

'Where is she?'

'Dead.'

Parker could have kicked himself. 'I'm sorry,' he said.

'S'okay,' said Brogan, 'you weren't to know.'

'It must be hard for your dad, bringing you up on his own.'

This met with no response, and Parker added, 'Sometimes, a lad needs a mother as much as a father. I expect you miss her?'

'She's been dead ages.'

'How long?'

'A couple of years.'

'Must seem a long time to you.'

He looked at the boy and wondered what was running through his head. The expression on his face as he looked at the photo – it was all that Parker could do not to pull him close and try to set his world to rights again. But he couldn't set his world to rights. Nobody could. Short of bringing his mother back to life and supplying him with the kind of background Parker tried to give to his own two boys, nobody could set his world to rights.

'What you doin' here?' said Brogan, bluntly.

Parker heard the sound of scratching coming from the box. 'I wanted a word with your dad, that's all.'

'He won't be back till late.'

Parker was sorely tempted to say he knew very well that Brogan's dad wouldn't be back at all because he didn't live there, but he resisted the impulse and said, 'Pity. I could have done with having a word.'

'What about?'

Cautiously now, Parker replied, 'Roly's Yard. I wanted to let him know I found you there the other day.'

'What's wrong with that?'

'How often have you been back?'

Guiltily, though not knowing why he should feel guilty about it, Brogan replied, 'Couple of times. Why?'

'What's the attraction?'

'Why do I go there, you mean?'

'Something like that.'

Brogan fell silent again, and Parker gave him time.

'I like it down there.'

'What do you like about it?' said Parker, gently.

'The birds. Roly gave me a Gouldian. You ever seen a Gouldian?'

'I don't believe I have,' said Parker, and Brogan went over to the table and picked up the box. 'I'm gonna keep him in my bedroom, and I've got to settle him down, so you'll have to go.'

He opened the door, as if expecting Parker to oblige by walking through it and out of the house, but as he got up from the chair, Parker merely said, 'I'll come up with you.'

'You can't.'

'I'd like to see your bird.'

'I don't like people going in my room.'

Parker could understand that. At Brogan's age, he'd also felt the need to exclude adults from his room, though there was nothing in there that warranted the ferocity with which he had sometimes protected his privacy.

He wasn't interested in invading Brogan's privacy, but he was interested in seeing what, if any, posters hung on the wall in his bedroom. Posters could give an indication of an adolescent's likely sexuality, though Parker was willing to admit that such markers often weren't as reliable as one might wish on the grounds that, six months ago, he'd been convinced that his eldest was well on the way to becoming the next Lily Savage. 'Tell you what,' he said, 'soon as we've settled the bird into his new home, I'll be off, I promise.'

It was a deal, of sorts, and Brogan accepted the terms. 'All right,' he said.

Parker followed him up the stairs to a bedroom at the front, and even as he entered the room, the way it was furnished and decorated struck him as inappropriate for a lad of Brogan's age. The wallpaper print of racing cars would have been more suitable for a boy of four, and he noticed a total absence of posters, CDs, or anything else that boys of Brogan's age tended to acquire. He had hoped to be able to draw him into conversation in order to learn more about him by asking what music he liked, what sports he played, who his friends were, but there was nothing in the room to give him a pointer as to where he should start.

He watched as Brogan tipped the bird out of the box, holding it in one hand as he fiddled with the wire on the door to the cage. It was a far cry from the multi-levelled cages of bamboo that Parker had seen at Moranti's Emporium. This cage was a cheap affair that had seen more than its fair share of birds.

He noticed there were no ornaments jammed between the bars and recalled that the cage in Gary's room had contained none of the paraphernalia that he had associated with birds. Maybe finches didn't like to look at themselves in mirrors, or maybe they had no need of the calcium that could be obtained from the shell of a cuttlefish. Parker didn't know and, what's more, he wasn't bloody interested: he had enough on his plate without filling his mind with trivia relating to the care of birds.

He watched as Brogan transferred the bird to the cage, and the minute he saw it, he remembered having seen similar birds darting around in the aviary. At the time, his mind had been on other things and he hadn't stopped to study them. Now that he was seeing a Gouldian at close quarters, he was taken aback: the bird was so brightly coloured, it seemed almost fluorescent.

'It's a lovely lookin' bird, Bro. Are they hard to keep?'

'They die easy. Moranti buys 'em sometimes, but they don't live more than a day.'

Minutes earlier, Brogan had told him Moranti had given him the bird. Parker now tricked him by saying, 'And Roly *gave* him to you?'

Brogan looked up in alarm. 'I didn't steal him.'

'The thought never entered my head. Just wondering, though. Why would Roly give you a bird like that?'

'He likes me.'

Parker wondered how best to phrase his next question. There seemed no subtle way of asking it. 'He doesn't . . .' He stopped himself. This wouldn't sound right, and he knew it. 'There's nothing he does that *worries* you at all?'

'Like what?' said Brogan.

'I don't know — things you don't like, maybe?'

Brogan fiddled with the clasp on the door to the cage. 'You'd better go,' he said. 'If my dad walks in and finds a copper in the house, I'll be in dead trouble.'

Parker watched as he lifted the cage and put it on the pale pink vanity unit. The bird saw itself in the mirror and hopped up to the reflection as far as the bars would allow. 'Brogan,' said Parker, and now he made a statement. 'Your dad isn't coming home, is he.'

'He is — he——'

'He isn't,' said Parker, 'and I want you to come to the station with me, just to look at some photos. Will you do that, Brogan? Will you come down the station? There's nothing to worry about.'

The boy was panicking now. 'I know what you're thinkin', Mr Parker.'

Parker doubted it, but didn't say so.

Brogan turned on him angrily. 'Roly isn't nickin' stuff to pay for feedin' his birds!'

Relieved, Parker suddenly smiled. 'I don't think that.' He shook his head to himself. 'I don't think that at all.'

Brogan had never seen the interior of a police station before, much less an interview room. He was taken into a room where a female officer, somebody Parker called Maureen, brought him biscuits and something to drink.

'Sit down,' said Parker, and Brogan sat, his nerves steadying now.

'Have a biscuit,' said Parker, and he indicated the plate.

Brogan took a biscuit and bit into it as Parker pulled two photographs out of a file. He put them on the table and said, 'Take a good look at them, Brogan. Recognize either of them?'

Brogan studied the photographs, and Parker noticed that he paused at the one of Gary.

'That's the photo you showed me in the car.'

'That's right,' said Parker. 'Do you know who the other boy is?'

'No.'

'Joseph Coyne,' said Parker. 'He and Gary used to work for Mr Moranti – just like you.'

Brogan took another bite from the biscuit, eating it as if it were dry in his mouth.

'He introduced them to Roly,' said Parker. 'And then they disappeared.'

In a voice that was muffled by crumbs, Brogan said, 'That's not Roly's fault, though, is it?'

'Brogan,' said Parker, gently, 'Joey is *dead*, and maybe Gary, too.'

Noticing that the comment had struck home, Parker indicated the photos once again. 'Have you ever heard Roly or Moranti mention these boys?'

'No,' said Brogan.

'Don't just blurt out the first thing that comes into your head – think about it.'

Brogan shoved the plate of biscuits aside. 'You've got it in for Roly. He doesn't know where they are.'

Parker exchanged a look with Maureen, then turned his attention back to Brogan. 'Where's your dad, Brogan?'

'At home.'

'He's never there.'

'How would you know?'

'I've called a number of times.'

'He's out a lot.'

'Does he sleep at home?'

'Yeah.'

'Don't lie to me, Brogan.'

He could see that the boy was beginning to get upset now, imagining all kinds of scenarios, no doubt. For all Parker knew, his dad might have primed him about not telling anyone that he wasn't living there most of the time. *They'll put you in care, so keep it shut ...*

'Nobody wants to cause you or your dad any problems, but we do have to make sure you're being looked after properly.'

'I can look after myself.'

'Where is he, Brogan?'

He clammed up, much as Parker had feared he might.

'I tell you what – you're going to stay at this station until we find your dad.'

He was getting nothing from Brogan now, just the threat of tears, and he said, 'Think about it, Brogan. There are two photos on that desk. It could easily be three.'

The threat of tears spilled over. 'He works,' said Brogan. 'Not all the time, just sometimes – the DSS doesn't know.'

'Where does he work?'

'He'll kill me if he finds out I—'

'Where?'

'Stockton's.'

'The wire-weaving place?'

A nod confirmed it, and Parker softened now. 'I'll go and have a word with him,' he said. He stood up. 'And while I'm gone, someone's going to talk to you. He's not a copper, so don't be scared, but he'll want to ask a few questions, find out how you feel about certain things. Okay?'

He got a nod from Brogan, who was still staring down at the photos, and then he left the room and contacted Hanson.

CHAPTER TWENTY-SIX

Hanson arrived at the station, and Parker led him down a corridor on the ground floor. The doors off it concealed a string of interview rooms, most of them occupied, and as Parker opened the door to the room where Brogan was being held, Hanson took stock of it.

In many respects, it was similar to others where he had interviewed prisoners when compiling the database, and he wondered whether Parker was aware of just how threatening an environment like this could be to a boy of twelve. The smallness of the room, the fact that there was no window — all these things could only serve to punch home the message that this was serious business. And then he wondered whether Parker had chosen this room intentionally. So far, Brogan had ignored all his warnings, and it was just possible, he decided, that Parker was getting tired, or desperate, or both.

He looked down at the lad, who seemed all the more tiny, sitting, as he was, behind a table that was level with his chest. The childish hands were clutching a half-eaten biscuit, and sitting beside the plate was an untouched plastic beaker of orange squash. 'Brogan,' he said, and the boy looked scared — disorientated, in fact.

Hanson pulled the chair round to the side so that the desk

didn't divide him from the boy, sat down, and said, 'Can I have a biscuit?'

Brogan pushed the plate towards him, and Hanson took one, bit into it and found it crisp, fresh out of a packet. 'Not bad,' he said, 'but my mum could make them better.'

Brogan put down his biscuit.

'How about your mum, Brogan? Could she make them better than that?'

'She didn't make biscuits,' said Brogan, and Hanson, who had intended to use whatever response Brogan gave, replied, 'What did she make? Anything?'

'Cakes,' said Brogan.

'Would you rather have a cake than those biscuits?'

He shrugged. 'Not bothered.'

'Not hungry?' said Hanson.

'Not bothered, that's all.'

Hanson turned to Maureen, saying, 'Don't suppose you could nip down the canteen and see if they've got any cakes, could you?' Once she — along with the uniform she wore — was out of the room, he said, 'My mum died when I was a kid.'

Brogan reached for the squash.

'I was older than you. Seventeen. I don't suppose I was a kid as such any more. But then, I don't suppose you are, either.'

Brogan was shutting him out, thought Hanson. Or maybe not. Maybe what he was shutting out was the pain of the conversation, his surroundings, his inability to handle the situation as a whole. 'When somebody dies, somebody as important as our mum, it makes us grow up fast. It did me, anyway.'

Brogan, who'd never thought about it in those terms, took a gulp of the squash.

'Thing is,' said Hanson, 'it doesn't much matter how old you are. You could be fifty, and it wouldn't matter. You'd still feel bad about your mum dying. But you ...' Brogan put down the plastic beaker. He wouldn't look at

Hanson. '... you must have been about eleven when your mum died.'

'Ten,' said Brogan. 'I was ten.'

'And now you're twelve,' said Hanson, 'but it doesn't get any easier, does it?'

It hadn't been his intention to make him cry, but he had the feeling that Brogan had needed to stop biting back the tears. He cried like a much younger boy, his hands balled up into fists which he rubbed against his eyes, and it was at times like these that Hanson hated his job.

He let him cry for what seemed a good while — long enough at any rate for Maureen to slip back into the room with a small iced cake. When Brogan had calmed down a bit, Hanson said, 'At least you've found a friend.'

Brogan, his face pale, stared at the small iced cake. 'Mr Parker doesn't like Roly.'

'No, but you do, and you wouldn't like him if you didn't have good reason.'

This sounded something like approval, and Brogan replied, 'He's great to me, Roly. You should see his yard.'

The memory of standing on that wasteground and listening to Parker's description of what lay behind those gates flitted into Hanson's mind. He said, 'Trouble is, you may not be safe at the yard.'

'That's just Mr Parker making it up.'

'Gary and Joseph were known to have gone to the yard.'

'That's not Roly's fault.'

'Maybe not,' said Hanson, soothingly. 'But Mr Parker has to check these things out, and until he's sure it's safe, he'd rather you didn't go there.'

He could almost guess at what was passing through Brogan's mind. On the one hand, he would probably be able to see the logic in that. On the other, he would automatically want to leap to Roly's defence, if only to convince himself that Roly really was his friend. He said, 'To tell you the truth, I can see

Mr Parker's point of view, but I can also see why you don't see any reason why you shouldn't go there. After all, Roly's just about the only friend you feel you have at the moment, and it's not as though he's ever done anything that worries you.'

He thought he detected something telling in the way that Brogan looked away a fraction, and Hanson spoke again, phrasing his words carefully. 'He hasn't, has he, Brogan? In the few weeks you've known him, he hasn't done one single thing you didn't like?'

'No,' said Brogan, but he couldn't help thinking back to the moment when Roly had given him the Gouldian.

'He's yours,' said Roly, and then he had kissed him, not on the lips, but the eyes.

Brogan had pulled away, not violently, but gently, more confused than afraid, and Roly had said:

'Look at the c-colour you've gone – like a little Scarlet finch,' and Brogan had reached for his throat as if there were blood on his feathered breast.

'*You shouldn't have done that. You shouldn't have kissed me like that.*'

'I th-thought we were friends?'

'We are,' said Brogan, 'but leave my eyes alone.'

Hanson watched him play with the small iced cake. 'Brogan?' he prompted, but Brogan pressed his fingers into the icing: two sad eyes, a cherry for a nose, and a smile that resembled a twist.

CHAPTER TWENTY-SEVEN

Over recent years, reports in the local press had portrayed Stockton's as being on the brink of liquidation, but as Parker drove under the barrier that had been raised to admit him, he saw no sign of the company going down. He wasn't there to question how Healey managed to keep the job quiet from the DSS. He only wanted to get it home to him that his boy was in danger.

The large prefabricated units that had replaced their Victorian predecessors seemed crammed to capacity with men, most of them working machinery that spewed out coils of wire in varying gauges, and Parker was directed to one of the units by a foreman who pointed Healey out, then left him to it.

Parker found Healey standing on a production line, lengths of wire streaming past like strands of silken thread, and although he made the right moves, he was working on autopilot, his mind elsewhere. Parker guessed he'd been doing the same job for years. He was built for it, the arms long and muscular, the face without humour. Brogan, thought Parker, must have taken after his mother, and he suddenly had an impression of a woman who was slightly built, her face pale, her eyes large, her hands, like those of a child, small and neat.

He walked up to Healey, and could barely make himself heard above the noise. 'Mr Healey?' he said, producing his ID.

Healey didn't bother to speak. He knew from experience that nobody could hold a conversation in front of one of the machines. With a truculent nod he indicated a door at the far end of the unit, and Parker followed him out.

They walked into a bitter wind, Healey reaching for cigarettes the instant he stepped outside: a reflex action, thought Parker, one born of true habit. He may not even have wanted a smoke, but years of taking whatever opportunity arose had forced his hand to his overall pocket for the fags he knew would be there. He offered one to Parker, who declined and watched the other man light up as a fork-lift shifted a stack of pallets across his field of vision.

'What's this about?' said Healey, and even then, Parker knew that Healey was no friend of the police. The man's face was not familiar, but Parker wouldn't have been surprised to learn that he had form. He'd check it out. 'You've got a lad – Brogan.'

'What about him?'

Parker wasn't about to dive in with the news that Brogan was currently at the station being questioned by Hanson. He decided to work his way up to that one, and started off by saying, 'I gave him a lift home the other day.'

Suspicious and defensive, Healey said, 'Where from?'

'Roly's Yard.'

'Never heard of it.'

'Neither had I, till I went down there to make some enquiries into a case I'm currently investigating.'

'What kind of case?'

This was where it got tricky, thought Parker. He wanted nothing more than to be able to say he was investigating the disappearance of two boys, that a known paedophile had unwittingly led him to Roly's Yard, and that he had taken one look at the place and had decided Roly warranted further investigation, but he couldn't say that – not unless he wanted to find himself up on a disciplinary. If he implied to a member of the public that he'd questioned Roly in connection with the missing boys, Roly would have good cause for complaint.

'I'm not at liberty to say,' he said.

'So what's the problem?' said Healey, and Parker wondered how to go about explaining what it was about the yard that had brought him here.

Finally, he said, 'Roly's Yard is a squat. It's got a massive aviary tacked on to the back of it.' He added weight to the words as he added, 'The kind of place a kid of Brogan's age might be attracted to.'

'Brogan doesn't like birds, not that I know of.'

Healey was missing the point, and Parker wondered how he could make it clearer without being too on the nose. 'Man lives there on his own, name of Roland Barnes.'

'Name means nothing to me,' said Healey.

Parker struggled on. 'During the course of my enquiries, I've had cause to call on him.'

'What are these enquiries?'

'I can't say.'

'What was our Brogan doing there?'

'I don't know.'

Lighting a fresh cigarette from the first, Healey said, 'Look, Mr . . .'

'Parker,' said Parker.

'What are you getting at?'

'Nothing. I'm just trying to let you know that your lad's hanging around with someone I've got my eye on at the moment.'

'What's he done, this bloke?'

'Nothing, that we know of.'

'He's not one of these . . .' Parker left him to find the words, and Healey said, 'He's not been touchin' him up – it's nothin' like that?'

There was nothing Parker wanted more than to be able to say exactly what he thought, but he couldn't do it. 'I'm not implying that. I'm just saying we're watching him at the moment.'

'Is he nickin' stuff? Is that what this is about?'

Again, Parker replied, 'Like I said, I can't say. We're just watching him, that's all.'

'So – he hasn't done anything that you know of, but you just don't like the look of him. Is that it?'

Parker began to lose patience. He couldn't believe that Healey didn't have at least some vague idea of what he was indirectly trying to tell him. Nobody could be that thick, but what they could be, and what Healey clearly intended to be, was uncooperative. 'Mr Healey,' he said, 'I'm struggling with this one – help me out. I'm constrained by the law with regard to what I can and can't imply, and I can't tell you what our concerns are because we don't have any proof. For all we know, Roly might be Manchester's answer to Mother Theresa, but until the Pope can confirm it, I'd rather play on the safe side and make sure you know that Brogan's been seen down his yard.'

'Sounds to me like you've got it in for the bloke.'

Parker's patience snapped. 'Right, Mr Healey, I spend my days trying to decide who to pick on next – that's the trouble with being a copper, there's fuck all else to do.'

There were times, thought Parker, when a little anger went a long way, and he was relieved when Healey said, 'Look, if it'll get you off my back, I'll have a word with him later.'

'Good,' said Parker, 'but later won't do. You'll have to talk to him now.'

'I'm workin'.'

'You're also claiming income support.'

The change that came over Healey brought joy to Parker's heart. On the one hand, the man was furious that Parker knew, on the other he was suddenly very wary. Parker thought he detected a note of something approaching respect as Healey said, 'Where's our Brogan now?'

'Down the station,' said Parker. He smiled. 'I'll give you a lift if you like.'

Healey threw the cigarette to the ground and crushed it as if he wished that he had Parker under his heel, but as Parker made for his car, he followed reluctantly.

Once they reached the station, Parker took Healey into the room where Brogan was being held. It was obvious to Parker that Brogan had been crying, and his heart went out to the kid, but Hanson seemed to have it under control: they'd walked in to find that he had his arm round the boy, comforting him.

'What the *fuck*'s goin' on?' said Healey.

'Mr Healey,' said Parker, and his voice held a note of warning, but the look that Healey shot Brogan told Parker that once he got him home, there'd be trouble. 'Your lad's had a bit of a rough time,' he said. 'Maybe you could ...' but Healey wasn't having any of that.

He took at step towards Hanson. 'Take your hands off him.'

'I'm not a copper,' said Hanson. 'I'm only trying to help.'

'Take your fuckin' hands off him.'

Brogan shrank away as his dad took a step towards them, but Parker grabbed Healey's arm and held him back. 'Lighten up,' he said. 'Nobody's hurting Brogan.'

Healey shook him off and grabbed his boy. 'You're comin' home.'

Parker had had enough of Healey for one day. He pulled him off Brogan, who clung to Hanson as if he were a lifeline, shoved him out of the interview room and pushed him up against the wall of the corridor. 'What the hell are you playing at?'

'You don't frighten me.'

'Then you have me at a disadvantage,' said Parker, 'because you frighten me.' He grabbed Healey by the throat and slammed his head against the breeze-block wall. 'People like me end up lying awake at nights through men like you – men who don't know the meaning of the words parental responsibility. You frighten me because the minute you walk out of here, you'll carry on as before. You don't give a *shit!*'

Healey was breathing rapidly, every muscle in his body tense. He clearly wanted to lash out at Parker, who loosened his grip. 'Come on,' he said. 'Have a go.' But Healey didn't have the guts, and Parker, mindful that there were people around, some of them suspects being led to and from the interview rooms, couldn't afford to take it any further. And he left it.

Even so, Healey pointed a finger inches from Parker's face. 'I want to speak to your superior officer.'

'And tell him what?' said Parker. 'That you've left your boy to fend for himself?'

Guilt, fear, denial – perhaps it was one or a combination of these things that made Healey respond with, 'I'm around.'

'You don't live with Brogan.'

'Don't be fuckin' ridiculous – where else would I be livin'?'

'You tell me.'

'I look after my boy.'

'I don't think so,' said Parker. 'Tell me, what kind of father are you?'

'What kind of question is that?'

'You leave him alone – he's *twelve*, Mr Healey. You leave him alone to fend for himself.'

'I was bringin' a wage home at his age.'

'You brought it *home*. I'm assuming there was somebody *at home* to receive it – a mother, a father. Just because he's got a roof over his head, you think he's sorted.'

'It's none of your business,' said Healey, but Parker said again, 'You don't live with Brogan.'

'Yes, I do,' Healey insisted, and Parker knew then that he was well aware that what he was doing was wrong.

'You know it's against the law,' said Parker. 'I could have you done, get Brogan put into care.'

'I look after him,' said Healey.

Parker replied, 'The other day, one of my officers tried to call on you. She saw a box on the doorstep. She opened the lid. There were a few bits of food in it. Is that what you mean, Mr Healey, when you say you're around, that you look after him?'

'I give him money. He doesn't go short.'

'He isn't starving, if that's what you mean, but I wouldn't say he doesn't go short. Still, Social Services will no doubt assess his domestic situation, and take a decision on his future.'

'You *bastard!*' said Healey. 'What gives you the right—'

Parker, who knew the only thing he could do was keep Social Services informed and hope they'd sort it out, said, 'I've got no choice but to let you take Brogan home with you right now. Believe me, if I had, I wouldn't do it – but if you so much as give him a sideways look, or spend one night away from that house, I'll know, and I'll come down on you like a ton of shit. You got that?'

Healey appeared to have got it.

'Where are you living?' Parker insisted, and Healey suddenly realized he didn't intend to leave it. 'Anton Close,' he said. 'Number nine.'

'There now,' said Parker. 'That wasn't so difficult, was it?'

'Look, I'll move back with Brogan,' said Healey, but he sounded reluctant and Parker said: 'You do that, and make sure you stay there. In the meantime, forget about your job. I'll contact Stockton's – tell them you've been headhunted.'

'Bastard,' muttered Healey.

'I'm not doing it to cause you a problem,' said Parker. 'I'm doing it so that you can be around, at home, to keep an eye on your lad and make sure he doesn't go back down that yard.'

'You still haven't said what the problem is.'

Parker couldn't even imply that Brogan was in danger without infringing Roly's rights and replied. 'I *can't.*'

For the first time since Parker had got him to the station, Healey softened. 'What's going on?'

'Keep him away from the yard,' said Parker. 'Hear me?'

Healey heard.

Brogan climbed out of the patrol car and wondered what was coming to him once it had driven off. His dad hadn't spoken a word on the way home, and when he flicked the light switch in the hall only to find that the house remained in darkness, Brogan braced himself. 'What's goin' on?' said Healey.

'They cut the 'lecky off.'

'When?'

'Two days ago.'

'How come?'

'Bill wasn't paid.'

'When did the final demand come in?'

'Ages ago.'

'You didn't say nothin' to me.'

'I did — I brought it round.'

'Jesus Christ,' said Healey. 'All right, I'll sort it.'

He went to the kitchen and fumbled around in a cupboard for candles, found some and lit one. The walls looked pocked, their every imperfection standing out in relief against the plaster.

Brogan watched as he opened the fridge and drew out a couple of pies. He put them on a tray and shoved them in the oven, forgetting that it ran off electricity and cursing when it wouldn't light. He dragged them out and put the pies on plates, handed one to Brogan and said, 'Can you manage it cold?'

They sat in the adjoining room, the candle on the mantelpiece, the pies on plates on their knees, and his father said, 'This yard . . .'

'What about it?'

'What goes on down there?'

'Nothin'.'

'Why do you go there?'

'To see the birds.'

'That all?'

'Why else would I go?'

Healey didn't know, but much though he didn't have any time for the police, he couldn't help thinking that Parker wouldn't be making a fuss like that for nothing. 'What's he like, this bloke?'

'What bloke?'

'Roly,' said Healey. 'Who did you think I meant?'

'Dunno,' said Brogan. 'Mr Parker maybe?'

'Don't push your luck,' said Healey, quietly. 'You know who I mean.'

'He's all right,' said Brogan.

'What's he up to?'

'Nothin'.'

'He's not . . .' Healey struggled to find a way of describing the only thing he really feared '. . . touching you up . . .'

'He breeds finches,' said Brogan. 'He pays me to clean the cages.'

'That all?'

'That's all,' said Brogan.

Healey spoke through a mouthful of pie, the pastry dry and sticking to his teeth. 'I don't want you going down there no more.'

'Parker's got it all wrong.'

'I don't care. I don't need Parker breathing down my neck, so give it a rest.'

He'd expected cries of protest, but got only a quiet look of defiance. Instead of rising to it, though, Healey made an effort, tried to see it from Brogan's point of view. 'You must get fed up, here a lot on your own.'

'It's quiet,' said Brogan, and he looked automatically at the photo of his mother.

Healey leant forward and picked it up off the mantelpiece, looked at it as if for the first time, and said, 'She was good to me.'

Brogan had seen this before, the surge of sentimentality that followed a violent outburst of the kind that had taken place earlier, at the station.

'She was a dreamer, your mum. She wanted a lot out of life – more than I could give her.'

She didn't complain, though, thought Brogan. She knew better than to criticize his dad – knew what she'd get if she did.

'We all start off with dreams. We don't expect to make a difference to the world – not most of us, anyway – we just expect that, somehow, it'll be different for us.' He put the photo down. 'I loved her a lot.'

Brogan suddenly saw him grab his mother and whirl her round a room that was far too small for happiness, for dancing, for forgiveness. Even so, she'd laughed like a girl, and he'd held her face in those overlarge hands, had kissed her, and Brogan had felt a stab of jealousy then – an unreasonable thing, but he felt it almost as deeply as he'd felt her death, as though a part of his mother was being stolen away from him.

'Looks like I'll have to come home,' said Healey. 'I'll nip off to Elaine's later – tell her what's goin' on.'

Brogan, who wasn't so sure that he wanted his dad around any more, said nothing.

'I'll tell her what's happened and ask her if she'd like to move in with us.'

Brogan cut the pie, a slow, rhythmical slicing of the knife, as if the knife were blunt or his hands were cold or both.

'Nothing much'll change, but you'll have us for company.'

Brogan chewed the filling, more gristle than meat.

'Well?' said Healey.

Brogan stopped chewing. 'She's not my mum.

'Nobody's sayin' she is.'

Brogan jumped to his feet, the plate crashing to the floor as he ran for the door. 'You killed my mum.'

'Brogan—'

'You killed her, you *killed* her – and I'm gonna tell Mr Parker—'

'Don't you run out when I'm talkin' to you! Don't you – Brogan!'

When Brogan returned to the house, he found the candle snuffed and his father gone. He relit the candle and found that his dad had left a note, the words 'Elane', and 'back layter', the only ones he could decipher. As he read it, he trod into the carpet the remains of the pie that had fallen from his plate. His dad had left it there as a statement. *You threw it, you clear it up.* There had once been a time when Brogan would have done so. Now, he left it. This was no longer his home. By inviting Elaine to live there, his father would drive all memory of his mother out of the house. There'd be nothing to stay for.

He tried to visualize what the room might be like if Elaine and her kids moved in. The chest of drawers that his mother had kept polished along with the dresser would be spoiled. Soon, there'd be scratches, figures drawn in crayon on the side, rings from mugs set straight down on to the surface without a coaster.

He took what was left of the candle up to his room where he balanced it on the vanity unit. The wax dripped down to form milky pools the colour of the moon, and the room was lit by a yellowish light that flickered and jumped and played. He reached into the cage and brought out the Gouldian, setting it free and noting that it made straight for the rail that ran round the room, an instinctive need to gain height and therefore safety.

His mother would have liked it, he decided. His mother would have bought him felt-tipped pens so he could draw it. She'd have pinned his every effort on to the door of the kitchen, and she'd have told him the drawings were great even if they weren't.

He went to the window and looked out on the houses opposite, their curtains closed tight on the early-evening darkness. He knew his dad well enough to have understood that there was no point arguing: no matter what he felt about it, he'd be back later, having spoken to Elaine, and ultimately, she'd move in with her kids, whether he liked it or not.

He drew the curtains closed, but one of them snagged on the runner. He pulled again and it came away altogether, a ragged, half-hung thing, so he yanked it down completely to leave the window bare.

From its vantage-point on the picture rail, the bird watched Brogan pull the remaining curtain from its runner. He threw it down on the floor on top of books he had owned for longer than he could remember. The pictures were brightly coloured, the words beneath them printed in large, bold letters. They lay in a pile on the floor, and on top of them strips of paper that Brogan had pulled from the walls. The plaster beneath was grey, cracked, and flaking. The house was old, parts of it damp, and it came away with ease.

It seemed to the bird that the boy worked with a frantic energy, stripped to the waist, his body glossy with sweat, and as the last of the wallpaper came away, he turned on the pale pink dresser with something approaching venom, emptying the drawers, tipping the cuttings from comics on to the pile, adding the small plaster figures of families carved from imagination.

He piled the rubbish into black plastic bin-liners and carried them downstairs, the bird flying with him, soaring over his head as he made for the back door.

Brogan shooed it back into the kitchen, where it perched on one of the units and stared out to a yard so different from the aviary of his birth. Here, there were no slender trees, just a strip of concrete twelve feet wide and half as long again.

The bird watched through the window as Brogan tipped the bags into the centre of the yard, put a match to the pile and set the rubbish alight. Dry and porous, the wallpaper ignited instantly, and as he watched his childhood turn to ash, Brogan decided to leave the house for good. Roly had said he was welcome at the yard whenever he liked. He'd take his Gouldian with him, and he'd go.

Having taken the decision, he shooed the bird back to his bedroom, snuffed the candle and sneaked out, closing the door behind him, leaving his bird in darkness. A short while later, he returned and closed the door to the cage. The Gouldian, coaxed back inside by the food, cowered on the litter as Brogan picked up the cage, and left the house for the yard.

CHAPTER TWENTY-EIGHT

Darkness did Roumelia Road no favours. The street lamps that had once lit the pavement were gone and the houses were stark, black shapes against an even blacker sky.

A truck had been parked by the wasteground. It reminded Brogan of something his mother had bought him when his hands were too small to hold it properly. He'd pushed it along the kitchen floor, the wheels spinning fast on the lino, and he had woven it through her feet as she polished the dresser.

The gates to the yard were closed and chained, but he knew that Roly was there. He didn't know how he knew until he thought about the birds and realized that they seemed settled. Some sat in the trees, watching, as he entered the yard and knocked on the kitchen door.

A light came on in the kitchen. Roly opened the door. He took one look at Brogan, reached out and pulled him inside without saying a word, then shut and bolted the door.

Minutes later, he and Brogan left the house, chaining the gates behind them. They walked across the wasteground, then slipped between the houses, and the men who were watching the yard radioed in to the station.

The news went straight to the incident room and Parker, who was off duty, was contacted at home. He was told that Brogan had left the yard with Roly, who had led him across the wasteground and almost up to the house where Parker's men were positioned, but he'd then led him down one of the many alleys that divided what was left of Roumelia Road from other derelict properties.

An attempt had been made to follow them, but Roly, who wasn't on record as owning a vehicle, had stopped at a row of garages that stood disused, the doors like bent tin cans.

The officers following them had been on foot. Roly had gone into one of the garages, had guided the boy into an ancient, battered Escort and had driven away. In short, Parker's men had lost them, but Parker, who was devastated by the news, made a better job of keeping his temper than Healey had earlier.

To do Healey credit, he'd called the police to tell them Brogan was gone, and Parker went to Arpley Street to find him there, worrying about his boy.

He sat on the arm of the couch, a six-pack at his feet, the density of the smoke in the room evidence enough of his concern.

'I'll kill our Brogan,' said Healey, to which Parker replied, more to himself than to Healey:

'You may not have to.'

'What's that supposed to mean?'

'Nothing, Mr Healey – just a figure of speech,' but Healey wasn't prepared to allow Parker to fob him off. 'What's goin' on?' he said.

Parker, who would have liked nothing more than to tell him the truth, still couldn't risk it. Not only might Healey cause him a problem by repeating whatever he said, but Parker, who now knew first-hand how easily Healey lost his temper, feared that he might go berserk if he knew the extent of his concerns. He said, 'When Brogan comes back, I want you to give permission for him to be examined by a doctor.'

Instantly, Healey grew aggressive. 'What for?'

Soothingly, Parker said; 'Alcohol, drugs, and just a general check-up. Okay with you?'

Healey couldn't be stupid, thought Parker. He must know the nature and purpose of such an examination, and yet he focused on the words *drugs* and *alcohol*, choosing to ignore that the result of such an examination might bring him face-to-face with facts that he might not be able to deal with.

'If you think it's necessary,' said Healey.

'I do,' said Parker.

He left an officer at the house, partly to ensure that he would be informed if Brogan *didn't* come home – this was Parker's greatest fear, that Brogan would disappear and that, somewhere down the road, someone would do as Hardman had and stumble on his remains.

He told Healey that he'd call on him the following morning, then went home in the knowledge that there was nothing more he could do: all cars were on the alert for Roly's Escort, but as he slept that night, he dreamed he could see it being driven down a road towards a wood. He was a helpless bystander, someone who could only watch as Brogan was placed on a scaffold. *What kind of game are we playing, Roly? What if somebody comes?*

The following morning, he was shaken awake by his wife, who said, 'Someone phoned from the station.'

Parker reached for the phone on his bedside table and phoned in. 'Brogan's back,' he was told.

Healey, mindful of Parker's warning and mindful also that Parker had left one of his officers in the house in case Brogan should turn up, had somehow managed to keep his temper when Brogan had let himself into the house at seven that morning.

He'd seemed surprised to see his dad actually there, but not quite so surprised to find the police in the house too.

The uniform had reported in to say that Brogan had turned up, but he didn't question the boy. Neither did Healey, Parker's last words to him having been, 'If he turns up – and let's hope he does – leave him to me.'

Roly had been seen returning to the yard and Parker was tempted to bring him in, but he had plans for Roly, and none of them included letting him know he was under surveillance. He probably suspected as much, but that was a far cry from knowing it for sure, and Parker wanted Roly where he could see him so that he could arrest him the morning they searched the yard. If he were to do anything to alarm him, Roly might do a runner, and Parker had enough on his plate trying to find Byrne.

Parker told the uniform to take Brogan down to the station, where he talked to him in the interview room in which Hanson had questioned him the previous day.

Hanson stayed in the background. He had wanted to be the one to talk to Brogan, but Parker wouldn't hear of it, though he'd taken a leaf out of Hanson's book by sitting next to the boy so that the table didn't form some sort of psychological barrier between them. 'Where've you been?' he said, gently.

'Roly's Yard.'

'Why did you go there?'

'I wanted to see Roly.'

Parker tried to talk to the boy in the way that he hoped a senior officer would talk to one of his own lads in the event of them causing concern, but it wasn't easy: his emotions were running high, and he wanted nothing more than to get it through to him what he, his father, and every member of the team had been through in worrying about him, searching for him, fearing the worst.

'We were worried,' he said, gently.

'Why?'

'We didn't know where you were.'

'I was all right.'

Parker, who could see full well that Brogan was all right,

replied, 'We weren't to know that, Brogan. For all we knew, something might have happened to you.'

'Well, it didn't,' said Brogan.

'Where did you go?'

'Nowhere.'

'You must have gone somewhere.'

Brogan couldn't deny the logic of that. 'Okay,' he said. 'We parked down a road in the country.'

'Where abouts in the country?'

'Dunno,' said Brogan, and he recalled the way the suburbs had seemed to melt into the darkness. Trees replaced the buildings, and hedges replaced the roads.

'Sounds like you went quite a way out of town.'

'It took a long time to get there,' Brogan confirmed.

'And when you got there, what happened?'

'Nothin',' said Brogan. 'We sat there, that's all.'

'Sat in the car?'

'Yeah.'

'All night?'

'Yeah.'

'You must have been cold.'

'I was, a bit.'

'And bored,' said Parker.

'A bit.'

'What did you do all night?'

'Nothin',' said Brogan. 'Just sat there.'

'Front or back?' said Parker.

Brogan didn't seem to understand. Parker said, 'Were you sitting in the front of the car or the back?'

'Both,' said Brogan. 'I mean ... we sat in the front at first, and then we climbed into the back.'

'What made you climb into the back of the car?'

'Roly said it was more comfortable.'

I'll bet he did, thought Parker. He looked at Hanson who shook his head a fraction, as if to say, 'Don't ask —

not now. You won't get an answer and all it will do is make him defensive.

'Why did you go to the yard in the first place?'

'Well,' said Brogan, 'I'd had a row with my dad, and Roly had said I could live with him at the yard if I wanted, so I went.'

'What about your bird?'

'Took it with me.'

'Where is it now?'

'At the yard. Hope it's all right.'

'Why shouldn't it be?'

'You never know,' said Brogan.

No, thought Parker. You never know. Mothers die. Dads go AWOL. Anything could happen in the world that Brogan inhabited. He said, 'I'm sure your bird'll be fine, but why did you leave it there?'

Brogan sensed a trick. 'How do you mean?'

'You wouldn't have left it there if you didn't intend to go back some time, and I thought you promised me you wouldn't go back down the yard.'

'I never promised.'

Parker bit back a desire to clip him round the ear, and said, 'That's true. You've never actually *promised* that you wouldn't go back to the yard. In fact, you've never actually said that you *wouldn't* go back to the yard — but I hoped, in view of everything I'd told you, that you might think carefully before you did.'

'I haven't done nothin' wrong,' said Brogan.

Parker spoke for Hanson as well as himself when he replied: 'Nobody's saying you have. We're just concerned, that's all.'

Taking him back a step, Hanson put in, 'You left your bird at the yard and you said you hoped he'd be okay. What did you mean by that?'

'Just what I said,' replied Brogan. 'I hope he's okay.'

'Why shouldn't he be?'

'Tiger wasn't,' said Brogan. 'But that wasn't Roly's fault.'

It was the first time Parker had heard of Tiger's existence. 'Who's Tiger?'

'Tiger finch that Roly gave me the first time Mr Moranti took me down the yard.'

'Ah,' said Parker, and he smiled.

The smile faded when Brogan added, 'He died.'

The way he said it, as if to say it didn't really matter, that *nothing could really hurt him any more*, wasn't lost on Parker. 'How did he die?'

'Moranti squashed him,' said Brogan. 'I took him back to the yard to see if Roly could make him better.'

'And he couldn't,' said Parker, quietly.

'We carried him out,' said Brogan, 'in a shoe-box.' He looked up at Parker, his face a complete blank. 'His wings fell off.'

Hanson was trying to visualise the scene. 'You carried him out in a shoe-box, and his wings fell off.' Softly now: 'How do you mean?'

'I lifted him out of the shoe-box. He was lying on cotton wool. I didn't like the thought of burying him in a shoe-box, it didn't seem right.'

Hanson could suddenly picture the boy standing by his mother's grave, the coffin being lowered, and Brogan wanting desperately to set her free from it, to bring her back to life.

'I lifted him out of the box,' said Brogan, 'but his wings fell off in my hand.'

'How did you feel when his wings fell off?'

'Dunno,' said Brogan. 'What did it matter? Tiger was dead. Roly said you had to cut the wings off, otherwise the bird inside stayed trapped.'

Hanson walked forward, crouched down in front of the boy. 'What did you think he meant by that?'

'Dunno,' said Brogan. 'Tiger was dead. It didn't really matter what I thought.'

But it did, thought Hanson. It mattered very much. The boy had been so stricken by the death of the bird, he'd blotted out the pain of it, had refused to feel it, and to such an extent that he hadn't even questioned the oddity of the bird having been dismembered. 'Then what?' said Hanson.

'We went back in the house, and Roly gave me Goldie.'

'The Gouldian finch,' guessed Parker.

'I call him Goldie.'

'Good name, for a Gouldian,' said Parker, kindly, and Brogan smiled a fraction.

'Hope he's all right,' he repeated.

'I'm sure he's fine,' Hanson reassured him. 'If you like, Mr Parker will go back down the yard and get him for you, bring him to you.'

'Back to my dad's?'

'No,' said Hanson. 'You won't be going back to your dad's for a while.' He didn't add that Brogan might not be going back to his dad's at all, though he thought there was a distinct possibility that by the time the authorities had investigated Brogan's domestic circumstances, it might well prove to be the case.

'Where am I goin'?'

'We're not sure,' Parker admitted. 'Some people are going to take care of you until your dad sorts himself out a bit.'

'Stops hitting me, you mean?'

Hanson and Parker looked at one another. Between them, they'd heard it all before, but it never got any easier. 'Does he hit you a lot?' said Parker.

'Only when I ask for it ... when I make him angry, mostly.'

It was Hanson who was angry now. Healey had robbed his son of his self-esteem, and to such a degree that Brogan felt he deserved the abuse meted out to him. 'Nobody has the right to hit another person.'

'Mr Parker hit my dad,' said Brogan, brightly, 'didn't you, Mr Parker?'

Parker fumbled for an appropriate reply and failed to find one. It was Hanson who fished him out of an awkward moment by saying, 'Was that what he did last night? Did he hit you?'

'No, he didn't dare. I think he's scared of Mr Parker.'

Parker smiled at that one.

Brogan added, 'He said he was going over to Elaine's to ask her to move in, and I couldn't stand the thought of her living in our house. She isn't my mum.'

Parker said, 'I don't expect he realized you'd take it that way.'

'He's the one you should go for, not Roly.'

'Why's that?' said Parker, gently.

'He killed her.'

'Killed who?'

'My mum.'

Hanson took his hand from Brogan's shoulder. 'Brogan,' he said, 'what do you mean by that?'

'He killed her,' he said. 'He battered my mum to death.'

After Social Services had collected Brogan from the station, Hanson and Parker spoke in Parker's office. 'Was it really necessary to involve them?'

'What choice do we have?' said Parker. 'His father can't be trusted to keep him away from the yard. I can't even trust my own men to keep tabs on him.' In an outburst of frustration, he went on, 'We haven't seen sight nor sound of Byrne since I took the surveillance team off him — God knows where he is, what he's doing.'

'When was the last time he was seen?'

'We know he went home after he led us to the yard. That's about it.'

'He hasn't been seen since?'

'Like I said.'

'You'll pick up the thread,' said Hanson.

'I hope so,' said Parker. 'He could be out of the country, for all we know.'

'Well, if he is, he isn't posing a threat to Brogan.'

'No, but he's posing a threat to someone ...'

There was no arguing with that, and Hanson didn't try.

Parker said, 'I asked his father to grant permission to have him examined by a doctor.'

'Did he give it?'

'Yes, though I'm not convinced he understands exactly what I was asking him to agree to.'

Hanson had grave misgivings: the only way they would be able to find out whether Brogan had been abused by Roly was by violating the boy's right to privacy, by degrading him, by perpetrating a different form of abuse. 'I'm glad I haven't got your job,' said Hanson. 'It must be one of the toughest there is.'

'You're wrong,' said Parker. 'Being a father is tougher.'

His words were a painful reminder to Hanson of something his wife had said. *I'm pregnant.* But she hadn't been pregnant for long. Besides, the child that she'd aborted hadn't been his. 'I wouldn't know,' he said.

'Take it from me,' said Parker.

The last time Brogan had seen his doctor's surgery, his mother had brought him. Now he'd been brought by a social worker, someone he'd only met a few hours earlier, her manner over-friendly, her smile determinedly bright.

She went with him into a consulting room that had changed since he'd last seen it. There were still the same white cupboards set against a wall, but the sink and mirror were new, and the beige and brown of the screen that concealed an examination couch had been replaced with a newer, whiter version.

Dr Freeman, too, had changed, his brogue shoes replaced by trainers similar to those that Brogan had seen on a documentary focusing on drug dealers. He sat behind a desk that was narrower than Brogan remembered, the paperwork neatly arranged.

The thought of Dr Freeman as a dealer made Brogan smile to himself, and Freeman misinterpreted the look. 'How are you, Brogan?'

Brogan didn't reply until he'd looked at his social worker as if for permission to speak. 'He's fine,' she said, 'all things considered,' and Brogan was reminded that the last time he'd been here, Dr Freeman had shone a torch down his ears and had gone on to write a prescription for a mild antibiotic. He'd then asked his mother *how things were going* and she'd replied in that shy way she had, lifting a hand to her cheek, feeling it hot as if the bruise that had last been there still showed. 'Fine,' she'd replied. 'All things considered.'

Freeman was aware that this was a difficult situation and he was anxious to make it as easy for Brogan as possible. 'I expected to see your father here.'

The social worker answered on Brogan's behalf. 'He didn't want him here.'

Freeman looked at Brogan. 'Is that true?'

'Dunno,' said Brogan.

'Well,' said Freeman, 'either way, I'm sorry to have to put you through all this.'

'Put me through what?'

Freeman's smile evaporated. 'Has anyone actually *told* you why you're here?'

'They said something about an examination.'

'Did they explain the nature of that examination?'

'How do you mean?'

Freeman turned to the social worker. 'Maybe you could give us a moment.'

'I was told to stay.'

'I want to talk to Brogan. You can come back in after that.'

Before she walked out, she picked up a bag that was woven and tasselled, a dolphin key-ring clipped to the plaited handle.

Freeman waited until she'd closed the door behind her before he said, 'Brogan, before I examine you, I'm going to explain exactly what the examination entails. Once I'm sure you understand what I'm going to do, and why, you can tell me whether you agree to me doing it.'

Brogan sat and listened, but he didn't speak.

'Do you understand, Brogan?'

Brogan nodded.

'Are you still in agreement?'

The door opened, and before Brogan could reply, his social worker walked back into the consulting room. She held a pale green envelope in her hand. It seemed an odd colour for an envelope, and Brogan couldn't take his eyes off it, not even after she'd handed it to Freeman. 'This is his father's written permission. If that's not enough, we can get an order from the court.'

Freeman drew the letter out of the envelope. Whatever was in it was typed, and Healey's signature was little more than a witnessed scrawl. Brogan wondered whether his dad had even known what he was consenting to.

Freeman read it, and handed it back to the social worker. 'I'm sorry,' he said, to Brogan. 'It seems you have no choice.'

CHAPTER TWENTY-NINE

Parker and Warrender turned up on Moranti's doorstep to find that the house was detached, modern, and situated on an estate that was owner-occupied. Parker guessed it to be worth pretty much what his own house was worth, and that wasn't a fortune by anybody's standards, yet he couldn't see the Emporium producing sufficient income to buy a house of this type and he wondered where Moranti had got the money.

He banged on the door and looked up to see the curtains tightly drawn. Within seconds of his knock, the pattern of one of those curtains was disturbed as they were pulled back.

He held up his ID, and Mrs Moranti drew away from the window to be replaced by her husband. He stared down at Parker and Warrender as if at an apparition, then he, too, disappeared from the window.

Once Moranti was safely in custody, Parker intended to have his house and the Emporium thoroughly searched, but he was no more hopeful of finding pornographic material there than he'd been of finding it at Byrne's, because something Hanson had said had stuck in his mind, was playing on it, in fact: 'Paedophiles sometimes rent premises under a false name. They keep their material there, particularly if it's the hard stuff.'

Most of the people with units on the market tended to

store a proportion of their goods elsewhere. As the Emporium was being searched, two of his men would be talking to other traders to see if they could find out whether Moranti had a lock-up that they knew of.

It was Mrs Moranti who came to the door, her husband behind her and struggling his way into a dressing gown, but it was Moranti that Parker addressed as he showed his ID and said, 'Get dressed, Mr Moranti. I'm taking you down to the station.'

For a moment, Moranti looked stunned, and it was his wife who addressed Parker in some European language, spoken very fast.

Moranti spoke in English, the accent heavy, the tone fearful: 'What have I done?'

There was something about the way he said it, something that told Parker he'd experienced this before, and suddenly, he was able to visualize Moranti as a boy, hiding behind his parents as they opened the door to men who stole them from their home.

Mrs Moranti appealed to her husband to do something, but if there was one thing that Moranti had learnt from the past it was that resistance was pointless.

'Etta,' he said, and Parker wasn't sure whether he had spoken her name or a word of reassurance.

'Go and get dressed,' he repeated, and Warrender materialized beside him.

They pushed their way into Moranti's house, Warrender threading his way down the hall and covering the back in case Moranti took it into his head to do a runner. Not that he'd have got far. Parker's men were all over the place. Moranti was going nowhere.

As he made his way to the interview room where Moranti was being held, Warrender caught up with Parker.

'Social services just phoned the station — Brogan's done a runner.'

'Where from?'

'Doctor's surgery.'

'Was he examined.'

'Yes.'

'Well, at least that's something.' Parker didn't have to think very hard to know where Brogan would go. 'He's bound to head for the yard — we'll pick him up in no time.'

He considered information that Warrender had accessed shortly after Brogan was taken into care. Much as Parker suspected, Healey was known to the police, but not for the reasons Parker had imagined: on more than a dozen occasions, he had put his wife in hospital, but he hadn't found himself in court as a result. Brogan's mother had refused to press charges.

'What did she die of?'

'Fell downstairs, apparently.'

They looked at one another.

'Discharged herself. Went home. Died of internal bleeding.'

Parker wondered what had gone on in Brogan's mind. Maybe his mother had fallen downstairs. Maybe not. Whatever the case, Brogan was clearly laying the blame for her death at his father's door.

He walked into the interview room and saw Moranti sitting on the very edge of a chair. 'Mr Moranti,' said Parker.

Moranti attempted to rise: his age and the fact that he'd been sitting there for twenty minutes or so had stiffened him to near immobility. 'Please stay sitting,' said Parker, and he pulled a chair opposite, the table between them.

Moranti sounded fearful as he said, 'My shop . . .'

'Don't worry about your shop,' said Parker. 'My men are there, and the birds won't starve for the moment.'

'What are your men doing?'

'Searching it,' said Parker, and he put a warrant face up on the table.

Moranti didn't look at it, and Parker added, 'When I came into the shop, you admitted that Gary had worked for you for a while.'

'What if he did?' said Moranti. 'Lots of boys have worked for me over the years.'

'Not all of them have gone missing, though,' said Parker. 'I asked you whether you'd ever taken Gary to Roly's Yard.'

'I told you,' said Moranti, 'I never take boys to the yard. I pay them to clean the cages, watch the shop. If I go out, they stay behind, see to the customers.'

Parker wondered how much more tense Moranti would become when he confronted him with information pulled from Nathan's statement. He produced the file on Gary and pulled out the library book, opened it at the page depicting the finch that Gary had kept and said, 'Do you ever sell this type of bird?'

Moranti took the book from him, looked at the illustration, and handed it back. 'No.'

'Never?'

'No.'

'Why not?'

'Who would want a plain green bird? Not people who buy from me. They want birds of colour, birds from exotic countries.'

'This bird came from an exotic country,' said Parker. 'Do you know what it is?'

'No,' said Moranti.

'It's a Woodpecker finch.'

Moranti shrugged. 'It's not very beautiful.'

'Maybe not,' agreed Parker. 'But it *is* an exotic finch.'

'You think so? I don't think so. I'd never sell a bird like that.'

'So who would?' said Parker.

'I don't know,' said Moranti. 'Not anybody I know.'

'There must be someone,' said Parker. 'Try to think.'

Moranti gave it thought, and finally came up with, 'A bird like that only true finch fancier would keep, someone who wants many different types.'

'Someone like Roly?' said Parker.

'Maybe, I don't know.'

'You've never seen a finch like that at Roly's Yard?'

Moranti shrugged, the gesture oddly dramatic. 'So many birds at Roly's Yard. Who can say? There might be many birds I never see.'

Parker could believe it. 'Mr Moranti,' he said, 'Gary had a Woodpecker finch. He kept it at home in a cage.'

Immediately, Moranti leapt to his own defence. 'He didn't get it from me!'

'In that case, where did he get it?'

Moranti just sat there, his eyes on the book, the illustration upside down to him now. Parker let him look at it a moment, and then, his tone of voice leaving Moranti in no doubt that he could prove the content of what he said next, he said, 'We have proof that you took Gary down to the yard. We also have proof that you introduced Brogan Healey to Roly.'

For a moment, Moranti said nothing, and then he began to cry.

'When did you first take Gary down to the yard?'

Moranti's reply was barely audible. 'Last Christmas. Business was good. I sell many birds.' He wiped at his face with the sleeve of the gabardine coat. 'Come, I say to Gary ... We go to buy more birds.'

'And you introduced him to Roly.'

Moranti didn't reply. Too frightened, thought Parker. 'Mr Moranti,' he said, 'did you know Joseph Coyne?'

Moranti could no longer speak. He closed his eyes, as if by doing so he might be able to stem the flood of tears.

Parker tried again. 'Mr Moranti.'

'Yes,' he whispered.

'Did he work for you?'

'Yes.'

'How long for?'

'Not long,' said Moranti. 'Joey ... he wasn't no good with the birds. He hold them like this ...' Moranti held out his hand and clenched the fingers tightly. 'He damage them. I say to him, "Joey, this no good, you have to find another job."'

'So you paid him off,' said Parker, but Moranti didn't respond.

'Mr Moranti?' said Parker.

Moranti shook his head. 'I don't pay him off, no ... He ...'

Parker finished the sentence for him. 'Joey disappeared.'

Moranti's hands fluttered nervously, as if he were trying to hold a finch that didn't want to be held.

'And when Gary also disappeared, didn't it strike you as strange that two of the lads who'd been working for you ...?'

'A little, perhaps.'

'A little?' said Parker. 'I'd have found it more than a little strange. I'd have informed the police. Unless, of course, I had something to hide.'

Moranti opened his eyes and the tears fell down unchecked. 'Over the years, I have many boys who work for me. They come. They go. Only Joseph and Gary disappeared.'

'How many have you taken down to the yard?'

'Most of them. All of them. I don't know.'

Parker opened the file on Gary Maudsley. In it, he'd slipped a sheet of paper, and on that sheet of paper was information that one of the team had accessed prior to Parker bringing Moranti in. He laid it flat on the table.

'When did you first come to England, Mr Moranti?'

Parker could barely hear his voice as he made the reply.

'Nineteen thirty-nine.'

'Why did you come?'

'My family feared persecution.'

Fair enough, thought Parker, and Moranti added, 'We were what you people might call travellers – circus people. Not very big. More a side-show.'

'So how did you make a living when you first got to England?'

'I started a shop,' said Moranti.

'The Emporium?'

'A second-hand furniture shop.'

It sounded such a far cry from the Emporium that Parker found it difficult to visualize Moranti running a business of that kind. As if guessing what he was thinking, Moranti said, 'One day, I sold a curious thing, a brass ashtray made from the casing of a shell. I collected more things like that, and soon, I realize there is more money in these strange things than in furniture.'

'The Emporium was born,' said Parker, drily.

'It's all legal – your men won't find any stolen property.'

'We're not looking for any.'

'What are you looking for?'

'Proof that you were procuring boys for Roly.'

Moranti's hands flew wide abruptly, the imaginary bird battering at the window to the room. 'I think,' he said, 'I want solicitor.'

'Very wise,' said Parker.

CHAPTER THIRTY

After Moranti had been taken down to the cells, Warrender took the opportunity to inform Parker that Gifford, the man he'd seen near the spot were the platform had stood, had been brought in for questioning. The address he had given hadn't checked, and Parker, who had made a note of the registration number of Gifford's pick-up, told one of his men to find out who he was and where he lived.

Information had subsequently come in that Gifford was the man's real name, but that his address was Crowthorne, Berkshire. It seemed to Parker a hell of a way for Gifford to have come if his only purpose in going to the wood had been to catch a glimpse of the remains. He had therefore given orders for him to be tracked down and picked up.

As Parker walked into the interview room, he weighed the man up afresh and concluded that Gifford, his face deeply lined from a lifetime spent working out of doors, had to be approaching his mid-fifties. He couldn't look at Parker, who got the impression that he was very much regretting having gone to the wood at all.

It took him a good ten minutes to get out of Gifford that he'd been the foreman of a road gang, and that he'd gone to the wood out of interest because he'd once worked on a road in the vicinity of Colbourne Wood.

'Which road?' said Parker.

'Ring road at Bickley.'

Parker knew the name, but couldn't think why. 'Bickley,' he said.

'Just on the edge of the Colbourne estate.'

Parker had it now – a strip of densely wooded land that was marked up on some of the older maps supplied by the National Trust. It had once divided Colbourne Wood from a further strip of land that was privately owned. 'Wasn't that strip of woodland bought by the Ministry of the Environment?'

'Yes,' said Gifford.

Parker wished he'd taken greater notice of some of the documentation supplied by the National Trust. Among the mass of information supplied at his request was material relating to the purchase of Bickley Wood, which had been bought by the Ministry of the Environment at about the time that Fenwick had purchased Colbourne House. Gifford said, 'The Ministry decided to build a ring road to keep traffic out of the centre of the town, but it wasn't built until eight years ago.'

'Why?' said Parker.

'Fenwick put up a battle,' said Gifford. 'He didn't want a major road on the edge of his estate.'

'Bickley didn't belong to him,' said Parker. 'How did he block it?'

'He promised his estate to the National Trust if they put pressure on the Ministry to change the route planned for the road. They didn't manage that, but they stopped it from being built for a good many years.'

'And how did they do that?'

'They pointed out that the woodland was ancient. But it didn't work for ever, and once Fenwick knew the road was about to be built, he threatened to bring in a particularly militant protest group.'

'And did he?'

'No,' said Gifford.

'Why not?'

'I don't know,' he admitted, but Parker thought *he* knew the answer to that one: Fenwick had been a recluse, and to have informed a militant protest group would have been to invite unwelcome guests to his doorstep for what might have turned out to be a considerable time.

'Go on,' said Parker.

'I was in charge of the men responsible for felling the trees. We were told to go in and make a start, which is what we did.'

'And?' said Parker.

Gifford thought back to the day that he and his men had rolled up to Bickley Wood with heavy plant machinery, the type of equipment capable of tearing trees from the ground by their roots, of slicing them into confetti if need be, of erasing all trace of woodland and leaving in its wake a smooth, flat surface, ready for the hardcore laid down in preparation for concrete and tarmac. They had arrived in anticipation of being met by the kind of protesters who could cause them a serious problem, the kind of protesters who had learned that direct action could delay the felling of ancient woods, the kind who would do rather more than simply stage a dig-in. But none had been there.

Gifford stared at the contents of his cup, wisps of steam curling from the liquid to evaporate, like his confidence. 'Maybe I shouldn't be saying this ...'

'We're dealing with murder,' Parker reminded him, gently. 'Anything you can tell us ...'

'We found a scaffold,' said Gifford.

Parker, who had remained standing throughout the proceedings, sat down. For some moments, neither he nor Gifford spoke a word, then Gifford swirled what remained of his coffee and knocked it back as if it were the stiff drink he no doubt wished it was. He put the cup on the table. It made an insubstantial sound, the rattle of hollow plastic on a laminated surface. 'I wanted to see the scaffold,' he said, 'to see if it looked the same.'

'It wasn't there,' said Parker.

'No, I know — and even if it had been, I wouldn't have been able to get anywhere near it.'

'Why didn't you come forward?' said Parker.

'I wanted to ...' said Gifford, 'but ...'

Parker didn't want to put him on the defensive so he raised a conciliatory hand. 'It's not important — you're here now.' He chose his words carefully. 'You called it a scaffold. Is that because the press referred to it as that?'

'No, it's because that's what they looked like.'

'They?' said Parker.

'There were several of them.'

Parker's conciliatory gesture became frozen for a moment, and then he watched his hand as it drifted to the table like the feather that had spun from Hanson's fingers. He could also see Gifford, but it was as if he were looking at the man through some telescopic device: he seemed small, and very far away.

'Most of the remains on those scaffolds were nothing but rags and bones. But one ...' Gifford grew quiet, as if the memory of what he'd seen would stay with him for life. 'It looked like something from a movie set.'

Parker, who knew first-hand what the remains of a partly decomposed body could look like, saw the scene through Gifford's eyes and wondered whether, like those of his men who had seen the remains at Colbourne, Gifford had dreamed the same dreams, had woken in the night to reach out for a partner who, no matter how she tried, couldn't come anywhere close to seeing the visions he held in his head.

'What did you do?'

'I called my boss.'

'Who was?'

'Pierce,' said Gifford, 'of Pierce and Newman.'

It was almost a household name, and Parker was acquainted

with it in the way that he would have been acquainted with the name McAlpine. He said, 'Was Pierce on site?'

'No,' said Gifford. 'He was based in London.'

'What did he do about it?'

'He came down to Bickley Wood, took a look at the scaffolds and told the police.'

'The area comes under our jurisdiction,' Parker reminded him, 'and I was a senior officer eight years ago. If anything of that nature had been found at Bickley or Colbourne, I'd know about it.'

Gifford stared into his cup and replied, 'I wouldn't know about that.'

'Take my word,' said Parker, softly, as Gifford stood up abruptly, the empty plastic cup wafting to the ground as if blown away by his torment.

'We were given a couple of days off and told to keep away from the place while the police checked out the area. By the time we got back to the job, the scaffolds had been removed. We never heard anything about them again. We were told that if we wanted to keep our jobs, we should keep our mouths shut and get on with felling the trees.'

'Why?'

'The boss didn't want anything to get in the way of the contract.'

Parker stood up and joined him at a window where wire mesh divided them from a courtyard and the buildings that stood opposite.

'How many men were there on the job?'

'Twenty-odd,' said Gifford.

'And all of you kept your mouths shut?'

'People told their families maybe – I don't know. I never said a word, not even to the missus.'

Parker was finding it increasingly difficult to believe that, if that was the case, the story hadn't found its way into the press. 'Are you asking me to believe—'

'We were told that the remains were plastic, a practical joke left by protesters to make us stop until they could get it together to occupy the trees.'

'And you all swallowed that?' said Parker.

'Listen, Mr Parker, eight years ago, the building industry was in even worse shape than it is today. Men like us were hanging on to our jobs by whatever means we could. We'd been told to fell a strip of woodland and we knew that if we did we'd be in work for another six months because that road had to be built and we were up for the contract. In circumstances like those, when somebody tells you you've stumbled on a practical joke, you believe it.' He paused, then added, *'Because you want to.'*

Parker could relate to that. His mind went into overdrive, searching for motivation on the part of the people responsible for slipping on to the site then seeking out and getting rid of whatever remains were discovered. He found it in the knowledge that, if the police had been called to the scene, the entire area would have been sealed off for as long as it took the police to conduct a thorough investigation. There would have been media interest, and media interest would have been like a gift from the gods to the type of protester that Gifford's boss had feared might turn up on the scene.

The idea that some businessman had taken it upon himself to arrange for the remains to be removed, buried elsewhere or just destroyed, outraged Parker, but he was no stranger to the lengths to which powerful and wealthy men were capable of going to ensure that their plans were never thwarted. He could even imagine the type of individual that Gifford's boss might be – someone who had started at the bottom, clawed his way up to his present position and wasn't about to allow a few bones to rob him of the potential for massive profit.

'What kind of man was your boss?'

'You wouldn't want to cross him,' said Gifford.

Gratified that he'd read the man accurately, Parker said, 'Where can I find him?'

Gifford smiled in a way that Parker couldn't read. 'He was younger than me,' he said. 'Money can't buy you health, Mr Parker.'

No, thought Parker, and it can't buy you morals, either. 'What about the men you were working with at the time? Are you willing to give their names?'

'I can't remember all of them, but a few, yes.'

A few will do, thought Parker, and he pondered on the likelihood of finding those remains. There was little hope, he decided. Men like Gifford's boss sometimes operated on the fringe of the criminal fraternity. He wouldn't have been averse to arranging for those remains to be slipped into concrete at any one of a dozen sites up and down the country, and there would have been the people to help him do it, men silenced by money, or by the knowledge that if ever they spoke out, Pierce might well arrange for them never to speak again.

'The remains,' said Parker. 'Were they children's?'

Gifford thought back to a scene that he had convinced himself had been erased from his mind by sheer power of will, and found that his will was weaker than he had realized. He looked at Parker in a way that suggested that, over the years, the scene had haunted him. 'It's been good to get it out,' he said. 'To tell someone.'

'You did the right thing,' said Parker.

CHAPTER THIRTY-ONE

Hanson arrived at Colbourne to find Parker waiting for him on the other side of the wood. He could hear traffic in the distance, the drone forming a backdrop to Parker's voice as he briefed him. 'The road we're standing on used to be known as Bickley Wood.'

It didn't look much like a wood. Not any more. The road ahead was a slip-road that led to a dual carriageway. Hanson listened as Parker told him what Gifford had said, ending with: 'We'll never know what was in that wood.'

'No, but we can guess,' said Hanson, and up ahead, the traffic thundered by, the wheels spinning effortlessly over the ground where Hanson imagined boys to have run in their last few moments of life. He could almost see their expressions of curiosity change to terror as it dawned on them that this was no game. They hadn't been taken there to explore some secret place. They had gone there to die and, in those last few moments, they would undoubtedly have fought. But where could they have run to? thought Hanson. At one time, there was no road, just a network of bridlepaths impossibly overgrown, and the trees so dense they couldn't see where they were going. Their killer would have known the area well, would have anticipated their every move, would have hunted them down with ease.

'Why?' said Parker. 'What possible pleasure could he have got from what he did?'

'We're all capable of the same behaviour. Fortunately, most of us indulge ourselves to a lesser degree.'

Parker found that impossible to accept. He replied, 'I don't know what kind of people you find yourself dealing with, but I can tell you for a fact that I don't know of any normal individual who indulges in that type of fantasy, much less behaviour.'

'Really?' said Hanson. 'How many men do you know who target a woman with the sole intention of making a conquest? They're not interested in the individual. They don't want to get to know her. They get their kicks from the thrill of the chase. Sometimes, they even back off at the point where the sexual act – the supposed *point* of it all – is about to take place. The conquest is made. Game over.'

It was difficult for Parker to equate what to him seemed fairly normal male behaviour with the thought of what had taken place in that wood. He was about to say so, but Hanson didn't give him the opportunity. 'Sherringham said the body had been dismembered.'

Parker didn't need reminding. He also didn't need reminding that Sherringham had suggested that dismemberment may have occurred before death.

Hanson added, 'When you were a kid, didn't you ever pull the wings from a butterfly?'

'I don't know,' said Parker. 'If I did, I grew out of it. I have no recollection of doing anything like that – if I did it at all, it must have been because I was too young to realize it was cruel.'

'Precisely,' said Hanson. 'But when you say you grew out of it, what you mean is that as you matured emotionally, you learned to empathize with another creature. You began to understand that it was capable of feeling pain, that it had rights, that it had value over and above that which you placed on it for your own gratification. The person responsible for dismembering Joseph Coyne hasn't matured in that regard. He's still pulling the wings off butterflies.'

'But the butterflies are boys,' said Parker, softly, 'and in this case, it would be more apt to say that he's pulling the wings off birds.'

Parker looked at a map that gave the approximate dimensions of what had been Bickley Wood. He stabbed it with a forefinger. 'There was once a bridlepath leading from the wood where Joseph's remains were found to the wood at Bickley,' he said. Hanson looked for evidence that, at some point, the path branched and led to a minor road. There was none, and that alone indicated that whoever had brought the materials and the bodies to Bickley would have had to have come from the direction of Colbourne House.

'There's something else I want to show you,' said Parker, and Hanson followed him back to the car.

Parker drove on to the dual carriageway but took the next slip-road off, and doubled back to the house.

The media had departed some days before, but the house, now empty, was being guarded by two solitary men in uniform. They acknowledged Parker, who led Hanson round to the back where a walled garden gave on to a gravelled path.

It led to the type of cottage that served as a reminder that there had been nothing romantic or easy about the life of a farm labourer at the turn of the century. Its doorway was small, the windows above and to the side of it minute, the walls bowing with age.

Parker led the way round the back to a garden that might once have produced a few meagre vegetables and said, 'According to our enquiries, Fenwick had an odd-job man, someone who cut wood in winter, mended frozen pipes, ensured that the boundaries of the estate were kept in good repair. He never paid him anything, but he let him use the cottage.'

Hanson looked up. The windows were so small, they looked like tiny black eyes.

'He stuck around for several years, on and off. Coming and going, turning up, disappearing. Fenwick didn't seem to have a problem with that.'

One of the small black eyes had been propped wide open with a ruler. 'Want to see inside?' said Parker, and Hanson followed him in.

It smelt a little damp, but that was all. Even so, Hanson found himself gulping at the air and holding it in his lungs in anticipation of a stench that never came. The walls, the floors and every available surface were covered in birdshit, but even as Hanson thought back to the way in which the upstairs window had been propped open, Parker said, 'It's circumstantial. That window's probably been open for years. There are rats, birds, mice — you name it.'

I can name it, thought Hanson. He said, 'When did your men come across this cottage?'

'The day the remains were removed from Colbourne Wood.'

'How come this is the first I've heard?'

'I've only just been informed of its possible relevance,' said Parker. 'You have to understand, I rely on reports from the men who are searching the area. All I was told was that a cottage had been searched at the back of the house, that it was derelict, that there was nothing of interest in it. I didn't connect it with Roly until the men who searched it heard about the yard and realized there might be a connection.'

'What made them make that assumption?'

As if by way of reply, Parker opened a kitchen cupboard to reveal its mesh-lined interior.

'Old habits die hard,' said Hanson, softly. 'Assuming they die at all.'

'And do they?' said Parker.

'Rarely,' admitted Hanson. 'In later years, the libido often decreases, and with it, the desire to indulge in the type of sexual act that can gratify the individual's needs.'

'So there *is* hope then,' said Parker. 'They *can* change?'

Hanson replied, 'An individual's sexuality and preferences are determined by many complex factors, very early in life. People can never rid themselves of that. The best that can be hoped for is that therapy enables them to learn to control their impulses.'

'How many succeed?'

'Very few.'

'Parker closed the cupboard, as Hanson added, 'Is this the first time you've seen this place?'

'Second,' said Parker. 'I took a look before you arrived. What do you think of it?'

'I think your men were justified in pointing out a possible connection,' said Hanson. 'When are you searching the yard?'

'Tomorrow,' said Parker.

'Do you need me around?'

'I'd prefer you to keep in the background.'

'That's what I thought,' said Hanson, who knew from experience that the last thing the police needed was a civilian at the scene of an operation of that kind. 'You can get me on my mobile if you need me.'

'You don't sound convinced that we might?'

'I think you're wasting your time,' said Hanson.

'So you keep saying,' said Parker, adding, 'We'll know for sure, soon enough.'

CHAPTER THIRTY-TWO

Parker left his men sitting in vans parked up at the top of the road, men who were unrecognizable as police, their casual clothes covered by overalls, the vans they sat in dark blue, unmarked, their windowless sides concealing the men within.

All was as Parker remembered it, yet nothing could have prepared him for the atmosphere of rot and desolation as he walked down Roumelia Road. The houses appeared to be weeping, a recent rain having run from the roofs to dribble down the walls. With their windows boarded up, they had the slightly stunned look of a recently blinded man, as though the realization that they would never see again hadn't quite sunk in, or wasn't to be believed.

He tried the gates and found them chained, then motioned Warrender and a couple of uniforms to appear, as if out of nowhere, and join him as he made his way to the front of the squat.

The properties opposite stood with windows boarded up, and Parker took a good look at what remained of Mousade Road. Its once prestigious shop-fronts seemed more derelict than any he'd ever seen, the names of former proprietors having weathered away from the signs so that it was difficult to tell what some of the shops might have sold or who might once have owned them.

These fading signs put Parker in mind of the type of inscription that one might reasonably expect to find on a memorial, the years having weathered the lettering to nothing, so that anyone reading them would find the names illegible. These cherished things, these businesses that had once represented a way of life, a source of income to a culture he could barely imagine to have existed, were gone for ever. He felt the loss as he knocked on the door to the squat.

There was very little furniture. Parker didn't have to see inside to know that. The sound of his knock wouldn't have echoed off carpets, off papered walls, off windows that were covered by soft thick drapes.

Behind him, his men stood prepared as Roly answered the door, and as he tried to close it on them, they forced their way into a hall that was every bit as stark as Parker had imagined. 'Roland Barnes,' said Parker, and Roly spat in his face as Parker, who didn't have grounds to arrest him, told him he was wanted for questioning in connection with the disappearance of Joseph Coyne and Gary Maudsley.

Parker couldn't have forced Roly to go to the station if he'd refused and he was relieved when the man appeared to come to the conclusion that further resistance was probably pointless. He walked out of the squat with two of Parker's men, and after seeing him driven away in the back of a patrol car, Parker, followed by Warrender, went through the hall and into the kitchen where Parker placed his hand on a tap and drew cold water, which he splashed against his face. Warrender stared around him in sheer, unbridled disgust as he took in the filth, the squalor.

All around them men were entering the property, pulling down the boards that blacked out the windows, letting light into rooms that had forgotten what it was to feel the sun on those plaster walls.

'You okay?' said Warrender, and Parker lifted the hand that had turned the tap to find it smothered in grease. There was nothing around that he could use to wipe away the filth. 'Go back to one of the vehicles, Neil, and get me something I can use to clean myself up.'

While he was gone, Parker left the tap running and searched the kitchen for keys to the padlock that chained the gate. He hadn't been averse to smashing them down if necessary, but he was aware that if he did so, the mesh that reached up to the roof would come down with them and the birds would escape. He wasn't a cruel man, and limited though his knowledge of birds might be, he was aware that exotic finches were hardly likely to be able to fend for themselves if they found themselves turned free.

Warrender returned from the car with a rag. 'It could be cleaner,' he said, but Parker took it gratefully.

'It's got to be an improvement on anything we'll find round here.'

He ran the rag under the tap, cleaned himself up, then used it to turn off the tap before tossing it into a bucket that passed for a bin.

'Where do we start?' said Warrender.

'We take a look round the house, just to get the geography of the place, and decide on aspects of it that seem likely to produce a result.'

He started with the room that faced the road. It was empty. Above him, the ceilings were high, the plaster mouldings intricate, and in front of him stood a fireplace of generous proportions. Its hearth was missing and Parker wondered whether a slab of marble had once stood in front of the grate. If so, it had been stolen, as had the fender that no longer surrounded it.

That fireplace would once have been a focal point for the family who lived here, thought Parker. He could imagine them sitting around it, velvet drapes at the windows, a nursery tea, then bed. Now there was only a blackened grate where once a fire had blazed, and the echo of his and Warrender's footsteps as they trod with caution on floorboards they didn't trust to withstand their weight.

They left the room, and made for the stairs, birds flying down from the bedrooms above even as they climbed. The way those finches flitted past, inches from his face, spooked Warrender. He saw nothing beautiful about them, and, left to his own devices, would have classed them as vermin. They could be sky-blue-pink for all he cared – they didn't belong here. He saw them as macabre.

The front bedroom was unused and devoid of furniture, the floor as bare as that of the room below, but the window wasn't boarded. At some stage, glass had been restored to the frame, and it took Parker a moment to work out what was strange about the birds that flapped at the window.

His immediate impression was of two finches lying flat against the glass. As if glued, thought Parker. And then he thought, No, not glued, but held into position. He took a step closer. They had been trapped between two sheets of glass that comprised a crude form of double-glazing.

Those birds didn't fly into that glass tomb, thought Parker, they were walled up. Instantly, he had a vision of the way in which Roly had crept up on them as they had fluttered at the glass, puzzled by their inability to fly through it and out to freedom. He would have jammed a second pane against them, holding them there. Then he would have reached for tools that had been placed by the window in readiness, and Parker imagined him using putty, wood, nails, or whatever else he needed to ensure that the birds remained trapped.

He wondered how long it had taken for them to die, and how much longer it had taken for them to become reduced to feather and bone. He found it bizarre that, despite there being barely anything of them, sufficient remained to keep the feathers intact. They looked like feathered skeletons, captured in flight, their skulls devoid of flesh.

They left the room and walked into a bathroom where mould had taken hold, and what looked like a map of Australia had grown on one of the walls. The bath stood in the centre like an afterthought, the enamel cracked and yellow, great streaks running like tears where water had dripped from the taps over the years. The taps themselves were masterpieces of craftsmanship, the chrome dull, but the fixtures strong – built to last, thought Parker.

A lavatory, its bowl blackened by bacteria, the water yellow and reeking, drove them out, and they walked into the bedroom that overlooked the aviary.

Warrender, who had always prided himself on having nerves of steel, felt afraid when he entered that room. He didn't know why. All it contained was a bed, a wardrobe and a chair, and there was nothing in these things alone to make him sick with fear. But all along the picture rail, which ran the length of the room, finches of every description were clinging to the walls.

Some remained quite motionless as he and Parker walked in; others flew past them towards the open window, and he found himself surrounded by the flapping, panicking wings. He backed towards the door as Parker made for the wardrobe and opened it to find that it contained nothing of interest, just a few clothes and some brand-new trainers, still in their white cardboard box.

He walked over to the window and stood as he imagined Roly might stand when looking out on his birds. Below him, men were making what amounted to a cursory search of the yard. They'd be lucky to find what they'd come for, thought Parker, who still felt the lack of a scanner.

The birds had become like leaves that were blown from one end of the aviary to the other. Each movement made by his men resulted in a counter-movement by the birds: when the men were still they, too, were still, huddling into the trees, packed closely, feather to feather, a shivering mass of fear.

Parker felt for them. These things were warm and real. They ate and breathed and slept. They didn't understand the implications of what was happening around them. They, like the boys whose remains he dreaded yet hoped to find, deserved more respect than to end up here.

He left the room, Warrender close on his heels, unwilling to be left there with so many little eyes, so many tiny claws. 'These birds,' he said, lashing out at them. 'I can't – they – Christ – *The way they fly in your face!*'

Parker shared his unease, but it wasn't the birds that made him afraid, it was the thought of what had happened there, in what he had come to believe was a house of death.

CHAPTER THIRTY-THREE

Two hours into the search, Parker noticed that the birds were growing fractious and he walked into the nesting shed to find a bag of seed.

Nothing seemed disturbed. The cages that lined the sides of the shed had been lifted away then returned to their rightful place, the plaintive cries from the hatchlings within making the men who had handled those cages extra gentle. 'Take them into the house,' Parker said, 'and keep them warm – the last thing we need is some animal-rights group accusing us of cruelty.'

He picked up a bag of seed that was standing by the door and walked into the yard with it, untwisting the ends and dipping his hand in to bring out a fistful of seed.

The birds, at first suspicious, began to swoop down in droves, and Parker looked up sharply, surprised by the sudden onslaught from the trees.

A finch flew on to his shoulder, and his first reaction, which had been to brush it away, was replaced by a feeling of pleasure. He couldn't explain why but he felt honoured, somehow, as though he'd been picked out for a moment as something special. He knew that, in reality, the only thing that had drawn the finch was that he had food; and yet the feeling remained, and after it darted away, his spirits dropped a fraction.

This was it, then: the lure of the birds, the lure that had

brought customers to Moranti and Moranti to the yard, along with the boys who had returned, never to leave.

He tied the ends of the bag and returned it to the shed, the birds, ever hopeful, like so many tiny missiles, darting past his face. He flicked them away, irritated by their persistence, and turned to find that Warrender had come out of the house and was walking towards him.

'We've covered everything obvious.'

'Anything?'

'Nothing,' said Warrender, 'just this.'

He held up a spool of tape designed to fit in an old projector. 'And one of the men thinks you should take a look at an alcove in an upstairs room.'

Parker went into the house with him, climbing the stairs as Warrender added, 'It looks as though it might have been sealed over fairly recently.'

Parker followed him to a room on the second floor. The windows faced the wasteground, chinks of light showing through the cracks and revealing a chimney breast divided by a couple of alcoves.

Warrender approached one, reached out and touched the plasterwork.

'That does look a bit recent,' Parker agreed.

A metal hoop, maybe an inch or so wide, had been screwed into the wall, level with Parker's chest. He wondered what it was. He couldn't think of anything the bracket might have held, but it was there for a reason.

A hole had been drilled beneath the hoop, a hole so small in diameter that Parker assumed it had been made by a nail. If so, the nail had come out. He peered at the hole, but couldn't see a thing.

Turning to one of his men, Parker said, 'Get a pickaxe.'

Moments later, the officer returned, carrying one as though born to the job of wielding it with considerable strength. His shoulders were broad and strong, the arms those of a labourer rather than of a man who had scored rather higher on the academic scale than Parker would have given him credit for. 'Go on, then,' said Parker. 'Let's see what you can do with it.'

He stood back and watched as the axe was brought to bear and the plasterwork fell away like marzipan. It was, he concluded, a DIY mixture with neither the strength nor the texture to withstand a determined effort to remove it, but the brickwork beneath it was solid enough: Roly might know little or nothing about plasterwork, thought Parker, but in bricking up that alcove, he'd done a near professional job. It was almost a shame to ruin it, but ruin it he would.

The pickaxe was coming down on the brick with steady, rhythmical blows, the man wielding it working up a sweat that soaked the back of his overalls. Once damaged, the strength of the structure was diminished considerably, and, five minutes into the job, one of the bricks fell on to the floor.

Parker shone a torch into the depths, half expecting to see a face, or what was left of a face, staring back at him.

But there was nothing.

He stood back and let the man finish the job, creating a hole large enough to allow Parker to get his upper body in there and shine the torch right round.

The alcove measured ten feet by three, and was maybe two feet deep. The interior walls had been painted brown at some point, but not in recent years, and there were still brackets at the sides where shelves had once rested.

'Anything?' said Warrender.

'Nothing,' said Parker, who couldn't quite believe it.

He pulled away from the alcove, brushing dust from his clothes, and indicated its twin. 'No point leaving it,' he said, and again he waited as the pickaxe pulled away the plasterwork to reveal bricks that had been laid every bit as recently as those that had sealed the adjoining alcove.

The pickaxe gained a purchase, hauling first one, then more of the bricks away to create the space that Parker needed, and once again, Parker leant in, shining his torch into an interior identical to that of the neighbouring alcove; the same proportions, the same brown paint, the same rusting brackets.

There was no smell. That was the first thing he noticed. And that didn't seem right, thought Parker, not when he stopped to consider what the beam of his torch had rested on. He saw a figure slumped on the floor of the alcove, its clothes instantly familiar to him. The bomber jacket, its zipper like a row of teeth, the dark-blue denim jeans – these were the clothes that Gary was known to have worn when he disappeared.

He pulled away, and turned so that his back was to the alcove. He closed his eyes for a moment, breathing rapidly, cutting the beam from the torch as if, by doing so, he could make the contents of the alcove disappear.

Hanson had been wrong, thought Parker. Very, very wrong. 'Hanson,' he said.

Warrender replied, 'What about him?'

'Get him down here. I want him to see what we've found.'

By the time Hanson arrived at the yard, vehicles he recognized as belonging to the press were parked up on the far side of the wasteground. He ducked under the net to find Parker in the yard, his suit dusted with powder. Hanson walked up to him. 'We've got company,' he said, nodding towards the gates.

'I know,' said Parker. 'I'm keeping them at bay with the offer of a press release.'

'What are you going to tell them?'

'As little as possible.' He turned towards the house. 'You said we wouldn't find anything,' but Hanson wasn't listening. This was the first time he'd actually seen the yard, and in studying the way in which he turned, very slowly, to take it in, Parker had a vision of the way in which Gary and Joseph might have done the same.

As Hanson scanned the yard, he saw a bird with plumage

that was green and cobalt blue. Its tail seemed impossibly long, the blue becoming turquoise, and he recalled the moment in the wood, his fingers releasing the feather, the way he had been unable to take his eyes off it as it spiralled to the ground.

The bird made for a hole where the mesh had come away from a fragment of guttering, and soared off over the rooftops, only to return. It seemed, for a moment, to hesitate, as if considering freedom, then squeezed back through the hole and into the yard.

'This way,' said Parker, and Hanson followed him into the house, eyes like vacuums, sucking in the details. The interior was more in keeping with the type of environment that he had come across before. Bodies hidden in alcoves, under floorboards or walled up, as those finches had been, were hardly unheard of.

He looked at the finches trapped in their tombs of glass, and Parker wondered whether, like himself, he was working out precisely how Roly had managed to fix them there.

It was the premeditation that Hanson found disturbing, that in order to have achieved such a feat, it would have been necessary for their killer to have prepared their deaths in advance. He felt it to be very much in keeping with the building of the scaffold, and he wondered whether he would find evidence of similar preparation in the adjoining room. He turned wordlessly from the window, and Parker led him through.

Here, as in the aviary, finches flitted past, and Hanson caught a flash of crimson and mauve.

Warrender seemed unduly upset by the birds. He swiped at them as if they were wasps, his face distorted by fear. 'You're not too fond of birds,' said Hanson.

'Don't mind them as a rule,' said Warrender. 'But these ...'

Hanson saw his point: he didn't mind birds either, but the way they came at them, out of the darkness, set his nerves on edge.

'There's an entire colony in the attic rooms,' said Warrender, 'some of them nesting, for God's sake.'

'Wonder why Roly allows it?' said Parker, and although Hanson knew the answer, he didn't reply. The birds were there for a purpose; they were part of the ritual. Their presence was not only welcome, it was essential to Roland Barnes.

Parker led the way into the room that faced the road, acknowledging his men as they stood aside to allow Hanson access to the alcove.

'Here,' said Parker, handing him a torch.

Hanson took it, the strong solid beam lighting the patterned wallpaper. Like Parker, he thrust his head and upper body through the hole. Like Parker, he shone the beam around the interior and, like Parker, he let the beam settle on the jacket, the jeans and the zipper.

He drew away from the alcove, the beam of light a circle on the floorboards at his feet. He and Parker looked at one another, neither speaking, then Parker turned to one of his men and said, 'Knock it down.'

They stood back as the pickaxe was wielded again, the overalled officer aided by others who clawed at the fractured bricks each time he rested, widening the hole, making it longer, deeper, revealing the alcove and all that it contained.

It seemed an age before the hacking stopped, but when it did, those present stood back and stared, unable, or just unwilling, to believe what lay before them.

The figure was now covered by plaster, dust, and fragments of shattered brick, and Parker thought back to the first time he'd seen it, when he had realized it didn't smell. He touched it gently, and stepped back as it slumped forward, rags spilling from the neck, the sleeves and the trouser legs.

He attempted to speak for them all, but was incapable of finding the words to describe what he was looking at.

Hanson stepped forward, touched the bundle of rags with a trembling hand, and looked up at him. 'It's an effigy,' he said.

✳   ✳   ✳

They walked out of the gates to waiting vehicles, and came face to face with photographers who had broken through the cordon to get what pictures they could.

Parker barked an order at the men who had failed to keep them back, a flash of light from one of the cameras leaving him in no doubt that, the following day, his photograph would be plastered all over the front page of some paper. The thought didn't please him. Not only did he object to being portrayed as having been caught unawares but he didn't much like the idea of one of his superior officers wondering why the scene hadn't been better secured in the first place.

'Mr Hanson?' said a reporter, and Hanson turned away. 'It *is* Mr Hanson?' the reporter repeated.

Parker climbed into a car, Hanson jumped in next to him. Warrender closed the door as the vehicle pulled away but remained at the scene.

'What a bloody fiasco,' said Parker. 'All we find is a bundle of rags. It's a joke.'

'A joke?' said Hanson. 'I wouldn't say that,' but Parker wasn't listening.

They sat in the back of the car, Parker exhausted and Hanson deeply disturbed by what they'd found. Whatever Parker might feel about that effigy, he decided, it was far from something that any of them could afford to dismiss as a joke.

Once they got back to the station, Parker led the way to the incident room where he briefed other members of the team: the outcome of the search was, in some ways, disappointing, but the news that an effigy had been found, clothed in an identical manner to the way in which Gary was known to have been clothed when he disappeared, was at least something. Parker said, 'Forensic will soon tell us whether the clothes are Gary's. If so, we'll be in a position to keep Roly in custody for as long as it takes to find out what's happened to Gary. If not,' said

Parker, 'we may have a problem keeping him in custody beyond tomorrow night. Same goes for Moranti.'

He was telling the team something they already knew. In itself, the effigy might well be evidence of a sick mind, but what Roly had done wasn't against the law and they wouldn't be able to keep him in on that alone.

Nothing had been found at the yard – nothing that was anywhere near incriminating enough and nothing of any interest had been found at the Emporium. None of the market traders had known whether Moranti rented premises elsewhere for storage purposes, and still there'd been no sign of Douglas Byrne.

Worse by far in Parker's view was the fact that Brogan was missing. He hadn't returned to Arpley Street and Parker pictured him scavenging for food in some back-street alley.

As he brought the briefing to a close, Parker turned to his men. 'Those of you who've been on duty for the past twelve hours ought to go home, get some kip.'

They all knew that he'd been on duty longer than any of them, and one said, 'What about you?'

'I'll stay on – have a crack at Barnes,' said Parker. And then he ended the briefing, taking Hanson with him, down to the interview room.

CHAPTER THIRTY-FOUR

Roly readjusted his position in a chair that wasn't designed for comfort. It suited the austerity of the interview room in that everything about it was hard, angular, and without colour.

In size, the room was barely large enough for Parker and the table that divided him from Roly. With Hanson, a detective and a duty solicitor present, Parker couldn't avoid the feeling that there was insufficient air, that the ceiling was pressing down on them, that the walls were closing in.

Roly had been at the station since early morning. He'd eaten when offered food, had asked for tea and been given it, but hadn't asked why he was there or why the yard was being searched. That was very telling, in Parker's view. People with nothing to hide were usually, at the very least, indignant about being dragged by force from their homes. They generally demanded an explanation and threatened to write to everybody from the chief constable to their local MP. Roly had spat in his face at the moment that Parker and his men had pushed their way through his front door, but other than that he'd been as quiet as a lamb; had seemed, in fact, almost resigned to the situation.

As Parker started the interview, recording the time, date, names, ranks and professions of those present, he reminded himself that Roly wouldn't know that the effigy had been found. Therefore, he watched for his reaction as he kicked off the proceedings by saying, 'You gave us quite a turn with that thing in the alcove.'

Roly kept his eyes fixed on a tape deck set into the wall and didn't react.

'Roly,' said Parker, quietly, 'that effigy was dressed in clothes identical to those that Gary Maudsley was known to be wearing the day he disappeared.'

Roly said nothing.

'Did you know Gary?'

'No.'

'Then how did you come by his clothes?'

Roly countered with, 'H-how do you know they were h-his?'

Point taken, thought Parker. Forensic would confirm it one way or another soon enough. 'Fair enough,' he said. 'But it strikes me as odd that you dressed that thing in clothes identical to those that Gary was known to be wearing.'

'C-coincidence,' said Roly.

'Maybe,' said Parker. 'How did you come by them?'

'F-found them.'

'Where?'

'On the w-wasteground.'

That was bullshit. Parker and everyone present knew it, but proving it might be a problem. 'Why stuff them with rags and brick them up in an alcove?'

'Houses are coming down,' said Roly. 'W-wanted to give the workmen a fright.' He took his eyes off the tape deck. 'They're knocking down my home.'

It could just be true, thought Hanson. He didn't for one moment think it was, but a jury might.

Leaving it for the moment, Parker said, 'It's not very pleasant to be evicted from your home. I know I wouldn't like it, especially if I'd lived there long. How long have you lived there, Roly?'

'Years,' said Roly, 'on and off.'

'When did you move there?'

'After I left the children's home.'

'You lived in a children's home,' said Parker. 'How come?'

'D-dumped,' said Roly, and Hanson picked up on the way he described what had happened to him as a baby. *Dumped*, he'd said. Not *left*, or even *abandoned*, but *dumped*.

Parker said, 'How old were you?'

'Two,' said Roly.

'Two years old,' said Parker.

'Days,' said Roly. 'Two days old. Somebody handed me in.'

'Where did they find you?'

'Shoe-box,' said Roly, and suddenly, he laughed.

'Why are you laughing?' said Parker.

'Don't know,' said Roly. 'Just seems funny, that's all — f-found in a shoe-box. Don't know ... just seems funny.'

It didn't seem funny to Parker, who couldn't have laughed if he'd tried. He couldn't imagine a baby being small enough to fit inside a shoe-box, but when he thought about it, he supposed it depended on the size of the baby concerned and the type of shoe-box. He thought back to the birth of his own two sons and found that his memory of what it had felt like to hold them in his arms for the very first time was somehow distorted; all he recalled was their weight — not that they'd each been so many pounds or so many kilos, but that for something so small they'd seemed incredibly heavy, as if he were holding the weight of the world in arms that had trembled with fear. He might drop them. He might fail them. 'This children's home,' he said. 'How long did you live there?'

'I w-went into f-foster care at nine, but w-went back to the home and left when I was s-sixteen.'

Thrown out, thought Hanson. Society's duty done.

'Where was it?' said Parker.

'Salisbury Road.'

The name meant nothing to Hanson, but it clearly meant

something to Parker who said, 'That's where the wasteground is – the one that divides the yard from Roumelia Road.'

'Yes,' said Roly, seeming pleased that Parker knew where it was.

'So you really have lived there a very long time,' said Parker. 'Not in the same house, or even in the same road, maybe, but right opposite the children's home.'

'Yes,' said Roly. 'They knocked it down a while back. Now they're knocking my y-yard down. I wanted to give them a sh-shock.'

'You'd have done that, all right,' said Parker. 'It scared the living daylights out of *me*.'

Roly smiled, and Hanson felt that the smile was essentially of the disarming variety – the sort of smile that would make a boy feel easy in his company. 'I'm sorry,' said Roly. 'It wasn't m-meant for you.'

'No harm done,' said Parker. 'We all like a bit of a joke.' He, too, smiled. 'Just don't do it again, eh?'

'I w-wouldn't do that, Mr Parker.'

'Good,' said Parker, 'only I wouldn't want any of my men coming across a similar shock – sensitive souls, some of them.' His tone growing serious now, Parker added coldly, 'You should see the state they were in when they saw what was left of Joey.'

Roly stopped smiling. 'I heard,' he said. 'You f-found him in a wood.'

'You're no doubt going to tell me you didn't know him, that he never came to the yard,' said Parker.

'He didn't,' said Roly.

'Good,' said Parker, 'because if we happen to find Joey's clothes down that yard, the council won't have to bother – I'll demolish it for them.'

A knock at the door to the interview room robbed Hanson of the opportunity to evaluate what Roly's response might have been, and Parker suspended the interview as one of his men poked his head round the door. 'Guv — I need a word.'

Parker left the room alone, returning seconds later to motion Hanson out of there. Hanson joined the two men in the corridor where Parker kept his voice down. 'Problem over at Byrne's place. Warrender's down there now.'

'Want me along?'

'No,' said Parker. 'By the time we're through, it'll be nearly midnight. You might as well go home.'

Home, thought Hanson. The guesthouse wasn't home — not any more. 'What about Roly?'

Parker had been on duty a good fourteen hours already and saw the rest of the evening stretching ahead like a long, bad dream. He was tired. He was disappointed by what the yard had produced, and short of Forensic telling him that the effigy was dressed in Gary's clothes, he wasn't over-hopeful of finding a means to keep Roly and Moranti in beyond tomorrow. 'We'll carry on in the morning.'

CHAPTER THIRTY-FIVE

Parker got himself down to the road that led to the shop only to find that he couldn't get any further. From beginning to end, it was swarming with people, some of them trying to get at the door that led to Byrne's bedsit.

He pushed through the crowd, made his way to the shop and saw one of his men pulling a woman away from the door. The dents around the lock were evidence enough of her anger, and his men had a job getting her into a car.

He ran up to Warrender, who was standing with two of the uniforms, as a jeer went up from the crowd, one of the women shouting, 'You want to spend our taxes looking after our kids, not protecting some bloody child molester.'

'What's going on?' said Parker.

By way of reply, Warrender handed him a copy of the evening paper. The headline said as much as Parker needed to know. The local press had reported that the yard was being searched, and had taken it upon themselves to publish Byrne's identity along with his address and an article divulging that he'd been questioned in connection with the disappearance of Joseph Coyne and Gary Maudsley.

Somebody's head would roll for this, thought Parker, assuming that he ever found out who'd given the information to the press. Chances were, he'd never know, and if the truth were told, this was one occasion when, despite the hassle it had brought to his door, Parker could sympathize. If he had a paedophile living within a few hundred yards of his sons, he'd want to know about it. 'Right,' he said. 'Let's get more back-up. Get these people shifted.'

He turned to the crowd and recognized some of the people that comprised it. Julie Coyne was there, her face drawn, her eyes hooded, the first signs of shock and grief manifesting now. Gone was the *he's-at-peace* look that she'd worn when he first broke the news. It was sinking in, and Julie looked ill. 'Get one of the lads to take her home,' he said to Warrender, and as he arranged it, Parker looked up at the bedsit. 'Byrne?'

'Still no sign,' said Warrender.

The crowd began to chant Byrne's name, staring up at the bedsit, hoping he was in there, wanting to tear him apart.

Back-up arrived in the form of further patrols, the crowd allowing itself to be pushed away from the shop. Warrender added: 'Mind you, one of the neighbours said she saw him burying something out the back some nights ago.'

Parker doubted that was true. Byrne knew full-well that he was under surveillance – or had been until Parker had first clapped eyes on that yard. He wouldn't be stupid enough to bury anything out the back, and the back, in any case, was under concrete. Right now, his van was standing on that concrete – Byrne, wherever he'd gone, hadn't taken it with him, mindful perhaps of the likelihood of his vehicle being spotted. 'We'll take a look,' he said, wearily, 'once we've got rid of this lot.'

It took some time to get the crowd to disperse, and Parker placed men at the top and bottom of the road to make sure that those who had stayed behind didn't congregate anywhere near the shop.

He then led the way to the side gate, lifted the latch, and walked round to the back. Byrne's van was still there, all right. 'Let's take a look at his bedsit,' he said.

He went to the front of the shop and hammered on the

door, then lifted the letterbox and shouted, 'Dougie, if you're in there, it's safe, open the door.'

Byrne didn't open the door, and Parker took the decision to have one of his men break the lock.

He fumbled for a switch as he and Warrender stepped through and into the square of space that stood at the foot of the stairs. 'Dougie!' he shouted, but there was no reply, and Parker and Warrender walked up the stairs to the bedsit.

They pushed the door and flung it wide, half expecting to see Byrne cowering on the floor, but the room was empty.

'Where the hell is he?' said Parker.

They left the bedsit and went down to the street. 'I'll check the van,' said Warrender, and he and Parker returned to the back of the shop.

Warrender produced a torch and shone it into the van. It was empty, so far as they could see, and he and Parker came away from it, Warrender shining the torch to the ground for some evidence of the concrete having been disturbed. So much of the information they got on any given case was a fabrication of somebody's overactive imagination that it didn't surprise either of them to discover that the concrete was much as they remembered it.

Then Parker took the torch and shone it in the direction of the bunker. This, too, was much as they remembered it. Except for one thing. 'That bunker's been moved,' said Parker.

'Doesn't look like it's been moved to me.'

Parker, who knew every brick on the wall of the house and where the bunker stood in relation to it, replied, 'It's been moved.'

Four of the men who had been involved in searching the yard arrived on the scene. Now, as then, they were dressed in dark blue overalls, and Parker directed them to the bunker. 'Over there,' he said.

They walked over to it, lifted the lid and peered in, finding it empty as Parker had known it would be. Then two of them got a grip and tried to lift it. It moved, but only a fraction and, try as he might, Parker couldn't imagine how Byrne had ever managed to shift it. It had taken two of his men to inch it aside, but Byrne had had the additional strength afforded by desperation. He couldn't afford *not* to be able to move it.

He had worked at night, thought Parker, mindful that the back of the shop was overlooked by neighbouring houses. But despite his every precaution, one of the neighbours had seen him. And thank God for that, thought Parker, who might not have bothered to search the bunker again.

A short while later the concrete structure was positioned several feet from where it had stood before, and Parker watched as his men began to dig.

Almost immediately, they came across something buried a mere two feet beneath the surface, and it took Parker back to that moment years before when he had expected to find the remains of Joseph Coyne and his men had uncovered the flyte case filled with clothing catalogues. They'd probably find something similar now. Byrne had done a runner, and had buried something he couldn't take with him. Stupid of him, thought Parker. He should have destroyed it, whatever it was. But then again, these were his treasures, his photographs of children.

The spade had slid into the soil as if it had recently been hoed and, in what seemed like minutes, it was swapped for a trowel.

The man using it leant down from the side of what was now a shallow pit, and worked with the care of an archaeologist who had stumbled on a find. He brushed at the soil with almost delicate strokes, and revealed a knot that sealed a plastic sack. The trowel was placed at the side of the pit and a knife was used to slit the plastic. Its sides sprang open like the petals of a large black rose to reveal the remains of a boy. Whoever had killed him had done what they could to ensure that it would prove difficult to identify the remains, but Parker knew who it was, and he was overwhelmed by a sense of failure.

For the second time in a day, Parker found himself saying, 'Hanson – get him down here – I want him to see what we've found,' and as he looked at that black plastic tomb, he swore to himself that he would never reveal certain details to the relatives, that he'd try to persuade them not to be in court when facts relating to what that body had looked like, and what the killer had done to ensure that it fitted in that sack, were made known to a jury. There were certain things, thought Parker, that the relatives of a victim should be spared.

As Hanson arrived at the shop, he noticed that paint had been hurled across the brickwork. The windows had been smashed, and the door had been scraped as if someone had dug their nails into the wood, had tried to claw their way inside to get at Byrne.

Maybe they had, he thought.

Warrender led him to the back of the shop and Hanson saw someone squatting down to take a look at the remains. 'Sherringham,' Warrender said, and Hanson saw him touch the plastic with a hand that seemed to be trembling. It took a lot to rattle a pathologist, thought Hanson, but Sherringham was clearly shaken.

He looked past him to see Parker standing by a bunker, its concrete sides and the timber lid giving it the appearance of a makeshift sarcophagus.

'Do we know who it is?' said Hanson.

'Gary,' said Parker.

'I'm sorry.'

'So am I.'

If Parker had looked tired earlier, he now looked completely exhausted. He leant against the bunker as if it were propping him up.

Hanson felt that he was being unfair in asking Parker anything at this stage, but there were certain things he needed to know to make the deductions that Parker would expect of him by morning, and he said, 'How long has he been dead?'

'Three or four days.'

'Byrne didn't murder him,' said Hanson.

'No,' said Parker. 'I realize that.'

In that case, thought Hanson, Parker must also realize that Gary had been kept prisoner somewhere, that Roly had been panicked into murdering him and had dumped the body in Byrne's back yard to focus Parker's attention back on Byrne.

Indicating the remains, Parker said, 'Would this fit in with what you make of Roly?'

Hanson, who still felt he knew too little about Roly to be able to determine what drove him, thought back to that alcove and the clothes found on the effigy. 'I think you can expect Forensic to confirm that Gary was kept in the alcove and that the clothes on the effigy are his.'

'That doesn't answer my question. I want to know why he did that. Why imprison him?'

Hanson gave the only answer he could at that particular moment. 'I don't know,' he admitted.

CHAPTER THIRTY-SIX

The following morning, Hanson walked into the dining room to find that only two of the breakfast tables were set. Business must be bad, he thought, though he doubted trade was seasonal.

He nodded an acknowledgement to the only other guest, then left him to his paper and sat down at a table by the window. In a sense, it was an unfortunate choice in that there had once been another table in exactly this spot, but that had been antique, its surface decorated with squares inlaid with different types of wood.

Mrs Judd walked through carrying a breakfast and set it down in front of the guest that Hanson had decided was a rep, the smell of hot croissants wafting across the room. 'Morning,' she said. 'Croissants?' and Hanson, who felt that he couldn't face anything much considering what he'd been through with Parker the night before, found himself replying, 'Fine.'

He had stood at the bunker with Parker, had tried to tell him that what had been found was entirely in keeping with what Roly was likely to do if cornered, and had realized in the end that Parker wasn't taking it in. He'd seen too much in too short a space of time. He needed sleep, time to think, time to come to grips with the latest development.

Whether Parker had heeded his advice to go home and get

some sleep, Hanson didn't know. He only knew that Parker had asked him to stick around a few days longer.

In the circumstances, Hanson didn't see how he could refuse, but in the knowledge that Parker had said he wouldn't be required at the station until early that afternoon, he decided that he might as well do something other than stare at the guesthouse walls all morning. His old school wasn't far from Bury. He'd always intended to take a look at the place, but he'd never been back. Time to pay it a visit.

The croissants, when they came, were disappointing — yesterday's offerings steamed back to life but barely passing for fresh. He washed them down with pale, milky coffee, and walked back up to his room, the aftertaste of chicory stinging the roof of his mouth.

He hadn't opened the curtains and the room was still in darkness, his bed as yet unmade. For a moment, he could almost imagine that Lorna was lying there, the bedclothes barely moving as she breathed. But they were bedclothes, no more, no less, and he wondered what subconscious desire had allowed him to push them aside when he woke, and leave them sculpted into a shape that looked like her sleeping form.

He straightened the bed abruptly, drew back the curtains and found that it was raining. It would have seemed odd if that hadn't been the case. Whenever he thought back to Manchester, and to what had become of his marriage, every scene he saw seemed set against a backdrop of rain, as if the sun had never once shone on their relationship.

He picked up the briefcase and opened the door that led from his room to the landing. He walked past Mrs Judd as he made for the stairs, then glanced back to find that she was watching him. She still hadn't placed him, but she knew now that he wasn't who he said he was. He didn't blame her for being suspicious of him, but wasn't about to enlighten her; he couldn't divulge what had brought him there to the very person whose presence in the house he so resented.

He left her to her thoughts, aware, even as he left the house, that she was in his room. If he were to return to it right now, she'd be poking around on the pretext of tidying it in his absence, but what she would really be looking for were clues.

Hanson's life revolved around looking for clues and he could relate to that. The need to know was a powerful force, one that had been driving him for as long as he could remember. He needed to know why he felt as he did about his current relationship. He needed to know why Lorna had left him for somebody else. He needed to know why he'd had to return and face the past like this.

And these were just some of the things he needed to know. If he thought about it, he realized that it was this same need that drove him to get to the root of his patients' problems, and Lorna had once accused him of spending every waking moment analysing what went on in the minds of sexual deviants and serial killers. 'It isn't normal,' she'd added. 'Why surround yourself with these people?'

He had defended himself with, 'I don't – they're referred to me by the NHS because people like you, people who are trained to deal with physical illness, don't know where to start when it comes to dealing with behavioural problems.'

In the infuriating way she had of making sweeping generalizations, Lorna had replied, 'Psychopaths are incurable. What's the point?' and he'd replied that certain physical illnesses were also incurable, but that didn't give others the right to end the misery of the victims against their will.

It had led to an argument that had become typical of their relationship, the subject matter gravitating towards more personal issues until, eventually, he had found himself retreating behind what, at the time, he had regarded as a civilized silence. He no longer regarded that silence as having been civilized; he regarded it as having been a mistake.

How many times since had he told patients to express what they felt, explaining that to bottle up emotions was unhealthy?

He had no idea. He only knew that he had never once given vent to his true feelings, had never once let her know how deeply she'd hurt him. The quiet rage that he'd kept contained in the years following her departure was pushing the lid of that bottle now, threatening to explode.

He had thrown himself more deeply into his work during his marriage, his interest in criminal psychology an addition rather than an extension to his everyday work at the clinic. As Lorna well knew, few of his patients were dangerous, or even particularly interesting if he were honest: the women referred by the courts or their GP had invariably stolen items they could well afford to pay for – cries for attention from people whom they had come to believe no longer loved or wanted them. The emasculated middle managers tended not to get out of bed one morning: they simply lay there, staring at the ceiling, impervious to the bewilderment, worry or even fury of the women they'd married twenty years before. Some left their jobs, their spouses, their entire past, only to be found in a doorway. If they were lucky, they were referred to him, or to someone like him, someone who could help them put their lives together again, not as before but in a way that was at least manageable, if only for the moment.

He found his work rewarding, and if the money was poor, then at least the rewards were substantial in terms of the minor triumphs that sometimes seemed to arrive on a daily basis – the agoraphobic who made it to the post box and back, the woman who found herself able to cuddle her kids for the first time in years, the lad who nerved himself to stand up to an abusive father.

Such was the bread-and-butter stuff of life, and he knew it to be small beer by comparison with those who achieved a first in the treatment of some major mental disorder, but what mattered to him was that what he did made an appreciable difference to somebody's otherwise miserable existence.

He only wished he could make an appreciable difference to his own.

*　　*　　*

As he headed out of Manchester in the direction of the school, he grew increasingly aware that the layout of the roads had changed a great deal since he'd last lived in the area. He reached for a road map, his hand dipping into the glove box and coming out with a wrapper from a high-energy snack bar. It served as a reminder that he hadn't made contact with Jan since the brief, stilted phonecall he'd made the day he'd arrived at the guesthouse, and questions she'd asked came to him now, questions she'd asked only recently, as if picking up on the fact that, of late, Lorna had been on his mind.

'Is she anything like me?'

'No, not really.'

'In what way?'

In every way, thought Hanson, but all he'd said was, 'You don't look alike, if that's what you mean.'

It wasn't what she'd meant, and he knew it. 'So what does she look like?'

'Small and dark.'

That would have to do for now, and she settled for it, although, when she'd come across a photo some time later, she had shown it to him saying, 'Is this Lorna?'

He had glanced at it quickly and looked away, angry at what he had perceived to be a violation of his privacy. 'Yes.'

She'd gone very quiet, and he knew he ought to give her the reassurance she no doubt needed, but anger had made him leave her to suffer. It was her own fault, thought Hanson. People who root through other people's belongings sometimes come across things they wish they hadn't seen.

'She's beautiful.'

He hadn't made any reply.

'Don't you think she's beautiful?'

'If you say so.'

She'd put the photo back, slipping it into the hold-all that he'd kept on the top of a wardrobe.

It hadn't been mentioned again until later in the day when she'd suddenly said, 'That holdall. The one on top of the wardrobe.'

'What about it?'

'I thought it was empty.'

'Well, it's not.'

'I never thought ... I ...'

He let her struggle on.

'I wanted it for gym, that's all. The handle's broken on mine. I didn't mean ...'

'You didn't mean any harm?' he'd said.

'No,' she'd replied.

'No harm done.'

But that wasn't true, and he knew it. Now that she'd seen a photo of Lorna she felt inferior, and that night, when he'd reached out to her, he had found her unresponsive. Again, he hadn't been able to bring himself to give the reassurance she clearly needed: the photo had been thrust at him without him having had the chance to prepare himself for seeing it, and he wanted her punished for the pain it had caused him.

He had turned off the light and when she spoke again, her voice had seemed to come at him from very far away. 'What does she do for a living?'

He knew his reply would fan the flames of the inferiority complex she was nurturing, but told her anyway. 'She's a doctor.'

Her response was very small, very quiet. 'Oh.'

He'd tried to sleep, but she wasn't finished.

'Do you ever—'

'Jan,' he'd said, 'I'm trying to sleep.'

'—hear from her?'

'No.'

'Maybe you should phone her some time, see how she's getting along.'

His patience exhausted, he'd replied, 'Maybe I should,' and she'd left it at that, turning away abruptly.

He wondered what she'd make of his not having phoned since he'd first arrived at the guesthouse, and decided that by now she'd be convinced that he was about to end their relationship. Maybe he was. If she'd asked him how he felt and what he wanted, he wouldn't have been able to tell her. Maybe that was why he hadn't called. Maybe he would never call again. Maybe he'd just drift back home after Parker had finished with his services and tell her he couldn't commit to more than he was already giving, that the house, the toad and the holdall were his and his alone, along with the mortgage, the finance on the car and the certainty that if he didn't sort himself out, he'd end up in therapy in late middle age: *I don't have anyone in my life. My life lacks focus and meaning. I just don't see the point of it all any more . . .*

He wondered what her response would be if he told her he couldn't commit, and it suddenly wasn't too difficult to imagine her taking the news calmly, then packing her things into something other than the holdall. Most of it would be items of clothing that largely belonged to him, in which case not only would he be saying goodbye to a relationship that was calm, workable, comfortable, he'd be saying goodbye to every sweatshirt he'd ever owned, and he wasn't quite sure he could cope with that. The house would be lonely without them. Lonely, cold, and devoid of the maroons, blues and greys that were tied round her waist if not left to hang round her shoulders.

He'd also go hungry or, if not hungry, malnourished, as he would, no doubt, revert to the junk food he'd eaten before he met her. There'd be no more salads as an accompaniment to the evening meal; no more fresh fruit brought home. No more wrappers pushed into the glove compartment of the Saab.

He picked up the wrapper, screwed it into a ball and pushed it into the ashtray, out of sight.

CHAPTER THIRTY-SEVEN

Mrs Maudsley opened the door, a pot plant in her hand. The African Violet, Parker thought, although he was no expert on these things. It was similar to one kept on the sill in his own kitchen, its leaves yellowing from too much light and water. He said, 'Do you think I could come in, Mrs Maudsley?'

She had been expecting him, really. Every minute of the past few weeks she had been expecting him. Parker could see it in the way she held on to the plant and made no effort to invite him inside, as if by preventing him from crossing the threshold she could somehow prevent the news from being true.

He led her gently by the elbow and guided her into a back room where she put the plant on the coffee table that held the magazines. 'Are you here on your own, Mrs Maudsley?'

Her eyes grew wide with fear. 'Why do you want to know?'

'Late last night,' said Parker, 'we found ... we found the body of a boy ... at a shop not far from here.'

'What did I do with my plant?'

Parker picked it up off the table and gave it to her.

'I don't know where I go wrong. I've had others, you know, and they've all gone the same way. First the leaves turn yellow and then they die. Everybody tells me I water them too much but it doesn't seem to matter what I do, they die just the same.'

She stroked the leaves as if she were performing some strange healing ritual, and then, quite suddenly, she pinched one so that an impression was left, a bruise that would never quite heal but would cause some essential part of the leaf to die away.

'Mrs Maudsley . . .'

'I don't know who this boy is you've found, but I do know it isn't our Gary,' and, as if the thought had only just struck her, she looked up, her eyes bright with possibility. 'He could be in London, couldn't he? That's where they go, isn't it, London?'

'Gary didn't run away, Mrs Maudsley.'

'It's his birthday, Wednesday. I'm putting on a tea.'

A tea, thought Parker, and he felt his chest constrict as if her grief were about to crush him.

She turned to a photo on a bookshelf, a photo identical to the one the police had released to the press. He had been an attractive kid, his cheekbones high, his complexion slightly freckled, but the expression on his face had struck Parker as being rather vacant, as if, during the split second that the photograph had been taken, he had somehow managed to glance into the future and had found himself to be absent from it.

'You should see what I've bought for his birthday. When he comes back, he won't be able to move in his room for the clothes and presents I've bought.'

Parker was lost for words. That small dismembered bundle would never be coming home.

By the side of the photo, there was a plaster ornament, a donkey labouring under the weight of a load that, in reality, it couldn't possibly have been expected to carry. He reached out and picked it up. It felt coarse in his hand and had about it a fairground cheapness that was in keeping with the rest of the room: the brown and yellow material that covered a wing-backed sofa, the grey nylon rug in front of a gas fire, its elements blackened through being lit by a twist of newspaper. He imagined the way in which the print would expand in the moment before the paper turned to ash, a chain of words that would fail to convey what impact the human tragedy would have on those left to suffer in its wake. Tomorrow, there would be fresh tapers made from today's news and somebody, somewhere, would be burning the words, *'missing boy found dead . . .'*

He knew that, whatever he said, she wouldn't take it in first time; that he would have to come back and repeat it, word for word. He'd seen it all before — other missing kids, other bewildered relatives plummeting into denial.

He explained that the pathologist had confirmed that the boy was Gary and she nodded and smiled. 'I see,' she said. 'I see . . .' She carried on stroking the leaves of the plant, still nodding and smiling, and seeing. 'Makes you wonder, doesn't it.'

'Excuse me?' said Parker.

'What he must have gone through.'

Parker found himself replying, 'Yes, it does, Mrs Maudsley, it makes you wonder very much.' Then he left, in case he, too, was bruised by an impression that would never quite heal but would cause some essential part of him to die away also.

CHAPTER THIRTY-EIGHT

Hanson drove up to the gates of the school and found the grounds silent, the pupils hidden behind the walls to classrooms that he could recall in detail. For a place crammed to capacity with young life, it seemed oddly quiet and intense.

In the distance, he could see the cricket pavilion, the nets and the strips of earth where the grass had been worn to the roots by inexpert bowlers. He recalled the lad who had ultimately become a county-level cricket player, had heard of him since and knew that he'd opened a sports shop somewhere in Hastings. It seemed an inappropriate end for someone whose talent had made his face instantly recognizable on advertising hoardings. He, like a number of old boys, had made his mark, had faded to obscurity, was one of those whose names were inscribed on a plaque in the headmaster's study.

Hanson, whose name had yet to be inscribed, didn't go into the school. He drove by, finding the roads unchanged, and finding also that what had been designated green belt had remained so. No one had given up a slice of their garden for development. No blocks of flats had sprouted up on a former village green. It was all a far cry from the estate he'd travelled from during his school days, the journey an hour-long bus ride with changes at the terminal in the centre of Manchester.

He'd walked these roads as a boy, finishing prep at school,

then lugging his books to the house where Parris had lived with the wife he'd murdered. He came to it now, and found it smaller than he'd remembered, though no less picturesque.

Parris would either be dead or approaching seventy. At any rate, Hanson couldn't imagine that he might have returned to the house where he'd committed the crime described by the press as *dreadful*. The expression seemed genteel. He couldn't recall having seen the phrase used in recent times. *A dreadful crime.* The press preferred more sensational terms today, and yet, they'd been right. The crime had been dreadful, not merely because of its violent nature, but because it had been committed by someone like Parris rather than by somebody long suspected of being psychotic. And therein lay the fascination, thought Hanson. People might die in drive-by shootings, and crimes of that nature were no less dreadful, but such cases didn't have legs. Not these days. What Parris had done had ensured that, over a period of weeks, his life and the lives of his closest relatives had been picked over by a press that had wanted to keep the story running. Here was a man whose background and qualifications were impeccable, a man who had taught the children of prominent local figures. What did those pupils think of him now?

Many had said, in his defence, that Parris had been a wonderful man, and not at all the type of person likely to take a hammer to his wife without good reason.

But what had been the reason — good or otherwise? thought Hanson.

The press had portrayed Parris's wife as a loving mother, an academic, a respected magistrate, and that was understandable, Hanson supposed. But she must have been something else as well as those good and commendable things, because Parris had been driven to murder her. There had been no other woman involved, no other man. No third party. No explanation. Just Parris, with his gentle air of regret, his willingness to admit to the crime, his refusal to blame anyone but himself.

Why?

He parked in front of the house, climbed out of the car, and approached a small, wrought-iron gate the height of his waist. In Parris's day, there had been no sign to warn the unsuspecting that they should *Beware of the Dog*, and even as he cast his eye over a garden that seemed every bit as well kept as he remembered, a Bouvier de Flandres loped from the back of the house, its coat steel blue, its face deceptively placid.

Hanson had seen that deadpan expression many times before and wasn't fooled: it was never the noisy, yappy people who bit, it was those who considered their options then exploded into action. He took his hand from the gate as more than mere precaution.

He looked up and saw the figure of a man emerging from the side of the cottage. He was middle-aged and dressed as if he were about to get down to the garden. He looked past Hanson to the Saab, and Hanson made a move away from the gate.

'Can I help you?'

He turned to face the man, an apology on his lips. 'I'm sorry, I was formerly the pupil of a maths teacher who used to live here. I was passing so I pulled over.'

The Bouvier lifted its lip in total, and meaningful, silence. 'I used to come to the house after school sometimes.'

This met with no response, and Hanson added, 'I didn't mean to stop, actually, I just ...' His words trailed away. The man looked at him. The dog looked at him. 'I'd better be on my way,' said Hanson.

'Hold on,' said the man, and Hanson turned back. 'You say my father used to teach you.'

The dog let his lip fall back into place. Odd, thought Hanson, how one simple act could transform it so totally. It now looked more of a family pet than the guard dog that it so clearly, genuinely, was.

'A long time ago,' said Hanson.

'Have you come far?'

'London,' said Hanson, 'though I'm working on something

in Manchester at present, so I decided to drive up and see my old school.'

'It hasn't changed.'

'So I see.'

They regarded one another a few seconds longer, the dog relaxing, the quietness of their voices having imparted the message that, essentially, there seemed to be no problem.

'Would you like to come in?'

'No, there's no need, really ...'

'He doesn't get many visitors.'

For a moment, Hanson wondered whether he'd heard correctly.

'I'm sure he'd be only too pleased to have a visit from one of his former pupils.'

'You're ...'

'Gus,' said the man, opening the gate, and Hanson recalled the press having made a mockery of the fact that Parris had named one of his sons Augustus.

The dog gave him the once-over, sniffing his shoes, his jacket and his trousers, then let him in, padding off to a corner of the garden, settling down, watching, head on paws, as Gus led the stranger into the house.

The wall clock had never worked when Hanson had gone to the house as a boy. Now, the pendulum swung and the hall was filled with a soft and comforting tick. The paintwork was relatively fresh but the hall had been redecorated in much the same colours as Parris, or his wife, had chosen years before.

He was led through and into a room that looked out on the garden at the back. In Hanson's day, it had been a sitting room. Now it was a bedroom, and, sitting in a chair, his back to him, was Parris. 'Father,' said Gus, 'you've a visitor.'

He led Hanson round the chair so that he was facing Parris.

My God, thought Hanson, he's so old. 'Mr Parris,' he said, 'it's Murray Hanson. Do you remember me?'

Parris took his eyes from the garden, allowed them to rest on him and said, 'Vaguely, yes.'

They shook hands, Parris's palm like parchment.

Hanson found himself totally unprepared. What *did* you say to a man who had shaped your entire life by one single act? And then he grasped that it hadn't been one single act but a series of acts that had shaped him: that every time Parris had paid him special attention, he had instilled in him the notion that much was expected of him and that he was capable of fulfilling those expectations.

He followed Parris's gaze to the garden and was disconcerted to find that, from here, he could see right out to the garden furniture, the cast-iron table, its four white chairs, the scene of his crime.

'Is that why you came?' said Parris. 'To see where I did it?'

'Father,' said Gus, but Hanson broke in with: 'No, but now that I'm here, I'd be lying if I said I didn't find it interesting.'

'You surprise me. Most people want to avoid the subject. It embarrasses them.' He turned to Hanson. 'Does it embarrass you, Murray?'

He had to think about it. It didn't embarrass him, yet if asked before the visit to consider whether he would have brought the subject up, he'd have replied that it wouldn't have seemed appropriate.

'No.'

'So why did you come?'

'I came to see the house. I didn't expect . . .'

'You thought I'd be dead,' said Parris. 'That was a reasonable enough assumption.'

'Now that I find you're not, I can at least thank you,' said Hanson.

'For what?'

'For extra tuition, for putting me well on the road to making a success of my life.'

'Is that what you've done?' said Parris. 'Made a success of your life?'

Hanson didn't reply straight away. Parris watched him thoughtfully, lowering his eyes when Hanson said, 'I suppose I have, yes, on one level.'

'And on what level might that be?'

Hanson was suddenly aware that if he were to reveal the nature of his work, Parris might feel he had gone there to study him. 'I'm a doctor,' he replied, and this wasn't entirely untrue. His thesis had related to criminal psychology and he would have been entitled to request that people address him as Doctor.

'Where?'

'London.'

He steered him away from the subject, asking after his health, accepting the offer of coffee, noting that Parris seemed tired, and feeling slightly alarmed when the old man returned to the subject of his occupation by saying, 'Why did you tell an untruth?'

An *untruth*. The word seemed to belong to another time, one in which people refrained from coming out with the darker word, *lie*.

'I'm not aware that I—'

'You said you were a doctor.'

'I—'

'You didn't go in to the school today.'

He'd totally lost Hanson now. 'I'm not sure I know what you mean.'

'The plaque,' said Parris, 'the one in the headmaster's study. You haven't seen it?'

'Is there any reason why I should?'

'Your name was inscribed on it some time last year. Something to do with *criminal psychology*, if I'm not mistaken.'

In all this time, he hadn't yet taken his eyes from that table and chairs.

The feeling of guilt that washed over Hanson was almost child-like in its intensity. He hadn't felt anything like it since being caught in some minor misdemeanour as a schoolboy, and it interested him to note the psychological effect that being in Parris's presence had on him. In his view, Parris would never be a murderer so much as a schoolmaster. Nothing could ever change that. 'I'm sorry,' he said. 'You're right.'

'Is that why you came?'

'No.'

'So why did you come?'

'I don't know,' admitted Hanson. 'Right now, there are things in my life ... I ... things I need to sort ... I can't explain.'

'A woman?' said Parris, and the guilt was replaced by embarrassment. Hanson, who had no difficulty discussing the finer points of whatever sexual deviation a patient might throw at him, knew he would find it impossible to discuss any matter relating to the opposite sex with his former schoolmaster. 'I was married,' he said. 'It didn't work out.'

'Ah,' said Parris.

Hanson rose to go.

'You're leaving?'

'I shouldn't have come.'

'You've only just arrived.'

'I didn't mean ...'

'Neither did I,' said Parris. 'On occasion, we all tend to find ourselves doing things we didn't mean to do.'

Hanson couldn't have wished for a better lead into the type of conversation that might have enabled him to ask Parris why he had murdered his wife, and yet he didn't ask. To have done so would have seemed an almost unforgivable intrusion. It therefore came as a surprise when, in the moments that followed, Parris inadvertently revealed his motivation, and by so doing, he articulated everything Hanson had thought and felt with regard to his own failed marriage.

He looked once again at the table and chairs, the paintwork recent, white, and terribly clean. Hard to imagine what it might have looked like after Parris had wielded that hammer, the mixture of blood and tea, and Mrs Parris's face pressed into the metal so that, later, when her remains were removed from the scene, it had borne the imprint of a single leaf of ivy, one wrought into the metalwork to scar her cheek in death.

CHAPTER THIRTY-NINE

After leaving Parris, Hanson drove straight to the station where Warrender handed him a copy of that morning's paper.

Much of the article was devoted to the search at the yard and the discovery of remains at the back of Byrne's shop, but Hanson's attention was drawn to a photograph on one of the inside pages.

It had been taken outside the yard the day before. It depicted Parker, who'd been barking a command at the men who had allowed the press to break through the cordon. This, in itself, was no problem. The problem lay in that Hanson had been standing beside him when the photograph was taken, and the text beneath the photo gave his name and occupation.

That's all I need, thought Hanson.

He wondered how Mrs Judd would react when she discovered that Mr Franklin the conference organizer was actually Mr Hanson the criminal psychologist, imagined being asked to explain himself, and imagined, also, being unable to do so.

A thought crept into his mind, and he quashed it as too appalling a prospect to consider. The Judds seemed short of money. What if they were to contact the press and tell them he was staying at the guesthouse under the name of Franklin? That had to be worth something, surely, especially if it came to light that he and his former wife had once owned the place.

He could imagine what the press would make of that, just as he could imagine what Parker might say. A thing like this could damage his career, not to mention the effect it might have on his relationship with Jan. She would want to know why he'd returned to his former matrimonial home, and he wouldn't be able to offer an explanation – he didn't have one.

At the thought of the potential consequences on both counts, he was enveloped by a wave of acute embarrassment, and he calmed himself with the assurance that the Judds were highly unlikely to contact the press. And then he wasn't so sure ...

As Warrender led him up to the incident room, he said, 'If the press track you down, don't make any comment, and don't give any interviews.'

'I don't intend to,' said Hanson.

Parker was in the incident room, briefing his men. Byrne's video shop had been cordoned off. Forensic were still down there. The remains had been removed the night before and had already been positively identified as those of Gary Maudsley.

Hanson took in the details then broke in with a question: 'Have Forensic come up with a result on that alcove?'

'Not yet,' said Parker.

They will, thought Hanson. 'What about the clothes found on the effigy?'

'Forensic are working on those, too. If hair and skin cells are found, and if they match those that have been taken from clothes found in the laundry basket at Gary's home, we'll soon know. Trouble is, that takes time, and I don't have that time.'

Hanson fell silent as Parker explained that, as things stood, they still had too little to go on. Roly's solicitor was putting forward the argument that nothing had been found at the yard or the squat, despite Parker's men having taken the place apart. What *had* been found, however, was Gary Maudsley's body, and this had been found buried at the back of a shop owned by a known paedophile, a paedophile who appeared to have done a runner. Roly couldn't be held simply because he'd made an effigy which he *alleged* had been intended to shock the workmen who were about to destroy his squat. Roly's solicitor was therefore pointing out that it was high time Parker either charged his client, or released him, albeit for the time being.

He had a point, thought Hanson, who followed Parker up to his office after he'd ended the briefing.

Once there, Hanson saw that Parker hadn't taken his advice *go home, and get some sleep*, or if he had, the sleep hadn't been enough. He sat in his chair like a much older man, the whites of his eyes almost totally bloodshot now.

'There must be something you can do?' said Hanson.

Parker replied, 'I can get an order keeping him for a further twenty-four hours. After that, I'll either have to charge him, or let him go. Same with Moranti.'

Hanson thought back to the statement made by Nathan Palmer. 'We know that Gary Maudsley went down to the yard, and Moranti admitted taking most if not all of the boys he's employed down the years to the yard.'

'It's not enough.'

Hanson was beginning to wonder whether anything would ever be enough. He knew that Parker had spent the greater part of the morning questioning Roly again, and he said, 'What's Roly thrown at you?'

'Nothing of interest,' said Parker. 'We found an old bit of film at the yard and on the back of it I managed to wheedle a little more out of him.'

'Film?' said Hanson.

'Home movie. Reel-to-reel. Done about thirty years ago.'

'What's on it?'

'Child's birthday party,' said Parker. 'Plenty of adults around. Balloons, streamers, jelly. It's all pretty innocent stuff.'

Let me be the judge of that, thought Hanson, who said, 'So what's his background?'

'Like he says, he was dumped as a two-day-old infant and,

like he says, he ended up in the children's home that used to be on Salisbury Road.'

Hanson had stood on the wasteground at the very spot where the children's home was purported to have stood. He had looked at the surrounding houses, and had been able to imagine what they must have been like in their heyday. These derelict, rambling houses had once been the homes of wealthy, professional people, and he couldn't imagine a children's home to have been built among them. 'Are you sure about the existence of this home?'

'I remember it,' said Parker. 'St Francis House.' As he spoke its name, Hanson saw the saint, his arms outstretched, a host of exotic finches feeding from his palms. 'Not that it was always a children's home,' said Parker. 'My information has it that it was three large properties knocked into one. You couldn't have distinguished it from any of the houses that surrounded it – not unless you saw the name on the door.'

Hanson, who could see the name on the door only too clearly, said, 'Do records exist of the children they had in their care?'

'In abundance,' said Parker. 'Warrender pulled what he could.'

'Which was?'

'We know that Roly was put up for adoption as a baby, but that nobody came forward,' said Parker.

'Unusual,' said Hanson. 'I'd have thought a baby had every chance of finding adoptive parents.'

'Hare lip,' said Parker, 'though you'd never know it to look at him now. Whoever operated did a good job, superficially at any rate. He still stutters.'

'That's not related,' said Hanson. 'A hare lip is one thing, a stutter is another.'

'Whatever,' said Parker, but already Hanson was on the look-out for anything Parker might say to indicate what had brought about that stutter. 'What else do we know about his background?'

Parker handed a folded slip of paper to Hanson as he added, 'St Francis House was initially run by a Church organization. It was taken over by the local authority in the late sixties. Roly was nine at the time, and Social Services placed an ad in one or the local papers. I've got a copy of it here.'

He handed Hanson a photocopy of the advert, and Hanson read the words:

> Roly is an attractive, brown-eyed boy of nine. Intelligent but shy, he needs a family who can give him the individual attention we feel he needs.

Hanson had to fight an urge to crumple the page. To have described a child as an attractive brown-eyed boy was almost an open invitation to a paedophile. But the ad had been placed thirty years ago, when people were less aware of the potential consequences of advertising for foster-parents to boys and girls who could be considered attractive, vulnerable and in need of individual attention. 'Who fostered him?' he said.

'Some local people – people called Timpson.'

Hanson, who was already planning to interview them with a view to finding out a little more about Roly's early years, said, 'Do they still live locally?'

'We don't know,' said Parker. 'They ... disappeared.'

For a minute, Hanson thought Parker was about to tell him that the Timpsons had been found dead, that their nine-year-old foster-child was assumed to have murdered them, but Parker added, 'Randolph Timpson was reported by a former foster-child who'd grown to adulthood bitter that he'd been abused by him. Roly was taken away from them, and the Timpsons simply evaporated. There's no record of where they might have gone.'

'Did anyone talk to Roly, find out what he'd been through while he was staying with these people?'

'Ah,' said Parker, and there was a subtext to that gentle, thoughtful *Ah*. 'This is where Social Services appear to have discovered a problem with their otherwise excellent records, which appear to be incomplete.'

I'll bet, thought Hanson, as Parker said, 'Funny thing is, there *is* a record of Social Services defending their initial decision to allow the Timpsons to foster the boy in the first place. Somebody seemed to feel that they were absolutely ideal.'

'Why?'

'Something to do with Randolph Timpson's line of work,' said Parker, drily. 'You might say, his *profession*.'

'And what was that?'

'Entertainer,' said Parker. 'Children's entertainer.'

Why do I see this? thought Hanson. Why do I see him giving the boy a balloon for *being good*, for consenting to perform some sexual act? Quietly, he said, 'I'd like a chance to talk to Roly.'

'And I'd like to give you that chance,' said Parker. 'Thing is, Murray, you know as well as I do, I can't risk it.'

Hanson was reminded that, if Parker were to allow him to talk to his suspect at this stage in the proceedings, Roly's brief might later claim that Hanson had somehow tricked his client into incriminating himself. There was a further complication in that any information gleaned by Hanson could be deemed inadmissible. Hanson wasn't a police officer. His function was to piece together a profile of Roly and increase Parker's ability to question him effectively. He said, 'Any sign of Brogan?'

'No.'

In the knowledge that Parker would be able to hold Roly if it transpired that Brogan had been abused during the night he spent with Roly, Hanson said, 'What was the result of the physical examination?'

'Freeman won't divulge the result to anyone but Brogan's father.'

'So why hasn't he done so?'

'Healey doesn't want to know the result.'

'Talk to him.'

'I've tried.'

'Let me try.'

'Be my guest.'

'Where is he?'

'Anton Close.'

Hanson hadn't heard the name mentioned before and Parker explained that this was where Healey had been living before Parker had insisted that he return home and take care of Brogan.

'Why's he gone back there?'

Parker replied, 'He didn't see much point in staying at Arpley Street once Brogan did a runner.'

'He hasn't gone back to the yard?'

'If he had, we'd know,' said Parker.

'That's where he'll head,' said Hanson, 'sooner or later.'

'We'll pick him up if he does.'

Hanson pictured Brogan, sleeping rough in town or hanging around the houses that surrounded Roly's Yard. He'd have seen the police activity and wouldn't have approached it, but once the police were gone, he'd return – Hanson was sure of it, particularly if he realized Roly was back. He said, 'Are the birds still at the yard?'

Parker had given orders that the mesh wasn't to be disturbed and found himself justifying that decision, as if Hanson might think him soft. 'If we'd pulled the mesh down during the search, they'd have been dead in a couple of days. I didn't want some Save the Budgie group breathing down my neck so I made sure none of my teams damaged the aviary.'

'They can't stay there for ever – that yard is coming down.'

'I'm trying to arrange for someone to come and round them up, take them to some pet shop or an aviary somewhere.'

Hanson wasn't so much bothered about what would become of the birds as what would become of Brogan if they didn't get it through to him that Roly was a danger to him. 'So the aviary still exists as such.'

'It's all pretty much as it was, except we've dug up the yard and returned the soil as best we can. Why?'

Hanson wondered how Parker would take his next suggestion. 'Maybe it could work in your favour if, for the moment, you were to release Roly from custody.'

'I don't see how.'

'Pull your men,' said Hanson. 'Release Roly. Watch the yard. I'll almost guarantee that the minute Brogan knows he's back there, he will go to that yard, provided there are no police in evidence.'

'Why should he?' said Parker, and Hanson thought of the way in which the long-tailed bird had escaped from the mesh, only to return to what it saw as security. 'Roly's all he's got,' he said. 'He trusts him.'

'What do we have to gain?'

'Everything,' said Hanson. 'The minute Brogan shows, we go to Anton Close, tell his father he's heading for the yard and that chances are, he'll ultimately go and stay with Roly when Roly sets up somewhere else.'

'How will that help matters?'

'Healey will have heard news bulletins by now, so he now knows something you couldn't tell him a few days ago, namely, that Roly is under suspicion of being, at the very least, implicated in the murders of Joseph and Gary. Healey will be terrified for Brogan's safety. He'll also realize there's real chance that his son might have been abused.'

'I think he knows that already. That's why he doesn't want the result from Freeman.'

'So force him to face up to it,' said Hanson. 'Tell him you can't do anything further because you don't have anything concrete to go on. Tell him that if Brogan's been abused you can get Roly off the streets.'

'Healey won't—'

'You don't know that,' said Hanson. 'You haven't let me try.'

Parker sat there, tired, and growing increasingly desperate. 'You think it might work?'

'It's the only option you've got right now.'

'Okay,' said Parker. 'I'll pull my men.'

CHAPTER FORTY

It seemed to Brogan many weeks since he had run from Freeman's surgery. In reality, it was a matter of a few days, which he had spent sleeping rough in the houses that surrounded Roly's Yard. He'd seen Roly arrested, and he'd watched the yard being searched, and if he'd eaten little, that was nothing new. He'd ventured out at night, walked into Manchester and stolen out of bins. He wasn't streetwise enough to know that if he'd gone into a burger bar or gravitated towards the type of area that boys who were sleeping rough found themselves drawn to from necessity, he'd have been picked up. He had no money, it was as simple as that, and he wanted to stay as close to the yard as he could, without being seen.

It was daylight when Roly came back. Brogan had imagined him walking across the wasteground, but that didn't happen. He watched from the window of one of the houses as a police vehicle drew up at the yard, and Roly got out. He walked through the gates, and the vehicle drove away.

Brogan left the house where he'd been hiding and walked across the wasteground to the yard. He knew that if the police were watching out for him, he'd be spotted, whatever he did, within the vicinity of the yard, but he was fed up with it all. A part of him wouldn't have minded if he'd ended up at the station and then back in care.

At least there had been food at the home, and people to talk to.

There were vehicles on the wasteground now, vehicles he associated with demolition. Workmen were piling out of them and, in the distance, he saw a crane arrive. The vast metal ball that hung from the jib seemed bigger than the houses it eclipsed as it rolled into view, and the workmen who watched it arrive seemed small by comparison. They didn't notice Brogan, but he noticed them. He also knew what the arrival of the crane signified: the houses were coming down.

He found that the gates were open and walked in to find the yard very different from the way it had been the last time he'd seen it. The concrete, such as it was, had been drilled away. It lay in large grey chunks in a mixture of earth and rubble, but there wasn't a finch out of place, and they watched him from the trees.

This was a boy who had fed them and they weren't afraid of him. He'd never been known to snap his fingers and whip them into a frenzy; he'd never been known to lash out and catch one among them as they flew.

They watched him cross the yard, and saw him enter the house, Roly letting him in then closing the door, as if the house were swallowing the boy.

The news that Brogan had returned to the yard came as no surprise to Hanson. That he had done so within so short time of Roly being released told him that Brogan must have been hiding in one of the other houses. Parker's men had kept an eye open, had even checked inside those houses, but they hadn't found him.

'He was there all the time,' said Parker.

'So it would seem,' said Hanson. 'How do you want to handle it?'

'We'll stick to our plan,' said Parker. 'I'll get down to the yard. You get down to Anton Close — see if you can persuade Healey to get the result from Freeman.'

If nothing else, thought Hanson, the exercise had flushed Brogan out of hiding. The police would be able to return him to care, and Social Services would do their best to make sure he didn't get the opportunity to do another runner.

Parker handed him a photograph of the scaffold. It was one that hadn't been released to the press, one that depicted what Hardman had seen when he peeled back the ivy with the tip of his scythe. 'If you don't get any joy out of Healey, show him that.'

As Hanson placed the photograph in the inside pocket of his jacket, Parker added, 'If that doesn't work, show him this.' He handed Hanson a photo of what had been found under the bunker. It was the first time Hanson had seen photographic evidence of what the remains had looked like, and in every respect it was worse than the horror of the scaffold. He wondered how the person who had photographed it felt, or whether they understood that they had to have some kind of defence mechanism that enabled them to push aside these visions of death once they came off duty. 'Let's hope I don't have to show him anything,' he said, and he echoed the sentiments Parker had felt when gazing down at the plastic bag that had held Gary Maudsley's remains. 'There are some things the public are better off not knowing.'

Healey answered Hanson's knock by flinging the door wide with arms that seemed too muscular for his otherwise average frame. He was nothing like his son, thought Hanson. Brogan had clearly taken after his mother. 'Mr Healey?' he said. 'Can I come in for a moment?'

He thought he detected a flicker of alarm. 'What's happened?' said Healey.

'Can I come in?' said Hanson.

A woman appeared in the hall behind Healey, her clothes not dirty but somehow in need of a wash, as if they, like the woman who wore them, were impregnated by the shoddy, tasteless surroundings.

Healey stood aside to let him in, and Hanson followed him down a hall in which the walls appeared to lean towards him. In looking at the pattern of the sunflowers, he found it difficult to imagine a room that the décor would suit. If the person who'd chosen it had hoped it would brighten an otherwise claustrophobic space, they'd been wrong. He felt as if he were hallucinating, the brushstrokes weaving and waving, but not even yellows as vibrant as these could brighten so narrow a hall.

In the only downstairs room, two young children sat in front of a television, and Hanson found the very fact that Healey made no move to turn it off intrusive. It didn't even appear to occur to him to turn down the volume.

Hanson followed him through the room and into a galley kitchen, its floor swamped with brightly coloured plastic toys.

The youngest child, a toddler, waddled in behind them, plucked at the string of a dog on wheels and tottered out of the kitchen, pulling it behind him.

Hanson glanced around the kitchen and couldn't hide his thoughts. Small, cramped and a total mess, he didn't doubt that it was in keeping with the rest of the house. He could imagine the rooms above, the bathroom the size of the kitchen, a mass of ducks, toy-shaped soaps, a scum round the rim of the bath.

'What's the problem?' said Healey.

'Brogan's been seen,' said Hanson.

'Where?'

'He's gone to the yard.'

Healey said nothing at all. He launched himself at the back door and Hanson said, 'Parker's on his way down there.'

Healey flung open the door and was about to step outside when Hanson said, 'We can force Brogan to leave the yard today, but we can't guarantee that we can keep him away.'

'I'll sort that, if and when,' said Healey.

'You may not get the chance,' said Hanson. 'The yard is coming down. Roly will move on. Brogan might follow. If he does, you'll never see him again.'

Healey was listening.

'Parker's got nothing on Roly. What he knows to be true and what he can prove to be true are two different things. He had to let him go and he'll have to *keep on* letting him go until he's got something concrete to put in front of a court.'

'That's not my problem.'

'It is,' said Hanson. 'You're the only one who can help us put Roly away.'

Healey stood in the doorway, half in, half out of the house.

'Mr Healey,' said Hanson, 'please phone Dr Freeman.'

Healey tightened his grip on the door. 'I can't.'

'Why not?'

Healey didn't reply, but Hanson knew the answer: if Healey were faced with the facts, he'd have to come to terms with a scenario that frightened him almost more than the prospect of his son going missing, of being found in circumstances similar to those in which Gary and Joseph had been found.

'How do you think I'm gonna feel if Brogan's . . .?' He couldn't finish the sentence.

'Brogan isn't an extension of your own masculinity,' said Hanson, but he'd lost Healey there — he saw it immediately. 'What I mean is, if it turns out that Brogan's been abused, it's no reflection on Brogan's masculinity or yours.'

'Don't come here talking your bollocks to me,' said Healey. 'You said I could help you put this bloke away. Tell me how.'

'By getting the result from Freeman.'

'What you mean is, if he's done what you think he's done, that gives Parker grounds to arrest him, get him sent down.'

'Something like that, yes.'

'You want to use our Brogan to get this bloke sent down. Why can't you use somebody else's kid?'

Hanson drew the photos out of the jacket of his pocket. He handed them to Healey. 'We would, if we could, but they're dead ...'

He knew that Healey would never have seen anything like those photos and he said, 'We know for a fact that they both went down to the yard. We can't do a thing about it. It's down to you.'

'What if ...' said Healey. 'What if Freeman ...'

'Please,' said Hanson, quietly, 'phone him.'

'I ...'

Hanson drew a mobile phone out of his pocket, handed it to Healey and said, 'Parker wouldn't be able to bring himself to beg, but I don't have that problem, Mr Healey. I've worked with people like Roly. *I know he'll kill your son.* So I have no reservations — I'm *begging* you to phone Freeman.'

Healey took the mobile phone. 'The number,' he mumbled, 'I don't know the number,' and Hanson, who'd encoded it, took it from him, pressed a couple of buttons, and handed it back to Healey as he heard the ringing tone. He heard Healey give his name and ask for Dr Freeman. He also heard Healey say, '*Tell me ... just tell me ...*'

The next few moments seemed to go on for ever for Hanson. He hadn't known what to expect in that he didn't know for sure what the result would be, and neither did he know how Healey would react if Freeman confirmed the worst.

Healey tried to speak, but the words wouldn't come,

and the phone fell to the floor as he put his hands to his face. There was no need to ask what Freeman had told him. Hanson knew the result. 'Come on,' he said. 'Let's bring him home,' and he led Healey out to the car.

CHAPTER FORTY-ONE

Roly led Brogan up the stairs, darkness leading to darkness, to the world of the rooms above that Brogan had never seen. He felt his way along the walls, unable to see a hand in front of his face until Roly opened the door to the back bedroom.

Here, as in the room below, a six-inch wooden ruler, its markings imperial and meaningless to Brogan, was jammed between the frame and the sill of a sashed window, finches diving from filth-encrusted pelmets to dart from the dark interior and into the cool grey light of Roly's Yard. They shot away like flashes of light on a slide-show, some smashing into the mesh-lined fence to spiral to the ground, others finding their footing and hanging on to the wire.

Brogan looked beyond them to where the jib of a crane reared above the houses like a mast. The metal ball hung dead and still, and then it began to swing, gathering momentum, as the driver positioned the crane.

The ball was swinging now, and gone was the impression of mass, of lumbering immobility; now it was agile, deadly accurate, and it hit the side of the house, the sound like a muffled explosion.

In seeing the front of the house cave in, it seemed to Brogan that the bricks merely sighed, then collapsed as if the breath had been sucked out of them. He saw through plumes of smoke-like dust the contents of the alcove, but the house was across the wasteground and he couldn't make it out.

'He kept me locked in an a-alcove,' said Roly. 'A-ll I got was water. I used to have to thank him. Sometimes, I was in that alcove for days. I used to have to shit in there. My clothes st-stuck to my skin. I scratched the walls and I b-begged him to let me go. He never would. But when I was good, he gave me birds — hundreds of beautiful b-birds. I couldn't decide how I felt about them. They were a c-constant reminder of what I'd had to d-do to get them. I h-hated those birds, but they were all I had — I l-loved them, too.'

Brogan stared out at the workmen. Some of them were walking towards the house. Others were already there, staring up at the alcove, and then, in the distance, he saw a car being driven across the wasteground, then swerving to a halt just yards from the house.

Parker had heard the thud of that metal ball from two blocks away. He'd never heard the sound before, and yet he knew what it was. He'd driven across the wasteground and now he jumped from the car. As he ran up to the workmen, the house collapsed a fraction. It was a barely perceptible sideways shift, but the bricks began to fall, and the driver of the crane yelled out, *'Keep back!'*

None of the men kept back, not even Parker, and as the driver ran towards them, Parker looked up at the alcove.

He knew that what they were looking at was all that was left of Byrne, and he realized also that Byrne must have returned to the yard in those few hours when neither he nor Roly were under surveillance. By Roly's own admission, the first time Byrne had gone to the yard, he'd been demanding money. Roly had probably told him to go back later, and he'd used what time he'd had to prepare the alcove. Byrne had returned, and had then been walled up alive.

Byrne must have known something, thought Parker. He must have tried to blackmail him. *Give me some money, or I'll tell Parker that Gary and Joseph used to come down the yard.*

He wondered what Hanson would make of the fact that Byrne had been found in the alcove. He may have been right with regard to the way in which Roly preferred to dispose of his victims, but the motivation for this particular murder had been different, and Roly had had neither time nor the motivation to build some scaffold in a wood.

How Roly had got him to that alcove was something Parker would probably never know, he decided. Maybe he'd convinced Dougie that he had money stashed in Roumelia Road. Maybe he'd knocked him unconscious and had bricked him up alive. But why do that? thought Parker. Why not simply kill him? He didn't understand.

The driver of the crane spoke to the foreman. 'Jacko,' he said, 'where's your mobile?'

The foreman fumbled in the pocket of a duffel coat. 'Who do you want me to call?'

The driver of the crane couldn't seem to make up his mind for a moment. 'Police,' he said, uncertainly.

Parker said, 'Don't bother.'

Even as he spoke, the back-up he'd requested on his way to the yard arrived with blue lights flashing. The workmen seemed so stunned by what they'd found that none of them commented – none of them seemed to wonder how the police came to be there so quickly.

Parker turned from the alcove and stared across the wasteground. Roly was staring back at him. He melted away from the window.

Parker took a step towards the yard, but even as he did so he caught sight of Hanson's car pulling up beside his own.

Healey jumped out of the passenger seat, and ran up to one of the workmen, yanked something out of his hands, a wrecking bar, thought Parker, who reached out to grab it from him.

Healey shook him off and ran across the wasteground, Parker close behind him. He tore the chain from the gates, kicked them wide, then burst into the yard with a cry that sounded as close to inhuman as Parker had ever heard.

He raced after Healey, diving into the yard with him as he started to smash it apart, renting great holes in the netting and the mesh. He wanted to stop him, but knew that if he tried Healey might lash out at him with that lethal metal bar, and so he watched as he pulled at the mesh with tearing, bleeding hands, the wire cutting his fingers, lacerating the flesh, and Healey weeping and shouting as the birds began to swarm.

He knew then that what Freeman had told him was the very thing that Healey had most feared hearing, and knew also that, at last, he had Barnes in his grasp. 'Healey,' he said, and just for a moment, he thought the man had calmed, but what had stopped him from smashing the yard wasn't the sound of his voice. It was the sight of Roly, who was coming out of the house.

Healey stopped dead at the sight of him, but Roly was watching his birds. They flew through the gaping holes in the mesh, and swept across the wasteground towards Roumelia Road. They flew across the jib of the crane and the roof of the corner house, swooping and gliding to freedom, thought Parker, freedom and certain death.

Roly stood in the yard and he watched his birds fly free. He didn't seem to notice Healey, who stood and stared at him as if he were seeing a demon. The movement he made towards Roly suddenly seemed fearful rather than savage, that of a man who is facing a predator in the knowledge that he has only one shot, that he has to make it count, and that if he gets it wrong he'll lose his life. He raised the metal bar, and brought it to bear with every ounce of strength in his possession, and Parker, who had been told of a phenomenon that he hoped he would never witness, witnessed it now.

The force of the blow split Roly's skull and his brains

spewed out like a liquid. It sickened yet fascinated Parker. Roly was still standing. Parker wouldn't have thought that was possible, but just for a moment, Roly stood, as if watching the last of his birds fly out of the yard.

And then he went down. Not as one who'd been hit with tremendous force, but slowly. He fell to the ground like a drowning man, the final submission of one who knows he'll never surface again.

Parker looked up to see Brogan staring down from the window. He pressed his fingers to the glass, those child's hands with the fingertips whitened by the pressure, and then he was gone.

Healey looked at the wrecking bar, the steel discoloured by blood, then threw it to the ground. He took a few steps away from it but he didn't run, and as Brogan burst out of the house, Parker suddenly saw it all through the eyes of a twelve-year-old boy.

The sky was empty. The birds had gone, and Roly was lying dead at his father's feet.

A blur of colour appeared among the grey. Parker focused on it. A fledgling, a Gouldian, had got in the way of Healey's attack on the yard.

It lay by the door to the shed. Brogan walked up to it, picked it up, and started to stroke the feathers, and as Hanson appeared in the yard, Parker looked at the way in which the boy was loving the bird. He was talking to it, coaxing it, as if he could somehow bring it back to life.

Uniforms cuffed Healey as Hanson led his son towards the gate. Healey didn't resist, but Brogan did. He wanted to stay with Roly. *Roly was my friend*, and he placed the corpse of the Gouldian by his body.

CHAPTER FORTY-TWO

The last time Parker's team had sat in this room with its semi-circular rows, they'd been watching footage relating to the appeal made by Gary Maudsley's family. Now they were watching the film that had been found at Roly's Yard.

Hanson sat at the back of the room, his thoughts very much on Brogan. Parker had wanted to question him, but Hanson had suggested that maybe he should leave it for the moment. Brogan was in shock. Now was not the time.

Parker dimmed the lights, then went to sit by Hanson, and as the lights went down in the room, the screen became a snowstorm.

Rather than clear completely, the blizzard became a sideways sweep of sleet. It swept across the footage, making it hard for those who were watching to see what was being portrayed. The film was old, thought Hanson, who knew that Parker had wanted to show it to his men the minute they got their hands on it, but had been delayed by the necessity of having it transferred from reel to reel.

The quality was desperately poor, yet it was possible for Hanson to make out a magician, his black moustache alarming and far too large to be real. He wore a top hat and a cape that was lined with scarlet, and in his hands, he held a magic wand.

A young boy stood beside him, a boy of nine or ten. He wore a skin-tight, flesh-coloured suit that gave him the appearance of a boy who stood naked but for the cape that was fixed round his throat.

The person who had shot the movie had been inexpert. The picture shook and drifted into and out of focus, but as the camera pulled back, Hanson saw that the magician was performing in a room decorated with streamers.

Red and blue balloons had been fixed to the corners of the room, and children sat cross-legged at the magician's feet, their parents in the background. They gazed up in wonder as the magician showed them an empty bamboo cage before covering it with a cloth, then removing it to reveal a Diamond Firetail.

The screen became a snowstorm for a second, then cleared, and Hanson saw children putting their hands to their mouths as the magician sawed through a box.

A boy lay in the box, his head moving, his feet visible and twitching, the limbs clearly clothing stuffed with rags. The children didn't mind. As the magician sawed through the limbs, they suspended their disbelief, and squealed in delight as the arms and legs thudded softly to the floor.

The film ended, and Parker turned to Hanson, 'Unfortunately, there's nothing untoward about the film. It's all run-of-the-mill Magic Circle stuff.'

'The boy in the box,' said Hanson, softly. 'It's Roly.'

Moranti sat in the interview room, and in his hands he held the bird that was invisible to the eye. He'd never seen Hanson before, and he seemed wary of him, as if sensing that events had somehow taken a turn for the worse.

Parker didn't introduce Hanson, but he noted his presence for the benefit of those who would ultimately hear what was being recorded. He then turned his attention to Moranti.

'Mr Moranti,' said Parker, 'you told me you came to England in nineteen thirty-nine.'

'Yes,' said Moranti.

'You told me your family were travellers.'

'Circus,' said Moranti. 'A very small circus — more a side-show.'

'Quite,' said Parker. 'And when you came to England, you adopted an English name.'

'I don't understand ...' said Moranti.

'Nothing unusual in that,' said Parker. 'A lot of people have done the same. They feel that it helps them integrate into the community.'

'I don't use that name any more.'

'No,' replied Parker, 'I realize that, but for many years you were known as Randolph Timpson. Morris Randolph Timpson.'

'What about it?'

'Yet you used the name Moranti, your *real* name, when you worked as a children's magician. Why didn't you use that name when you applied to the local authority as a potential foster-parent?'

'It made me sound more foreign,' said Moranti. 'I thought that might go against me.'

Something would have gone against him, thought Parker, but it wouldn't have been his nationality: it would have been what came to light when the authorities checked his background. 'Not all records were destroyed during the war,' said Parker. 'You have a record for child molestation. Any local authority worth its salt would have checked whatever records were available, and they would have discovered that. Is that why you changed your name when you came to England?'

Parker suspended the interview to allow Moranti time to compose himself.

He knew the implications of what he'd done, thought

Hanson. He knew that, at the very least, he'd be charged with procuring the boys whom Roly had murdered.

'Why did you do it?' said Parker. 'You must have known that by taking them down to the yard you were as good as signing their death warrants?'

'I didn't know what he did with them. I thought he want to film them, that's all.'

'And why would he want to do that?'

'For Byrne,' said Moranti.

Byrne distributed the videos under the counter, Parker guessed. 'Good money, was it?'

'It wasn't done for the money,' said Moranti.

No, thought Hanson, who knew enough to know that money wouldn't have been the prime objective: Moranti would have got as much of a kick out of those films as Byrne had got from the photos in those clothing catalogues.

He caught Parker's eye as if to ask permission to put a question to Moranti, but Parker just wouldn't risk it. He shook his head a fraction, then went on to ask what Hanson had, in any case, intended to ask. 'Tell me, Mr Moranti, when Roly was a child – when Roly was in your care – what did you give him for doing what you wanted him to do?'

For a moment, Hanson wondered whether Moranti was going to deny what Parker was proposing he had done, and Parker, who wasn't averse to spelling out the precise nature of the sexual acts he was referring to, said, 'We can get hold of the man who reported what you did to *him*. Once a court hears his evidence, a jury will no doubt come to the conclusion—'

'A bird,' Moranti blurted. 'Roly always love birds.'

Little wonder, thought Hanson, that Roly would for ever associate these birds with his earliest sexual experiences.

'And tell me,' said Parker, 'how did you punish Roly if he *refused* to do what you wanted?'

Moranti declined to answer, and Parker said, 'You'll only be telling us something we already know.'

'I lock him in an alcove,' said Moranti.

'How long for?'

Moranti gave that oddly dramatic shrug. 'A while.'

'An hour, a day, two days, perhaps?'

Moranti looked at Parker, as if suddenly believing him to have access to information relating to the most private details of his past. 'A week, sometimes. Maybe longer — it's all a long time ago, I don't remember.'

Parker said, 'You're asking me to believe you locked him in an alcove for weeks at a time on occasion. He'd have died.'

Quietly now, Moranti said, 'I gave him water.'

'How?'

'A feeder,' said Moranti. 'I rig up a feeder . . .' and Hanson knew in that moment that Forensic would come back with the information that Gary had been kept in the alcove at the yard, and the mystery of the bracket and the hole that was drilled into the plasterwork would be solved for Parker. In his mind's eye, he saw a bird-cage and, fixed to the bars, a bracket designed to hold a water-feeder. A metal tube protruded from the water-feeder, and the bird sipped water from it. The bracket on the wall of the alcove had also held a feeder. The tube was slotted through the brickwork, and Gary had drunk from it.

Hanson saw the look on Parker's face and knew that he shared his vision of Gary's last weeks of life. He also guessed he was blaming himself. *If only I'd found him sooner. If only I'd searched that squat the day I found Brogan at the yard . . .*

In reality, Parker couldn't hold himself to blame, but shaking off the feeling was going to take some doing. He would need to talk it through with someone who could rationalize it for him.

During the silence that followed, Hanson thought about Byrne. Roly had kept Gary alive by giving him water, but he wouldn't have risked going to Roumelia Road to show the same mercy to Byrne. He knew he was under surveillance, and Byrne had died in that tomb. In many ways, thought

Hanson, he'd been more fortunate than Gary, who'd been kept alive for weeks. When Roly realized that Byrne had led Parker to him, he would also have realized that the yard was bound to be searched. Having already dealt with Byrne, he had released Gary from the alcove, had killed him, and had taken his remains to the bunker to focus Parker's attention back on Byrne. The scaffold that Roly had no doubt been in the process of completing would never be used ...

Parker had collected himself to a degree, but when he spoke again it was in a voice that suggested he was having to force out the words. As if they wouldn't come. As if the horror of Roly's Yard were somehow constricting his throat. 'You said the boys were filmed.'

Moranti played with the invisible bird, a bird that was all the colours of the world.

'Where are the films?'

Moranti knew it was over. He pressed a thumb hard against the palm of his other hand. The finch was crushed by the impact. Parker saw it die. 'Lock-up garage,' he said.

'Tell me where,' said Parker, and Moranti broke down.

Parker stood with Hanson at the back of the room. They were alone. The semi-circular rows seemed filled with ghosts.

The screen was before them, a dull, lifeless grey, but Parker slotted a video cassette into a machine at the back of the room.

Earlier, he had gone to the lock-up rented by Moranti, and in it he had found more videos than Bryne could ever have hoped to stock in his poorly kept shop. Some had been imported and were nothing to do with the case. Others, such as this one, were all the evidence he would ever need with regard to what had become of Joseph Coyne.

'You ready?' he said, to Hanson.

'Ready,' said Hanson, and the screen now came to life.

Initially, all Hanson could see were swarms of exotic finches. They filled a dusk-streaked sky, and dipped down into trees, and he took the scene to have been shot in some tropical forest. But there was something about it that didn't ring true. The trees were too English, and there were other give-aways, like a pylon that was accidentally caught for a fraction of a second before the camera zoomed in on the figure of a boy. He was naked, bar the cape that streamed from his slender throat, and he was running for his life, the glimpse of a granite house in the background informing Hanson that this was Colbourne Wood.

Parker paused the video. 'You don't have to watch the rest.'

'I've seen worse,' said Hanson, and Parker resumed the screening.

It answered the final questions with regard to what had become of Joseph Coyne, and it was something that Parker intended should never be public knowledge.

CHAPTER FORTY-THREE

There had been nothing further that Hanson could do at the station, and he returned to the guesthouse to discover that he had a visitor. He recognized her voice even before he walked into the dining room to find her sitting by the window, as she always had. 'Lorna,' he said.

Mrs Judd stood up. 'I invited her in. I hope that was all right?'

It seemed bizarre to see them talking like old friends, almost as if it were Mrs Judd, and not he, who had shared this house with Lorna.

'Murray,' she said, and she looked much the same. A little older, perhaps, but that was all. She was dressed in a V-necked sweater, along with a navy skirt and those gold button earrings, as though she'd only just bought the scarf with the pattern he'd found it so easy to recall. 'You look well,' he said, but she wasn't to be distracted by his attempt at making small-talk.

'*What the hell are you doing here?*'

'I could ask the same of you.'

Mrs Judd slipped from the room and it struck him as the only sign of sensitivity she had shown in all the time he'd been there. At least the woman knew when she wasn't wanted.

'I read it in the paper. You can't imagine the shock I got.'

Hanson knew then that the Judds had told the press where he was staying.

'I don't know,' said Hanson. 'I don't know what I'm doing here,' and then he thought back to something Parris had said earlier. *In all the years we were married, I never once told her how deeply she'd managed to hurt me.*

Hanson had observed that it was never wise to bottle these things up, that people who put their feelings away with the intention of dealing with them at a more convenient time often discovered that their feelings dealt with them before they got round to it. 'How are you, Lorna?'

'Don't you think your behaviour is rather odd?'

He sat down, the table between them in much the way that the antique table with its pattern of inlaid wood had been between them years ago.

'Not to me.'

'Enlighten me, then,' she said. 'I've had some of our friends on the phone, asking me what you're playing at.'

Hanson wondered who those friends might be. Most of the people they'd known were colleagues of Lorna's, and none had been friends of his. 'I can't say I'm terribly worried about what anyone else might think.'

'Then at least tell me why you chose to stay here, of all places.'

Hanson looked past her to a wall that he'd practically rebuilt at one stage. The plaster mouldings that matched those in the bedroom above were white now, one or other of the Judds having slapped a coat of emulsion over the intricate detail that he'd picked out with such care. 'I like the place,' he said. 'It meant something to me.'

'It meant something to me, too, but I wouldn't dream of booking in as a guest.'

'I wanted to see what had become of it,' said Hanson. 'I wanted to see what someone had done to the rooms I restored with such care.'

She looked at him as if she could barely remember what a state the house had been in when they had purchased it.

'We were lucky,' said Hanson, softly. 'If not for the fact that the house was falling apart, we'd never have been able to afford it.'

'I found it cold,' she said.

'Such great rooms,' said Hanson. 'Big. I'll never have a house like this again.'

'What are you talking about?'

Hanson thought back to Parris, and wondered whether, if Lorna hadn't been sitting there, he'd ever have looked her up to say what he had wanted to say for years: 'You took me for every penny, Lorna. Stripped me of the house, and what little money I'd managed to put aside.'

She was staring at him now, as if someone who was capable of behaving in what she considered to be so strange a manner might be capable of anything.

'But worse than that, you stripped me of my dignity, my self-esteem and my happiness.'

'I don't know how you work that one out.'

'You carried on an affair in this house, slept in our bed with people who knew me, people who told me what was going on. Have you any idea how I felt when I found out?'

'*Keep your voice down, Murray!*'

Hanson was well aware that one or both of the Judds were probably listening but had no intention of keeping his voice down. 'Are you happy?' he said.

'That's a strange question.'

'Maybe ... but I'd like to know if everything you did to me was worth it. Tell me, Lorna, I'd really like to know.'

'I'm happy enough,' she said, and he smiled as he replied, 'I'll take that as a no.'

He thought back to those last few moments with Parris, who had observed that it was possible for a person to be too civilized, too understanding and too reluctant to give vent to justifiable anger. *It isn't civilized, Murray, it's weak, and it's the weak who resort to murder, not the strong ...*

'I met a former teacher of mine today.'

'I didn't come here to talk about some former teacher.'

'He murdered his wife,' said Murray. 'For years, I've thought about him on and off, wondering what became of him, but it wasn't until the last few months that I really began to wonder why he did it.'

'I spent our entire marriage listening to you talking about what motivates people to kill.'

'But recently,' he continued, 'I've thought of little else. I'd almost became obsessed with it, *and now I know why.*'

She looked towards the door, finding consolation in the thought that the Judds were close to hand, should she need them.

He reached out, took her hand and found it cold. '*I wanted to kill you, Lorna.* I've never told you that, but I wanted to make you a cup of tea, take it into the garden, and watch you lift the cup to your lips as I crushed your skull with a hammer.'

She jerked her hand away, and stood up, the chair falling back as she took a step away from him. 'You're sick,' she said. 'I always knew you were sick.'

'Not sick, Lorna. *Normal.* We all have these feelings. Most of us never act on them. The few who do are sometimes referred to people like me, that's all.'

Mrs Judd entered the room, the sound of the chair having drawn her in from the hall. She stood in the doorway. 'Is everything all right?'

He stood up and caught the scent that Lorna wore. There had once been a time when the scent had aroused him. Now, he couldn't imagine himself ever having made love to her. 'Everything's fine,' he said. 'Lorna's just leaving.'

He followed her out to the hall, needing to be the one to open the door, to watch her cross the threshold, to close the door behind her. 'Goodbye,' he said, slamming it closed, flicking the lock that he'd fitted when they'd first moved into the house. He was shutting her out, consigning her to the past.

He turned to find that Mrs Judd was backing away from him. 'Don't worry,' he said. 'I'll get my things, and then I'll be on my way.'

'What about your bill?' she said.

Hanson replied, 'I take it you were paid by the press for telling them where I was?'

She didn't deny it.

'So let's call it quits,' said Hanson.

Hanson arrived home to find the cottage in darkness. Not a good sign, he thought, and he visualized the way in which Jan might have tried to come to terms with the story run by the press.

Most of the papers – and Hanson had now seen the majority of them – had published a photograph of the Judds standing at the door to the house that he and Lorna had shared. No doubt the press would get hold of Lorna in due course, but he was no longer worried by what she might say. He was, however, worried about what Jan would make of it all. She was bound to fear the worst, thought Hanson, and that was fair enough. In her position, he, too, would think the worst. She had probably imagined that he had been drawn back to the house he had shared with Lorna because he still loved her, and the implications of that would have made any woman with an ounce of pride pack her bags.

Something about the lack of light from within the rooms of the cottage made him reluctant to turn his key in the door. He didn't want to walk in to find her gone, and he suddenly realized how badly he'd behaved. He hadn't told her what he was doing because he hadn't understood it himself, and he had hoped to get away with it without her ever knowing. Plenty of people embarked on affairs for similar reasons, thought Hanson, and most were caught out, as he had been, by events they hadn't envisaged.

He walked round the side of the cottage to the garden at the back. At first, he found it difficult to make out the shape at the bottom of the garden, and then he saw her, sitting at the foot of the rockery, and he walked over.

'Hi,' she said, but she didn't look up, and Hanson touched her hair. It was damp in the way it was always damp whenever she'd been to the gym, and he noticed that she was wearing a couple of jumpers. 'No sweatshirt?' he said.

'I put them all in your drawer.'

The subtext wasn't lost on him. She had given them back, and her clothes were packed, ready to be moved.

'I'm sorry I didn't phone.'

'You obviously had your reasons.'

She still wouldn't look at him.

He crouched beside her, sitting on a boulder that he'd picked up from the side of the road earlier in the summer. Between them, they'd stolen boulders from all over the country. Some rock. Some granite. Some smooth and others jagged. The result was a mildly guilty conscience and an outstanding rockery. It was hard to imagine that a garden once so neglected could be transformed in such a short space of time, and it wasn't just the garden: in looking back at the cottage, he saw how much work they'd done on it together. It was nowhere near the size of the house in Bury, but it was big enough for two.

'Where's the toad?' he said.

'I haven't seen it for ages.'

'Time of year,' said Hanson. 'He'll turn up, next spring.'

'Give him my regards.'

'Give them yourself.'

She looked up at him now. 'Murray, what's going on?'

He didn't feel up to telling her why he'd gone to the house, not tonight, but he'd tell her in the next few days, and then he'd suggest that maybe it was time that he stopped behaving like an emotional fuckwit and admitted that he wanted to make a commitment. 'There was something I had to sort out,' he said. 'I couldn't make a commitment to you without doing it, so I went back.'

It wasn't much of an explanation. Plenty of women would have pushed him for more, but not her. 'You hurt me,' she said, simply.

'I was hurting myself,' said Hanson. 'You got caught in the cross-fire. I'm sorry.'

'Do you still love her?'

'No,' said Hanson, truthfully, 'but a part of me will always love the house.' He smiled. 'Think you can cope with that?'

'Only if you promise not to make a habit of going back.'

'I think I can manage that,' he said, and she followed him into the cottage.

CHAPTER FORTY-FOUR

Parker and Brogan stood with their backs to Roumelia Road, the shell of the house half hidden by plasterboard screens, and they watched as Roly's Yard was being dismantled.

The house looked smaller, somehow, as if the place had been crushed on more than an earthly level, and the aviary, now stripped of the boundaries that had defined it, melted into the gardens on either side. Its surface resembled nothing so much as a mass grave, great trenches having been dug its length and breadth, and the trees, the fencing, the mesh had been ripped away.

The birds were gone, and Brogan didn't have to see the evidence to know that, without exception, all were dead. If the cold hadn't killed them, native birds or lack of the type of seed they required were bound to have done so, and he pictured their remains as a scattering of colour in the gutters and gardens of the city and its suburbs. People would come across these strange, fragile creatures, and, in realizing that they were not indigenous to the country, would wonder how they had come to be in so grey a place to die.

Workmen were tossing debris into the skips, rolls of mesh, bricks, slabs of concrete. They touched these things as if they were contaminated, their hands gloved, their eyes averted as if afraid of what they might inadvertently pick up. None of them spoke. None of them wanted to be there, and it showed.

Parker didn't blame them. Within hours of Roly's death, Forensic had reported that the clothes found on the effigy had belonged to Gary Maudsley, and tests done on the alcove where the effigy was found had revealed that Gary had been imprisoned there prior to his death.

Parker had assumed that Roly had imprisoned Gary in order to give himself time to build a scaffold. Hanson, however, had had experience of killers who suffered from the type of psychosis he believed Roly to have suffered from, and he was as convinced as was possible under the circumstances that Roly wouldn't have imprisoned Gary until the scaffold had already been erected.

Upon hearing Hanson's opinion, Parker had experienced a vision of the future, a vision in which someone like Hardman came across the scaffold intended for Gary.

Unless they were acquainted with the details of this particular case, they wouldn't be able to work out what it was, or what the person who had built it had intended it to support. Chances were, they'd knock it down, considering it to be a project that had never been completed, and, in that regard, they'd be right, thought Parker. The scaffold could only ever have been complete once Gary was lying on it.

He recalled asking Hanson why Roly had imprisoned Gary in the first place, and Hanson had put it down to the fact that, as Moranti had imprisoned Roly for refusing to perform certain sexual acts, it was just possible that imprisonment of his victims had played an important part in the ritual of the kill.

Parker had left the questions of *why* Roly had felt it imperative to follow a particular ritual, and had turned his attention to the question of *where* he had murdered Gary. The question had been answered when Forensic came back with a result on bloodspecks found on the walls of the room where the effigy had been found. The blood matched Gary's.

There were further traces of blood found in the cracks on the bath at the yard, and the press had revealed that the police believed his body had been dismembered in the bathroom before being transported to the bunker in the back of Roly's car. Therefore, the workmen were only too aware that the pieces of debris they handled might well hold traces of unimaginable horror, traces barely visible, but there ...

A non-stop rain produced a steady stream of sludge that rolled from the yard to the road. It slid by their feet, lapping at the soles of their shoes, threatening to deepen but never doing more than sliding by, and as he side-stepped some of it, Brogan felt the house behind him reaching out as if to draw him into the alcove, its former tenant having vacated the premises in favour of sacred ground.

The distant rumble of heavy machinery drew their attention. The driver of the crane killed the engine and jumped from the cab. He spoke to the workmen briefly, then approached Parker and Brogan.

Brogan recognized him as the man who'd driven the crane the day the contents of the alcove were revealed, and it seemed strange to him that he should be willing to come back at all. Perhaps it was the money, or perhaps, like him, he had to lay the ghost, finish the job.

'It isn't safe,' the driver said. 'You'll have to leave.'

'We're going,' said Parker, his arm on Brogan's shoulder. He led him away from the slow-moving sludge that was all that remained of the yard. 'I'd better get you back,' he said, and they headed for the car.

Social Services had found temporary foster-parents for Brogan. They looked okay to Parker, but how could you tell? In view of the foster-parents that had been found for Roly, Parker had grave misgivings, but the only alternative was for Brogan to stay in a children's home and, in view of recent publicity, Parker wasn't altogether sure he'd be any safer there. He said, 'If you have any problems of any description, you come straight to me, you understand?'

'What kind of problems?'

Parker didn't believe that Brogan was still so naïve in view of everything that had happened and said, 'Anything that troubles you, anything at all.'

Brogan turned for one last glimpse of the yard, and saw, as the crane rolled into position, the way in which the workmen stood well back, goggles and masks in place.

'What are you thinking?' said Parker, but Brogan doubted he'd understand if he were to tell him that he hated to see the yard like this, that he'd give anything to see it with its boundaries defined and the tall slender trees weaving their fragile branches through the mesh.

Over recent weeks, the gaping wound in his belly seemed to have expanded a fraction, as if to accommodate emotions he could barely comprehend, emotions that related to his mother's death, the murder of Roland Barnes, the desecration of the yard, keeping them safe until such time as he could pull them out, turn them to the light, examine them, and put them back, no less painful, but a great deal better understood.

He turned away.

EPILOGUE

There were weeds pushing through in the flowerbed that circled the lawn of the foster-home where Brogan was now living. They crushed the stem of some flowering shrub, its petals a splash of purple, bleeding on to green. Brogan had watched it burst into flower over the past few days, and it was as if the soul of a Gouldian had taken possession of the soil to dictate the colours the petals would become.

Parker's car drew up at the gate and Brogan watched from a downstairs window as he climbed out and made his way to the house.

Moments later, he was led into the room by his foster-mother who said, 'You've a visitor, Brogan.' Then she took Parker's jacket and disappeared, leaving them alone.

Parker stood by the window, its curtains of crimson velvet pinned well back to leave an unimpeded view of the garden. 'How's it going?' he said.

'Fine,' said Brogan.

'Back at school?'

'Yeah, I'm back.'

'Sticking to it, not slopin' off?'

'Stickin' it out. My foster-parents see to that.'

'Social workers'll be pleased.'

It had been some months since Parker had last questioned

him to put the final touches to his statements, but during that time, Brogan seemed, if anything, to have grown slightly more child-like, as though the events of the past few months had made him curl in on himself.

He looked at Parker shyly. 'That all you came for — to find out how I am?'

'No,' said Parker, quietly. 'I came to tell you your father was in court today. Ultimately, it'll go to Crown Court, and you'll be called as a witness.'

'Will he go to jail?'

That was a tough one, thought Parker. Healey hadn't been much of a father to Brogan, but, at the end of the day, he *was* his father, and Parker wasn't sure how Brogan might react to the news that a jail sentence was almost inevitable. Healey was pleading manslaughter on the grounds of diminished responsibility. He might just get away with it, thought Parker, but not if the Crown Prosecution Service came up with medical records relating to Brogan's mother, and not if they then persuaded a jury that, at the moment that Healey had grabbed the wrecking bar, he'd intended to do rather more than wreck the yard. Several seconds had elapsed between the moment that Healey had seen Roland Barnes walk from the house to the yard. Roly had stared at the finches as they flew across the crane, and Healey had sneaked up on him like a cat sneaks up on a bird, had crushed his skull with a single blow, had hit him from behind.

'It's hard to say,' said Parker. 'He's pleading diminished responsibility, and even on a bad day, a judge would have to agree that there were mitigating circumstances, but the problem is . . .'

He stopped. Brogan deserved the truth. Better to hear it now than to harbour hopes and have them crushed. 'He's going down,' said Parker.

There wasn't much of a reaction from Brogan, and Parker prompted him gently, 'You okay?'

Brogan faced a mirror that hung above the mantelpiece. The window at Parker's back was reflected in the glass, a small domestic finch huddling on the sill. Brogan kept his eye on it and said, 'Don't make no difference to me. He wasn't around much anyway.'

'No – well ... he did his best.'

Brogan didn't reply, and Parker wondered what was on his mind. 'Want to talk about it?' he said.

'That man ... that man you found in the alcove ...'

'Douglas Byrne?'

'Maybe Roly never meant to hurt me. Maybe he killed him to stop him from killing me.'

'Brogan ...' said Parker.

'He was good to me, Roly. He gave me birds. He was ...'

He stopped, and Parker forced himself not to stride across the room, grab him by the shoulders, and shake the truth into him.

'He was my friend,' said Brogan.

Quietly now, Parker replied, 'He wasn't much of a friend to Joseph and Gary.'

'That was Byrne,' said Brogan, and Parker knew that now was neither the time nor the place to argue. Eventually Brogan would understand just how close he'd come to meeting a fate similar to that of the boys whose disappearance had occupied his every waking moment for as long as he could remember, but at present, Brogan believed that Roly had been a friend to him at a time when he had no one. He appeared to be plucking up the courage to ask something else, and Parker gave him the space to do it in his own good time.

'How many ...?' The words trailed to nothing before Brogan tried again. 'Were there any more?'

Parker thought back to enquiries that had been made with the firm that had employed Gifford. Pierce and Newman had kept no record of there having been anything unusual found at Bickley Wood. Pierce was dead, and Parker only hoped that he had taken his secret with him into hell. 'There are certain things we can never hope to prove,' he said, and even as he said it, he realized that Brogan would cling to the remark, feeling that it was proof enough that Roly hadn't harmed anyone, and wouldn't have harmed him.

It was very quiet in that room, very still.

'Roly wouldn't have hurt me,' said Brogan. 'He liked me.'

Parker choked back the urge to get it through to him that Roly would have killed him in the end. 'You're a lucky lad,' he said, and he held out his hand.

Brogan took it, shook it uncertainly, and felt that although Parker's grip was firm, it felt like a letting go, as if he were saying goodbye.

'I won't be back.'

He let himself out, and after he'd gone, Brogan went to the window and looked down on the finch. It was one he hadn't seen since the previous spring, a domestic bird, rather dull by comparison with the exotic species down at the yard, and he had the strangest feeling, as if he were the bird, perched on the sill, divided from the room by a window that had been closed against him. He saw a few slender trees in the reflection, finches flying through the branches, a backdrop of Manchester sky.

The bird stared in through the window, the boy stared out through the glass, and it seemed to the bird as if Roly's Yard had been superimposed on his face.